MW00974471

# CIRCLE OF TRUST

Close Enough to Kill — Book 2

JACQUELINE SIMON GUNN

Copyright © 2016 Jacqueline Simon Gunn
Circle of Trust
By Jacqueline Simon Gunn
ISBN: 1533259186
ISBN 13: 9781533259189

*For my two favorite men, my dad and my husband…*
*Philip Simon and Joseph Gunn*

"All extremes of feeling are allied with madness."

— *Virginia Woolf*


"I have little left in myself — I must have you. The world may laugh — may call me absurd, selfish — but it does not signify. My very soul demands you: it will be satisfied, or it will take deadly vengeance on its frame."

— *Charlotte Brontë*

Dear Oliver,

If I could crawl inside your head, what would I see? A tormented man wondering who he should be?

You said you didn't mean to hurt me, perhaps this is true. But I don't know who you are, my thoughts are askew.

You have broken me and broken me, I am beyond repair, and you're carrying on like you haven't a care.

That's too bad, Oliver, you underestimate me. The woman you knew before will no longer be.

I have no choice, you've left me none. That's too bad because you are finished, you're done.

Bye-bye, Oliver, it's such an itsy-bitsy shame that I had to watch you writher and wither in pain.

That's what you get for betraying me, knifed in the chest, bleeding thick like the sea.

In the back of my mind it is you I will miss, so I lean in and give you one final kiss.

I feel your lips, dead and dry, but you feel so good, I let out a sigh.

I so enjoyed watching all that blood quickly seep. I especially liked looking inside the wounds so deep.

Ta, ta, Oliver, bye-bye... I bet you never thought I'd decide you must die.

Love, Emily

# CHAPTER 1

*Bbbrrring! It should* be illegal to call anyone before 9 a.m. during the winter.

A dreary morning. Kadee could see the drab colorlessness of the sky through the slits in her blinds. An endless monotony of blah.

*Bbbrrring.* She pulled the comforter all the way over her head, scrunched her knees up to her chest and tried to ignore the noise. It was one of those mornings where it was too cold. The wind whipped about, giving off that ghostly sound that it creates when it's speeding between the city buildings, making getting out of bed a gloomy prospect.

She peeked at the phone. Yvonne Tracy's name appeared on the caller ID. Kadee had not seen or talked to Yvonne since they met in the fall for their picnic underneath the large oak tree. Part of her felt an attachment toward Yvonne; part of Kadee feared her; part of her was fascinated.

*Maybe I shouldn't pick up.* One eye still closed, the other open, her mind groggy from sleep.

But she had been wondering how Yvonne was doing. She had even contemplated calling her a few times. Kadee felt a deep kinship toward her, their shared betrayal by Noah created an empathic bond. There were days when Kadee felt so alone in her despair. The memories of Noah, their relationship, his death, her almost going to prison, all overwhelmed her. Sometimes she thought Yvonne was the only one who could possibly understand how she felt, having suffered similarly.

Then there was her book: *Circle of Betrayal.* Yvonne sent Kadee a final copy in the mail. Kadee knew the premise, but she hadn't read the actual pages until Yvonne sent the book: a real page-turner.

Yvonne had named her female protagonist Emily Goodyear, whose narrative resonated with Kadee. Emily's voice spoke to so much of what Kadee felt, she couldn't help but identify with her.

But there was one looming hitch: Emily Goodyear was a murderer. She slaughtered her fiancé, Oliver, after she found out he was having sex with another woman. That character's name was Elle, and she resembled Kadee. Of course, the story had been written as fiction, so Kadee couldn't be sure where the lines between Yvonne and Emily and her and Elle were drawn. The book could have almost been a memoir, and the question of whether or not it was the truth, frequently ricocheted around in Kadee's mind.

Kadee often ruminated about their exchange that day in the park when Yvonne showed her the draft of the book. Since that day Yvonne explained the plot. Kadee played out the sentences they spoke to each other over and over in her head trying to decide what she believed.

She had said to Yvonne, "Sounds like the truth."

And Yvonne had responded, "It is."

But there was the note that Yvonne had sent with the book. Her handwritten message had implied that it was a work of fiction, that she was just using the characters to get some of her feelings out, which made perfect sense.

Of course, it made sense.

Besides, Kadee did not want to believe that someone she admired as much as Yvonne, someone she saw as strong and secure, was a murderer.

She opened her other eye, brushed her hair off her face and answered her phone. "Hello, Kadee? Hi, it's Yvonne. How are you?" Yvonne spoke in her calm, composed tone.

Kadee enjoyed hearing her voice. "Hey Yvonne," her voice hoarse from sleep. "I'm doing OK. How are you?"

"I'm well. I really am. " She paused for a moment. "Oh, did I wake you? I apologize."

"No. It's fine," Kadee croaked.

There was silence on the line.

Yvonne continued. "I'd like to see you. There are some things I'd like to talk with you about. Can we meet for lunch?"

"Sure." Kadee's interest was roused.

"And can you please bring the copy of *Circle of Betrayal* that I sent you? You did receive it, didn't you?"

"Yes. I did. I enjoyed it. I'll bring it with me."

"Wonderful. I had a feeling you'd enjoy it. I've made some revisions. I'll give you an official copy once it's published."

"OK." She felt a smile form.

They agreed to meet the next day at a diner along First Avenue midway between their Upper Eastside apartments.

It was just the previous month that Yvonne had sent Kadee a finalized copy of her novel. A tall, tanned man with a crew cut arrived at her door one day. He wore a brown UPS uniform. His thick fingers handed Kadee a small package. He asked her to sign, then left without another word.

Kadee went back in her apartment, opened the mysterious package. It turned out to be Yvonne's book. Kadee saw the pages of Yvonne's manuscript that day in the park. But this was her own official copy. A signed copy.

The manuscript had a shiny cover that was mostly blank, something laminated from an office supply store, a brown cover with the title *Circle of Betrayal* and the byline *Y. E. Tracy*. She stared at it for a few minutes. She wasn't sure if she wanted to know what was written on those pages. But then she couldn't resist.

She opened it and flipped through the pages. A note stuffed between the first and second page fell out.

She unfolded the note. In thin, black marker, it read:

> *Dear Kadee,*
>
> *I hope you enjoy my book. I wanted you to have the opportunity to be the first person to read it. I know we both suffered tremendously. It has been very hard to put the pieces of my life back together.*

*I can't tell you how therapeutic the writing has been. Without it, I may have sunk into a deep depression. I was able to use the fictional characters to get at some deep feelings that I didn't even know I had. Who knew writing could rouse such a catharsis? I found it so helpful that I have started a second one. Anyhoo, I think of you often and hope that you, too, have found some way to work through what happened. And please, let's keep in touch.*

*Best Wishes, Yvonne*

Kadee had devoured the book in two days. The moment she had closed the book, she then wrapped it in a rag and hid it all the way in the back of her underwear drawer. Part of her had been hiding it from Alex. Part of her had been hiding it from herself. If she put it away, buried it, left it in its own compartment maybe she could deny the two big haunting questions: Was the book really fiction? Did Yvonne murder Noah?

*No, categorically, no, she couldn't have.* Kadee kept telling herself. *Her note explained the truth: The book was a type of therapy, an emotional outlet to release her pain.*

But she just couldn't be sure; the annoying question of what the truth really was kept seeping into her consciousness uninvited, making her wonder on and off if Yvonne really had killed Noah.

After Yvonne's call Kadee felt wide awake, her curiosity piqued. She imagined what Yvonne wanted to talk about. But she was also a tad apprehensive.

*It will be nice to see her,* she told herself. As she swung her legs off the bed and stepped onto the hard-wood floor, her feet flinched at the cold. Shaking off the shivers, she slipped her feet into knee length, furry knit socks and ambled into the kitchen to wake herself up with a fresh pot of coffee. She had some time to relax before she needed to leave for her internship. As she watched the brown, oily fluid — the elixir of the gods, as far as she was concerned — fill the glass pot, she decided not to allow her mind to get into her typical cerebral warfare, mulling over what Yvonne wanted to talk about all day. *NO.* She had important business to do. She would wait and see what happened.

Kadee now worked as an intern for the New York City Police Department. Following Noah's murder, Gibbs pulled some strings. Kadee was soon employed as a forensic consultant. She was helping with crime scene investigations. It was a fortuitous twist of fate. Through her personal tragedy, something good happened: Kadee was presented with the opportunity of a lifetime.

That particular morning turned out to be challenging. She arrived at the station with layers of clothes. In a feeble attempt to protect herself from the sub-freezing temperatures, she even wore a pair of wool stockings under her pants. The city wind whipped itself into a frenzy. No matter how much clothing she piled on, she felt naked and exposed to the elements.

She puffed warm air onto her hands when she arrived. She took her hat off, relieved to be inside. She went into her little office, where files were sprawled across her desk. She had been going through some cold cases, seeing if she found something that had been missed. She put the floor heater on and began peeling off layer after layer. She was mid-peel when Poole came in.

"Stop. Bundle yourself up. We're heading out." Poole's voice gruff. His nose, a swelling of color, bright red. He wore a navy blue knit hat pulled all the way down below his eyebrows. It skimmed the tops of his eyes. "There's been a stabbing." He watched Kadee's jaw drop. "You ready for this?"

She nodded *yes*. It was her first official onsite investigation.

Poole held the door open for her. He shook his head. "For fuck's sake, it's cold."

Kadee had been working alongside Poole and Gibbs for almost a month. She knew they had a tendency to bicker like an old married couple. So, she wasn't surprised when she got into the car with them and the wrangling started immediately. Kadee listened, her breath blew little clouds of white into the air. She knew better than to interfere with their banter.

The victim: Jacob Temple, a 44-year-old psychologist. He was found by his wife, a real estate agent. She had been away for the weekend. When she arrived home, she found her husband stabbed to death, a fork sticking out of each of his eyes.

Poole jumped to the conclusion that the victim's wife had done the deed. Of course, they would still run a full investigation. They had to. But he was positive his instinct would turn out correct.

Gibbs was used to this kind of gut reaction from Poole. He found it amusing, particularly because Poole was correct on the lower end of thirty percent of the time. Not a very accurate gut instinct. Plus, Gibbs realized Poole was bringing into the mix a bit of personal bias: a bitter divorce.

Kadee remained silent, enraptured, her head flicking back and forth as she watched them argue like an old married couple.

"Come on, Poole," Gibbs' mouth released large clouds of frost with each exhale. "You always go for the partner. We haven't even seen the crime scene yet."

Poole shot Gibbs a quick glance, averting his eyes from the heavy New York City traffic for the briefest of moments. "For fuck's sake, I know that. I'm just sayin. There's a good chance it's her. It's basic statistics."

"When you make an assumption like that it's bound to cloud your judgment is all. We haven't even met the wife." Gibbs laughed at his sneer. "Shit, you're probably already thinking about handcuffing her."

Poole hated when Gibbs was right, especially about Poole's predictability. "Fuck off!"

Gibbs laughed. Kadee joined in once Poole chuckled along. Gibbs changed the subject to basketball.

Kadee leaned back into the car seat, wrapped her arms around her chest for added warmth. *Blah, blah, basketball.* She tuned them out.

They pulled up alongside the curb right in front of the victim's apartment. A perk of traveling in a police vehicle: They didn't have to drive around for hours looking for that coveted New York City parking spot.

Jacob Temple was a well-known radio psychologist. Kadee had listened to his show a few times. She got annoyed at the way he dished out advice. He gave simple explanations for what she felt were complicated questions. She knew there was a limitation to what could be done in a five minute on-air conversation, but it still irritated her. So she didn't tune in often.

He and his wife, Fiona, lived in Kadee's neighborhood. She knew the building door and window frames, an elegant brownstone with red wood adorning the front of the two-story building. Planters spilling the dried corpses of autumn flowers lined the sills of the two first-floor windows.

She saw Jacob Temple at her gym a few times. He even smiled at her once, made eye contact while she stretched and he ran on a nearby treadmill. The Upper Eastside was a like a small town within a big city, every few blocks being its own neighborhood. And like a small town, neighbors from the 'hood would see the same people at the same grocery store, the dry cleaner, the local restaurants. And sometimes, like small-town neighbors, they overheard personal information about each other. Sometimes they knew information that really should have been private.

Jacob and Fiona occupied the entire first floor of the brownstone. Kadee looked up the long flight of stairs that led to the front door. She had always adored brownstones. But now they reminded her of Noah. Although the veneer of the building appeared relatively different than Noah's, the overall architecture and aesthetic was the same. And now with it being the scene of a murder, she could not help but associate the apartment with him.

Kadee used to fantasize about living in a brownstone, thinking that someday, if she was ever able to afford it, it was just the sort of building that she would want to be her home. But as they walked up the long flight of stairs, Kadee had memories of going to Noah's apartment. She wondered if she could ever untangle herself from the memories of Noah and disconnect from them. She shook her head, tried to rid herself of the gruesome images.

She placed her right hand across her chest. Sometimes she really missed him.

She hated *that.*

From the outside the brownstone appeared to be a comfortable, peaceful place to live. She grimaced as they made their way through the outer door into the hallway. It didn't matter how the building looked from the outside. Although it may have appeared luxurious and safe, it could never protect its residents from the harsh reality of life: Everyone, no matter their financial comforts, came face-to-face with heartache.

The crime scene unit had arrived a few minutes before them; they had already begun their investigation. The front door hung ajar. Poole peeked his head in, made eye contact with Fiona. She motioned her hand: *Come in.*

Fiona, a tall, substantial woman, stood at five-foot ten. She wasn't overweight, just large-boned and strong looking. Her tan velour jogging suit fit snug around her body. She rippled as she walked. She had a thick mane of reddish hair, wavy and long. Her eyes, brown and swollen, looked as though she had been crying for days.

Jacob Temple lay on the floor of his den drenched in blood. A sea of crimson soaked over angry wounds on his chest and throat, one fork in each eye, the metal handles suspended.

Kadee never witnessed a real crime scene before. Of course, she had read about crime scene analysis in her forensic science class, and she had viewed images as part of her education. But being in the room with a murdered body was sickening. The gashes. The crying flesh, open, hanging, exposing blubbery insides. The sight, ghastly. The stench, worse. The air, thick and sour, reeked of rot and death. She palmed her nose and mouth, a trickle of vomit inching up her esophagus.

Gibbs came to her side and offered her smelling salt. It did not help much.

Jacob was a tall man with long, thin legs and a lean, muscular upper body. His coarse brown hair flowed thick over his neck. Congealed blood covered the dark strands. The crime scene investigators discovered that he had hair implants.

Kadee cringed inside when they revealed that information. In some ways being a murder victim abolished the person's right to privacy. Of course the implants were nothing compared to some of the things that were exposed during an investigation. That was certainly the case when it came to Noah's murder. That would also be the case with Jacob Temple.

Poole stood over the body, tried to get a better look at the injuries. Even this longtime career detective recoiled from the awful scene.

Jacob Temple's shirt was off, his chest hairless and covered with small lacerations. The slash across his neck left a gaping hole, flaps of dark red and black surrounded the wound. Long lines of dried blood trailed down from his eyes. The two forks deep inside his eyeballs left a pool of red on the wood floor of the den.

The three sat down on a large red sofa to question Fiona. She sat across on a matching red love seat. A deep red that echoed the blood that had drained from her husband and all the tragedy that came with it. She tore at a tissue bit by bit. The tiny pieces floated to the rug like a snow flurry on a sad winter day.

Fiona's voice and demeanor didn't match her body. She looked so strong, but her voice was soft and meek. She partially covered her mouth with her hand when she spoke. It made it hard to hear her. Her eyes, dark, saucer-like and pleading. At the time it was hard to know if it was just a reaction to the shock or her natural comportment. But she reminded Kadee of a girl trapped in a woman's body.

Fiona had been away visiting her family in Miami. They would have to confirm her alibi, of course, but it appeared that she could not have been the murderer. It was obvious even without forensics that Jacob had been dead for at least twelve hours, and Fiona had only just arrived home. Kadee thought Poole sighed upon hearing that Fiona's whereabouts were accounted for at the time of the murder. Or perhaps it was just that she imagined he was disappointed. Regardless, he continued to ask Fiona some difficult questions.

Fiona's eyes, two fixed circles, the tears poured out of the corners, trickling down her face as she responded to Poole's inquires. Her distress, palpable. Kadee could feel it: impenetrable brokenness.

"Ma'am, is there anyone you can think of who would want to hurt your husband?" Poole kept his voice steady and unemotional.

Fiona — chin down, eyes up and glued on Poole — spoke with a cracked voice. "He talked to so many people on his show. Some of them were crazy." She wiped her eyes, smudging the mascara underneath, like the makeup of an aging rocker still desperate for attention from her dwindling concert crowds.

"Was there any caller in particular that your husband mentioned or one that you noticed, one that stood out to you?"

She sniffled. "There was one Detective... Poole you said, right?"

Poole nodded.

"Detective Poole. There was one recently. It's hard for me to think right now. But there was at least one I can think of. I don't know her full name. I just remember Jacob mentioning her. I... I...," she burst out in moan as she doubled over and sobbed.

Kadee could feel her own eyes welling up. "I'm so sorry for your loss, Mrs. Temple. I know this is very hard."

She looked up at Kadee, wiped her eyes. "What would you know?"

Kadee's mouth parted. She looked into Fiona's eyes, wanting to say: *I do know. I wish I didn't. But I do.* She swallowed. Fiona took a heavy breath. Her eyes met Kadee's, "I'm sorry. I'm just..... on edge."

Kadee nodded.

Fiona turned to Poole. "The caller is a woman. She used the name Beth. She called almost every day. Well, every day that Jacob was on the radio. She sent him a package over the holidays. A thank-you gift for all of his advice. But I think she was in love with him."

Poole took notes. "Do you know what her sickness was?"

Kadee glared at him. Poole was the type who thought a person had to be seriously mentally ill to seek out therapy or any other mental health support.

Poole noted Kadee's disapproval. He grimaced. "Do you know why she was calling the show? What she needed advice for?"

Fiona mumbled, her hand partially covering her mouth.

The three leaned all the way forward, straining to hear her.

"I think Jacob said she was a middle-aged woman. Fiftyish. She couldn't stop thinking about an ex-boyfriend." She swallowed.

"Lots of people call the show for that kind of stuff. But her relationship ended when this Beth was thirty. So over twenty years ago. Can you believe she had never moved on? It sounded creepy to me."

Poole wrote as Fiona talked.

Kadee's interest piqued, wondering if Beth switched her obsession from her ex-boyfriend to Jacob Temple.

Fiona looked up. "Truthfully, I think a lot of the women that called the show had a crush on Jacob. He has… had…" Fiona choked back a sob.

Poole said, "It's OK, ma'am." He nodded for her to continue.

"He had such a nice voice. Jacob just had a way with people…" her lips dropped into a frown.

"Did anyone ever threaten your husband?"

"I don't think so, but I don't really know to be honest." She sobbed again. "I always worried something would happen to him. I never liked him doing that show."

"What about his family? Parents, siblings? Other close relatives we could talk to?"

She sniffled. "No. No. No one. Jacob was an only child. Both of his parents are gone. His father about a year ago and then his mother just about six months ago. It happened so close together. It was very hard on Jacob. The last year was a terrible time for him… for us… and now… this…"

Fiona got up to retrieve more tissues when a skinny blond woman holding a cat on a harness stuck her head in the door. "Fee? Fee?"

Fiona turned, made eye contact with the woman. The woman placed her cat on the floor. The two hugged.

Fiona hysterical, "Oh, Sally." Her long arms wrapped around Sally's slim back. They held the embrace until Fiona calmed down.

Sally was a tall, bony blond, her face skeletal and her eyes, dark sunken bowls that seemed to take up most of her face. She appeared to be in her late forties and looked like she hadn't eaten in days. Sally looked at Poole, Gibbs and Kadee. "I'm Sally Stringfellow. The upstairs neighbor." Her eyes frozen-looking, her voice flat. "This is Pip. My feline companion." She patted Pip's back.

Pip looked like her alter ego: a plump orange tabby with a belly that swept the floor as he walked. Fiona went into a cabinet, leaned down, gave Pip a cat treat. It was obvious that the two women were familiar with each other.

Fiona turned to the detectives. "Pip's named after the male character in *Great Expectations*. Charles Dickens' novel. Sally's a writer."

"Oh. Right." Poole noted. He looked at Gibbs, one eye squinted with a sarcastic gleam.

He turned toward Sally and started with some routine questions: Did she hear anything strange? See anything strange? Basically, did she know anything that could provide a lead in the case.

Sally responded "No" to each question.

Sally lived alone. They hadn't determined the time of the murder yet, but the Crime Scene Unit estimated that it happened some time the day before. Sally said she had been alone all day and night, writing. She had no one to account for her. Of course, that didn't mean she did it, but it did mean they couldn't eliminate her as a suspect. She lived right upstairs. She probably knew the Temple's comings and goings. As far as Poole was concerned, something off about her sent up a red flag.

Sally was odd, her eyes wide with a frozen gaze — but shifty, too. She barely blinked, yet her eyes twitched about. Her stiff manner, like an ice-covered statue, appeared rigid and weighty in movement.

While Kadee observed her, Poole ran through his questions.

"Ma'am, you said you were home all day and night."

"Correct." Her eyes wandered around Poole. "Pip, Pip, come here darling, darling." She looked like she might strain herself as she picked up her cat and placed him on her lap. She stroked his back while Gibbs kept an eye on Fiona.

Poole huffed over the cat nonsense. "You didn't hear anything?"

"Nothing," her eyes zigzagged. "Nothing."

"What were you doing all of that time you were home?"

"Writing and sleeping. Same thing I always do when it's freezing out, same thing I always do. I don't like going out in the winter if I don't have to, if I don't have to," her voice hollow.

"Did you speak to anyone on the phone?"

"I don't think so. I don't have many friends. I'm a loner type. A loner. Well except for Fee," she looked at Fiona. "Fee is my closest friend, closest."

Fiona nodded, buried her face in her hands. She started sobbing again.

"I'm socially awkward. But Fee, here, well... she understands me, understands me. And so did Jacob, so did Jacob." Though a few tears rolled down Sally's cheeks, her eyes remained two dark, bottomless pits void of any emotion. "I hope you find who did this to him. It's so scary, so scary."

"Is there anyone you can think of who would want to hurt Dr. Temple?"

"Could be a caller from his show. I used to listen in sometimes, sometimes. There are some really damaged people in this world, and Jacob helped many of them. Maybe someone he spoke to on his show, on his show."

Kadee noticed Sally's eyes were expressionless when she wailed, placed her face onto Pip's back, and cried into his fur. It seemed incongruent. She went from flat and unemotional to passionate and out of control.

Of course, she could have been in shock, but Kadee jotted down some notes. She wanted to think about her observations of Sally. Her intuition told her that something wasn't right, but she did not know what. Sure, they had only one meeting, under extraordinary circumstances, but her intuition hit high alert.

In the meantime, Poole gave Fiona and Sally his card. Poole already felt suspicious about the relationship between Fiona and this Stringfellow character. There was something there to be uncovered. Maybe relevant to the case, maybe not.

One thing Poole loved about the work: discovering all the dirty secrets people kept. One thing that constantly pissed him off: needing evidence. It was crucial, his personal motto, but sometimes the whole proof thing really got his ire going. Sometimes he wished he could just handcuff the suspect he felt was guilty. In this case it was Fiona Temple, even though she had an alibi. He didn't trust her.

He asked the women to call if they thought of anything. They both nodded in agreement. Fiona walked them to the door. Sally remained in her chair petting and talking to Pip.

The trio went back outside. For Kadee, the blast of cold air provided a relief after the intensity of the crime scene. Poole huffed. "For fuck's sake, that woman's tendency to repeat everything she says is annoying. She must drive her friends batty."

Gibbs laughed. "She's a quirky one all right. I did enjoy her cat. Pip's a great name for a cat." Gibbs had three cats. Poole always joked with him that he was one cat away from turning into a crazy cat lady.

"You and your feline fetish. Looks like she feeds all of her food to the cat. She's as skinny as a rail — a step away from the grave — while that cat is fat as fuck."

"But cute," Gibbs teased. He knew Poole hated cats almost as much as he hated his ex-wife. He couldn't resist poking at him. Poole took himself too seriously sometimes.

"Whatever, Gibbs. There's something about those two that rub me wrong."

"Yeah. Maybe." Gibbs' eyes pensive. He opened the car door.

They stopped for takeout sandwiches — though Kadee had little appetite — then headed back to the station.

She sat in the back of the automobile, her arms wrapped around her chest. Thoughts about Noah's murder came into her mind. Having read Yvonne's book, she had an image of what he looked like right before he died. *But of course, that's not really what he looked like. The book is fiction.*

Yvonne was a descriptive writer. The murder scene in the book crafted a vivid picture. Even if it was just an imaginative re-creation, it was a dramatic one. Kadee closed her eyes trying to clear her mind of it.

# CHAPTER 2

The following afternoon, Kadee had her lunch date with Yvonne at the diner on First Avenue. She still had mixed thoughts about whether or not Yvonne killed Noah. Even though Yvonne wrote her that note about the story being fiction, the details and perspicuity of the narrative made it feel so real. She wanted to believe it was fiction. Oh, how she needed to believe that. For the most part, she did. But that part of her that could never quite let go of things kept her wondering.

Was it her intuition or some cerebral game she played with herself? She couldn't be sure. Regardless, she looked forward to seeing Yvonne.

Kadee had been working through her grief, trying to move on and get past what had happened. It wasn't easy. She assumed Yvonne was experiencing similar emotions. It had only been four months since Noah's murder. Yvonne had to be suffering, too. Or maybe Kadee needed to believe that.

Loss is an inevitable part of life. Kadee knew that intellectually. But knowing something in theory is very different than having the intimate knowledge that only life experience offers. Once some time passed and the initial shock wore off, Kadee was alone trying to sort through her feelings.

Kadee had heard in a lecture once that the grief process was more difficult when the relationship that was lost was conflicted. The mix of a loving attachment with intense anger, for the same person, made the course of moving on complicated.

Noah's death, so sudden and tragic, took a while to sink in. She needed time to accept what had happened. In the beginning, she recognized that he was gone, but it didn't really hit her until a month or so later.

One evening while sitting in a class presentation about intimate relationship homicides, the truth of what happened hit her. Her stomach knotted. She could feel a heaviness in her throat. She felt panicked, her heart racing, her breath shallow. She went outside into an open space — immediately — she felt she might die. She left the presentation, wandered aimlessly through the west side of Manhattan, feeling lost and confused.

Everything she saw seemed unreal, almost like an illusion. Nothing meant anything. Life itself, a transitory state, filled only with moments that taken collectively make up a life. But what did it all mean anyway? Each thing, errands, school, work, even barbeques, holidays and birthdays. It all seemed so senseless, a made up distraction, a calling away from a truth about life. That it is short, fleeting. That it could end in one split second.

Loss and trauma have a way of making it hard to avoid this truth. Kadee had mixed feelings about Noah, but one thing was clear. His loss called her attention to the reality of life, made it so poignant that she couldn't avoid it. She was in a full-blown existential crisis.

After dashing out of class and drifting around Manhattan for almost three hours, unaware of how much time had passed, Kadee finally went home. Her legs were tired, and her heart hurt. It wasn't just Noah's murder, though that was a lot of it. It was also the loss of life in general. There was an emptiness, a hole, a nothingness. When she finally meandered home, she tried to sleep away the pain.

She felt a little better the next morning. Sleep often helped her regain her balance. But she wondered if she would always feel — be — just a little broken. Or maybe, she wondered, *everyone is just a little broken.*

*Everyone is just a little broken.*

It felt strange, in a way, Noah had hurt her so much while he was alive, but his death felt like the tragedy of her life.

Of course, this was complicated by the fact that she also felt relief over his demise. This bit really distressed her. It was an uncomfortable reality. One that Kadee tried to deny, but couldn't. He had been murdered. How could she allow herself to feel anything but devastated.

Kadee had been seeing a new therapist. She decided against Dr. Ramirez because of her connection with Yvonne. She was seeing a young male therapist, Dr. Wright. She got the referral from her professor. Dr. Wright was in his early forties, short with a pot belly and dark and clear eyes. They glistened. He possessed an even and undemonstrative manner, much like Yvonne's, but those eyes communicated an almanac of emotions. In that way, Dr. Wright reminded her of Noah.

In fact, Kadee saw Noah in a lot of people. Walking down the street, riding the subway, dining in a restaurant. She wouldn't even be thinking about him when suddenly she would suspect she saw him, only to discover it was a stranger. It would cause a jarring pierce to her heart whenever that happened. Dr. Wright was helping Kadee through her grief process. He told her that she had to talk through and be honest with herself about all of her feelings, even the ugly ones. The only way she could integrate the loss, and move past the hardest part of the sorrow, was to be honest with him, and most important, with herself. Kadee was hopeful that things would get easier with time.

The Yvonne dilemma was a whole other can of worms. Kadee hadn't told anyone about Yvonne's fictional admission, not Dr. Wright, not Alex, not even Vanessa. Kadee didn't know what to believe. Most of the time she just tried not to think about it. But then the unwelcome question about the truth would pop into her head. She would go back and forth and back and forth trying to make sense of the whole thing.

*If it wasn't the truth, why would Yvonne say that it was? Maybe she meant the story was true with the exception of the murder scene. Maybe that part was just her fantasy.* Certainly Kadee had thought of killing Noah. Not in the elaborate fashion that Yvonne's protagonist Emily went into, but it could have been a variation on imagining what it would have been like as a way to work through her rage toward him. Then again, the amount of detail made it seem real. *Well, isn't that what good fiction writers do? They use descriptive language to make something in their imagination seem authentic on the pages,* she would remind herself over and over. She hated how her mind would not let go of things.

*It's fiction, Kadee, FICTION.*

But no matter how many times she repeated that to herself, yelling at her own thoughts, she just couldn't quite convince herself. The nagging uncertainty remained. And she hated that.

The vivid description of the murderous act in Yvonne's book jumped out at Kadee. She had nightmares where she could see exactly what happened. Her sleeping mind placed Yvonne in the role of Emily Goodyear. The dream images showed Yvonne, her dark hair pulled back, grabbing the huge butcher knife, looking crazed, stabbing Noah over and over. His face racked with terror and pain as he witnessed someone he loved, someone he trusted, take his life. This paradox of passion transformed a violent, deadly act, through its intimacy, into the ultimate betrayal.

In the book, Emily detailed the moment when her eyes met his, and she could see the terror register across his face. The exact moment she knew that he knew that she was going to kill him. She described feeling powerful. He had taken her strength, but in that moment she got it back. Yet, she also described a disturbing sense of closeness with him.

Emily Goodyear narrated that moment in the book: *It was an intimate moment when our eyes met. I was the last person he would see before he left this world. He would leave by my hand, keeping us forever bonded. As his blood splattered all over me, I could see the inside of his body through the wounds. I could feel his fluid all around me. It felt warm. I stood over him, blood everywhere, and I knew in that moment that I would never be closer to anyone than I was with him. As I watched the last bit of life ooze out of him, as he took his very last breath, I wiped his blood across my face. I never felt more connected to anyone than I did in that moment or relieved that someone I loved was gone.*

Emily didn't describe any remorse either. The book sort of just ended after Emily got away with murder.

Kadee walked into the diner. Yvonne, already seated at a table, sipped her tea, her pinky finger raised in the air as she lifted the cup to her mouth. She noticed Kadee, stood up and waved her over.

It was an odd moment for Kadee. She observed herself in a quick moment of self-reflection. She thought she would feel some discomfort upon seeing Yvonne, the question of if she was a killer still unanswered. But she actually felt warm when she noticed her waving, glad to see her, almost like she was a long-lost relative with whom she had reconnected. Kadee smiled with her whole face. The safety she had felt in Yvonne's therapy space washed over her.

Yvonne walked to Kadee and pulled her close, hugged her tight as can be.

Kadee hugged her back.

They sat. Kadee noticed that Yvonne changed her hair again. She had almost down-to-her-waist long, pin-straight hair. Thick, too, it was as thick as Vanessa's, but straight instead of curly.

Yvonne noticed Kadee noticing her new hair. She tilted her head, ran her fingers through and said, "Do you like it?"

Kadee's eyes widened, surprised by Yvonne's transformation. Yvonne looked so different with long hair. Then Kadee realized that she wasn't wearing her glasses either. The two alterations together made her look almost unfamiliar.

"Yes… yes, I do. It looks nice."

"This was just the change I needed. You know, after everything that happened, I suppose I thought a bit of a physical makeover would help me with…with the harder part, the psychological process of letting go and moving on. Starting over. You know what I mean? Don't you?"

"I totally do. It's been very hard for me too."

"It's so good to see you, Kadee. I feel like we have been through so much together… when I think about you, I always say to myself that you are probably going through the same thing as me… missing Noah… but feeling betrayed too," she paused. "It's very difficult, the two together. Isn't it?"

"I'm so glad to hear you say that. It's hard to even describe the conflicting feelings. It's like I feel so awful that he's gone, but I'm still angry. And then I feel guilty for being angry. I even feel relieved. How can I feel those things? He's been murdered for Christ's sake…" she paused. The word "murdered" rolling off her tongue reminded her that she still wasn't sure if Yvonne was Noah's killer.

*Maybe I should just come right out and ask her about the book. But what if she says it's true? I'm not sure I want to know if the answer is going to be yes. There's no way she did it. No way. It feels so nice to be with her.*

They chitchatted. Kadee enjoyed the conversation. Yvonne seemed so… normal. Certainly if she was a killer, Kadee would sense something. Even if she wasn't emanating some murderess vibe, at the very least Kadee would be able to tell something was off.

Their food arrived. They both ordered the same cheeseburger and fries, winter comfort food.

Kadee rolled her fry in ketchup, looked up at Yvonne, "So what is it that you wanted to talk to me about?"

Yvonne swallowed the delicate bite of her burger, her eye contact unwavering. "So you liked my book?"

"Yes… yes I did. Oh, here…" She reached in her bag, retrieved the book and handed it to Yvonne. A chill emerged throughout her body. *Here it goes; I will finally know the truth.*

"I knew you would." The sunlight reflecting off the building across the street flickered in Yvonne's eyes. She wore her hand like a visor across her forehead, took the book in her other hand, placed it in her purse. She took another bite of her burger. Kadee waited for Yvonne to continue talking. Her chewing seemed to last an eternity. "I'm writing another one, and well," Yvonne paused, sipped her tea. "Well, I thought maybe you could help me."

Kadee squinted. "How?"

"Well, I remember you were researching stalking and cata-thy-mia. Did I say that right? Catathymia? I never heard of it before you told me about it."

Kadee nodded, her eyes inquisitive.

"Well, I was wondering if you could go over some of your research with me. You see, in this next book, my character is going to first stalk and then kill her victim. I need to under-stand what makes someone become a stalker. You know, so the character seems real. Fiction writers do that sometimes, consult with experts."

Kadee's palms sweated as she ruminated more about the possibility of Yvonne killing Noah. "I can lend you some of my research, if you think that would help." She took her sweater off. "By the way," her voice box shook a little, "what happens to Emily? Does she feel guilt or remorse? It wasn't clear in the first book."

Yvonne gave a thin smile. She tilted her head. "Well, I'm not sure Kadee. I didn't give it much thought, actually. Once she killed him, it was just over. One. Two. Three. And it was done. But I'd like to think she had some guilt." She lowered her voice a little. "She would be a psychopath if she didn't. That wouldn't be good."

"It's not that cut and dry. You know human behaviors don't fit into compartments. I remember you said that a few times in our… um…" she looked down at her fingers, "in our sessions. Criminality is just like any other personality feature. It has gray areas and individual variability. It's loaded with contradictions. You know this."

"Yes, I suppose I do. I mean, I never worked with criminals, but I know this from my clinical work." She paused, stared into Kadee's eyes. She wasn't blinking. "I think Emily did feel guilt. I think she really did. She killed the man she loved, after all. She had to feel something."

Kadee couldn't stop herself. She wanted to believe, needed to believe that Yvonne was not a killer. She needed to just come right out and ask her already, removing the large unspoken elephant that sat between them.

Kadee felt the words on the edge of her mouth, but she chickened out. She skirted around the question. "Does she miss him, Yvonne? Does Emily miss Oliver?" Oliver was the name Yvonne assigned to the murder victim in her book.

"Yes, I think Emily does miss Oliver. He did deceive her, though. He broke her heart into itsy-bitsy, tiny little pieces, so I think part of her will always feel that he deserved it. But, yes, I think sometimes when she's alone and really thinks about him, she misses him. He was the love of her life. I think she will always love him. I mean, always *would* love him." A laugh emerged from her throat. "It's funny to talk about Emily as if she were real."

*Here's your opening. For Christ's sake, just ask her already.*

She gulped. "Yvonne…" she stopped, pondered the words. "Yes?"

"I… I don't know the right way to ask this… and, truthfully, it's a little uncomfortable for me, but I need to know something."

"OK. Please don't feel funny. You can ask me anything."

"Um… well… that day in the park when you told me about your book, I said that it sounded like the truth, and you said it was… It has been bothering me ever since. What did you mean when you said it was the truth?" she whispered. "What does that mean exactly? Does it mean that you killed Noah?" She wrapped her arms across her chest.

Yvonne's eyes widened. "Oh my, Kadee. Oh my dear... I didn't mean that I..." she lowered her head and her voice. "I didn't mean that I killed him. I would never be capable of doing something like that. I can't believe you have been carrying that around with you since the fall. My dear..."

"I'm sorry. I didn't really think you did it, but with what you said in the park and then... well, your book... it's very descriptive... that murder scene..."

"When I said it was the truth, I was referring to my feelings. Emily is a fictional character I created to work through my own emotions. I made her up, put her in an imaginary situation and then used her narrative to access my own hurt and pain. That's why it was so therapeutic. I feel a little funny about this... I thought you understood what I meant." She put her hands up to her face. She was flushed. "And the murder scene... well... I just took what I knew from the detectives' descriptions and the crime scene photos. We both saw those images." She looked down, shook her head. "I wish I could get those pictures out of my mind. Writing about it did help a bit. Anyhoo, I suppose it must be decent writing if you're saying it was very descriptive."

"Wow... a huge relief." She exhaled all the tension that had been building inside. "I was afraid to ask you, but I am so glad that I did. And it *is* good writing. I related to a lot of Emily's story. So your next one is going to be about a murder too?"

"Yes, yes. That's why I wanted your input."

The waitress came back. She had a thick sweater over her uniform. It must have been cold in the diner, but Kadee felt hot, still recovering from asking Yvonne that question. She regained her equilibrium. The relief of knowing the truth lifted the world off her shoulders.

Kadee asked for the check. She had to head over to the station. "I can email you some of that research tonight, if you'd like. Unfortunately, I do have to get going. It was so nice to see you though. I'm glad we cleared the air. Maybe we could meet up again soon?" Kadee shifted through her bag, looked for her money.

"I would really like that Kadee… and yes, please email me what you can. Listen, there's something else I wanted to tell you."

"OK," Kadee placed a twenty-dollar bill on the table and looked at Yvonne.

"I was waiting for the right moment to tell you. I'm dating John Poole."

Kadee froze, cocked her head a little off-center.

"You know John Poole. Detective Poole. We started seeing each other a few weeks ago. He told me you were working with him. Small world, right?" She smiled.

"Yeah, small world," she digested the information. "Wow, that's… um… how did that happen?"

"It was a funny thing really. As part of my letting-go process, I decided to stop by the station one day to show my gratitude for all of his help. Detectives don't have an easy job. It's a lot of responsibility and, well… I just wanted to express my appreciation. We got to talking. One thing led to another. He asked me to go for coffee, and then that led to a lunch, then a dinner. Now it's official. We're dating. He's been good for me. Just what the doctor ordered."

"Wow. It's so strange how life happens. I'm glad he's making you happy."

"Oh, he is. He really is." Yvonne took her hand, tossed her long hair off her shoulders. It draped down her back. She grabbed her bag and got up from the table.

Kadee stood up. They were standing face to face. Yvonne's large-heeled boots made her almost as tall as Kadee, who wore flat-heeled boots.

"Well, let me know if you need more information after I email you the research. I'll add references for a few books too. I think that would be enough for a work of fiction."

Yvonne leaned in, took Kadee's money off the table and handed it back to her. "Please."

"You sure?"

Yvonne smiled, "Think of it as a thank-you in advance for all the research you're going to send me."

"OK. Thanks. I'll get you next time."

Yvonne hugged Kadee. "Thank you, Kadee. It was so good to see you. Let's talk next week or something and do this again. Or I may see you down at the station before then."

"Good plan and great to see you too."

# Chapter 3

Jane Light sat glued to her television. The information about Jacob Temple's murder was all over the news. She leaned on her threadbare couch, the white foam stuffing pushing through in numerous spots. It looked hideous, and felt even worse to sit on. But, she couldn't part with it. In fact, Jane Light had difficulty throwing anything out.

Her pre-war one bedroom apartment on the Lower Eastside was filled with piles and piles of old magazines and newspapers, old clothes, boxes filled with bills and paperwork, things she had been collecting over the last nineteen years. She had a hard time moving around her apartment. The clutter, squeezed into the apartment like an elephant stuffed in a lion's cage, hogged all the free space she had.

She reached behind the couch, pulled out her knitting needles. Knitting held her together, her sanity just a snag away from oblivion. She was weaving together a blue scarf mixed with green. Already long enough, she had planned to finish the ends that day, but when she learned about Jacob, she decided to continue making it longer. And longer still.

The six o'clock news had just started when her buzzer rang. She made her way through the maze of boxes and objet d'trash, hit the buzzer. She opened her front door to hear her Fresh Direct delivery man huffing and puffing as he trudged his way up the five flights of stairs with the boxes of groceries she had ordered.

A short stout man with a thick mustache and a strong voice entered. As Jane moved aside to let him pass, she didn't notice him recoil at the smell, a single smell that choked out all other odors in her apartment. Something like dirty laundry mixed with unwashed feet with an undertone of soured milk. Jane didn't notice it much. Or at all. He asked where he should place the three boxes. Jane pointed to a naked piece of floor to the left of her refrigerator. He placed them down, had her sign and hurried off.

She quickly put the perishables away, leaving a steak out for her dinner. She went back to watch the news. Jane could not fathom how nineteen years had passed since she first met Jacob Temple. She had been thirty years old at the time. Idealistic and hopeful, with long brown hair. Her figure, curvaceous. Jacob and she had met at a bar one night. He was younger than her by five years, handsome and charming. She liked him immediately.

Jane's hair was still long, though gray strands dispersed rather generously among the brown ones. She looked older than her forty-nine years. Her full breasts hung low, the nipples practically touching her stomach. She didn't care for bras. She was thick in the middle. She didn't care for diets. More than anything, though, she had lost her liveliness. Her *joie de vivre*. Her eyes used to sparkle. Her lips, pink and smiley. Now she had deep lines around her mouth and eyes, her skin, pale and tired looking.

She had been calling Jacob's show for months, disguising her voice just a bit and using Beth, her middle name, to hide her identity. She missed him so much. When she discovered he was on a call-in radio show, she couldn't resist. She had felt so dead. She had felt that way for years, ever since Jacob ended their relationship and insisted that Jane never contact him again. Hearing his gentle voice nourished her soul. It made her feel alive. Talking to him on the show reminded her of how she felt when they dated.

"I Will Always Love You" blared from her phone, knocking Jane out of her trance. The song, Whitney Houston's version, was the ringtone Jane had set for her sister, Vivian. In fact, it was the ringtone she had set for everyone in her contact list. It was her favorite song. It was her and Jacob's song.

No one else would be calling her at this time, but she checked her caller ID to confirm that it was, in fact, Vivian. She could be highly annoying and melodramatic, but she was well-intentioned. Jane hesitated, took a deep breath, then answered the phone using her cheeriest of voices.

"Jane, it's Viv," as if her nasally voice could ever be mistaken. She sounded like she had a clothespin perpetually clipped on her nose.

"Hi Viv. How's it going?" Jane's voice, falsely elated.

"Did you hear about Jacob Temple?" She didn't wait for a response. "He was murdered! Muuurrrddderrred!" She had a tendency to draw out words when she was distressed.

"Yes, I heard." The cheeriness drained from Jane's voice.

"He was muuurrrdddderrred!"

"I know."

"How on God's green earth can you sound so calm? He's been killed. Once they start investigating, you know they're gonna find out about you… about what happened. You need to call them first. If you call them first, you won't look guilty."

"How's that going to change anything?"

"If you call them first and just tell 'em the truth, they're more likely to believe you. I mean, you've been stalking him for years and calling in to the show."

"They have no way of finding me." Her voice flat, completely unconcerned.

"You've been calling that show almost every fuckin' day to talk about some guy — some unrequited love — and that unrequited love is *him*!"

"Yeah, I get that, but they have no track on me."

"I know you can be thickheaded. But really? What about caller ID? Huh? What about that? What if they find out about that restraining order?"

"That was a long time ago."

"But there must still be a record of it!" Vivian calmed herself. "Listen. I just don't want you to get into anymore trouble. You've had enough problems. Unless you did it! Did you kill him? Oh my God! Did you?" Vivian put her hands on her waist and tapped her foot, half expecting Jane to say that she had killed him.

"Vivian. Please. Calm down. I loved him. Talking to him on that show made me feel alive for the first time in I don't know how long. You know that. I've been doing better since we've been talking. I'm devastated by what happened."

"I know, honey. But please, Jane, please call the police. Let's be honest. If they unravel the truth, it doesn't sound good. Just go there or call them and have them come to you. Tell them the truth. Besides, the stuff you know about his past might help them find the killer. Jacob's killer. Do it for Jacob. OK?"

"Yeah, OK. I will."

"Love you, Jane. I'll call you tomorrow."

"Love you, too."

# Chapter 4

After her lunch date with Yvonne, Kadee headed over to the police station. Poole and Gibbs had asked her to accompany them to question Oscar Piedmont, the station manager for *On the Couch with Jacob Temple*. Poole had called over to let him know they would be coming. Aside from Piedmont's whereabouts at the time of the murder, they were hoping to get more information on some of the callers. And they wanted to retrieve the recordings of the show.

It was more than 20 blocks from the diner to the precinct. Kadee planned to take the subway. It was freezing, but after her conversation with Yvonne, she decided she needed air. She put her red hat on, wrapped the matching scarf all the way around her neck and over her mouth and nose. She commenced her journey.

She felt tremendous relief finally confirming that Yvonne did not kill Noah. But her presence roused unresolved feelings about him. Yvonne was a connection to him, to that part of Kadee's life, a part of her past that was painful. At the same time though, sharing her grief with Yvonne comforted her. She walked quickly, the wind biting like a wild animal at her nose, as she thought about how nice it was to feel understood without having to say much at all. Yvonne knew her emotional struggle intimately. This made her company soothing.

She thought back to the days that followed her picnic with Yvonne when she first learned of her book. She *had* contemplated going to Poole and Gibbs with Yvonne's fictional admission, but she felt an attachment to Yvonne. She admired her, trusted her. It was hard to separate the way she felt about her prior to her admission with how she felt about her afterward. *Thank God I didn't I tell them. Thank God. They would have thought I had gone off the deep end.* Her cadence accelerated as the gusts of frigid air pushed her from behind.

Besides — and she hated this part — if Yvonne *had* done it, she understood why she would have. She herself had considered the very same thing: killing Noah Donovan. Of course, letting your imagination run wild with some disturbing inner craving, like a steam engine that has run off the tracks, was far different than acting on it.

At the time, Kadee was so emotional about the whole thing, her judgment, and even her morality was compromised. After a few weeks passed and Kadee hadn't told anyone about the book, she decided that the best tactic was denial. Naturally, this wasn't an intelligent long-term solution. Kadee wasn't good at suppressing her feelings.

But at the time, it seemed like her only option. She didn't know what the truth was. How could she take action? So she pushed her thoughts somewhere deep into her subconscious. She tried her damnedest not to think about Emily Goodyear or Yvonne.

It's nearly unbelievable how the mind exercises strong denial. But when faced with information that is overwhelmingly traumatic, this type of defense mechanism is almost like the reflex of hands coming forward when someone falls, automatically defending the body from greater injury. The arms extend and the hands hit the ground for protection. The same way denial happens, without reflection, to keep the person safe from psychological harm.

Kadee sort of knew she was in denial, though. Her self-awareness and her desire to know the truth often made denial hard. Her thoughts would seep into her mind, even the unwanted thoughts. Sometimes no matter how strong the will to deny is, the will to know is greater.

She hadn't realized how heavily the whole situation weighed on her until Yvonne relieved her burden by explaining the truth. How could she be so fucking stupid, even contemplating that Yvonne actually killed Noah? She had been tormenting herself with some internal back and forth mind fuck, when all she had to do was ask Yvonne what really happened.

*For the love of God, Kadee, sometimes you really are your own worst enemy,* her mother's criticism echoing in her head.

Liza Carlisle would always say that to her when she was a young girl. "Kadee-love, you are making a big deal over nothing. Sometimes you really are your own worst enemy."

She hated when she had one of those grown-up moments, and had to recognize that her mother was right.

*Sometimes I think you look for shit to worry about to use as an existential exercise program. The more you ruminate, the better you get at it or some messed up variation on that.*

She stopped in a convenience store to get water and gum. Her mouth felt like sandpaper, dry from the winter air. She stuck a wad of Trident peppermint in her mouth. She walked the last block to the station.

It was so cold her toes could have fallen off and she would not have felt it. But the walk gave her the opportunity to process her feelings. It was a good day. She finally learned the answer to the question that had been haunting her, and it was the truth she had hoped for. It was nice to spend time with Yvonne. She thought they would get together again soon. That was that. She needed to re-focus her mind on who killed Jacob Temple.

Kadee opened the door at the station, her eyelashes dusted with traces of frost. Her cheeks, two splotches of red.

Poole gave her a look, "For fuck's sake, Kadee, did you walk here? You look frozen. It's negative five with the wind!"

"I know. Hindsight and such." She cupped her hands and warmed them with her breath. She gave Poole a look, a real look. He was in his early 50s, more than ten years older than Yvonne. Bald and tough, a nice man, just rough around the edges. The type that said whatever was on his mind, however he wanted to say it.

Poole was nothing like the charming and magnetic Noah. Maybe Yvonne wanted someone less complicated. Noah was riddled with internal conflict after all. His suave demeanor concealed the depth of his inner chaos. Maybe Yvonne saw Poole as trustworthy, the type of man who was easy to read, who would love her forever — exclusively.

Maybe he was just a step in Yvonne's moving-on process, or perhaps they would end up in a long-term committed relationship. Regardless, Yvonne had said that he was good for her. Wasn't that all that mattered? You just never know what attracts two people. Whatever Yvonne saw in Poole was her business. She deserved to be with a man who appreciated her, valued her and would never take her for granted. Poole seemed like the type of man who would give her that level of devotion.

She thought about her own moving-on process. She was with Alex now. Unlike Noah, he was consistent, stable and loving. There were no late nights lying in bed worrying, ruminating, wondering what was happening, sitting at her computer, looking through his Facebook, the stale smell of cigarettes lingering into the next day. No, Alex made her feel secure, loved, like the most fabulous woman in the world. She liked who she was when she was with him. And she loved him. But sometimes in the most private part of her head, a part that she completely despised, she still pined over Noah.

She hated that!

Poole, Gibbs and she entered the police car and headed south toward Jacob Temple's midtown recording studio where they were meeting Oscar Piedmont. It was a large office building, twenty-four floors, cement and steel, with an exterior comprised mostly of windows.

When they arrived, they hurried into the building to escape the blustery air. The studio was on the ninth floor. After exiting the elevator, Gibbs pulled on the heavy steel door, which opened to the reception area. A young ponytailed brunette with thick bangs and blue eye shadow waved them in. A pair of glasses hung from the tip of her nose.

"Hi, awfficers." Her extra-heavy New York accent prodded an inside chuckle out of Kadee. *The Bronx or Brooklyn?* "Can I get you any cawfee?"

Poole responded for all of them. "No thank you, ma'am."

Poole was about to ask her a few routine questions when a thin man, average height with jet-black hair and thick-rimmed red glasses rushed over to them. Clad in a shiny black shirt, with an extra-long collar and dark jeans, he introduced himself.

"Hi Detectives, I'm Oscar Piedmont. We spoke on the phone." His voice quick and shaky.

The three introduced themselves, each shook Oscar's hand. It felt warm and sweaty.

"Come this way." Oscar guided them through another doorway, down a long, narrow hall, through another doorway, into the recording studio. A small framed poster of Jacob Temple hung to the right of the door. A steel plate underneath read: *On the Couch with Jacob Temple.*

Inside, cable cords snaked around the room connecting the recording and transmission equipment. Stacks of boxes on one side of the room mirrored two small beige couches on the opposite side, a large flat-screen television dividing them. Behind that stood stacks of CDs of the show, each sectioned off by the month going back two and a half years to the show's beginning. During airtime, Jacob's producer would sit at a desk on the opposite side of the tech equipment while Jacob sat in a small adjoining room with line-of-sight to his producer through a picture window.

Oscar motioned for them to sit on the couch. He pulled two desk chairs over. He sat on one and Gibbs on the other. Poole and Kadee sat on the couch. Together they made a circle.

"How can I help?" Oscar blurted out, his voice high-pitched and squeaky.

Poole began, "What was your relationship like with Dr. Temple?"

"It was mostly a professional relationship. But, we did work closely. As you can see," he motioned his hand around the small studio.

"Did you ever meet his friends or family? Did you know anything about his personal life?"

Oscar pushed his thick-rimmed glasses up on his nose with his front finger. They looked too heavy for his face. "A few times, I met him outside of work. You know, for special occasions."

"For example?"

"Um, I was invited to his birthday dinner two years in a row and I went. He invited me to a dinner party last winter and I went. Over the two and a half years we worked together, I'd say I could count on one hand the times we spent together outside of work-related things."

"What about working with him? What was that like?"

"Well… it was just fine. I mean, I enjoyed working with Jacob," he paused to think. "To be honest," he paused again.

Poole leaned forward. "We need to know the truth, Mr. Piedmont."

"To be honest, he could be difficult sometimes, but I guess most people are if you spend enough time with them."

"Can you elaborate?"

"He was concerned about how he looked, and he talked about himself just a little too often. It got on my nerves sometimes. Then he got those hair plugs. They looked hideous, in my opinion, but he was thinning on top, and well… he didn't want that. He thought it made him look old. Then last year he started with Botox injections to his forehead. I thought it made him look sort of, well… at first it was fine, but then he had a few too many, too close together and his forehead… it didn't move."

Poole took notes. So did Kadee and Gibbs.

He pushed his glasses up onto the bridge of his nose again. "You see, I'm from Kalamazoo, Michigan. Moved to the city three years ago. People are different where I'm from. It took me awhile to get used to the fast-paced, competitive city-living. I guess Jacob was just trying to keep up his image. But he was a little too preoccupied for my taste, and then… well… I guess it's just not what I would have expected from a psychologist," he paused, looked thoughtful for a moment.

Perspiration had accumulated along the sides of his face, pasting down his hair. He stuck his fingers under his glasses and wiped away the sweat.

"All that being said, I did like Jacob. He grew up in a small town somewhere in upstate New York, moved here for graduate school. I always thought he felt he had something to prove. It's not easy being a celebrity. Everyone is always in your business, assuming your life is perfect. Of course, that's not true, detectives. I think Jacob was just trying to keep up his image, you see. But even with that, he was still likeable. He was always good to me."

Poole wiped his hand across his bald head. Kadee knew that he was tossing around what Oscar was saying.

"Mr. Piedmont, you seemed to know Dr. Temple quite well. Anyone you can think of who would want to hurt him?" Poole asked.

Oscar broke eye contact. He tilted his head up, looked at the ceiling.

"Mr. Piedmont," Poole leaned in.

"I don't know. There were a few regular callers on the show. One man called a few times agitated after his wife left him. He blamed Jacob. But, well….it wasn't Jacob's fault. The guy just seemed angry. He needed someone to blame."

Poole skimmed back over his notes. "Do you remember his name?"

"Yes, I believe he called himself Thomas."

"Anyway we could find this Thomas?"

"Well… no, not really. We don't register the numbers of people who call. It's a way to allow people to keep their anonymity. But he's on the recordings. I guess that won't help much." He folded his hands together almost like he was praying, placed them on his lap. He looked down. "What a terrible, terrible thing. I don't totally believe it yet. Maybe I never will. He talked to so many people; I guess it could have been anyone." Tears streamed down his cheeks and over his chin. Each tear left a spot on his shirt. Oscar placed his head in his hands and cried. Poole gave him a few minutes before he continued.

Oscar looked up, his glasses splattered with tears. He got up to get a tissue. He wiped the lens dry and sat back down. "I want to help, but I'm not sure what else I can tell you."

"This is just routine, Mr. Piedmont, but where were you two days ago? The day Dr. Temple was murdered?"

"Well…" he folded his hands in his lap again. "I was with a woman."

"A woman?"

"Yes, a woman."

Poole looked at the others. "You are going to have to be a little more specific."

Oscar Piedmont sweated. His black shirt blacker under his arm pits. "Well… I can't, detective. At least not until I check with her. I know this sounds fishy, but this woman… she has a husband. It could ruin her marriage if this comes out."

"And it could make you a murder suspect if it doesn't," Gibbs chimed in.

"Well… oh, yes, I see. I mean, I know. I have receipts from our date. I can show you a credit receipt from our dinner." He pulled out his wallet, produced a receipt. It had the date of the murder on it. The restaurant was in New Jersey. He produced another receipt for a car service into and out of New Jersey for the same date.

It temporarily assuaged Poole, but he wanted the whole story. He thought there was something going on with Oscar Piedmont. It may have had nothing to do with Jacob Temple or everything to do with Jacob Temple. Either way, Poole meant to get to the bottom of whatever it was that Oscar Piedmont wasn't telling.

"We will need the name of that woman. It's our job to get to the truth. No matter what. Do you understand?" Poole got up. Gibbs and Kadee followed his lead.

"Well… yes, of course, Detective. I want you to find out who did this as much as you want to find out." Oscar Piedmont stood up too. "There are the recorded shows you asked for," he motioned to three boxes of CD's. "I hope you find something."

Gibbs handed him their card. "We'll be in touch."

Oscar Piedmont nodded, "OK." He walked them to the front door of the ninth floor. When Kadee looked back at him, he had removed his glasses. He rubbed his eyes with his knuckles.

"Boy, that was one nervous guy. So what do you think?" Gibbs asked as they got into the car.

"I think it was hot as fuck in there. My balls are sweating." Poole said. He looked back, gave Kadee a glance. "Oh, sorry, Kadee. I'm not used to having a woman with us."

She waved away his concern. "It's fine, I have a brother. I'm used to it."

Poole turned to Gibbs. "He seemed genuinely upset, but he was hiding something."

"That was obvious. But as I always say, everyone has secrets. There's nothing like a murder investigation to find out the truths behind people's lives." He glanced back at Kadee.

She nodded in agreement.

"I want to know who this woman is. There is something going on there, a story we should know. Let's follow up at the restaurant. Maybe take a ride over there and ask the staff."

"I agree. We can pull Piedmont's picture off the Internet… No doubt there's a story there, but it doesn't mean it has anything to do with Temple's murder. Don't go getting all tunnel-visioned.

There are too many possible suspects in this one. He was a celebrity. We need to be thorough. Go through everything."

Kadee nodded. Gibbs always seemed so rationale.

"For fuck's sake, you two, I know that. I'm just saying he's keeping secrets, that's all. I'm saying we need to investigate him further."

Gibbs looked at Poole and nodded. "Agreed."

He reached over, flipped the radio on. *Bring Me to Life* by Evanescence played. Amy Lee and Paul McCoy's voices alternated bellows.

*Bid my blood to run*
*(I can't wake up)*
*Before I come undone*
*(Save me)*
*Save me from the nothing I've become*

When they arrived back at the station it was close to 5:00. Kadee decided to spend a couple of hours listening through the CD's before she went home. She sat in her tiny office, door closed, head set on. A large glass window on the door provided a view of the main part of the office.

She noticed Gibbs getting ready to leave. He peeked his head in to wish her luck going through the recordings and to say goodnight. Kadee smiled and wished him a good night back. She really liked Curt Gibbs. There was something honorable, something very even and fair about him. She thought he was a thorough investigator.

She listened through the first show. Jacob Temple had a hearty voice, sexy, with a compassionate tone. He sounded like he really heard what the callers said. But then he would blow it by giving out generic advice. But then again, it must have been hard to advise someone he didn't know at all. So much of the nuanced information that happens in person was lost on the radio.

Kadee thought of what Oscar Piedmont said about Jacob being preoccupied with his appearance. She wondered what that really meant about who he was. Clearly, being a celebrity could be hard on the ego, always being in the spotlight with the public interested in your private life. Maybe he just felt pressured to perform the role. On the other hand, he may have been a vanity-driven ego-maniac. It was always so hard to know the truth about people from other people.

Jacob Temple talked with a woman who possessed a loud, hysterical voice. She sounded like she had phlegm stuck in the back of her throat, almost like she needed to swallow really hard. She yelled to Jacob that she thought she was dying. In fact, she had been to fourteen doctors for this pain in the back of her neck and a rash covering the front of her chest just above her breasts. No one could give her a diagnosis.

"I know I'm dying, Dr. Temple, I just know it. But how can I accept it, make arrangements and such, if no doctor can figure out what I'm dying from. You know what I mean?"

"Yes, Trisha. Yes, I can hear how hard this is for you," Jacob responded, an easy tone.

"Thank you for saying that. Thank you. My family won't listen anymore. They think I'm a total fruit cake, a nutty one." She chuckled, a phlegm-filled chortle. "Bet they'll feel pretty crappy when they're standing at my funeral."

"I'm sure. Maybe you could try telling them how afraid you are."

"Dr. Temple, I'm scared outta my wits. They know that. But they still think I'm a fruit cake. Until they have medical proof, a blood test or CAT scan or something, they ain't never gonna believe me. That's just how it goes with my life."

"I'm sorry no one hears you. That's very hard, to feel so alone."

"Yes, thank you. It is. I haven't had an easy time of it, either. I have had one serious medical problem after another. I'm always in pain, but they can never figure out what's wrong. It ain't easy, Dr. Temple. My life just ain't easy."

"I understand Trisha." His tone, warm.

"But now I have you to talk to. Can I call again? I have another doctor's appointment at the end of the week. Can I call and tell you about it?" Her cheerful response was masked by a garbled sound, like she had marbles in her mouth.

"Sure Trisha, I'd like that. Please do."

"Thank you Dr. Temple. Thank you. You are my guardian angel."

"You are most welcome, Trisha, and thank you for phoning into *On the Couch with Jacob Temple*." His voice morphed from a calm, even tone to a high-pitched overly enthusiastic sound. Kadee's stomach rolled over.

*What a phony.*

*Stop it, Kadee, you don't know that.* She just hated when her mind made those judgmental leaps.

The next call ran through her head phones. The woman introduced herself as Beth. *Beth*, the woman Fiona Temple mentioned. Kadee listened. She concentrated. Then she looked up for a second and noticed Yvonne in the main office next to Poole. Her hand placed coquettishly on his shoulder.

*They are a bit of an odd couple. Stop it… he makes her happy. Just stop it.*

Yvonne raised her arm, smiled, waved toward Kadee. Kadee greeted her through the glass window, a hand gesture and nod. *She really does look happy.* Kadee became momentarily preoccupied with observing the interaction between Yvonne and Poole. In some ways her fascination had to do with wanting to understand Yvonne's moving-on process, as a way to better figure out her own.

Beth's voice broke her musing when she gushed, "Thank you, Jacob. It is OK if I call you Jacob? Isn't it?"

Kadee stopped the recording, backed it up to the previous segment and listened again. She used his first name. Kadee regained her focus. It wasn't just that she used his first name, it was how his name sounded rolling off her tongue. A touch of warmth, a touch of familiarity. The way the "b" hung in the air, dancing for an extra second. Kadee believed people said the names of those they loved slightly differently than their usual tone. She heard love in the way Beth said 'Jacob.'

She backed the recording up, listened again, backed it up, listened again.

She looked out of the glass, noticed Yvonne hanging like a kitten on Detective Poole. For a flash, she saw Yvonne with Noah instead of Poole. Kadee placed her hand on her chest. She ached.

She backed the recording up, tried to concentrate on her work instead of her personal life. *Kadee, love, sometimes you really are your own worst enemy.*

She felt convinced that this caller Beth felt some sort of attachment toward Jacob Temple. Was it real or imagined? Did she know him personally or did she develop a fantasized intimacy through their phone calls? Of course, none of that meant Beth was the murderer. But it was curious.

Yvonne motioned a finger toward Kadee, said *one minute* with her lips.

Kadee nodded. Mouthed back: *OK.*

*I guess they do look kinda cute together.*

# Chapter 5

"One, two, three… four, five, six… One, two three… four, five six… One, two, three… four, five, six…"

Jane Light had the compulsion to count everything in sixes. Six stairs up. When she would reach six, she would start from one, count six more. Six knitting stitches, six bites of food, six wipes after using the toilet, six blows to put out her candles, six sips of tea, six, six, six.

Some days were worse than others, depending on how anxious she was. The less she needed to count the better. She couldn't stand the days when she had to keep counting. It would nearly drive her nuts, but it was compulsive. When the urge came, she couldn't stop.

The counting started immediately after Jacob broke it off with her. She couldn't stop counting the months they had spent together, one count for each of the six months that she had spent with Jacob. They were the best months of her life. Jane thought if she kept counting the six months of ecstasy, he would come back to her. Somehow her counting could control the outcome. Somehow, if she repeated the numbers long and hard enough, it would bring him back.

He never did come back, though. She just kept counting, never giving up hope that one day he might change his mind, and they would be reunited. Even now that he was dead, she couldn't stop repeating the numbers. She knew rationally he could never come back, but emotionally, she couldn't let go. So, she kept doing everything in sixes. The need now even more urgent.

## 1996

Nineteen years earlier, Jane was on vacation in South Beach, Miami, with her girlfriends. They holed up at the Clevelander Hotel on Ocean Drive right along the ocean front. A little bit of a dive, it was nothing like the more luxurious places along Collins Avenue. But it was affordable and in a prime location for partying.

The rooms small, the walls thin, you could easily hear the people staying in the adjacent rooms. A smell lingered in the air of the narrow hallways, something like stale cigarettes mixed with the yeasty scent of fermented alcohol.

The downstairs part of the hotel housed two bars. A small cramped one inside with a line of bar stools and rows of alcohol bottles. A television hung on the wall, sports played on the screen. The outdoor bar, much larger, had two separate bar stations. Cocktail waitresses strutted around, butt cheeks bursting out of revealing uniforms, busy taking drink orders. A medium sized pool, small stage, dance floor and a few scattered tables filled the space.

A constant, uninterrupted parade of people walked, talked and drank along the sidewalk in front of the hotel. It was the kind of endless, pulsating crowd that caused dizziness if you stared at it for too long.

Loud music blasted all day. It started around lunchtime and carried on into the wee hours. It was steamy and hot. People dressed in as little clothing as possible. The sound and smell of sex emanated off the small island, filling the empty spaces with the subtle whirl of gyration, making it seem as if everyone had an aphrodisiac pulsing through their veins.

It was her friend Carol's last weekend as a single woman. Carol, a petite, curvy, red-head, had shoulder length curls and eyes the color of the sky. She was getting married the following weekend. Jane, Carol, and two other girlfriends — Mandy and Star — came to South Beach to celebrate.

They met two guys earlier that day on the beach right near the hotel. The six of them spent the afternoon together. They lounged, enjoyed margaritas and the limitless blue sky.

Star, a confident woman, was sexual and forward. A tall, thin, brunette, taut body and a beauty mark just to the right of her nose. Star knew just how to look at a man and talk to a man. She laughed at just the right moments, touched them in just the right way. It always seemed like she knew how to make a man want her undivided attention.

Star spent the day flirting with both men, who looked as though they would break out into a small war any second to redeem Star as the prize. Mandy and Jane were used to Star's need for attention, but it still annoyed them. Star was both a marvel and an annoyance. She literally attempted to usurp the interest of every man they came into contact with. But it was impressive.

The bar at the Clevelander was packed at around 10 p.m. when the girls arrived after a dinner on Lincoln Road. Star spied their new friends who were seated at a round table, white outdoor plastic. They had four extra chairs saved for the women. Star flipped her head side to side, brushed her long hair over her shoulders, stood tall, chest out. She walked slightly in front of her three friends toward the table. They sat down.

One of the two, Wyatt, a painter with a huge afro, sported a black wife-beater that showed off his perfectly sculpted arms. The other, Thomas, a tall, red-headed architect, had a face full of freckles and a shy smile. They were also on vacation from New York. Both lived in Brooklyn.

They ordered drinks from a skinny, tanned cocktail waitress. Her breasts covered with only two small triangles of fabric, held together by the thinnest of strings. Jane thought for sure one of her boobs would pop out before the end of the night.

After a few drinks, Star took her right leg, placed it on Wyatt's lap; her short-shorts exposed her long, sculpted thigh muscles. She giggled as Wyatt told her a story about how he had beat Thomas at a 5K road race in Prospect Park. Wyatt rubbed her leg, "Yep. I beat him, even though Thomas runs more than I do. In fact, I barely run. I cycle." He looked at Thomas and laughed.

Thomas did not look happy, his face reddish, almost like his freckles were all stuck together. He bit the side of his lip. Jane thought he felt irritated. He seemed to be Wyatt's shadow. She could see why. Wyatt was charismatic, sexy. Thomas, quiet and awkward. But Jane felt kind of bad for him. She knew how he felt; she always felt second to Star.

Jane was an attractive girl in her childhood, and as a woman she was no different, but she didn't feel attractive. She sort of felt not good enough. She grew up the artistic type, in Short Hills, New Jersey, living in a home with corporate banker parents.

Her father wanted her to study business, but she wanted to be a writer. "Nonsense Jane, writing is not a career. It's a hobby. You're chasing a pipe dream if you think you're going to make a decent living as a writer."

"But Daddy, please, I don't want to study business. I'm not good with numbers. I'm a good writer. You can ask Mrs. Stiles. She entered the essay I wrote for her class into a high school senior's writing contest. She encouraged me to pursue my writing. She says I have real talent, Daddy."

"I'll approve two or three writing classes, but I'm not paying for you to slack off for four years and then not be able to find a job when you're done with college."

Jane looked to her mother for support, but she always said the same five words: "Listen to your father, Jane." Then she would lean over and kiss Jane on the cheek.

Jane enjoyed writing song lyrics, essays and short stories. She had even written part of a novel. Late at night after everyone was asleep, she would sit with one of her spiral notebooks and write *and* write. Sometimes, if it was a weekend night, she would stay up writing until the birds began their early morning songs. It was the only way she knew how to get all of her feelings out. She had pain. Emotional pain. She couldn't describe it verbally, but she could illustrate it through written words. Writing was her solace, a savior, a reliable, constant source of comfort.

And she was good at it. At least she thought she was. Her English teachers seemed to think so too. But her parents' comments affected her. As time passed, she wondered if her father was right. Maybe it was just a hobby. The contradicting input made her head spin.

Being a teenage girl sucked. Once she hit her senior year and began applying to colleges, she grew more and more baffled by life, by her choices. By expectations from not only others, but herself. She had dreams, big dreams, imaginings of being the next Danielle Steel or maybe even the next Emily Brontë or J.D. Salinger. Her literary heroes called to her to join them on library shelves.

But her dreams collided with the reality her father demanded of her. Maybe, she began to wonder, just maybe her parents were right and she would never be one of the great writers she aspired to be. Maybe she needed to be more practical and go into a secure career like business.

The whole college decision-making process propelled her into a premature adulthood, one for which she was fully unprepared. Now she was supposed to make grown-up decisions about a life she felt continually moving out of reach. Nothing about it made sense. She would enter the university as a girl, and she was supposed to leave a woman with a career and her own apartment. Maybe even a husband. It was hard to fathom. Jane felt sad and confused almost her entire senior year of high school.

Things were compounded by the fact that Jane was introverted, not the best personality trait to earn popularity in high school. Other kids hung out together, went to movies, pep rallies, school dances, and parties. They learned how to kiss for the first time, maybe sensual touching and heavy petting, maybe even sex. But Jane was most comfortable with her spiral notebook, living in an imaginary world filled with made-up characters.

Classmates at school thought she was strange. She believed them. It didn't matter how pretty she was, her full cheeks, long eyelashes, thick hair, didn't matter. Her intelligent, witty humor, or the way she could play the guitar without any lessons, her love for animals, her sincerity. None of it matter after awhile.

Carol Ann Ashman was her next-door neighbor from the time she was born. Her best friend. The Ashmans and Lights were friends for a number of years before Jane and Carol were ushered into this world on the same day. Twin friends to the world, but more different than two people could be. They did everything together. As little girls, the two were inseparable.

When Vivian was old enough, she started playing with them. Vivian had an ease about her that Jane didn't. She intuitively knew how to act with other kids. She didn't carry the social awkwardness that Jane did. Jane admired Vivian for that. Despite the fact that Jane was four years older than Vivian, she looked up to Vivian. A part of her wanted to be Vivian. Or at least, be more like her.

By the time Carol and Jane started middle school, Carol had a bunch of girlfriends. Even one boyfriend. They kissed on the mouth a few times, then graduated to French kissing. Carol told

Jane everything: how it felt, the chills she had, the tingling sensation in her vagina, even that he felt her breasts over her shirt. Jane wanted to be like Carol, too. She'd have given a finger, to be like Vivian or Carol. But try as she might, Jane could not shake her awkward behavior.

During high school, Carol had a big group of friends. She didn't spend much time with Jane, but because they were next-door neighbors and their parents were friends, they still saw each other occasionally. Unlike some of the kids at school who teased Jane, Carol was always nice to her.

A few times, she even tried to help Jane dress better. Jane always wore big T-shirts, sweaters, or sweatshirts. She had a magnificent figure. Carol admitted that she even wished she had a figure like Jane's. Carol helped her wear clothes that accentuated her body, her tiny waist, thin coffee table legs, her large boobs. With Carol's help, Jane started to dress in more form-fitting clothes. She no longer looked like she had just rolled out of bed, but despite the outer transformation, she still felt shy and uncomfortable.

Carol and Jane both got into Rutgers University, both planned to be business majors. When they arrived, the beautiful, but enormous, campus swallowed them both. For Carol who was so well-liked, so popular in high school, the anonymity of the large campus intimidated her.

But for Jane, who liked the personal obscurity of the campus, the school allowed her to finally thrive. She was able to join a few writers' groups and planned on doing her minor in English literature. Jane had the feeling, for the very first time, in a very long time that she just might find her place in college.

Carol and Jane decided to be roommates for their first year. They got along so well, each balanced the other's weaknesses. They remained roommates through all four of their college years. Though they didn't always hang out together — each had her own friend groups — their bond never wavered no matter how different their interests were. They remained close friends. And great sources of comfort for each other as they both navigated through the trials and tribulations of growing from girls into young women.

After college, they both moved to Manhattan. Carol decided to go for her MBA at New York University's Stern School of Business. Jane took a job at a small accounting firm. She pursued some writing classes on the side. She really wanted her MFA in writing. She hoped that if she worked really hard, she would have a published novel out within a few years. Maybe, just maybe, that would prove to her parents that she was a good enough writer to make a career of it.

But Jane had trouble keeping herself together. Without imposed structure, she found it difficult to finish tasks. She would churn out hundreds of pages, get close to a completed manuscript, then find herself unable to finish. It felt like she didn't know how to end the story. Sometimes she thought she might be afraid to say goodbye to her characters. She could not figure out why, but her motivation to finish would transform into a creative paralysis whenever she neared the denouement of the story. Several unfinished novels sat on a shelf collecting dust.

About four years after graduating from college, Carol's friend Mandy got Jane an interview at the *Daily News* as a writer and editor. Jane was ecstatic. She absolutely hated her job at the accounting firm. She still hadn't published a novel. Wondering if she ever would, she had become increasingly hopeless. When Mandy got her the interview, the possibility of change — hope — breathed new life into her.

Jane got the job. It was only part time, but it was better than nothing. She quit her accounting job. Found another part time job as a hostess at a nearby Italian restaurant, a supplement to the *Daily News* job. She lived frugally, but felt more satisfied with her life path. At least she was finally getting paid to write.

Mandy Dolan, an attractive brunette, possessed heavy-lidded green eyes that made her look sleepy. Her deep raspy voice added to the just-woke-up appearance. A tad overweight, she would always be cursed with ten extra pounds: the bane of her existence, as she would describe them.

Mandy worked as a reporter for the *Daily News*. Carol and Mandy were good friends. They had met a couple of years prior when Mandy moved into the apartment next to Carol's, a small walk-up building on East 64th Street between Second and Third Avenue.

Carol and Mandy met Star at their step aerobics class. It was 1994. Step aerobics was the newest fitness trend. Carol and Mandy went three times a week unfailingly. Mandy hoped to burn off those extra ten pounds. That's where they met Star.

Star Brewster was their instructor. They would ask Star for fitness and weight-loss tips after class. Eventually, they started going for coffee, then Friday night happy hours. Soon enough, Star landed a leading role in their lives.

Carol adored Star. A daring, fun and free-spirited woman, she would try anything, say anything. She had no care for what others thought of her. Jane could see the appeal. In some ways, she admired Star's lack of self-consciousness, but the same personality trait, made her a careless friend.

Star liked sex and a lot of it. It was not unusual for her to hook up with a guy she met at a bar and take him home the same night. She was cavalier about it too. She often told Carol, Mandy and her, "Oh, yeah, I fucked what's-his-name last night." She rated the sex on a scale from one to ten; one being awful and ten being fucking awesome. Worth answering his phone call.

Jane had never known a woman who could be so detached from the act of sex. Most of the women she knew felt something after having intercourse, even if it was only for fun, not necessarily the making-love type, sort of speak. But not Star. Star could fuck like a man. Star could fuck for the pure physical pleasure of fucking. No emotional investment. Men seemed to flock to Star too. It was as if she doused herself in a pheromone that shouted, "Capable of fucking with no strings attached."

When Star found out that Jane was a virgin at thirty years old, she made it her personal conquest to get Jane laid. Jane was hesitant. She wasn't a virgin because she was saving herself or anything like that. She was a virgin because she felt so awkward around men. Sure, Carol told her about sex, how it felt, how to do it right. She had read oodles of romantic fiction. But the whole taking your clothes off and spreading your legs, the penis going in and out, the whole climactic convulsions bemused her. What if she didn't do it right? What if she looked ugly naked? What if her vagina smelled? What if it hurt? She didn't tell anyone her fears. Not even Carol. She would just say she hadn't found anyone she wanted to do it with yet.

Star didn't like that explanation. "You're thirty years old! How could there have been no guy worth riding in the last thirty years? How is that even fucking possible?" she chuckled, but she wasn't joking.

Jane felt cornered. She felt so awkward next to Star, but Jane wanted Star to like her. "It's a strange thing. I know what you're saying. I guess I'm just picky."

"For just a fuck? I could see picky for a relationship, but for a simple fuck? We need to find you a guy so your hoohah doesn't shrivel up. A decent looking guy with a nice dick would do. Trust me. You'll like it."

Jane gazed downward, picked lint off the bottom of her shirt. She felt so exposed. Star's brazenness left her feeling timid. She didn't know what to say to her. She didn't know how to respond without sounding stupid or immature. She felt so childish, so inexperienced. She had lived most of her life vicariously through the characters in her books and Carol's stories.

Truth be told, she did want to have sex. She was very curious to see what it was like.

She sipped her beer, a long sip. She looked into Star's eyes. Big and brown and hard. Her chin raised, her head tilted sideways. Cocky.

Carol responded for Jane, "Come on, Star, back off. Jane will do it when she's ready. We're not all as brave as you are."

Star glanced at Carol. "She'd be having more fun if she was like me. You all take sex way too seriously. If you break it down, it's basically just a physical act that feels really fucking amazing. Besides, I love seeing the guy wanting me. That look in his eyes when I know he's just dying for me, that he just might keel the fuck over and drop dead if I didn't let him have me. Now that is one fucking God damn rush."

Carol, Mandy, and Jane listened to Star. There was a detachment about her, but also fearlessness. Jane felt a strange duality. Part of her thought Star was just about the coolest woman she had ever met, but another part of her thought Star was a cold-hearted, callous woman who didn't care about anyone but herself.

Carol was close with Star. Jane followed Carol's lead most of the time, especially when it came to social interactions. She trusted Carol's judgment over her own, so she tended to disregard her negative feelings about Star. Instead she saw her as free-spirited and outspoken. But she recognized that Star absolutely needed to be the center of attention.

That night the girls joined Wyatt and Thomas for a wild time on South Beach turned out to be the night that Jacob came to Jane's rescue.

# CHAPTER 6

Yvonne walked toward Kadee's small office. Kadee observed Poole admiring Yvonne. His eyes fixed on her, a smile across his lips. *He loves her,* Kadee thought.

Of course, Poole would love Yvonne. She, herself, held a deep respect and esteem for her. She admired Yvonne, imagined her as someone who had control over her life. Her easy-going demeanor, calming voice, effortless poise, she was the type of woman most men wanted: confident, smart, compassionate, attractive, independent, without a trace of arrogance, pretense, or ostentation. A proud woman whose personality maintained the balance of a gymnast. Not someone who would compromise who she was for a man. Ever.

Of course, Poole would love her. Noah certainly did.

Envy, the green-eyed monster, that pesky feeling that creeps up on you like a mosquito. A seemingly minor annoyance, a tickle, a tingle, a sensation that you can brush off, flick away. Until it stings you — BAM — biting with purpose, leaving you itchy and throbbing for days.

Envy, that feeling that lingers when the man you loved, loved someone else.

It wasn't Yvonne's fault. She was just being herself, and for whatever mysterious and inexplicable reason, Noah chose her to marry.

But it wasn't inexplicable, was it? That was a big no; it was not.

The hard part was believing there was a rationale behind Noah's choice. That Yvonne had something that Kadee didn't. Or worse: Yvonne *was* something that Kadee wasn't. Kadee never wanted to covet what someone else possessed, especially not internal attributes. But there was something really damaging about what happened with Noah, how he carried on sexual intimacies with her, while he was in love with Yvonne. Knowing how fantastic Yvonne was made everything worse.

If she didn't know Yvonne, if she was some random woman, she could have fabricated numerous excuses why Noah chose her: He needed a weak woman, or at least one weaker than Kadee; or Noah couldn't be with a woman as strong as Kadee. He needed an uneducated woman. He needed someone needy.

*But Yvonne is none of those things. She's a secure woman.*

Or maybe he needed a woman his mother picked, a Manhattanite version of an arranged marriage. He definitely couldn't stand up to his mother.

*But Belle Donovan didn't approve of Yvonne.*

Or perhaps Yvonne was more into the kinky sex than Kadee. He was certainly sexually preoccupied and needed a woman who would indulge all of his sexual fantasies.

*But Yvonne didn't seem the type. Too well-contained, proper.*

She knew Yvonne, at least to some degree. Kadee realized that some of her ideas about Yvonne were hunches, emotional extrapolations from the little bit she did know of her. But Yvonne was a living, breathing person who she had spent time with. She believed she had a sense of who she was. And that woman would never lower her dignity for a man the way Kadee felt she had with Noah. Never. That pained Kadee. Not that she wanted Yvonne to diminish herself, but she honestly trusted that Yvonne never would, yet Kadee had.

Of course, *Circle of Betrayal* told a story about a woman with some vulnerabilities. The narrative of Emily Goodyear purportedly expressed some pieces of Yvonne's inner struggle. It was fiction, but Yvonne admitted that it was written as a way to work through her feelings. So there was some truth in it. Some residue of Yvonne's feeling that she wasn't Noah's (Oliver's) "favorite."

Regardless, Noah had planned to marry Yvonne. No matter how Kadee looked at it, she felt that she was the one who was second best. He used Kadee for sexual gratification while he preserved Yvonne as his pristine wife.

*Always see your mistakes as an opportunity for learning,* another one of Liza Carlisle's life instructions. There was nothing she could do to change what happened. Her best resolve was to learn from her errors, forgive herself, and Noah — tougher to do — let go, move on, and make better decisions going forward. All good hypothetically, and as a researcher, Kadee valued theory. But, in real-life, it was an arduous process. Like most constructs, it sounded good on paper. But the practical application was like climbing a mountain without a coat in a blizzard: a grueling psychological task, an uphill battle that required discomfort, will and persistence.

She had definitely started to move on. She was with Alex now. Not that she wanted her defining feature to be her man, but she was open to loving him and allowing him to love her. Noah stripped her of her guard. True... he broke her down. But instead of becoming even more self-protective, she learned that she could be open, and she stayed that way. It allowed her to enter into a loving, stable, and committed relationship with Alex!

She hadn't really confronted her envy toward Yvonne. It tapped occasionally from her subconscious, knocking for her attention. She pushed it back down. But after lunching with Yvonne and seeing her with Poole — not in the role of therapist, but in the role of woman, a-woman-with-a-man — that green-eyed monster emerged from the deep place where it was buried. It howled like the ghost of Christmas past, or Kadee's past, for immediate consideration.

She didn't *want* to be envious of Yvonne. She enjoyed her. She thought they would spend more time together. She admired her. Her mind moved into supposition mode, deferring to her propensity to intellectualize: *When does admiration and desire become resentment? Or How?*

The door opened. Yvonne knocked as she came in. They made eye contact and held it for a moment. And the green-eyed monster evaporated.

Kadee was glad she came in. *Maybe spending more time with her is the best solution for figuring this out. Of course, she is not perfect. Maybe*

*I'm idealizing her, imagining her as flawless because she was my therapist. Maybe I'm still seeing her as the nearly inhuman, super-heroic object that I needed when I was seeking her therapeutic help. She has issues and conflicts, just like the rest of us. Why ever Noah chose her, it doesn't have to mean something is wrong with me. We aren't going to be loved by everybody all the time. We can't choose who loves us. The best we can do is just be who we are and hope for the best.*

"Hi Kadee." She smiled.

"Hi,"

"Kadee," she paused. She was doing something weird with her head. She moved her neck around, from right to left. She looked like she was trying to see something. Her long neck snaked about. What was she looking at? Or around? All there was between them was empty space.

Kadee's eyes narrowed. "What is it, Yvonne?"

Her eyes looked lifeless. For a moment, Kadee thought she was in a trance.

"Yvonne?"

"Oh, yes, yes, sorry." Yvonne shook her head like she was clearing out cobwebs. Her voice had that soothing tone that Kadee enjoyed hearing, but it didn't match up to Yvonne's physical demeanor.

"What were you just doing? Are you OK?" Kadee's brow furrowed.

"Oh, nothing. Nothing." She blushed, looked like herself again. "John and I are going to dinner. I've had a taxing week. Things have been really stressful, really stre– well... I didn't want to say too much at our lunch. I don't want to burden you with my problems."

Kadee said nothing. Yvonne looked sad. Kadee wasn't sure what to say.

Yvonne took a deep breath, sighed. "Anyway, I would love it if you joined us. John is a nice man, and I would love for all of us to have dinner. I think it would be a nice time. I really do." She gazed out at Poole, a smile formed on her mouth and eyes. "So will you join us?"

"Oh, thank you for the invitation. I appreciate it. But I have a ton of work to get done. Maybe another time…"

"OK, Kadee. OK. Yes. I understand. I really do." She did the weird neck thing again.

"Yvonne?"

"Kadee?"

"Yes?"

"Kadee do you think Oliver loved Elle more than he loved Emily?" And there it was, the question haunting Yvonne. Elle, the name assigned to the character of the *other woman* in Yvonne's book, Kadee's fictional counterpart. Yvonne's question, a variation of the same one Kadee had asked herself: *Why had Noah loved Yvonne more than he had loved her?*

Yvonne continued, relieving Kadee of having to make up a comforting answer. "I… well, I was just thinking that if Emily was more like Elle, if she was a little sexier or maybe freer, maybe things would have been different. You see, I think Emily wanted to be more like Elle, but she didn't know how."

"And maybe Elle wanted to be more like Emily."

Yvonne sat down next to Kadee, her eyelashes fluttering. "This has been bothering me."

"Me too… Listen, Yvonne, I think if we talk about this openly, it will help both of us. Noah hurt us. He was messed up. And I don't know about you, but I feel unsure of myself in a way I never have before."

"Life is hard, isn't it? You just never know what will happen. And just when you think everything is tied up, secure in a tidy little package, all dressed up with a pretty pink bow, just when you think you know a thing, suddenly nothing is what you had expected and you realize you really didn't know anything at all." She bowed her head. "It's all been so confusing."

"He lied and manipulated both of us, and you knew him waaay longer than me. I could only imagine the shit he told you."

"He told me he loved me. I believed him."

*Me too.* Kadee thought.

"I believed him. How naïve of me. I was going to marry him. I thought he was the love of my life. How downright silly of me. My ex-husband, Dustin, had an affair, too."

"Oh. I'm sorry, Yvonne."

"You know this has really affected my ability to trust myself. No matter what happened in my life, I was always able to trust myself. My instincts. Two men in a row carrying on indiscretions makes me feel like I made up some story. Almost like a fiction, I wrote in my mind that had a beginning, middle and end. It feels like I manufactured some ideal life that was a made-up invention that I needed to believe was the truth. Do you know what I mean? Noah's version of our story had you in there. My version didn't even realize that there was another character dictating my fate. *The* truth, *a* truth, and reality are not always the same.

Naturally, I knew this from clinical work, but... I guess, I don't know... It's been very hard."

*She's more devastated then me. What a fucking dick he was... jeez, I hate these thoughts. I know he was killed, for Christ's sake, but he was such a dick. We're allowed to have ugly thoughts. Dr. Wright says it nearly every session. Noah really messed Yvonne up. If he were alive, I'd kill him. How's that for a bad thought.* "I really understand. I've had a hard time trusting myself too. But I knew something wasn't right from pretty early on. For you, it must have been even harder... well, I'm guessing anyway. I'm guessing you totally trusted him and probably had no idea who he was at all. That's just the type of situation that would make *anyone* question *anything* they *ever* believed was real."

"It was a shock. A real shock. I trusted Noah with all of my heart. I had a hard time believing the truth. And after my heart was broken into itsy-bitsy, teeny-tiny pieces, after that I just became so confused about what the truth really is. Or if truth really exists. The line between truth and reality has blurred. I started thinking that maybe we just make up the truth as we go along. Maybe that's the truth. I don't even know what I'm thinking or feeling half the time anymore. When I don't know, I just make something up. It's like in my fiction writing. I create details to help the story make sense. If done well, it sounds real, like the truth. I think we all do this in life." She paused, a tear trickled down the side of her cheek.

Kadee put her hand on Yvonne's shoulder, bolstering Yvonne's spirits, which allowed her to continue.

"Life can get really hard. Sometimes it feels like there is no order to anything that happens to us. And that's scary. I think we create new ways to understand these things by assembling them in a way that helps them make sense to us. But that doesn't mean that the arrangement we decided in our head is the reality. It's a truth we have fabricated. Like I imagined a new truth." Her lips twisted. "Noah was a faithful, loving partner. But that wasn't the reality. It was a fiction. I would never have accepted an engagement from an unfaithful partner. At the time of my engagement, my truth was that Noah was a wonderful man. That I was lucky. I decided it was the truth. It was *my* truth, but it wasn't the reality, was it?" she bowed her head, took a heavy breath.

"It's all become so hard to sort through, Kadee. Sometimes I have awful dreams. Nightmares. Noah's murder has been very traumatic," she paused, stared into Kadee's eyes. She pulled her hair away from her face, draped it along her back.

Kadee looked into Yvonne's eyes. She saw such sadness. "I have nightmares too. The whole thing has been... well, terrible. I can summon no good words to describe it. I think we have to do our best to put our pieces back together. And Yvonne... I don't think Noah loved me more. In fact, I don't think Noah loved me at all. I believe he loved you. However you look at it, you were the one he proposed to. You were the one he planned to marry."

"Yes, but he was unfaithful. He was dishonest. He told me things, and I believed him. I believed every word that came out of his mouth. I'm a fool." Her lip twisted at the corner.

"No. You're not. You are an amazing woman. I admire you. Please don't let Noah's craziness make you think otherwise. Are you seeing a therapist? I've been talking to someone, and it's really helping me. You know, being with Alex now... well... being with someone who loves me has been therapeutic too. To feel loved is so important. Maybe the most important."

Yvonne's eyes narrowed. "Do you think there's such a thing as loving someone too much? You know the expression, 'love him to pieces,' or 'love him to death'? Do you think a person can literally love another to death? Love them so much that it kills them?"

"It's a metaphor."

"But what if it's not a metaphor? What if we can love someone so much. So completely. So totally. With every single ounce of our being. What if that person is the reason we get up in the morning, the reason we want to live and breathe, our one and only. Our everything. What if we couldn't take it, and we just want to devour them, eat them, consume them, so they become a permanent part of us. And what if our need for them becomes too much to bear and we start to hate them because we love them too much? Isn't that loving someone too much?"

*Noah has really messed her up. Or maybe she was always like this.* "What are you getting at?"

"It's something I've been trying to figure out for my next book. I *am* seeing a therapist, and it is helping quite a bit. The writing has also been a valuable therapeutic tool for me. My therapist actually suggested writing a memoir, which I have thought about. Perhaps it would help to tell my story and maybe it would help other people who have been similarly deceived. But I have already started this second mystery book. So that's what I'm working on now. It's brought up a lot of interesting questions about love and hate and murder. And since killers are your specialty I was curious to hear your thoughts."

"I see. I agree with your therapist. A memoir would probably be the most therapeutic. You know, get down to the nitty gritty of what happened. Tackle it directly. But the second fiction sounds intriguing too."

"The topic *is* titillating. What do you think about the 'loving someone too much' question?"

"I think there are different ways to love someone."

"Do you think loving someone too much can cause hate, which leads to rage and then murder? So in a way the act of murder would be the result of this type of love. The loving-too-much type of love."

It was a gripping hypothesis. "Wow, I guess fiction can open doors to some dark questions for the writer."

"It does seem to do that. So… what do you think about my question?"

Kadee mulled it over for a moment. "I think it could. Absolutely. Love and hate do share feelings of obsession for another person. But like we've discussed before, there are always gray areas. Nothing is ever that simple — you know A leads to B which leads to C — there are all sorts of other factors. But it is fiction, right? You can make up whatever you want in that case, can't you?"

Yvonne was just about to say something when Poole opened the door and interrupted her.

"Yvonne," he looked at her, his eyes soft. Kadee had never seen this side of Poole. He almost looked like a dog, with a leash in his mouth, salivating as he waited for his owner to walk him. "You ready, gorgeous?"

Yvonne stared at Kadee, a wince of sadness gleamed. "Sorry to cut this conversation short. To be continued."

Kadee nodded. *Yes*

Poole placed his arm delicately over Yvonne's shoulder. Yvonne looked like an animated character coming to life; the corners of her lips raised into a smile. She looked back at Kadee one more time, then turned to Poole, "Yes, dear, I'm ready."

Poole looked at Kadee. "Have a good night. Good luck with those recordings."

"Night." As she watched them leave the office, Poole's arm wrapped all the way around Yvonne's petite frame, Kadee felt a surge of emotion — sadness, anger, guilt, grief — all coalescing into a tumbling knot deep in her abdomen. She folded her arms on her desk, buried her head into the nook, trying in vain to hide from her past, her present, her future.

It was all too much. She was still so angry with Noah, despite that he had been killed. She could not comfortably reconcile the fury with the grief. But he truly emotionally demolished Yvonne. Kadee felt selfish for experiencing even a modicum of self-pity; at least she knew on some level that she couldn't trust the bastard. But Yvonne... she believed him. Every word that he let flow from his lying tongue, Yvonne believed him.

But... she had lied to Yvonne too. *You tried to let that fact slip your mind, trying to ignore your own responsibility in this.* If she hadn't given Noah that pseudonym when she was in therapy, Yvonne likely would have surmised that they were involved with the same man sooner. At the very least, she wouldn't have been misled by

Kadee too. It wasn't just Noah's crafty subterfuge making Yvonne question her own perception, Kadee had also deceived her.

"FUCK," she screamed as her words bounced back and forth off the walls in her small office.

She had to get out of there. Her self-punitory thoughts were suffocating. It was an emotional ambush, too many feelings simultaneously. *Why was I born without the capacity for prolonged denial like most other people? For Christ's sake, my emotional world is too accessible. It must be some sort of freak genetic mutation.*

It was freezing out, but she didn't care. She walked with her coat open, no hat, no gloves, almost like she was rebelling against the temperature, while also punishing herself for what she had done. Or didn't do. For not telling Yvonne, for staying with Noah, for even getting involved with a man like him. For wishing he was dead, for being glad he was dead. For envying Yvonne when clearly the woman was suffering more than Kadee, had lost more, too. From the way Yvonne sounded, Kadee wondered if the whole debacle hadn't permanently damaged her. The pain of the cold bit at her nose and fingertips, but she made herself walk the 16 blocks to her apartment anyway.

She got home, stuck her hair in a tight ponytail, immediately got into gym clothes. She put on some calming music, the sounds of a waterfall. Her thoughts whirled through an involuntary cycle of self-loathing, a washing machine in the spin phase, dirt squeezing out of every emotional crevice.

*Always see your mistakes as an opportunity for learning.* Her yoga mat was out. She was in downward dog, deep breaths. She was sick of Noah and the train wreck that followed affecting her.

Just as she maneuvered into a head stand, blood engorging, relieving her angst, she heard the key to her front door. The crackle of it opening. She dropped her legs onto the mat. It was Alex. They had dinner plans. She had totally forgotten until he walked in the door.

An hour later, Kadee and Alex were cozy, sipping Chardonnay at an Italian restaurant. She felt more relaxed. Maybe it was Alex's presence, maybe the wine, perhaps some combination. She wanted to tell him a little about the thoughts knotted in her head. But right as she was about to say something, Alex surprised her. He got down on one knee in front of everyone in the restaurant.

He proposed.

# CHAPTER 7

**1996**

Wyatt Jones rubbed his right hand up and down Star's naked legs. Jane observed, fascinated. They looked so comfortable with each other, like they had known each other for years. She so wished she possessed that easy way about her. She wished she could feel that ease of familiarity with someone unfamiliar. Especially a man.

Star laughed and laughed. She swung her long hair across her shoulder effortlessly. An inviting gesture. Wyatt took her hand, nodded his head toward the dance floor. They both got up.

Wyatt winked, "We are going to get it on." He meant they were going to dance, but it seemed clear that he knew the words he chose had a dual meaning. With Star's hand placed in his, they made their way onto the crowded dance floor. He pulled her waist close. They rubbed up and down along each other's bodies, moved with the rhythm of the music. A dance mix roared out of the stereo system.

Carol and Mandy started talking about Carol's wedding plans.

Thomas McPherson pulled his chair closer to Jane. "So... you enjoying your trip, Jane?"

She looked into his eyes. She felt shy. She looked away, then looked back. "Yes, it's really beautiful here. I wish we were staying longer."

He nodded. "So you're a writer, you said?"

She shrugged her shoulders. "Sort of. I mean, yes. I write for the *Daily News*, but I'm also working on a novel."

"Oh, excellent, excellent. I've always wanted to write a book. I'm very artistic. Wyatt always acts like he's the artistic one, but architecture is a form of art too."

"Oh, yeah, definitely. You're creating buildings, that's really creative."

He turned his chair. His body faced her.

She followed his lead, turned hers to face him.

The cocktail waitress came back. Her boobs still concealed by the small triangles of fabric. They ordered another round. Jane and Thomas both ordered a shot of whisky with their beer.

Thomas put his hand on Jane's thigh. She looked at his hand, felt self-conscious. She wasn't really attracted to him, but he seemed nice. She let him keep his hand there. That's what she thought Star would have done. Star's words, "a decent guy with a nice dick," floated through her mind. She looked at Thomas, a bashful smile. *Maybe tonight's the night. Maybe I will wake up de-virginized,* she thought.

The shots came. They downed them. They ordered another.

Thomas talked about his distaste for women who dressed provocatively; he felt it was a tease. Jane wore a knee-length skirt with a sleeveless button-down top. Practically a full overcoat compared with what most of the other women wore.

His head high and straight, his tone braided with condescension. "I just think women are wearing less and less clothes. I believe women should show a certain... well, a certain propriety. The way some of these women are dressed. It makes it look like they have no respect for themselves. Look at your friend Star for example," he motioned toward the dance floor where Star and Wyatt grinded their crotches together. "Her shorts are so short she might as well have left them home. They aren't covering anything. It's not respectable for a woman to dress in such a manner. And when I hear women complaining that men objectify them," he took a long sip of his beer, "whatever, whatever, whatever, it just makes my stomach curdle. I'm thinking, what do you think is going to happen if you're leaving your house practically naked."

He leaned down, kissed Jane on the lips, then said, "I wish more women were like you, Jane. You seem to respect yourself. You seem more traditional. I like that."

It felt strange. The kiss came from out of nowhere. He went from attacking women's rights to act however they want to blaming them for being objectified. Then he separated Jane from the other women. He made her different, then kissed her on the lips.

It felt unnatural. His lips were coarse, in need of Vaseline or Chapstick or something. But Jane enjoyed hearing that Thomas preferred her to Star. She really did enjoy hearing that. It was the first time any man had ever said anything like that to her before. She felt all warm inside, or maybe it was the shots. Either way, she felt really good. Her confidence boosted, her back arched, her head tilted, her lips formed a smile.

He leaned in, kissed her again. This time he slipped his tongue all the way into her mouth, stiff and straight. He rolled it over hers. It was an awkward kiss. Jane rolled her tongue around his, but it felt forced and mechanical, not warm and natural. He extended his arm around her shoulder, pulled her closer. It was harsh, not gentle. Jane didn't like it. After continuing for a moment, she finally felt so uncomfortable, she pulled away from him.

He tried to pull her close again, but she resisted.

"What's the problem?" he asked, a chill in his tone.

"Oh, nothing, nothing." She wasn't sure what to say. She glanced over at Carol who was still talking to Mandy and not paying attention to Jane and Thomas.

He responded for her. "Is it the PDA? I bet you're not into public displays of affection. A nice traditional woman like you wouldn't be, would you. I should have known." His tone aloof. "Do you want to go upstairs?"

Jane's eyes widened. She was not savvy at all, but she knew there was something she didn't like about Thomas. He was pushy and arrogant, almost angry. Although the thought of losing her virginity on South Beach was romantic, even titillating, something she could imagine one of her protagonists doing in one of her novels, she refused to lose it to him. She knew for certain that she did not want to be alone in a hotel room with Thomas.

She needed to be diplomatic. Carol always talked about men's egos. She didn't want to hurt his feelings. "Um, not right now. OK?"

"Do you mean no? If you mean no, then just say no. Don't string me along all night with the old 'not right now' bit. I hate that!"

"OK." She took a heavy breath, another sip of her beer, said as sensitively as she knew how: "I mean no, Thomas. I'm sorry. I don't want to go upstairs with you."

His faced turned bright red, his nostrils expanded. His tone oozed contempt. "You're just like the rest of them, Jane. I thought you were different. Sitting there in your conservative shirt and your covered thighs, giving off the pretense of respectability. But it's all a sham. Isn't it Jane? You're not like *them*, you're worse than *them*. You are a succubus camouflaged as a woman of propriety. At least *they* aren't hiding behind the safe façade of decency. You are the poster girl for duplicity wearing a uniform of virtue while the whole time your only goal is to seduce a man, make him want you and then toss him out once you've snagged your ego boost."

Even with the music blasting, Carol and Mandy heard Thomas' tone. They couldn't really make out his words, but his sneering was unmistakable. Jane, tears forming in the crests of her eyes, looked over at Carol. Jane jumped up and ran toward the bathroom, just as Star and Wyatt returned to the table.

It turned into one of those mysterious chain of events that happen in life. Each event alone seemed of little significance, but taken together each one led somehow fatefully to the next. Suddenly the end result becomes life changing.

Jane fled from Thomas, his horrible words corroding her thoughts. She hurried to the bathroom to wash them off. She looked down, tried to get her eyes to stop watering.

At that same moment, Jacob Temple, got up from his chair at the bar. He headed toward the bathroom. When...

*BAM...* they knocked right into each other.

Jane looked up at Jacob, startled by the jarring of her body bouncing off of his. Tipsy, she jolted backward, lost her footing. Jacob Temple caught her by the shoulders. He steadied her, rescuing her from falling. "Whoa," was the first word that Jacob Temple said to Jane.

She blushed, embarrassed.

"Are you OK?"

She looked up at him. He stood a full head taller than her. She nodded. *Boy, is he handsome.* She immediately looked down, feeling ever so conscious of her clumsy social skills.

Jane couldn't stand herself right then. If she had any social grace at all, if she had the ease that Carol, Vivian or Star had, she would know what to say to this striking man who stood before her. She looked up for a second. He smiled down at her. A warm smile, his eyes sincere and playful. She tingled all over; a thousand little needles prickled her from the inside.

She looked down again. "Yes, I'm OK. Sorry for knocking into you. I'm a total klutz."

He smiled wide. Jacob had a big smile, his eyes lit up his face. He responded simply, "Me too."

She took air into her chest, looked up at him. Their eyes met. Jane's whole body felt warm and tingly, like a firecracker had exploded inside her. It bounced around from her head down to her toes. She felt like a character in one of her books. But this wasn't fiction. This was actually happening. She pinched the inside of her arm twice.

"Let me buy you a drink. What's your name? I'm Jacob, Jacob Temple." He put his right hand out.

"I'm, um… I'm Jane. Nice to meet you." She smiled sheepishly. *I hate this outfit*, she thought.

He seemed to think she looked just fine. They both went to the bathroom, then met back at the inside bar. Jacob bought a round of blue martinis. The music pulsed with such force. Jane felt the bass pounding in her throat. It had been like that all night. But it didn't bother her until she was with Jacob and actually wanted to be engaged in a real conversation.

He must have read her mind. Within just a couple of minutes of screaming over the music, he asked Jane if she wanted to go for a walk along the beach.

She immediately agreed. *I must be dreaming. This can't be happening? He's so handsome. Is this really happening?* She gave herself another inconspicuous pinch.

They walked along the ocean's edge. It was so peaceful. The sky, a mantle of calming darkness, clear and infinite. The waves crashed along the shore, echoes of tranquility, sounding smooth and rhythmic. The undertow pulled back and forth, sifted water through their feet and tickled their toes. The water mated with the sand over and over as it had been doing since the dawn of time. In that moment on that beach, life seemed eternal and everything interconnected.

The ocean always seemed bottomless and mysterious, sort of romantic to Jane. She believed that humans originated from the water and that the ocean held the answers to the big questions about life. She could have written a romantic scene in one of her novels just like this one. They walked along the edge of the water sharing thoughts and ideas with each other.

She felt very far away from the dreadful experience with Thomas and her lifelong sense of gracelessness. She actually felt, perhaps for the first time, comfortable, content, and able to be herself in the presence of a man.

They strolled along. Jacob took Jane's hand. His palm, warm and moist; he weaved his fingers through hers. When he did that, she felt a tingling deep in her vagina. She had never felt anything like it before.

Jacob wasn't just handsome, he was a sensitive and compassionate person. He was twenty-five at the time. He had a few thin lines around the outside corners of his eyes. The type that were premature for someone of his age, but reflected some worries or struggles that made him have a sensibility about life that was beyond his years. There was an honesty about him too. Unlike many people Jane knew, Jacob had no problem expressing his imperfections.

He shared intimacies about his life with Jane without pretense, without false pride. He told her that he grew up on a farm in rural upstate New York. His family was poor. He moved to Miami at eighteen for college after being awarded a scholarship to play basketball for the University of Miami. He admitted to Jane that he loved the weather in Miami. The winters in upstate New York were dark, and brutal, but he felt a bit out of place in Miami, a way of life world's away from the farm he grew up on.

Jacob swung their joined hands, looked downward, met Jane's eyes. His voice deep and even. "There's just a superficiality in Miami, very different from the culture at home, from the way I grew up. It took me awhile to get used to the lifestyle here.

There's a lot of emphasis on looks and money here. We didn't have much at home, but I never felt ashamed about it. My father taught me to be proud of hard work and discipline. To feel good about what I did, instead of what I had... like what kind of car I drove or what designer jeans I had or didn't have. That never mattered until I moved here.

"Down here, how you dress, how you look... that's what's important here. Honestly, I personally don't see the importance, but I want to fit in too. You know? I don't like feeling out of place. I want to fit in. It's not so easy for me, trying to balance who I am with who I think my parents and my friends want me to be. It's hard sometimes." He smiled down at her, squeezed her hand. "I can't believe I said all that. You're really easy to talk to."

Jane decided right then, that she was totally and completely in love with Jacob Temple. *Tonight is the night. I will be de-virginized by the man of my dreams. This is better than I could have imagined or wished for. Jacob must be my soul mate. This must be why I've had so many problems with men in the past. It was all part of a larger life plan, one that led me right here, right now. I was always meant to be Jane Beth Temple. Everything makes sense now. My whole life makes sense now... Jane Beth Temple... Mrs. Jane Temple, Mrs. Temple... Boy, do I like the sound of that.*

Without thought or reflection, Jane stood on her tippy toes and kissed Jacob on the lips. He leaned down, kissed her back. He took his shirt off, placed it on the sand. He took Jane's hands, guided her until they were both sitting.

He rubbed his hand along the side her face, through her hair, tenderly touching the long strands. He let them flow through his fingers. He leaned in, kissed her again. This time he slipped his tongue into her mouth. His tongue moved slowly, wrapping around hers.

Jane felt tremors course inside her. Her body shook with pleasure, one she had never experienced before. A tingly blast of warmth mixed with an electric sensation. She wanted to take her clothes off. They kissed, their arms wrapped around each other. They continued kissing, exploring each other with their hands.

Jane wanted to feel him closer. She laid down, pulled him next to her. They rolled around kissing. Sand stuck to their clothes and moist bodies. All she noticed was the pulsing of her vagina, a strong throbbing that excited her. She wanted him to touch her down there. She took his hand and moved it between her legs. With the tips of his fingers, he rubbed her inner thigh up and down, from the top all the way down to her knee. Back and forth, slowly, affectionately, like he wanted to feel all of her.

Jane experienced a pleasant sort of tension. She felt it building and building. Her body shook. He moved his hands, slipped them under her shirt and bra. He massaged her breasts, spent extra time with his fingers circling her nipples. They became hard. She arched her back, kissed him. Her lips felt connected to his, the kissing became faster, more urgent, the desire increasing.

She couldn't take it anymore. She grabbed at the top of his jeans. She wanted him to be naked and on top of her. She never wanted anything so desperately in her entire life.

He whispered, "Here?"

She said, "Yes."

Jane saw him look around. There was no one else on the beach near them, but she knew someone could walk by. But she couldn't take the mounting tension. She didn't think she would be able to walk back the way she felt: her legs weak, her stomach like a pinwheel, her whole body emanating heat.

"It's OK," she whispered.

He took his hand and rubbed her vagina with two fingers back and forth. He removed her panties, massaged her entire pelvic area, moved his hand around so he could also feel her behind. His hands caressed her naked body. He raised her skirt so he could see her nakedness. He continued to touch her all over. He placed his hand into her vagina again, watched as her back arched when he massaged her clitoris. Jane pulled at his pants again. She wanted him.

He removed his jeans and underwear, mounted on top of Jane. He entered her. It was a moment of pain for her, but it was a good sort of pain. Once he was all the way inside, it didn't hurt at all. It was the best thing she ever felt in her entire life. He thrusted in and out, she wrapped her legs around his back. He went deeper. She never felt such a closeness with someone before. She felt connected to him, like she was the ocean and he the sand, touching, penetrating, connecting over and over.

She felt hotter and hotter, her breathing changed. She panted. Her vagina crackled with sensations, like a kaleidoscope scattering an array of shapes and colors everywhere. She panted harder and harder, the tension building and building. She stuck her nails in his back. She couldn't take it. More tension, a little more, a little more, then… a long release. Her body quivered with an ecstasy she never could have imagined.

She hung onto his back. A few seconds later, she felt him pull out of her. She watched him ejaculate into the sand. *A decent looking guy with a nice dick*. Star's words flashed through her mind. Jacob had a perfect dick…

Jacob was perfect.

He leaned over, kissed her. She felt like she had a cartoon bubble over her head, red and pink hearts swarming about. *This is love. This is definitely love*, she thought. Jacob had his face close to hers; he ran his fingers through her hair as he gently removed bits of sand, which covered them nearly completely.

She lost herself in his eyes. *Heaven. This is Heaven on Earth*. Then…

*Jane Beth Temple*.

# Chapter 8

Jane knew she would have to go to the police. Eventually. Vivian was right. Vivian was always right about those types of things. She could be a real pain in the butt, always telling Jane how to live her life. But deep down, Jane knew her intentions were good. Vivian wanted her to get it together.

But she wasn't ready to go in just yet. She couldn't believe what her life had become, what she had become. She was ashamed. She knew when she went in to tell the truth, the reality of what she had become would have to be revealed. Besides, a large part of her couldn't really wrap her head around the real truth: Jacob, the love of her life, was dead.

He was never coming back.

She knew he was dead. Of course, she knew *that*. It was hard to deny with it being plastered all over the news. He's dead, he's dead, he's dead, he's dead, he's dead, he's dead. She would say it in sixes, trying to force herself to accept the truth. But it roused such a deep pain. It stirred from the pit of her stomach, extending through every part of her body, an ache, an empti-ness, almost like a limb had been amputated. A piece of herself was…gone.

The world, her world, suddenly became smaller, and it al-ready had been small without him. But now that he was no longer alive, her world felt like a small hole, a crawl space, in which she was trapped and had no hope of getting out of. Knowing he was alive, somewhere in the same city as her, and knowing that be-ing reunited was a possibility, gave her some comfort. She liked thinking about him just being in the world somewhere, living his life alongside of her. Now that he was gone, there was no hope that they would be together again.

She tried to console herself with thoughts of the afterlife. Maybe that's when it would happen. Maybe that's when they would be together again. A large part of her believed that that could be why he was killed. Maybe his destiny had been fulfilled in this life, and he had transitioned to the next to wait for her. It made sense to her. It fit within her larger ideal that she was always meant to be Jane Beth Temple. Thinking about his death this way soothed her soul, quieted her impatience. She had been waiting and waiting. She waited for the last nineteen years, five months and three days for her destiny to be fulfilled.

But in the meantime, this life, the one in which he was per-manently gone, this life was that much emptier. A feeling of meaninglessness sucked at her, pulling her into a void, a vacuous space where there was nothing. She would go to the police. She promised Viv that she would. But not yet. She needed more time to accept what happened. She needed time to grieve.

Her counting had reached an all-time high. Once she left her apartment, she could mostly control it. But while at home, the counting had become a real problem.

She showered. She lathered shampoo through her hair, counting each rub, *one, two, three, four, five, six, one, two, three, four, five, six.* "I should go to the police station. Viv's right," she said to herself. "One, two, three, four, five, six." But after an hour in the shower, when she finally sated her compulsion to count, she said to herself, "Not today. I'll go. But not today. Today, I'm going to my writing group. That's what I'm going to do today." She dried herself sixty times. Six dries, ten times, until finally she was out of the bathroom and getting dressed to go to her group.

Jane had one published novel *The Dandelion Whispers:* a romance novel that she finished while dating Jacob Temple. It was picked up by a small publishing house and received good reviews within its genre. Since then, Jane had not been able to finish another manuscript. Being with Jacob inspired her, gave her confidence, a sense of meaning. Once he left her, she lost her focus again. She had more than twelve mostly-completed manuscripts, but she didn't know how to end any of them.

She did get some work as a freelance writer. She didn't have a problem finishing those assignments. But she could only take one project at a time. Jane became overwhelmed easily. She had hoped going to the writers' group, being with other writers, would help motivate her to finish her books. So far, mission *not* accomplished.

She chose a group on the Upper Eastside. It was close to Vivian's, she told herself, but that wasn't the truth. The truth: It was close to Jacob. In fact, Jane did a lot of things on the Upper Eastside, always hoping that one day the stars would be aligned just right and they would meet again. Jane really believed that being with Jacob Temple was her destiny. She didn't know how it would happen, but she truly believed the relationship would come full circle. That one day, like the seeds of the dandelion that take to the air to find a home to root and bloom, the wind would blow the right way, allowing their love to blossom again.

Of course, Vivian told her that that was absolutely certifiably nuts. Those were her exact words: absolutely, certifiably nuts. But Jane had an innocence about her, a childlike naïveté. Or maybe she could not fully accept that he was gone from her life and never coming back. Whatever it was, it basically stopped her entire life. It left her permanently stuck at thirty years old. The age she was when Jacob left her.

If one thing kept Jane motivated, it was staying close to Jacob. If she couldn't be near him, she would have to settle, at least until he came back, for a once-removed sort of closeness. If Jane was a master at anything at all, it was finding ways to remain inconspicuously connected with Jacob Temple.

That's why and how Jane met Sally Stringfellow. She had followed Jacob and Fiona on Facebook since 2007. Facebook was a gift from God, Jane thought. It was a way to remain attached to Jacob while also being totally discreet. She believed it was a sign that they were meant to remain connected. It was certainly easier than any sort of physical following. She knew more about his life. Some nights she spent hours looking through Fiona's pictures, and there was little threat of her being caught.

It was easier than she could have ever dreamed. Fiona used her page to promote her real estate business. Jane used the name Jane E. Ess. She set up her profile page, hung a few generic pictures and sent Fiona a friend request. A day later, Fiona accepted. She told herself that if Fiona accepted her friendship, it was a sign from the universe that she and Jacob were meant to be. She told herself that, and she believed it. It was her truth. The only truth. So when Fiona accepted, she took it as evidence of her destiny with Jacob.

She followed Fiona's posts, checked who her friends were. She looked for other writers, and various group pages they joined. Fiona's friend Sally Stringfellow was a writer. She lived upstairs from Jacob and Fiona. She sent Sally a friend request. Sally accepted.

It was one of the easiest things she had ever done. Before Facebook, she could not believe what she used to go through to stay close to Jacob. After the restraining order, she had had to be very very cautious. Facebook alleviated a lot of her stress. It made staying close to Jacob, and following her destiny, nearly effortless. It had to be a sign from the universe. It just had to be.

She knew she needed to be smart about it. It was a peculiar incongruence in Jane's personality organization; despite her inept understanding of social nuances, she held a superior understanding of exactly how to navigate her relationships with people close to Jacob. In this one particular area, unlike any other area of her life, almost like a savant, she maintained the balance of a tightrope walker. She knew how to get close, but not too close. Close enough to satisfy her desire to still know

Jacob, indulging her fantasy that their special connection still existed somewhere in the universe, but far enough that no one would know who she was.

The group met at Eliza Tinkle's apartment. Eliza Tinkle, a retired English professor, had authored two books on the didactics of writing. Somewhere in her late sixties or early seventies, Eliza had a thick head of gray hair with a few errant brown strands, small brown eyes, and thin lips. She had been divorced four times. She acquired her luxury apartment through her latest divorce settlement. Although not a wealthy woman, her apartment suggested otherwise.

Eliza started the writer's circle three-years earlier, the same year she had retired and finished her divorce. No husband and no job, she needed something to fill her time that included socializing. Jane assumed it was also a way to keep teaching without the pressure of academia.

About two years earlier Sally posted an update on her Facebook page which said that she was going to Eliza's group. Jane waited a couple of months, then contacted Eliza about joining. Eliza welcomed her into the group without hesitation. Jane saw it as another sign from the cosmos that Jacob and she were meant to be.

Most weeks they discussed their writing, passed each others' work back and forth for feedback, or spent the entire two hours reviewing one group member's manuscript. Occasionally, Eliza would give an informal lecture, instructing them on a particular area of the writing process. Usually from a lesson proffered in one of her books. There were usually six of them: Eliza, Jane, Sally and three other women, Alala, Miriam and Callie.

Jane arrived at Eliza's building for her group. She wondered if Sally would be there. It was only two days after Jacob had been found murdered. Maybe Sally would be too upset to go out. Or maybe she would be busy helping Fiona with the arrangements. She saw all of the posts on her and Fiona's Facebook pages. People offered condolences and words of prayer and support. Jane voyeured the pages. She imagined that she received messages, same as Fiona and Sally. She imagined that she was still an important person in Jacob's life. Oh, how she needed to feel that. She hoped Sally would come to the group, to share with her in the grief process. It would help Jane feel close to Jacob.

Eliza's apartment was on the twenty-third floor. Jane got into the large steel elevator, pressed six and twenty-three. She was alone in the cart. *Thank goodness*, she puffed out a sigh of relief. It always made her self-conscious when there were other people around her and she had to pretend that she pressed the six by mistake. She always wondered if someone could see through her facade, if someone would construe the truth about her compulsion.

She entered Eliza's apartment, everyone was seated in her living room. Eliza and Miriam sat on the two loveseats, steel gray, matching Eliza's hair. Alala and Callie on the big black sofa. Sally sat between them, crying. Alala had an arm wrapped around Sally's bony shoulder. She patted Sally's head. Coffee, juice, bagels, some spreads, and donuts sat on the dining room table.

Pip sat on Sally's lap. She rubbed her hand back and forth along his thick coat of orange. Jane felt awkward right off the bat, the same way she always felt whenever she arrived into a room of people. But she felt clumsier than usual. Her tongue, heavy and lifeless. She was getting all mucked up. What she thought she *could* say competed with what she *wanted* to say. It crisscrossed in her mind. For a moment, she felt utterly clueless.

She wanted to say that she had suffered the greatest loss, that the love of her life — the man she was supposed to be with for all eternity — had moved onto the next phase without her. Now she would suffer alone until it was her time to die, when she believed they would be together again. But she knew she couldn't say *that*. She definitely could not say *that*.

She scanned the room, watched their mouths moving. She heard the dull noise of talking as though she had plugs in her ears. She held her breath for a moment, her chest heavy, like she was diving in the ocean, water pushing against her chest desperate to force the air from her lungs. Then, as if she had finally come up for air, she let out a sigh, and pulled in a deep, refreshing breath. She hoped it was imperceptible to the others.

She walked toward Sally… slowly. She knew she had to give her condolences. She counted each step, *one, two, three, four, five, six*. She thought about Vivian: *What would Viv say?* Then she knew. When she imagined Vivian walking toward Sally instead of her, she knew how to handle the situation.

She approached Sally, petted Pip. Sally always insisted that Pip be greeted. Jane leaned in, hugged her. "I'm so sorry, Sally. I'm so sorry."

Sally reached a gangly arm around Jane's back, her voice crackly and small. "Thank you. Thank you, Jane, Jane."

Jane sat on the black chair next to Eliza. They spent the group, sitting in their circle. They consoled Sally, and talked about the tragic demise of Jacob Temple.

Sally explained that the detectives didn't have any leads in the case and that Fiona was devastated. Jane listened, her eyes huge. She hung on Sally's every word. Getting the story from the inside, not the story portrayed by the media, made her feel a special bond with Jacob.

Eliza urged Sally to eat something. She served her a bagel with cream cheese. Sally picked tiny pieces off the bagel, but didn't put any of it in her mouth. She let out a throaty cough, then explained, "Fiona called the lead detective this morning. There was no evidence, no evidence at the crime scene, crime scene."

Miriam leaned forward, her voice deep and raspy. She blurted, "None at all? No fingerprints? DNA?"

"Nothing. Not yet anyway." Sally paused, picked at her bagel. "But they do think it was someone who knew Jacob, knew Jacob."

Jane leaned forward. "Who would do that to him?" *Damn, that didn't sound right. Too personal. You have to pretend you didn't know him. No one can know about your special bond with Jacob.*

"I know Jane. He was such a wonderful man, wonderful. It's horrible, horrible."

Jane felt her heart sink. *Sally knew him,* she thought, *Sally knew him and got to see him every day.* A thin film of water coated her eyes. *One, two, three, four, five, six…*

Callie put her hand on Sally's leg, her voice soft and mild. "How do they know that without any evidence?"

"The way he was killed was so violent. It's scary. There were no signs at all of a break in. The killer had to have known him, known him." Sally looked down and shook her head. "Plus, the detective told Fee that they can tell by the way he was killed. The forks in his eyes suggest it was personal, was personal."

The room fell silent. Jane was confident they were all thinking the same thing: a Pandora's Box that she was sure no one planned to open. Sally had written a memoir that detailed her tragic past. When she gave them each a copy, she insisted that they never discuss the contents. She wrote the book to share her story and as a way to rid herself of her trauma. She said adamantly: "I never want to discuss it, discuss it."

Jane could understand why. When Jane finished the terrifying story, she thought it was a miracle that Sally was even alive. She thought about Sally as soon as she learned that Jacob had been killed. The instant she saw it on the news.

Sally knew of murder in a way that most people pray they never experience. When she was just twelve years old, her entire family had been killed. Sally survived because she had pretended to be dead. And the killer bought it.

Sally waited a whole day in her house. Her parents and two sisters dead around her. She waited. Stayed in the position that he left her, petrified. He had banged her repeatedly over the head with a ceramic vase that eventually smashed to pieces. She felt the blood trickling down her back, but she was afraid to move.

She stayed still, afraid he would see she was alive and finish her off. So, she waited a whole day until she was sure he was gone. Then she stumbled to the police station.

Sally was placed in the custody of her aunt and uncle, her mother's step-sister and her husband. They lived in Manhattan. The city was nothing like the small town she grew up in. A rural area in the middle of Pennsylvania. It was an adjustment and a difficult transition to go through. She was already so traumatized by the loss of her family, by everything she witnessed. She feared for her life.

Unfortunately, her aunt was one of those people who thought if you didn't talk about something, it would just go away. She would not let Sally discuss anything that happened. Sally was left alone, deeply frightened by life, missing the family she could never see again. And she had no one to talk to.

It turned out her uncle was a psychopath. That's what she called him in her memoir. He sexually abused her for years. He even pawned her out as a prostitute to his friends on occasion. He sodomized her repeatedly. Sometimes he shoved his dick so deep down her throat and with such force that she choked the whole time. She had trouble swallowing. She could barely eat. Even now when she swallowed even a small amount of food, her throat reacted involuntarily. She would choke.

She had had years of therapy for it. If she cut her food into really small pieces, she could eat sometimes. But at forty-five years old, it was still a problem for her.

Her uncle made her repeat everything he said during his sexual assaults. If he said, "Suck it hard, baby." Sally had to say,

"Suck it hard, baby." If she didn't repeat it back in just the right way, he would slap her across the face and make her repeat it over and over until he was satisfied.

One day when she was seventeen years old, he came at her, his pants down, his dick full. The swollen head touched her stomach. He pushed Sally's head downward. "Suck it."

Sally had had it.

She grabbed a fork off the table, stabbed him three times in his neck and then ran out of the apartment away from him. She ran all the way from the Lower Eastside, where they lived, to Covenant House in Midtown on the West Side. A safe house for runaway teens.

The counselors helped her. They called the police; her uncle was arrested and convicted. His new home: a luxury six-by-eight in Rikers Island. Sally was almost eighteen at the time. The counselors at Covenant House helped her with legal aid. When Sally turned eighteen, she inherited her parents' money.

She had thought her parents were poor. Though they lived in a comfortable home and they always had food and clothes, it seemed that she had just a little less than her friends. And from what she surmised from the television shows she watched, her family seemed poor in comparison. The way life was depicted through television was very unfamiliar, very different from her life and life of the people she knew.

Apparently this was not the case. She didn't know how, but the legal aid lawyer discovered that Sally had inherited 1.5 million dollars from her parents.

Her memoir went on to describe more difficulties Sally endured from eighteen through forty-three years old, when the book was published. Her uncle was released from prison. Sally lived in a constant state of fear for many years. She worked as a prostitute for a while; she didn't know how else to make a living. She knew that 1.5 million wasn't going to last for the rest of her life. She couldn't let a man get close to her emotionally. She could have intercourse, no oral, but she didn't enjoy it. In fact, it disgusted her most of the time. She could barely eat. She was always getting sick from lack of nutrition.

Jane didn't know how Sally was even standing. Jane doubled over with stomach cramps a few times just from reading it. It was hard to take in. In fact, if Jane hadn't wanted to know Sally so badly, she probably would have stopped reading it by the tenth page.

Toward the end of the book, Sally talked about meeting Jacob when she went to look at the apartment in his brownstone and how he really listened to her. She described his kindness and his empathetic way. She found him to be a natural healer. She wrote that Jacob and Fiona "saved her."

Jane thought about Sally as soon as she heard about Jacob because she could not imagine Sally having to go through another trauma, another murder, another loss. It seemed so daunting. Sally's life was unfair. How could so much happen to one person? And why, why was it like that? It didn't make any sense. Just like Jacob's abandonment of her nineteen years ago made no sense. Life remained a mystery to Jane.

But there was a darkness in Jane, a side that exists in everyone, a side that could be frightening for some. It terrified Jane. She did not like when she had *bad* thoughts. She did not like that at all. Whenever she thought, *that person is ugly*, or one time she thought, *I'd like to shoot that guy in the head*, after he cursed at her on the subway, whenever she had thoughts like that, she pushed them all the way out of her consciousness. They were bad. She didn't want to have them.

When she heard about Jacob, one of those bad thoughts emerged, teetered on the threshold of what she would allow her mind to be aware of. Sally had stabbed her uncle with a fork. Jane remembered that vividly from the book; it was a very poignant part. But she went back and read it again to double check. There it was: Sally had stabbed her uncle with a fork. *It was probably a coincidence.* That's what she told herself. But then there was a moment when her body got that hot, uncomfortable feeling. The feeling she always got whenever she had a thought that she did not want to have. She did not like that feeling. So, she pushed Sally and the fork incidence out of her mind. For the most part it was forgotten.

Miriam's voice broke the long, painful silence, startling Jane back to the present. "Aren't you scared Sally!" Miriam put her hand on her forehead, scrunched her whole face. "What if the killer has a key or something? What if he comes back?" She immediately covered her mouth after she said that.

"I know. We are having all the locks changed, the locks changed." Sally eyes grew wide and frozen, her pain evident to the group.

When the group dispersed, Miriam had her arm around Sally, as they all made their way to the elevator. Jane leaned over, hugged Sally, squeezed her fragile frame tight to her body. "I'm so sorry, Sally. If you need anything, let me know." Jane leaned down, rubbed Pip's back. Six quick rubs back and forth. Her fingers massaged his soft coat.

"Thank you, Jane. Thank you for your kind words, kind words."

Jane walked down the twenty-three flights of stairs. It was better than going into the elevator, pressing the six, and risking that one of the women would recognize her urge. She walked down while she counted each set of six stairs. The counting uncontrollable, like the sensation of hunger: a need that emerged from the most primal of instincts. That's exactly how it felt right then, but it also stopped Jane from thinking about anything else. She just counted one, two, three, four, five, six, over and over until she opened the door into the lobby, then walked outside.

When she got to the sidewalk, she observed the oddest thing. Well maybe not the oddest thing she *ever* observed, but it was unexpected. Even surprising. It was probably something she wasn't supposed to see too. So she hugged the side of Eliza's building, kept her body in the little alleyway. She peeked her head around the front to see.

It was Sally walking Pip on his little cat harness. Fiona next to her. Jane guessed that Fiona came to meet Sally after the group. Fiona wore a bright blue hat. It looked striking next to her red hair.

Sally stretched her neck all the way up and kissed Fiona on the mouth, then pinched the right cheek of Fiona's tushy.

Fiona brushed Sally's hand off of her, and created a little more distance between them. They continued to walk. Jane was pretty sure she heard Fiona say, "Stop, Sally. Not here." She was pretty sure that's exactly what Fiona said.

And Jane was pretty sure she heard Sally respond: "Sorry, Fee. You're right, you're right. I just can't help myself."

# CHAPTER 9

Alex looked up at Kadee. He kneeled on his right knee and held the shimmering diamond up toward her. His dark eyes warm and vulnerable. The moment caught her off guard. It was so unexpected.

She looked at him looking up at her.

He waited for her answer.

So were the occupants at the neighboring tables. It was a small restaurant. His position on the floor, with the ring shining, flickering as the light bounced off of it, roused the other guests' interests. Kadee and Alex became the center of attention.

Kadee's face flushed. She felt hot. It all happened so quickly, and it felt a little surreal. Out of her peripheral vision she could see a woman with dark curly hair and thick rimmed glasses, at the next table, nodding her head, telling Kadee to say *yes*.

*I have to say yes*, she thought, and with that came: "Yes. Yes." She nodded her head. "Yes, Alex. Yes."

He slipped the ring on her left ring finger. It glowed, flickered tiny sparks of fire, a stunning accoutrement on her long, elegant finger. She gazed upon it. Alex stood up. They kissed, embraced, in the middle of the restaurant. Their audience clapped, joining in their joyous moment. Kadee felt like they had become the evening's entertainment. Kadee flushed from embarrassment, but the attention was to be expected: Everyone loves a happy ending.

*But would this be a happy ending?* Kadee wasn't so sure…

They ordered a chocolate mousse for desert and a bottle of champagne. Alex smiled at her across the table. His eyes, sparkling and emotive, had a subtle longing — he loved her. She knew that. But did she love him? Well, yes, of course she did.

*But…*

In that moment she could not hate her "buts" more. But she assumed Alex's feelings were simpler. Alex, a rational, level-headed person, loved her and wanted to spend his life with her. It was probably that basic for him.

But Kadee was complicated. Consequently, the whole "love him, spend my life with him" question was ambiguous. But she had to say yes. Of course she did. A room full of people watched. Observed. Their every movement magnified in those moments. It would have been humiliating for Alex if she hadn't said yes. And she loved him. Of course she did. If she wasn't thinking about spending her life with him, then what the fuck was she doing with him at thirty-five years old anyway?

Yvonne's question about loving someone too much entered her mind. She recognized it, was annoyed by it. But it was there. It had been there. It was what was behind that nagging sensation she had been trying to ignore over the last few months. Her love for Noah, *if it was even really love*, but those feelings, those crazy, head over heels, follow him home at night, can't stop thinking about you feelings, she didn't think she had those feelings for Alex.

It was a more solid, secure, comfortable-sort-of-feeling, kind of like he was home. Alex was her home. If Alex and Noah were houses, Alex, was definitely her brownstone: her stable, solid, permanent residence. Noah, more like a chalet in the Swiss Alps: sexy, elusive, good for adventure, but definitely not for life. Definitely not. Positively. Unequivocally. Indubitably. *Not* for life.

Anyway, she hated Noah. Maybe she did love him at one point, but then she hated him, loved him and hated him, thought of killing him, as a matter of fact. She never would have married him. Not that he offered her the choice. But given the option, her answer would have been no. Incontestably. Irrefutably. *N-O.*

With Alex, there was only love. Of course he did get on her nerves sometimes, but that was to be expected. Spend enough time with anyone and they will get on your nerves. But she loved him. Of course she did. She had said *yes.* That was the right answer. Of course it was.

"What's wrong, honey?" Alex looked at her.

She saw a barely visible wince in his eyes, perhaps even a touch of fear. Her heart hurt for a second.

"Oh, nothing... Nothing Al," she smiled warmly, reached for his hand across the table.

He knew her.

"Kade... come on... Tell me. What are you thinking? This is what you want? Isn't it?"

She just loved his deep voice and the way he spoke to her, with such ease, such familiarity. *He's home*, she thought.

"Oh, yes Al… YES. Of course. I'm sorry you just caught me so off guard. I was thinking about work crap before you asked me, so I'm just trying to get my brain to shift gears. You know me. It's always busy up here," she pointed to her head and smiled.

He cupped her hands in his, smiled. "Yeah, I know, honey. You're always thinking. I never know what you're going to come up with. It's one of the things I love about you. But think about this from now on. My job is to make you very happy. I promise you."

She leaned across the table and kissed him. His lips were warm and tasted like chocolate.

*He's home*. He's *her* home.

Alex had moved in almost immediately after they started dating again, not long after Noah's murder. Well, he wasn't really moved in. He still had his own apartment, but he was there practically every night. He had clothes in the closet, a gym bag, and his own key. His mail might still be going to his own place, but he was living with Kadee. Her home. *He's home.*

They went back to the apartment after dinner, facing a list of people they wanted to call to share the good news with. Alex called his parents first.

Kadee went in the bedroom, called her own parents. She flipped open her lap top while the phone rang. Yvonne had sent her a message on Facebook.

Two rings, her mother picked up the phone, "Hello."

"Hi, mom, whatcha doing?" Her brain still hadn't fully registered that she was going to be married. She held her hand out and admired the ring.

"Hi, love. Dad and I are out to eat with the Martins. It's a beautiful night here. A balmy seventy-five degrees. Nice breeze. Your kind of weather." Kadee's parents had moved to North Miami a few years ago when they both retired. Her mother always tried to entice Kadee into moving down there with them.

"Tempting, mom, with this ridiculous cold front we're having. It was warm today, twenty-three degrees," she said with sarcasm. Then she blurted out, "Mom, I'm engaged! Alex proposed tonight. I said yes. We are officially engaged!" She mouthed the words officially engaged a few more times after she said them aloud.

"Oh, Kadee, that's wonderful news! Oh, my baby, congratulations." There was some noise on the line, like the phone was moving around. "Lee, Lee, Kadee and Alex got engaged. Our baby is getting married," she heard her mother say to her father.

More rustling, then her father got on the phone. His deep voice sounded festive. "Congratulations, baby! I told your mother this was going to happen soon. You know her, always worrying. She thought it would never happen. I told her that was nonsense talk. I'm so proud of you, baby. So proud of you."

"Thanks dad. Love you," her voice thin. He was proud of her. The words stung. And then *the* burning question: Did she even deserve Alex while Noah was still occupying a space in her head?

"Love you too. Here's mom."

The text of that Facebook message sat in front of her, but she couldn't read and talk at the same time. She wanted to apologize to Yvonne for lying about Noah's name *again*. Saying she was sorry over and over would not absolve what she did. Her mistake. But the guilt, it gnawed. She hoped a discussion with Yvonne would be reparative for both of them.

"Hey, mom. I love you. Let me go. I have a bunch of people to call, and you're out anyway. We'll talk over the weekend. OK?" She felt a little twitch in her throat.

"We'll talk about plans and things."

"OK, mom." She held her hand out, looked at her ring again. *Planning a wedding, planning our wedding*, she thought. *He's my home.*

"Love you."

She heard Alex still talking on the phone in the other room.

She made the text as large as her computer would allow. And read:

> *Hi Kadee,*
>
> *Nice to see you on here. Facebook is a funny thing, isn't it? It's like being connected all day long 24/7, just floating along in cyberspace. John and I had a wonderful time tonight. He says he really enjoys working with you. That's good for you, right? Maybe they'll offer you a permanent position, Detective/Doctor Carlisle, LOL. Anyhoo, I just wanted to remind you to email that research. I have been typing away. I enjoyed your pictures. I hope you don't mind that I took a quick peek. Hello to Alex. Are you two living together already? I thought you might be from your pictures. He's very handsome. Good for you, Kadee. Hope you have a good night.*
>
> *Your friend, Yvonne*

She could see that Yvonne was currently on Facebook. They were both on at the same time, right then. Alex's voice rang jubilantly through the door. He was still on the phone.

She assembled her response to Yvonne.

*Hi Yvonne,*

*I'm glad you messaged me. To be honest, something has been bothering me since our lunch...I feel that I have contributed in some way to the difficulties you are having overcoming everything that happened with Noah. I know I've said I'm sorry a number of times, and maybe it's just words, but I really feel terrible that I lied about Noah's name. I don't know how you feel about that, but I just can't help wonder if I also have caused you to not trust your instincts (trust yourself, as we discussed).*

*It was wrong of me. Of course, I could never have foreseen the chain of consequences that would unravel as a result. But I just wanted to say I'm sorry again. You're a terrific woman, a better woman than me. I hope you'll find a way to move past this and experience happiness in your life.*

*PS. I will email the research in the morning.*
*And yes, Alex and I live together.*
*Cheers,*
*Kadee*

She felt better having expressed her feelings of regret to Yvonne. She wrote that Alex and she had just gotten engaged, then deleted that part of the message. She knew Yvonne was distressed; she didn't want to end her message of remorse with her own celebratory news. *That would be selfish.* So she erased it. She hit "Send," and the message was off.

Or maybe she wasn't ready to announce it yet. *Ugh*. She did not like that thought. The whole conflict, utterly ridiculous. She loved Alex and she had imagined them spending their lives together. She had. She did.

What did it matter that she wasn't done thinking through what happened with Noah. How could she be? She had been deceived, a victim of Noah's cunning duplicity, and he had been killed. Just because she wasn't over the events that transpired, which were both dramatic and traumatic, didn't mean she wasn't over *him*. Besides what she felt toward Noah may have been passionate, powerful, even obsessive, but was it really love. Emphatically not love.

Then came the "loving someone too much, loving him to death" question. *Again*. Sometimes, she wished her own thoughts would require some sort of formal invitation before they intruded. Getting to the point where you supposedly love someone so much that you want to kill them certainly is not a healthy attachment. Isn't that what happens in passionate homicides? Yvonne was right, wasn't she? The love turns to hate leading to an unbearable state which gets released only through murder.

*No*. She did not love Noah.

She looked at herself in her bedroom mirror, held her left hand across her chest so she could see the glimmer of her ring, sparks darting out from different angles. She loved it. She loved him. She felt warm. Her heart felt warm.

She was just about to sign off Facebook and go join Alex in the living room when she received a friend request from Yvonne. She accepted. Yvonne had read her response message, but hadn't written back. It wasn't a note that needed a reply. Kadee recognized that she was looking for some kind of pardon from Yvonne. But in reality, the only resolve for her guilt was self-exoneration: forgiving herself. She signed off.

Meanwhile, Alex was nearly manic; he was so excited that they were officially engaged. He popped a bottle of champagne and brought a glass to Kadee in the bedroom. He tapped his against hers, shouted, "Cheers, honey."

She closed her computer, tapped his glass back. "Cheers, sweetie." She was angry at herself for even harping on Noah and the mess that her life had become during that time. It was the past now. Perhaps, if not for Noah, she wouldn't be with Alex. They reconnected because he helped during her arrest. Besides, she was able to be vulnerable because of her experience with Noah. *Maybe that's what the Noah fiasco means in terms of the bigger picture of my life. Sometimes we just don't understand the meaning of the tribulations of our lives until we look back and can put all the seemingly haphazard events together.*

Alex hopped onto the bed, pulled Kadee toward him. They both lay down. He caressed her face with his hands. He kissed her lips. Soon they kissed harder and faster. He removed her shirt and bra, then her pants.

She pulled his body close, as close as she could possible pull him. She wanted to feel his strong body next to hers. She removed his pants and boxers. They lay naked, kissing, embracing. She pulled him closer again. While his body touched hers, she felt protected. His broad shoulders and muscular arms enveloped her; she always felt such security wrapped in his arms, like nothing could touch her. He sheltered her from the ills of the world. *He's home.* She let herself feel the sanctuary of his love. He entered her. He felt so good. For the rest of the evening, Kadee didn't think about anything but their engagement.

At the crack of dawn, Alex did his usual: chugged down coffee and oatmeal before heading off to the gym. He tried to get Kadee to go with him, but she said she had too much to do. She had a dissertation meeting with Dr. Puffin, her chair. She needed to prepare for it. A true statement, for the most part.

It was too early to call Vanessa or Hailey. Vanessa, her best friend and a hopeless romantic, would be thrilled that the engagement was official. Vanessa not only wrote romantic fiction, she loved real-life romances. Besides, Vanessa adored Alex. She couldn't wait for them to be engaged.

Kadee sent them both texts. She wrote that she had some news to tell them. She asked if they could all meet for dinner that night. Vanessa would probably know what the news was. She had helped Alex pick out the ring. And they had selected just the right one.

Vanessa had been dating a new man for the last month. Henri, a French pastry chef who lived in the West Village. Vanessa seemed optimistic. Of course Vanessa always was in the beginning. Her nature: hopeful and optimistic. Even after years of dating disappointments, she never became cynical or jaded. She believed love was possible. Every guy she dated for more than a few weeks became *the one.* Kadee hoped Henri would be *it.* She hated seeing Vanessa constantly let down. If anyone deserved love it was her.

Hailey and Dean were working on their marriage. Hailey still had a little of that judgmental edge to her, that touch of bitterness still permeated. It kept Kadee and Vanessa a little distant from her. Kadee still loved her. They had known each other since college. Besides, when it came down to it, Hailey did the right thing. She risked her reputation and came forward on Kadee's behalf during Noah's murder investigation. Kadee would remain forever grateful for that.

The whole experience changed Hailey. It gave her pause for reflection. She finally admitted that her bitterness caused problems in her personal relations, especially her marriage. It also forced her to admit her multiple indiscretions to Dean. He forgave her. They were seeing a new couples therapist. As far as Kadee and Vanessa knew, she recommitted herself to Dean. No more clandestine extracurricular activities. She seemed almost… happy.

Kadee munched on her peanut butter toast, perused through the news on the Internet. She opened up her Facebook page. A new message from Yvonne sat in her mailbox. Written at 3:41 a.m.

*Wow 3:41 a.m.! She must be having trouble sleeping. Restless nights are awful.* She tossed her toast onto the plate, clicked on the message. She read:

> *Hi Kadee,*
> *I enjoyed hearing back from you. You are very sweet apologizing again, but it is really not necessary. None of this is your fault. You're also healing and I don't want to be a source of unrest for you.*

*Noah hurt both of us and we both need time to mend. Please don't undermine what you went through with him. I was there with you and I remember.*

*It's true that I'm going through a rough patch, but it's not your burden at all. I hope you believe that.*

*Anyhoo, did you and Alex get engaged last night? It looks like you did from the pictures he tagged you in. I wasn't sure because you didn't mention anything when you wrote to me last night. If so, please accept my sincerest congratulations. I know part of you is still working through your feelings about Noah, but I'm glad you have moved on and committed to a good man.*

*Love,*

*Yvonne*

Kadee sat back in her desk chair. Yvonne didn't blame her. That was a relief. But the guilt still lingered. Somehow she felt responsible. It was the end of Yvonne's message, her words, her congratulations. It jostled Kadee, helped her connect some dots. It gave her insight. She wanted to experience the elation that usually corresponds with becoming engaged to someone you want to spend your life with. But how could she allow herself to be joyful? Did she deserve Alex's love? She still thought about Noah. Maybe she never really loved Noah. But he certainly rented a lot of space in her head, like the house guest that overstays their welcome. Then there was Yvonne. Where was the fairness of it all? How could she let herself move on, be content with her new man and new life, when Yvonne was still so broken?

Sure Yvonne was dating Poole. It appeared that she enjoyed his company. But she was not the same woman Kadee had known before Noah's murder. The truth about Noah and Kadee must have cracked her, shattered something inside that she hadn't been able to put back together. It left Kadee feeling accountable. But she wasn't really? Was she? Noah's deception was intentional. It held a purpose that only he benefited from. Kadee never meant to hurt Yvonne. If she had known the truth about Noah, she would have marched right into Yvonne's office and told her. Immediately.

She had to let it go. Had to. Staying stuck in the entanglement only caused her more distress, more unhappiness. In some twisted manner, it also kept her connected to Noah-fucking-Donovan.

She had to let him go too. Didn't she? Whatever they experienced, it wasn't love. Not like what she had with Alex. In fact, Noah wasn't even half the man Alex was.

Noah was a man with a disturbed relationship with his mother, which led to unhealthy relationships with every single woman he ever came into contact with. Yvonne was fucked from the very beginning. She met him as a young girl. Yvonne had explained their whole history to Kadee that day underneath the large oak tree in the park. And then Emily Goodyear's relationship with Oliver, which paralleled much of the Yvonne-Noah story, told a similar tale.

Yvonne knew Noah for a long time. Of course, she trusted him. They spent time together over the years. She met his mother. She saw him with friends and in various situations over many years. Certainly Yvonne was having a hard time. She believed he was who he had pretended to be, who he wanted her to think he was: a facsimile of a loyal man, one who loved her. His *favorite*.

Yvonne believed him. She rested her future with him, only to learn that the man she loved was a veneer. Hidden underneath the real Noah Donovan skulked a person she didn't know at all.

That certainly would obliterate the foundation of anyone's sense of reality, making them feel that everything around them was illusory. For sure, it would take a looong time for Yvonne to recover. That wasn't Kadee's fault. She may have told that lie, but she never pretended to be someone she wasn't. Not the way Noah had.

Her face wrinkled. It was the way Noah was killed, by his own mother. The same woman who gave him life, took it away. If anyone had their trust violated, it was Noah. Wasn't it? She rested her hands on her temples, elbows on the edge of the desk. Her mind spun, a cacophony of ideas that wouldn't synchronize.

It sounded like Belle Donovan controlled him throughout his life. But in that last action, when she murdered him, she committed an unspeakable act. Kadee wondered what could possibly have gone through her mind when she decided that he had to die. She sat up, wrapped her flannel top tight against the chill that crept in.

How could she be angry at Noah for what he did to her? Or to Yvonne? He was also a victim? Perhaps the greatest victim. He lost his own life to the woman he trusted most: his own mother. He was exploited from the beginning. It was the first time that idea entered her mind, the disharmonious guilt and rage finally made sense.

She was angry at Noah, but she also felt guilty for her feelings. He was raised in an acrimonious relationship. It's all he knew. His version of normal, and it ended in his murder. She understood, perhaps for the first time, that although Noah's behavior was manipulative, he couldn't help it. He was a product of a toxic home environment. That didn't excuse what he did, but it explained why he did it. And he was killed as a result. The bitter end. She just couldn't justify the rage. It didn't seem fair.

She always had that over-empathizing problem, that affinity for taking care of the underdog. From her mother, for sure. Liza Carlisle always helped her students that came from less fortunate circumstances. She extended herself, twisted herself into a pretzel if she had to, trying to help them. Talked to their parents, helped with difficult course work, attended their sporting events, college applications. Her mother was the ultimate teacher of the year.

She took in all of those stray animals too. One year, her mother found a bird's nest with three abandoned chicks. She took them in, raised them herself. Along with their two dogs, three cats and even a baby groundhog they named Polly. Liza Carlisle had rescued Polly from the neighbor's trap. She fed her with a bottle. She would explain to Kadee: "It is our duty as human beings to help others — people and animals — who need it."

Her mind leaped: *How can I help Yvonne?* She didn't really know what she could offer her. She was also still digesting everything that happened. But from the few interactions they had, it seemed obvious that Yvonne was having a harder time than she. Yvonne said that she didn't want to burden Kadee with her troubles. She seemed the type to bottle up her emotions. Perhaps the best Kadee could do was to offer an ear.

And with that, she responded to her message.

*Hi Yvonne,*

*I appreciate your words. I just want you to know that I think I understand what you're going through. I am here to listen (and it's not a burden) if you want to talk. I know you have a therapist, but if you ever need an extra ear, you can borrow mine.*

*Noah's duplicity has made me question everything I thought was real, and it sounds like (from our conversation at the station) you are struggling similarly. Maybe it's not my fault, but I feel that we as human beings have to help each other. Please do not feel ashamed to reach out for support if you need it.*

*And yes, Alex and I are engaged! Thank you for the congratulations. He is a great man. Things are looking up for me. They will for you too.*

*Cheers,*
*Kadee*

# Chapter 10

**1996**

Around 4 a.m., Jane and Jacob walked back to the Clevelander. Jacob draped his arm around Jane's back as they strolled along Ocean Drive steering through the clusters of people. Drunken laughter echoed all around them. They discussed plans to stay connected. Jacob still lived in Miami, but he would be moving to Manhattan to begin graduate school the next month.

If there was any question in Jane's mind that Jacob and she were meant to be together, it was eliminated as soon as she found out that he was moving to New York City. This was the greatest indication, an undeniable message from the universe that she was meant to be Jane Beth Temple.

Jacob did most of the talking. Jane dangled on his every word. Despite the busyness on the streets, she barely noticed anyone around. His presence cloaked her from the outside world. The only world that existed was the one shared alone between the two of them.

He kissed her. "I can't believe you have to leave tomorrow. It's just my luck to meet you on the last night of your trip."

She shrugged her shoulders. "I know. I wish I was staying longer." Jane didn't feel her usual awkwardness. She felt so comfortable with Jacob. For the first time, the haze of her life lifted. The world, her world seemed to make sense. "But you'll be in New York soon. And we'll talk every day, right?"

"Yes, we'll talk *every* day. I know it's only a month, but it seems far away. I've never met anyone like you before." He looked down at her. Their eyes met.

Jane tingled all over. "I've never met anyone like you before, Jacob. I feel like I have always known you, though. Maybe from another life." She smiled.

He pulled her closer and smiled, as they continued to stroll along. "I was worried about moving to Manhattan. It was such a hard transition for me when I moved from Roxbury to Miami. I was pretty depressed my first year. And I know Manhattan is very different than Miami. The hardest part is that most of my friends are here now. I'm leaving a lot behind. I was real worried that I would get depressed again. I'm not so good with change. I definitely didn't want to go through another hard time like that. "

She squeezed his hand. He tickled her palm with his finger.

He continued. "Oh, I do have one friend who just moved up there. So, I know one person in New York City. But now I have you to look forward to. How far do you live from Columbia University? You said you live downtown, so pretty far, right?"

"It's far, but not too far. Columbia is all the way uptown, but you'll just be a subway ride away. With the subways in the city, nothing is that far. Besides, it's closer than Miami." She smiled. "And we can always have sleepovers. I can't wait for you to get there. It's like the city will be lonely without you when I go home, which is totally weird because I didn't even know you until tonight."

"I think I know what you mean."

They arrived at the front of the hotel. "Will you come up?"

"Aren't you sharing a room with your three girlfriends?"

"We have two rooms. I'm sharing with Carol. She won't mind."

"I would like to spend the rest of the night with you. As long it won't bother Carol."

"Trust me, she'll be fine with it. Plus, then you can meet her in the morning."

They got upstairs. Jane stuck her key in the door, turned the lock. Star's voice hollered from inside Jane's room. Star was supposed to be in the adjacent room with Mandy. Star yelled and yelled.

Jane knocked. "Star?" She slowly opened the door.

A cloud of confusion washed over Jane. Her eyes scanned the scene. Star, naked except her red thong panties, Thomas McPherson perched on top of her. His shorts sat on his ankles. His bare ass hung in the air.

Star screamed, "Get off of me! Get the fuck off of me or I will fucking kill your pathetic ass!" She squirmed.

Thomas didn't budge.

"Star? Star?" Jane said.

"Jane! Oh my God! Jane help me. Get this useless excuse for a man off of me. He's trying to rape me. Get him off. Get help!" She yelled. Her breathing labored as she wrestled with Thomas.

Thomas shouted, "Go away, Jane. You wretched wench. This is between me and Star. It's just a sex game. Go away."

Jane didn't know what to do. "Star?"

"Jane, he's a piece of shit liar. He's so fucking gross." She spit in Thomas's face, kneed him in the balls. "Get the fuck off of me. You fucking loser. I will kill you."

Jane and Jacob looked at each other.

Thomas fell onto the floor. He held his balls in agony.

Star got up, grabbed the sheet and covered her body. She went toward the door. Thomas grabbed her feet. He pulled her to the ground. "Now you're going to get it. You ubiquitous whore. I am going to fuck you up the ass so hard you'll bleed."

Star on her stomach, scrambled to get away. "Help! Fucking help me!"

Jacob went in, grabbed Thomas' hands, yanked them off of Star's ankles. Star got up and ran out the door.

Thomas got up, turned and punched Jacob right in the face. "Who the hell are you? Batman? Go back to your bat cave. This is none of your business."

Jacob stumbled back a few steps.

Jane screamed, "Jacob, Jacob!"

Jacob got his bearings back, leaned forward, cracked Thomas right in the nose. Drops of crimson trickled down his face. Thomas looked furious. Jane could almost see actual fumes of smoke leaving his ears. He released a bloodcurdling sound.

Carol, Mandy and Star came to the entrance of the room. Thomas picked up a beer bottle, slammed it on the dresser, cracking it. He took the broken glass and stabbed Jacob in the stomach. "How dare you lay a hand on me! No one lays a hand on

Thomas McPherson and gets away with it. Especially not some jock-looking loser like you."

He let out a shallow laugh, sounding maniacal. He stabbed Jacob again, then rushed toward the door.

Two Miami Beach police officers came up to the room and stopped him before he could flee the scene. One officer, with blond hair and a thin mustache, slammed handcuffs on Thomas McPherson. He read him his Miranda rights while escorting him out. Jacob bled through his shirt, Jane ran over to him. "Oh, no Jacob... oh, no!"

He looked down at the red splotches on his T-shirt. He rubbed his stomach. "I'm OK, Jane. I'm OK. The wounds are pretty superficial."

But he winced. Jane didn't believe him.

Jacob looked at Star. "Jane, is your friend OK?"

"Yeah, I think so. Just really upset. But Star's tough. She'll be OK. I think we should go to the hospital. I'm worried about you. He stabbed you. He's crazy."

"I'm OK, really, I am." He leaned in and kissed Jane.

Star observed the kiss. She came over, introduced herself, and thanked Jacob for rescuing her. A damsel in distress, suddenly Jacob became her prince. True to her nature, Star wanted Jacob's attention. Not even the severe circumstances of nearly being raped could squelch her absolute need to be noticed. But things were not going her way.

Star smiled, arched her back, played the innocent coquettish card with Jacob. Or tried to. He respectfully asked if she was OK; he showed concern for her well-being. But he completely ignored her sexual overtures.

Star did not like that. She moved closer toward him, brushed her breasts along his arm.

He moved toward Jane, placed his arm around her.

*Jane Beth Temple.*

"So I'm guessing you two fucked? Did you finally have your cherry popped Jane?"

"Star!" Carol yelled.

"I'm just fucking asking Carol." She smirked at Carol and then Jane and then Jacob. "She's a thirty-year-old virgin. Or was?" she winked at Jacob.

"It's none of your business. Don't embarrass her."

Two police detectives materialized at the door of the hotel room. They asked to come in to get the details of what had transpired.

Star invited them in. She explained that she fell asleep with Wyatt Jones after they had had sex. Next thing she remembered: she woke up to Thomas McPherson lying on top of her. His pants were off; he groped her and attempted to force her to have sex.

The lead detective had a thick bush of black hair and dark skin. He wrote down everything that Star said. He asked Jacob for a statement. After gathering all of the information, he asked if they wanted to press charges. Jacob said *no*. Star said *yes*.

Star had to go down to the station to press formal charges. Carol and Mandy went with her. The second detective, a bulky man with a sunburn, said to Jacob, "I think you should have a doctor look at that. Lotta times those types of wounds go deeper than you think. You don't want to get an infection."

Jacob nodded and thanked him. When they left, he and Jane went to the twenty-four hour pharmacy. They got some disinfectant spray and bandages. Jacob didn't want to make a big fuss about it.

He said to Jane, "I grew up on a farm. I've had my share of gashes. I'll be OK. I can go see the doctor tomorrow. I don't want to spend the little time we have sitting in the ER. OK?"

She leaned in and kissed him. "OK."

*Jane Beth Temple.*

While Thomas McPherson sat in a jail cell surrounded by what he called vagrants, his nose bloated to the size of a golf ball, he vowed to get back at the man he blamed for getting him there. No one would humiliate him like that and get away with it. No one.

He found out from the police report that the man's name was Jacob Temple. He never forgot his name and he never forgot the shame he suffered at his hands. The rage stewed within him for years. It percolated. He just couldn't let it go. Then one day, he discovered that Jacob Temple lived near him on the Upper Eastside. A celebrity on the radio and married to his old friend, Fiona Peoria.

# Chapter 11

Saturday afternoon Vivian arrived at Jane's unannounced. Jane disliked when Viv did that, but she knew Viv was just trying to help her. She buzzed her in. She dreaded the argument that would ensue as soon as she told Vivian that she hadn't gone to the police yet.

She had been feeling disoriented since the day before when she witnessed the kiss between Fiona and Sally. She couldn't figure out what it meant. She kept trying to stop thinking about it. It made her feel foggy, almost like she was trapped inside a cloud that was about to burst with a downpour. One, two, three, four, five, six, she kept counting. If she focused on her counting maybe the picture in her mind would evaporate.

But the image of that kiss tugged and pulled at her insides. She felt restless and uncomfortable, as she wondered if Fiona and Sally had been having an affair. If so, had Jacob known about it. She had one of those dark feelings again, when she wondered if Fiona and Sally had killed Jacob so that they could be together.

She had a slight chill, almost like there was more to that thought. A memory. Something. But she didn't like thinking Fiona and Sally killed Jacob, so she pushed it out of her mind. She placed it in a compartment of her subconscious where she placed all of her darkness.

Sexual preference wasn't always so cut and dry. Viv explained that to Jane nineteen years ago when Fiona left her girlfriend Stacy to be with Jacob. That was when Fiona tricked Jacob into leaving Jane.

Jane knew a lot about Jacob's life. More than she probably should. Even though much of what she knew caused her distress, she felt compelled to know as much as she could. It was the only way she could keep their relationship alive in her mind. It may have been imaginary. Viv had told her as much. She said that Jane was making it all up, that it was over with Jacob. Done. Finished.

But Jane believed they were eternally connected. Everything she did to stay close to Jacob was based on this belief. Her absolute unwavering conviction that their bond was everlasting and that they would be together again.

Fiona caused Jacob to move out of alignment with his stars nineteen years ago, when she and Jacob first got together. Fiona's actions interfered with Jane's destiny, causing Jacob to abandon Jane. He never would have left her on his own. It was Fiona that interrupted her future. She couldn't be angry with Jacob. It wasn't his fault. He had to be with Fiona. She was pregnant with his baby. He was just doing the honorable thing. Jacob, a man of integrity, couldn't leave Fiona when she was pregnant. He just couldn't.

It was confusing though when she found out that Fiona had taken an accidental fall down the long flight of stairs in front of their new brownstone and had a miscarriage. Jane thought Jacob would come back to her then. Without the baby, he no longer had an obligation to Fiona. But he stayed.

Jane called and called. She begged him to come back. She reminded him of his promises. She reminded him of their destiny. At first he was responsive, wavered back and forth, said he still wanted to be with Jane. But then for reasons Jane didn't quite understand, he became increasingly distant. He stopped taking her phone calls. Eventually he got a restraining order against her.

Jacob and Fiona had met at the gym one day. Jacob told Jane about her. He said she was a friendly woman who lived in his neighborhood with her girlfriend, Stacy. He told Jane that it was innocent. A budding friendship. He was still pretty new to the city. He didn't have many friends. He enjoyed his conversations with Fiona. She was funny, smart and into fitness like him. Over the course of a few months their friendship evolved. The casual chitchat while on the treadmill eventually turned into lunches and the occasional informal dinner.

Jacob was involved with Jane at the time, and they were totally in love. Jane trusted Jacob. So when he told Jane that Fiona and he were just friends, she believed him. Besides, Jacob said that Fiona was in a committed relationship with a woman. She lived with her girlfriend. Jane never questioned it.

It happened one night at dinner. It had to have been that night because Jacob said that they had only had sex that one time before she became pregnant. Jacob almost never drank. When he did, it was a very small amount. But that night he had six vodka martinis. Fiona kept ordering and, for some reason, one which Jane still didn't understand, Jacob kept drinking. He became totally drunk. In fact, he wondered if Fiona had slipped him a pill or something because he felt like he could barely walk.

Fiona lived right next to the restaurant. Jacob was so intoxicated that she suggested he stay at her place so he didn't have to stagger home. Fiona lived with her girlfriend. He assumed that Fiona was not at all interested in him. He further made an assumption — an erroneous one — that he was safe with her. He told Jane that at the time he thought it was *no big deal*. Of course his thinking was influenced by the alcohol. But he really believed it was an innocent invitation.

This was not the case. And like dominoes, one falling piece of Jane's life led to the next falling piece and the next and the next. Until the end result was Jane's whole life collapsing in one final descending blow: Fiona's pregnancy.

Jacob told Jane everything that happened. He felt so guilty; although he knew it would hurt Jane, he wanted her to know the truth. So, he spilled it all. It started as soon as they got upstairs. Fiona kissed his neck and rubbed his penis over his pants. He said he tried to stop her. He gently nudged her hand away, but she kept going. He'd nudge her away and she'd slowly put her hand back. She rubbed him so that he naturally just became aroused. He tried hard not to be aroused. But the way she just took control, there was something about it. Then with the pollution of the alcohol in his system, he just couldn't think clearly.

Eventually she opened the front of his pants, pulled them down. She massaged him until he stood with his pants off, totally exposed and completely erect. She kneeled down, took his penis, wrapped her mouth around the whole thing. She moved her mouth back and forth, slowly, back and forth.

Jacob admitted to Jane that he was aroused. How could he not be? But the evening got away from him. He knew what he did was a betrayal, but he wanted to be honest with her. Jane felt physical pain when Jacob told her the rest of the story. Imagining Jacob with another woman was just about the worst thing she had ever heard, but she wanted to know the truth.

Jacob didn't want to tell her anymore of the details. He wanted to be honest, but he knew the more he said, the more it would hurt her. And he already felt awful about what he did. About the whole situation.

But Jane insisted that he tell her. She begged him. "Pleeeazzze, Jacob. This is very hard. But I want to know. I want you to tell me. Pleeeazzze."

He looked at her. "I– I just– Jane. I don't want to hurt you more than I already have." He touched her cheek.

She looked into his eyes. They were glazed with such sadness. "I need to know. I want to know. Please."

He held her hand and continued, as sensitively as he could.

Fiona took her own pants off. She did it so fast. Jacob looked away and when he looked back he could see that she was naked from the waist down. After that, Jacob told Jane, he just didn't have any control. He tried really hard to stop, but he just couldn't. He wasn't even attracted to Fiona. He definitely didn't love her. It was just pure sexual arousal.

Fiona knew just how to get him aroused. Once she was na-ked, once he saw that, he couldn't stop himself. He told Jane that she pulled him down, she took him inside of her and then it happened really fast. He told Jane it was really fast. He barely remembered being in there.

He quickly pulled out, rushed to put his clothes on. He stum-bled to the door, hurried out. He felt so out of it. He thought she might have drugged him, but he didn't know. It could have just been all the alcohol. Either way, he said he barely remembered walking home. He passed out on his couch with all of his clothes on. Even his shoes.

When Jane told Vivian the story, Viv said, "That's total bullshit Jane. Buulllshhitt! He cheated on you, and now he's playing all Mr. Niceguy to try to get you to forgive him. What a sensational story too. It's a good one. You gotta give him that. He didn't really cheat because she's a lesbian and practically raped him. It's a good one." She shook her head, her nasally voice slightly raised. "He's a man, Jane! Give me a break. He fucked her. That's cheating. Sorry, I know it hurts. I really am sorry, but it's true."

"But he didn't have to tell me. I asked him to tell me every-thing and he did. He wanted to be honest because he loves me."

"That's such a crock. He was probably afraid you'd find out. You're all up in his shit. He probably assumed you'd figure it out or something. Trust me, he's not as perfect as you think. No one is as perfect as you think. Not even Jacob fuckin' Temple."

"I know he's not perfect. I mean, I'm not an idiot. But he's my perfect and I'm his, so we are perfect together. He made a mistake. I have to forgive him. He told me the truth. He's my soul mate. I know you think that's silly, but I believe it's true."

"It's not silly, it's asinine. Assiniiinne! But I do know you love 'em, and he's pretty OK as far as guys go. Although that story is pretty fuckin' wild. I have to say. But forgive him then. You love him and you want to forgive him, so do it. I wouldn't, though. Just saying."

Vivian came in, huffed and puffed after the five long flights of stairs up to Jane's apartment. She didn't waste any time once she was inside. She could be so high-strung. She practically vibrated angst. Sometimes she made Jane nervous. She immediately started moving Jane's stuff around. "You've got to get rid of some of this clutter. It's not normal. I can't even move in here. How do you live like this?"

"Viv. Leave it. We've talked about this. I need this stuff. It's for my writing."

"Bullshit. Just bullshit." She started to go into one of the boxes.

Jane almost never raised her voice, but right then she felt a yell emerging in her throat. She tried to swallow it. She did not like it when she got angry, but it wouldn't go down. "Viv!" she yelled. "Viv, leave it. Leave it alone! It's my stuff. Leave it!" She swallowed really hard. The anger finally went down.

Vivian's eyes grew wide. "OK, fine. Fine. I'll leave your stuff."

There was a moment of silence. Jane knew it was coming.

"You didn't go to the police yet, did you?"

"No... I didn't... but I will. I promise I will."

"Did you know they have no evidence? I saw it on the news and read it in the paper. And they believe it was someone who knew him. They say the forks in his eyes suggest it was personal. Those forks are pretty awful," she paused for a breath. "I don't know, maybe they think it was someone with a vendetta against him. Or just someone who was really enraged with him. They weren't specific about that. But there was no evidence at the crime scene. None that they found yet anyway. They said on the news that they were still investigating the scene. There was no break-in either. Then today, I heard that they have a person of interest, but they didn't say who. It could be you, Jane!"

"That's crazy talk. How would they even know I exist? I haven't been with Jacob in years." That chill came again, along with the image of the kiss that Sally planted on Fiona's lips.

"You probably know more about him than his damn wife. Don't you care about who did this? You want to tell 'em what you know, don't you?"

"It's just really hard right now. It's hard for me to really admit that he's gone. I feel, well… I feel really confused. And I feel really ashamed. How can I tell them everything I've done? Then everyone will know the truth. I know it all makes sense to me, but it might not to them. What if they think I'm crazy? You've said it yourself… You've told me I'm nuts. I'm all mixed up. But I know I have to go in, and I will. I just needed a few days. Don't you understand that?"

"Yeah, I do. I'm sorry I called you nuts. I didn't really mean it. Not like that anyway. I just always wanted you to let go of Jacob. He had moved on, had a whole life without you. You're my sis. I just wanted the same for you. You know… a life."

Vivian leaned over and hugged Jane. Jane hugged her back. She loved Vivian, but deep down she knew she didn't really understand. Sure, Jacob had moved on. She could understand what Vivian said. But in Jane's mind, that was only a temporary situation. But she knew what Viv meant.

Vivian had been married for nearly twenty years to Gabe, her college boyfriend. Her path had been very straight. She was one of those lucky people whose stars were orderly, always in the right place. She went to college, studied business, met Gabe, got her MBA, got married. They bought an apartment. They had one kid, Veronica, and two dogs. She couldn't expect Viv to understand.

Vivian looked Jane straight in the eyes and continued. She seemed genuinely concerned. "But you need to go in. You really have to trust me on this. I'm not sayin' you're nuts. I'm not sayin' that… just sometimes… you live in these made-up worlds where everything works out and is all happily ever after and shit. Things aren't like that. And Jacob was murrderrred. You get my drift?"

"Yeah… I get your drift. But can you stop using the M-word. Every time you say it, it hurts my bones. Can't we say transitioned or passed on? Something like that instead?"

"Sure, Jane. Sure. But that's what I mean about these nice little worlds in your books. You and your made-up characters can use euphemisms all you want, it doesn't change the reality of what happened?"

Jane nodded, but her eyes had a dazed look.

"Jane? Jane?" she tilted her head. "Do you understand what I'm sayin?" She put her hand on Jane's leg.

Jane had that weird chill again. It passed through quickly. "Yeah… yeah, I understand what you're saying. I'll go in on Monday. I promise I will."

"Do you want me to go with you? I could take a long lunch or even a half day."

"Thanks, but that's OK. I'll go alone."

"But you will go on Monday?"

"Yes. On Monday."

Jane would go to the police station on Monday. She wouldn't tell them everything. She would tell most things and ask that they keep her identity confidential. If possible. She didn't want everyone to know. She was worried. But she wanted to help them find out who did this to Jacob. It was for him that she went. She knew it was going to be an uncomfortable experience, but for him she would do it. She just hoped that she could stay focused and that she wouldn't keep getting that body chill.

But her thoughts and emotions became pretty muddled on Monday when she saw Yvonne, that woman that Jacob knew, down at the station.

# Chapter 12

Kadee arrived for her dissertation meeting. Dr. Puffin sat at his desk. Kadee had been doing research on catathymic homicides for close to a year. Dr. Puffin helped with organizing her thoughts, so she could formulate her hypotheses, and begin writing her literature review.

He wore a towel around his neck. His silver hair, matted from water. He swam laps nearly every morning. He was fit and lean, looked younger than his age, despite his long silver beard.

He reminded Kadee of an ancient Greek philosopher. The combination of his gray beard, which hung down passed his chin, his tall stature and his tendency to speak slowly and thoughtfully shouted teacher of wisdom. He also had that touch of social awkwardness that many scholars have, almost like he was removed and unaffected by the trivialities of everyday life, spending most of his time pondering and thinking about abstract questions.

His quirkiness appealed to Kadee, and she trusted him as her mentor. She aspired to be as astute and perceptive as he was. He smiled as soon as he saw her. His eyes always had an inquisitive look, almost like he was in a constant state of fascination. Even when engaged in the ordinary, everyday chitchat, he still had that look. Sometimes Kadee wondered what it would be like to live in his brain; no doubt she would need little outside stimulation if she swarmed around inside his head.

Kadee brought in some of the material she had researched having to do with obsession, stalking and catathymic homicides. The Jacob Temple case sat in the back of her mind. It appeared from the crime scene that it was a passion-driven murder. She wanted to pick Dr. Puffin's brain about that too. But first she was going over a research question that she was thinking of pursuing as the focus of her dissertation. He was intrigued by the ideas she raised. According to the research, perpetrators usually feel relief after a catathymic homicide. The internal tension during the emotional buildup phase becomes so unbearable that once the act of murder takes place, the killer often experiences relief. Kadee was curious about alternative possibilities. She wondered if after the initial murderous act, it was possible for the tension to build again, toward another victim, or even a number of victims, leading to a spree.

He sat back in his chair, rubbed his right hand down his beard a few times. "I like the direction you're going with this. Unfortunately because catathymia is a complex psychodynamic process, which is largely unconscious and therefore difficult to document, it has received little attention. Wertham described the process first in 1937, as you know, and well… it just hasn't received the merit it deserves."

Kadee nodded in agreement. "Wertham suggests that the perpetrators have insight following the offense, that they have some sense that the act was wrong, or at least that they reacted based on their emotions, that they reacted to their passion without having any control. It almost seems from the research that they usually only kill one person: the one they blame for their distress. But, what if their tension is more complicated, or if the murder itself compromises their internal resources? What if the crime itself causes them to unravel further? What if the crime itself is a trigger? I mean, I know it is way more complicated than I'm saying. But, I'm trying to figure out the chances that this type of murderer would kill again. I mean, would Betty Broderick have killed again if she hadn't been caught? Or Jodi Arias? This is what I'm trying to figure out." She cupped her hands, placed them on her lap.

He leaned forward, then settled back into his chair. His eyes lit up. "I see what you're saying, an important inquiry into the mind of a murderer, indeed. But I think you're trying to answer an unanswerable question… and I adore unanswerable questions, as I think you know. But this one has plagued forensic experts for decades. I think your question is really about predicting dangerousness. How can we predict if someone will kill? Is this an accurate representation of your query?"

"Yes, Dr. Puffin, in a general sense."

He retrieved a huge binder from his bookshelf and handed it to Kadee. "Here's some of the best research I have read on predicting dangerousness. But even the best still offers little solid method. There are studies and profiles looking at what particular factors lead to specific types of crimes, and though there are some predictors, none seem to be solid. The exception would be past violence. There is evidence that violent offenders are more likely to commit violent acts than non-violent offenders. But when you are situating this within the context of a catathymic act that is committed toward someone the perpetrator knows, as in the case with Betty and Jodi, well, it becomes more complicated. Theoretically catathymia is thought to be an internal tension arising from a real or perceived relationship with the victim. It's based on the real or perceived attachment. Theoretically, it should end when the person is eliminated. But as you know, theory can be, well… in cases such as this when we are trying to narrow down a specific behavioral pattern, theory and research can be quite pedantic. Real life always has those confounding variables. The gray areas, as you often call them."

"Exactly. So, what if doesn't end there?"

"Then, perhaps it doesn't fit into the category of Wertham's catathymia. Perhaps you want to create your own construct of catathymia, look into the forensic cases and pull out homicides that sound catathymic from repeat offenders and extend the definition to include repeat murderers. That would make for a fascinating dissertation topic."

Kadee thought his idea was brilliant. Shifting through her ideas with him helped her organize her theory. An ambitious topic, but an original one, and she felt up for the challenge. She jotted down a few notes. The sound of notebook pages rustled.

Her mind moved to Jacob Temple, his blood covered body, his wife crying, the eccentric upstairs neighbor, Oscar Piedmont, Beth, the radio show caller, Thomas, and the forks in Jacob's eyes.

"Dr. Puffin, can I ask a general question, one that is not directly related to my research?"

He stroked his beard, nodded up and down. "Of course Kadee. Please do."

"Do you think anyone is capable of murder?"

"Given the right set of circumstances, anyone can commit murder."

Her eyes narrowed. An image of Noah being stabbed burgeoned: a faceless Emily Goodyear superimposed on a picture of Belle Donovan holding the knife, fresh blood dripping down her willowy frame.

Dr. Puffin tilted his head. "What is it, Kadee? Is there something else? I get the feeling your questions are personal? Or perhaps you're asking about Jacob Temple? Those forks in his eyes? As I'm sure you know, that's very personal."

"Oh, no… I'm fine… every so often this all gets to me. So much violence. It's scary sometimes to think about how people can just snap, and how unpredictable it all is. I guess I'm just trying to find a way to predict the unpredictable." She scratched her head. "And yes, the Jacob Temple murder… I was at that crime scene. A gruesome sight to say the least." She looked down, tried to get the image of Jacob Temple on the floor of his den with the forks in his eyes out of her mind.

Dr. Puffin adjusted his seating position. "We know it was someone who knew him for sure, just from the way he was killed."

"Yes."

"And no sign of forced entry?"

"Right."

He rubbed his beard again. "There is some symbolic significance to those forks in his eyes."

"Right. Any thoughts what they mean?"

"Perhaps Jacob Temple saw something he shouldn't have or didn't see something he should. It's too soon to tell, but that was my first thought when I read about it."

Kadee nodded in agreement. She felt sad thinking about his death. It reminded her of Noah's murder. Jacob was also youngish, tall with dark hair, and most likely killed by someone he knew. His life taken by someone he trusted. She blew her wispy bangs off her face.

She finished writing her notes, scheduled her next meeting with Dr. Puffin and left. Her mind drifted as she made her way down to the subway, then back to her apartment. There were people scattered throughout the railcar as it grinded through the underground passage. She noticed a woman wearing a pair of red stilettos, crimson suede with a long high heel. She couldn't imagine what the woman was thinking when she decided to put those shoes on. It was only twenty degrees out, with big splotches of ice scattered everywhere.

She stared at the ruby heels, seeing them and not seeing them at the same time. She thought over her conversation with Dr. Puffin. If anyone was capable of murder that meant she was too. Well, she already knew that. She thought she had killed Noah for Christ's sake. But if she had killed Noah, it would have been in an altered state. Not as a conscious decision. She had thought of killing him, but she never would have been able to go through with it. Morally, she just couldn't justify taking someone else's life. She didn't have that right. But if it happened in a fit of rage, there would be no time for reflection. Perhaps no amount of virtuous beliefs could stop that.

The voice of Emily Goodyear offered Kadee some insight. Of course, Emily was fictional, but it was an unfiltered narrative exploring the mind of a killer. She had heard that writing good fiction was almost like being an actor. The author slipped into a character and tapped into a particular emotional experience (role) in order to express some truth about life. Perhaps because of Yvonne's training as a psychiatrist, she was able to write the internal process of a passionate murderer with great perspicuity.

The woman in the red stilettos got off at the subway stop right before hers. She watched the heels scurry out of the car and onto the cement platform. Kadee looked down at her brown Uggs: solid, secure, and safe. If Alex and Noah were shoes, Alex was definitely her Uggs; Noah, more like a red stiletto, good for a day or two, maybe even a month, but definitely, categorically, undeniably *not* for life.

She got off the subway. Vanessa and Hailey had both called while she was underground. She listened to their messages as she walked from the subway to her apartment. They both knew of her engagement. Vanessa had spoken with Alex and Hailey had spoken with Vanessa. They both left congratulatory messages. Both said yes to a celebratory dinner.

It's funny how fast news travels sometimes. She slipped into a morbid fascination, which happened occasionally no matter how hard she wrestled against it. She wondered what would happen if she was ever murdered. How long it would take for news of her demise to travel. She assumed Alex would be the one to find her. He would come home one day and there she would be, dead on the floor, blood streaming out of her the same way it had poured out of Jacob Temple. *How awful for him.*

*How would it happen? Don't go there. Don't go there.* A momentary battle of synaptic firing, and her thoughts went there even though it terrified her. A knife, a gun, maybe a strangling. She rested her hand, fingers spread out, along her collarbone. *Now that would be agonizing.* Her body tightened. *Kadee, love, you shouldn't read about all of this violence. It will give you nightmares.*

*Thanks, mom.* She stopped her thoughts, pulled her head out of the quicksand before she suffocated in panic. She tried to better understand the criminal personality to prevent murders. Sometimes she couldn't help but wonder what it was like for the victims.

That night, they all went to dinner: Vanessa and boyfriend Henri; Hailey and husband Dean; Alex and Kadee. They met downtown in the Meatpacking District at a Spanish tapas restaurant. They sat in front along a large window. Snow fell outside, puffs of cotton in a steady stream. A thin blanket of white accumulated along the sidewalk. They toasted with champagne, and indulged in sangria, more champagne, delicious food, and the easy rhythm of a piano playing. It was an evening to savor, a festival for their engagement.

After dinner, Kadee and Vanessa went to the bathroom together. A small space, three stalls, electric blue tiles, the synthetic smell of air freshener. Once inside, Vanessa pulled her curly hair away from her face. "What is it, Kade?"

"Nothing. What do you mean?" She felt a twitch in her throat.

Vanessa sighed purposefully. "I know you. I can tell when your wheels are spinning. Is it Alex?"

Kadee went into the stall, started peeing. "Ness, I'm fine."

"Kade…"

Kadee had confided in Vanessa that she still had mixed feelings about Noah. She was over him and she knew she hadn't really loved him, not the everlasting, for life, sustaining love, kind of love. But she wasn't over what happened. They had talked at length about the difference between obsessive crazy-love and the solid, secure type. The type she felt with Alex, her brownstone, her Uggs. Vanessa assumed this was what was on Kadee's mind.

"You seem distracted."

"What do you mean?"

There was a flush. Kadee came out of the stall.

Vanessa looked at her. "This is the right thing."

"I know."

"Do you? Is the Noah stuff still bothering you?"

"Well, not bothering me. But it's still there. It's going to take a while to be fully over what happened. But I'm working on it with Wright every week in therapy. And I'm happy with Alex. I am. I'm just tired. I had an early meeting with Dr. Puffin this morning, and I spent the day knee-deep in research. I'm just a little tired." This was the truth. She also felt uncomfortable talking about Noah at their celebration dinner.

"OK." Vanessa's eyes intense. She wasn't convinced. "But if there is something, anything, you know you can talk to me, right?" Vanessa rested a hand on Kadee's shoulder.

"Of course." Kadee felt the burning that precedes tears. She wasn't even sure why she was ready to cry.

Vanessa noticed Kadee's eyes turn red and knew tears would come. She decided to change the subject to help her friend keep the night upbeat. "By the way. I got a friend request and message from Y. E. Tracy — that's right, Yvonne Tracy — on Facebook this morning. She wanted to connect. She said that she wrote a book and that she was working on a second one. She knew that I was a writer too. Said you had mentioned it in a therapy session or something. She was looking to connect with other writers."

Kadee scratched her head. "She say anything else?"

"I think it's strange… her writing to me. Or she's strange. Sorry, I know she was your therapist and then everything between the two of you with the drama with Noah…" she paused, seemed thoughtful. "I remember that day you went to meet her in the park, I remember you said that you hoped to get some sort of closure with her. It seemed that you two had a nice relationship. I even thought to myself that maybe when some time passed, the two of you would be friends."

Kadee glanced at Vanessa. "That *is* a little strange. Did you accept her friend request?"

"Not yet. I was going to, but I thought I should ask you about it first. Her message was kinda weird. She asked about you and Alex? If you had gotten engaged. It seemed… don't know. Why would she ask me instead of asking you?"

Kadee took her sweater off, pushed her hair away from her face.

Vanessa touched up her lipstick. "You look flushed."

"I'm fine. It's a little warm in here. Listen, Yvonne is really messed up over Noah."

"Do you talk to her?"

"Well, sort of. We just started talking. We met for lunch and have been messaging on Facebook. Oh, and she's dating Detective Poole. Which is totally bizarre, right? So I've seen her at the police station too."

"Whaaat? She's dating Poole? The gruff one, whose always adjusting his crotch? That *is* bizarre. Talk about opposites. Is there something else with her? Do you talk about…" she looked down, "Noah? That must be hard."

"We have talked about Noah some. It's brought up mixed feelings, but in some ways, it's been helpful too. I feel… um… guilty though."

"Guilty? You didn't do anything wrong."

"Yvonne seems really distraught. I mean, I know grief is a process, but she seems unsure of herself. Like she's lost her confidence. Something about the look in her eyes and the way she carries herself, her posture, her gestures. She's not the same. And I… I… can't help but feel partially responsible. I lied about Noah's name. If I hadn't done that, maybe things wouldn't have ended so… um… so badly."

Vanessa guffawed. "Badly? That's an understatement."

Kadee ignored her. "She says she doesn't blame me. But whether *she* does or doesn't is almost less important than the fact that I blame myself."

"Kadee, you always do this to yourself. You did the same with Noah. Blamed yourself. What happened isn't your fault. You were a victim, too." She reached over and hugged Kadee. "Is that what's eating at you tonight? You've gotta let this go, hon. You didn't do anything wrong."

Vanessa felt warm and comforting. "Thanks, Ness." She released the embrace. "Talking with Yvonne has just brought up a lot of stuff I was suppressing. But it's good. I need to get this all figured out so I can really move on." She shook her head. "Though I'm not sure Yvonne will ever fully recover. I hope she will."

"She probably just needs more time. Time heals all wounds, right?"

"I don't know. I just don't know."

"It's still strange her sending me a friend request."

"She's using the writing as therapy. She's probably trying to form a network with other writers. Part of her moving-on process, I'd guess. I can ask her about it."

"I'll just accept. It's always good to network with other writers."

"Maybe it will help her in some way. How's it going with Henri? You two look cozy."

Vanessa beamed. "All's well. This might be it. He may be *the one*."

Hailey opened the door and came in. "What are you doing in here? You've been gone for like ten minutes, leaving me out there with the men." She grinned.

Kadee said. "Just the usual girl stuff."

Hailey looked into Kadee's eyes. "What is it?"

"Nothing… really. We were just talking about Yvonne."

Hailey squinted one eye. "What about her? Is it the Noah stuff *again*?" She groaned. "I told you when we discussed this last week that you've got to let this go. He chose Yvonne to marry. That's that. Right?"

Vanessa gave Hailey a light tap on the arm. "Hailey! That's an awful thing to say."

"Well, he did. I'm just calling a spade a spade. I said it from the very beginning: Noah was never going to marry Kadee. Yvonne was more the type that guys like Noah marry."

"What does that say about Kadee? Type. What a crock."

Kadee glared at Hailey, tears burned in her eyes. "You know this is a sore spot for me. I have been tormenting myself with thoughts about why Noah chose Yvonne instead of me. I shared my feelings with you, and now you're throwing it back in my face."

"I don't mean anything by it, Kadee. I'm merely stating the truth. I want you to be able to move on. I'm just trying to help."

Vanessa scoffed at Hailey. "You're so insensitive. Yvonne has nothing on Kadee. Besides, Noah wasn't faithful to Yvonne. He wasn't a good guy." Vanessa folded her arms, satisfied with her dig at Hailey's own marital indiscretions.

Hailey's eyes pierced Vanessa. "Being unfaithful doesn't make someone a bad person. He was using Kadee for sex. Sowing his oats until he was ready to marry Yvonne. It happens every day. Guys having great sex with one woman while the whole time they are prepared to marry another." Hailey licked her lips.

"Riiight." Vanessa said sarcastically.

"He told me he loved me. I believed him. He told Yvonne he loved her. She believed him. The man has been murdered.

Do you have any idea how painful this is for me?" Kadee's voice quivered.

"I understand, Kadee, and we talked about this. Over and over. Honestly, I think it's a little disrespectful to Alex. You... *We* are here to celebrate your engagement to Alex — your fiancé — and you're in here talking about Noah."

Kadee and Vanessa looked at each other and then back at Hailey. Silence. Hailey broke it. "Yes, I know the irony in me preaching about emotional fidelity."

Kadee squeezed her nose. She felt tears coming. She was not going to allow herself to cry in front of Hailey. "I love Alex. This has got nothing to do with him." She swallowed. "Let's change the subject. This is supposed to be a celebration. I don't want to argue."

Hailey pursued her lips. "Yes. Let's."

Awkward silence.

Hailey broke it again. "So when is the wedding? Have you decided yet? I hope you're planning on a designer dress. I'll go shopping with you if you'd like. There are a few places I can take you..."

Kadee listened and nodded, pursed her lips into a smile, listened and nodded. She looked right through Hailey. *What an absolute bitch. I cannot believe she said those things to me. I knew I never should have told her my private thoughts. Sure, she has been making more of an effort to be kinder and less judgmental. Clearly, not enough to trust her with my inner feelings. I am not going to let her get to me. No.*

She couldn't talk to Hailey about her wedding. Alex and she had discussed a small destination wedding, or possibly eloping.

Her parents would be disappointed, but they would recover. They had just gotten engaged and already everyone was asking for the date.

Kadee knew Hailey would be appalled at the idea of anything less than a traditional ceremony. She wasn't in the mood to explain herself; she certainly did not want to get into *another* tiff with her. Especially not on the night of her engagement celebration. She politely acknowledged Hailey's words as they flew in one ear and out the other.

As they walked out of the bathroom, Vanessa whispered to Kadee, "Don't listen to her."

Kadee squeezed Vanessa's hand. "Don't worry. I wasn't planning on it."

Later that night when Kadee and Alex got home, he mentioned that Yvonne had sent him a friend request along with message on Facebook. Alex was one of those people who used Facebook for networking, as well as staying connected with friends. So he kept his page open; he didn't have secure privacy settings, affording anyone the privilege of seeing all of the information he posted.

Kadee admonished him a few times. With all the forensic experts that came for lectures, she knew the Internet made people more vulnerable to things like stalking. In fact, it was a breeding ground for pedophiles, stalkers and murderers. Alex was strongminded. Like many good attorneys, he could argue his position so well that by the time the discussion finished, he made you wonder if you even had a clue about what you were saying in the first place.

"What did Yvonne say in the message?" Her stomach knotted for a second. She wasn't sure why.

"Not much. She was looking to connect, knew we had gotten engaged and was sending congratulations."

"Did you respond? I told her we had gotten engaged. She saw your pictures when you tagged me. So, she knew already." She thought about Vanessa saying Yvonne asked about their engagement. Kadee wondered if Yvonne was having a hard time knowing that Kadee was moving on while Yvonne was still heartbroken.

"Not yet, but I was going to. You seem annoyed. Would you rather I didn't?"

"No, go ahead. I'm just being silly. It's just Yvonne's still really messed up over Noah and everything that happened. I feel a little guilty that I'm so happy. That I have you. I guess I just feel sorry for her, for what she's going through."

"Your mother and the stray kids and animals again?" He smirked. He always teased her about having become like her mother, adopting Liza Carlisle's save-the-world philosophy.

"Al, I'm serious." Her brow wrinkled.

"I know, sweetie. Just relax," he uncorked a bottle of red wine. "Let's have one more drink before we turn in." He poured two glasses; they both plopped onto the couch.

"She's dating Poole. Isn't that wild?"

"What? She's dating Poole? Wow. Crazy how things happen. He was the lead detective in her fiancé's murder investigation..." He thought for a moment. "Well, I guess it makes sense in a way. He helped her, and she probably found that attractive. It sounds

like she *is* moving on with her life then. You've got to stop worrying about everyone else. She's a big girl. She'll be OK."

"Yeah… I'm sure you're right." But she wasn't sure.

"I was going to send a polite note back to her. I think it's
rude not to respond at all?"

"Yeah, I guess you should."

They lounged on the couch, sipping wine. Alex put the
TV on, flipped through, landed on a rerun of *Goodfellas*. They
watched until the end, finishing off the whole bottle of Merlot
before going to bed just before 3 a.m.

The next morning, after Alex left for the gym, Kadee sipped
her coffee and glanced through Facebook. She saw that Yvonne
had liked their engagement photos. Yvonne writing to Alex and
Vanessa seemed a bit odd. Yvonne didn't know either of them.
She assumed that Yvonne was lonely, maybe feeling estranged
and in need of human contact. Kadee wondered if Yvonne had
friends that she spent time with. It sounded like Noah was her
closest friend. For many years. Perhaps he was all she had. *Awful.*

But still there was something unusual about her reaching
out to them. Wasn't there? She felt something, an intangible sensation, a nagging itch with no identifiable source. Her curiosity piqued. She signed onto Alex's Facebook to read Yvonne's
message.

> *Hi Alex,*
> *I see you and Kadee got engaged. I just wanted to send a quick*
> *note to say how happy I am for the two of you. Kadee has been*

*through such a hard time, but I guess it all works out in the end.*
*It's funny how that is. Isn't it, Alex?*

*Anyhoo, Kadee and I have been talking some, which has been*
*really lovely. She goes on about you so much that I feel like I know*
*you already. \*wink, wink.\* I'm sure we will meet soon. By the way,*
*I just love the photographs of the two of you in the restaurant, right*
*after you popped the ole question. You make a delicious couple. I*
*look forward to seeing more pictures.*

*Kindest regards, Yvonne*

Kadee rested back into her chair, arms crossed, thinking, a
vague sense of uneasiness. *But* why? The message was innocuous
enough. Although that comment — *a delicious couple* — sounded
a little creepy. Yvonne certainly had a unique way of expressing
herself.

Maybe Kadee felt possessive over Alex, worried that he
and Yvonne would form some sort of clandestine attachment.
Or that he would get to know Yvonne and prefer her to Kadee.
Same as Noah. *That's a big no.* Her relationship with Alex was
entirely different. He really loved her. He would never leave
her for another woman. Yet, still there was a subtle feeling
nestling, indistinct. It crept along the inside of her skin. She
rolled up her sleeves, scratched at her arms to chafe away the
hebbie-jebbies.

She didn't want Alex to talk to Yvonne. When she came to
that conclusion she hated it. She never wanted to see herself as
the insecure, domineering type. Ever. Besides, Yvonne wouldn't
betray her. It's not like she purposefully stole Noah from her.

But her mother had trusted her father and her teacher-friend Ramona. The two eventually engaged in an affair.

*No.* She trusted Alex. Her parent's marriage was estranged at the time of that affair. It was short lived and a mistake. Her mother forgave her father, and their bond was as strong as ever. She didn't want to react, become guarded and worried that she would be hurt like her mom was. The truth was she didn't want Alex and Yvonne to be messaging back and forth. But the thought of herself as controlling was even less appealing.

She wanted to be the easy-going type. She *was* that type. *I am that type.* And with that, she decided to let it go. Alex would probably send a quick, respectful response acknowledging her message, and their dialogue would be done.

She gnawed a cuticle and switched her attention to some of J. Reid Meloy's research on stalking.

# Chapter 13

Saturday night. Yvonne arrived home after a dinner date with John Poole. The snow floated down in small flakes, dense and steady, leaving a coat of glistening white frosting along the sidewalk and treetops. She sipped tequila, jingled the ice against her glass, and admired the scene from her window. She had planned to stay the night at John's apartment, but her interactions with Kadee weighed heavily on her mind. She wanted to be alone.

She turned from her window, hummed Beethoven. She began going through some of her clothing. She was tossing out most of her conservative attire. She wanted a new look, a sexier, more chic, lady-of-the-hour look. That's what men wanted. Dustin wanted that. Noah wanted that. Although it was painful for her to look back, the truth was that her brother, James, had wanted that, too. His girlfriend was one of *those* girls.

Of course, James would find himself with a beautiful, smart girl. He was so well-liked, so charming and funny. Bettina, his girlfriend, who eventually broke his heart, the one who Yvonne blamed for James' suicide, was one of those fabulous girls. One of *those* girls who could leave a man drowning in desire just by looking at him.

Bettina knew how to spread her legs, too. *Those girls always do.* She folded one of her polo shirts, paused for a moment, then tossed it in the garbage bag. Yvonne would hear them having sex through her wall. Boy, that Bettina knew how to cry out with pleasure. Yvonne tried to mimic her sounds when she was with her first boyfriend in college. Clearly, she wasn't so good at it because Derrick eventually left her. Dustin left her for Madelyn. The hardest one to swallow? *Noah.* He preferred Kadee. Of course, he would. She was everything Yvonne wasn't.

However, things were going to change. She was so sick of not being good enough. Now, she had the power to change that. She would become that spectacular, brilliant woman. She was certainly more intellectually sophisticated than all of those other women. She would use her brains, making sure no woman ever stole her life from her again. She had already begun her plan. It appeared to be going smoothly. She was going to make sure *that* continued. *No more pussy footing around what I want. No more.* She tossed out a blazer with shoulder pads. *It's my time to score.* She paused, reflected, then went to her desk. She wrote something down.

She blamed Kadee for everything that happened. *If* Kadee hadn't lied about Noah's name in her therapy sessions. *If* she wasn't so beautiful, so interesting, so adventurous. *If* she had stopped seeing Noah when she should have, clearly he was only using her to boost his own ego, because Yvonne was constantly rejecting him. *If* Kadee didn't indulge Noah's dark sexual fantasies. *If* Kadee didn't do all of those things, Noah would still be alive.

It was Kadee's fault that Yvonne killed Noah and that her mind, once seemingly an integrated whole where she was able to think through things rationally, was now an abyss, a dark hole with her thoughts now scattered into fragmented, itsy-bitsy pieces.

In some ways, she had never felt so free. Killing Noah opened up a door in her psyche that had been tightly fastened, where she kept all of the rage that accumulated over the years. The murderous act unlocked her violent proclivities.

Watching Noah as he begged for his life, after everything he had done to her, all the years he'd betrayed her trust, how he'd treated her as worthless, hows her love had held no value for him, the killing empowered her. The blood trickling out of his body released her, relieving years of built-up tension that she wasn't even aware she carried.

Yvonne was a new woman. A killer. A murderess. But also a woman who wasn't going to shove her feelings away to protect everyone else anymore. She was so tired of taking care of everyone else's feelings. Now it was her time to think of herself. *My time to score.*

She knew she was toying with Kadee by telling her the truth, but in the form of fiction. Yvonne knew it would keep her in that sort of limbo between knowing and not knowing. Having been privy to Kadee's interior dialogue as her therapist, Yvonne knew that was a particular vulnerability for her. She knew it would drive her a little crazy. She couldn't resist the temptation to needle at her psychologically. Oh, it felt so good to be the one in control. The superior one. The one who was manipulating all of the pawns in her own private chess game. For once in her life, she was doing exactly what she wanted to do, and she felt fantastic.

She did, however, need to be cautious. She wanted to be a part of Kadee's life. At least for the time being. As much as a part of her hated her with every ounce of her flesh, she also loved her. She couldn't quite reconcile the two feelings, the love with the hate. Instead of feeling like a fluid stream with one on each end, her emotions drifting somewhere in the middle, where love and hate exist simultaneously, she flipped from one dramatic extreme to the other. Some days she loved Kadee so much she wanted to devour her, and other days she hated her so much she thought she just might kill her.

In fact, she thought she just might kill Kadee if she didn't behave according to Yvonne's plan. She wasn't sure; naturally she would have to be really careful with that decision. With the triangle between Kadee, Noah and her, she could be a person of interest in that case. But she *was* sleeping with the lead detective now. Unlike Noah, she was positive that she had this one wrapped around her itsy-bitsy, teensy-weensy little finger.

*I am fucking the shit outta him.* She released a venomous shriek from her lips whenever she said that to herself. She loved cursing. She had never let herself use vulgar language before. It was so thrilling to toss profanity around without a care.

The one thing that she couldn't get rid of was the image of Noah's eyes as he pleaded in terror for his life. It both pleased and bothered her. At first, the image disturbed her. She had loved him for many years after all. In the wake of the aftermath, guilt haunted her. But after a few weeks passed, she recognized a level of satisfaction from that look he had, like she had finally accomplished a fulfilling project, and she could just sit back and relish in her achievement.

The two emotional experiences sat separate in her psyche. Sometimes, the guilt would come on and envelope her in a blanket of fragility. Now, though, she would brush that right off. She was never going to allow herself to be vulnerable to someone else's careless whims again. So any remorse she felt, now transformed into blame. It fueled her anger, made her feel justified. Her favorite flavor of blame: Kadee. She originally blamed Noah. But, he was dead now.

Though the guilt still manifested, instead of being registered as a difficult emotion, it became a hallucination. Yvonne had an intrusive visual image of Noah's eyes that came from out of nowhere and felt real. She would be out to dinner with John, when, with no apparent trigger, Noah's brown irises, the pupils a pinpoint of black from terror, would emerge. They seemed real. They weren't a picture in Yvonne's head; instead they were a hallucination that actually bounced right in front of her. They blocked whatever was behind them.

On Friday afternoon while she talked to Kadee, Noah's eyes moved up and down, blocking whatever part of Kadee's body they were in front of. Whenever Yvonne saw those eyes, she became petrified, thinking that somehow Noah was there watching her, reminding her of what she did. She exercised tremendous concentration, pushed her eyelids together, held them tight for a few seconds, visualized something else. Wiping the air clean of him.

It was fair to say that Yvonne had a traumatic reaction to the murder. But she would not let herself feel powerless over any emotions ever again. So instead of letting herself feel her remorse, possibly even turning herself in or going for help — something constructive — she channeled all of her energy into being a more sophisticated perpetrator.

Maybe she would kill Kadee. Maybe she wouldn't. She didn't have to decide right then. That was the beauty of her new way of life; nothing mattered other than whatever she decided to do in the moment. Oh, the jubilation.

She stopped for a moment. The corners of her lips formed a grin. *Pierce your skin, watch you bleed.* She rushed to write it down. Now that she had started her second book, ideas flowed freely into her mind. She had notes all around her apartment that would eventually be consolidated into her story.

There was no more planning, no more worrying, no more anticipating, and no more emotional consequences. She could just make it all up as she went along. Except for the intrusion of Noah's bobbing eyeballs scaring her into her old reality a few times a day, she was free from any and all moral authority and obligations.

She had never been more exhilarated.

Being close with John made everything easier, too. She could not believe how easily she seduced him. He was putty in her hands. *He will believe just about anything lil' ole me tells him.* A hoot emerged from her belly whenever she thought that. She loved the experience of her laughter now. It was a deeply visceral experience. She could feel the bitterness leaving her body as the sound bellowed out of her mouth. An emotional detox. Marvelous.

Undoubtedly it was her newfound ability to be sexually open that whipped John around her finger. She had Kadee to thank for that. *Those* girls always knew just how to fuck a man. Kadee had taken Noah that way. Kadee spread her legs in any and all positions, things Yvonne had been uncomfortable doing. Well, not anymore. Her new womanhood included indulging in all of those sexual experiences that she used to think were shameful. She was a murderess now. There was absolutely no reason to maintain any semblance of purity.

She did enjoy John's company. He was a decent man, but she was not going to allow herself to invest any emotional commitment in him or any man ever again. She would be respectful of him. She did enjoy the companionship. But for the most part, she was using him as part of her plan to get away with murder.

He trusted her. *Ha!* John Poole trusted her. That was the icing on the cake. John Poole revealed details about the cases he worked on to her. She had learned just how to finesse him, too. She read his moods, used her clinical training to recognize when the best time to ask him questions was. She knew exactly when he was the most likely to divulge information. As a matter of fact, he had spent a good deal of time that evening telling her about Jacob Temple's murder.

She just knew she could get away with almost anything at this point. She pulled off Noah's murder without a hitch, and she hadn't even been a trained criminal then. She always wanted to feel superior at something. To maintain unsurpassed talent in some area of her life. But there was always someone just a little better than her. It had pained her so. She tried to use her clinical knowledge to rationalize away her inferior feelings. But they festered underneath the surface, a nagging allergy, always there, flaring up when exposed to an irritant.

Getting away with Noah's murder empowered her. It left her with a sudden potency, which was unmatched in any other area of her life. The part of her that still held a modicum of rationality knew killing someone was wrong. She had moments, particularly when Noah's eyeballs intruded, when she became disturbed by her own urges.

But the energy. The force. The feeling of power. They were stronger.

They dominated her emotional world, fostered her new identity. A murderess. Using all of her cleverness, she would refine her skills. She snickered, tossed out a few pairs of old panties.

She stripped down to her bra and panties, peered at herself in her full-length mirror. She looked at herself from the side and turned slowly until she faced the mirror. She looked upon her new self. She grasped her breasts and pumped her pelvis at her reflection, practicing groans of ecstasy: *Ooohhh, Ahhh, Ooohhhh, Aaahhh. Yes. Yeeesss!*

She used the video recordings that Belle Donovan had taken of Noah with the other women as training videos. The one's Kadee had sent to her back when Yvonne was her therapist. She watched them over and over, particularly Kadee's. She rehearsed the leg spreads, facial expressions, and sex sounds.

Yvonne took her fingers, pulled the string of her new thong panties out of her butt. She found them uncomfortable, but it was a small price to pay for her evolution into one of *those* women.

While her hips gyrated at her reflection, she took her hands, fingers spread, ran them through her thick black hair. "Thank goodness for extensions," she said to herself. "I had wanted my hair to look more like Kadee's, but it looks even better than hers does."

She wasn't going to allow anything to stop her. She held the control now. *My turn to score.* She wanted to be in a relationship with Kadee; she was going to do whatever it took. She picked up her cell phone to call her, pausing to pull the string out of her butt crack again. "Do *those* women find these itsy-bitsy, teensy-weensy strings annoying, too?" she wondered aloud. *No more.* She took the panties off, removed her bra. She threw on a satin nightgown.

She walked back to her mirror to have a look at herself. Maybe she should start by using the Facebook messages to get close to Kadee. Less obvious than a phone call. She had even sent a message to Kadee's best friend, Vanessa, and Alex earlier in the day. She wanted to become close with the people in Kadee's life. This would make it easier to collect information about Kadee. It would also make it easier to be as close with Kadee as possible. The more people in the circle the better. Her face lit up. A new idea. *Proximity. Yes, proximity.* A wily grin stretched across her face. She went to her notebook and added a few lines to her plan.

She went back to the mirror. Examined her body. Her phone rang. It was John. *Ha!* They had only been apart for an hour, and he was calling. She had never had a man who was so attentive before. She cocked her head at her reflection, stared into her own eyes. She decided to let the call go to voicemail.

She would call him back, but she had something she needed to take care of first. She hummed again, reached all the way in the back of her filing cabinet and pulled out a large manila envelope. She went into the kitchen, dumped the contents in the sink, took a lighter and started burning page after page.

The yellow glow smoldered at the end of each sheet until it disintegrated. Yvonne took her laptop, placed it on the kitchen counter, kept her eyes on the flames in her sink. She logged onto Facebook.

She scrolled through Kadee's home page, stared at the engagement pictures again. Yvonne's eyes dark, her jaw clenched.

Alex and Vanessa still hadn't responded to her. She was sure they would, but she hoped it happened sooner than later. Yvonne couldn't be sure how she would feel or behave if she had to wait too long.

The small flames were taking a long time to burn up all that paper. So she decided to call John back while the pages smoldered.

He picked up on the first ring. "Hello, handsome," she said, her eyes vacant. As they spoke, she watched those pages burn, disintegrate, the fire consuming each one. Eventually becoming… nothing.

# Chapter 14

**1996**

Jane and Jacob spoke every day during the month between their meeting and his move to New York City. They also emailed throughout the day, short messages, to stay connected while they were apart. Jane had two boxes full of their exchanges. She printed them out and saved them. So when Jacob destroyed her by ending their relationship, Jane spent days lost in time reading and rereading all of the letters between them.

It didn't make any sense. The Jacob she was in a relationship with and the Jacob that filed for the restraining order weren't the same person. Even with all of her efforts to know everything she could about his life, there had to be an important piece missing. There had to be something she didn't know that tied the before and after together.

When Jacob had moved to New York, the relationship progressed like lightning. It was late summer. Jacob had started his graduate program at Columbia University. Although he was busy with classes, they managed to be together at least four times a week, sometimes more. Jacob called and emailed every day. After only about a month, he told Jane he loved her. She loved him, too. Boy, oh boy, did she love him. Her feelings toward Jacob were more powerful than anything she had ever felt before in her life.

The sex was good. But it was so much more than that. Jacob made Jane feel alive. He understood her. He listened to her. He accepted her just as she was.

Jane was so used to feeling insecure, uncomfortable, and inferior. Jacob built her up. He made her feel like she was the most fantastic, beautiful woman in the world. Finally, Jane felt confident. She could hold her head up, be proud of who she was.

And he was romantic. Boy, oh, boy was he romantic.

Vivian always told her that real life love was nothing like the love that she read about in her romance novels. She understood what Viv meant, but the way she felt with Jacob made her feel the same way as the characters described feeling in her books. He was always attentive; he sent cards in the mail, just because. He was affectionate; he always held her hand as they walked down the street. He played with her hair, kissed her constantly and told her over and over how lucky he was.

The days they were apart were difficult for Jane. She didn't really know how to handle those feelings. She felt a deep desire, a longing, a painful sort of ache. It wasn't just emotional, she felt it physically too. A throbbing she felt in her bones.

But the pain felt good sometimes, in a strange way. She had never longed for anyone before. Sure she missed her parents and

Viv when she first got to college, but this was different. Her yearning for Jacob filled her up, sparked life into her, made her feel wide awake. All of her nerve endings felt raw. She experienced *everything* more intensely. It just felt so good to rejoice in that depth of emotion.

Even when it was painful, it teetered on the edge of pleasure.

When she told Vivian how she felt, Viv said, "Do not tell that man all of these feelings. It's too intense. You're gonna freak him the fuck out."

"But he loves me. I can tell Jacob anything."

"Not this. You're gonna have to trust me on this. You don't have to tell 'em every single thought you have. It's good to keep a little mystery goin. You know what I mean?"

"Kinda. But Jacob said he always wants us to be honest with each other. He says he wants me to trust him with my feelings. And I do, Viv. I do."

"This isn't being dishonest. You're not lying to the man. It's just holding back a little. You've only been together a few months. He seems like a nice guy, but you don't really know 'em yet. You don't wanna freak 'em out? Do you?"

"Well… no… I don't want to do that."

"Then write it down in your journal or something. And one day, if you get married or somethin', then you can tell 'em."

"OK, Viv. I can do that."

And just like that, Jane finished her very first manuscript.

Then came the night, *that night*, when Jacob strolled in and told her what happened with Fiona. He cried as he disclosed the whole awful truth as he knew it. Of course, there are two sides to every story and naturally Jacob only told his. Jane believed every word of it.

"I'm so sorry, babe. I can't believe how careless I was. I never meant for this to happen. I always thought that we would… that we would… be married. You are the one, Jane. You. But she's having my baby…" he heaved. "Oh God, this is terrible. I can't believe what an idiot I am." He put his face in Jane's chest and sobbed.

She took her hand, rubbed it back and forth through his thick hair. She kissed his head, tears streamed down her face. "But you don't have to marry her, Jacob. You can help her with the baby, but you don't have to marry her. People do that all the time."

He shook his head while it remained imbedded against her chest. "No, I can't do that… I can't … I've told you about my family. My father would disown me. He would never accept that. I hate the values I was raised on, but I cannot go against my father. I just can't. I am a weak man, babe. I don't even deserve you."

"That's not true Jacob. You're not weak. You're doing what you believe is right even though it's not what you want." As soon as those words spilled out, a dark feeling washed over her. Anger. Or maybe something worse. She didn't like that. So she rationalized: *I can't be angry at Jacob, I just can't. He is doing the right thing. Most men would leave her alone to raise the baby. He's doing the right thing, thinking about the well-being of his unborn child.*

She rationalized those dark feelings right out of her mind.

Then Jacob Temple said something that stayed with Jane for nineteen years. Unbeknownst to him, it was a string of words that would feed right into her wish and belief that they were eternally connected and meant to be. "Maybe someday, we'll be together again…" He lifted his head up, ran his fingers slowly down the side of her face and kissed her. They kissed and cried, and hugged so tight, and then kissed and cried some more.

The moment that Jacob walked out of Jane's life remained frozen in her in mind. It repeated itself over and over, sometimes intrusively, other times purposefully. But the image never erased. The strength of her feelings never subsided. It lasted only seconds, but imprinted itself in her psyche as the most painful and most significant event of her life.

As she watched his body move out the door and down the stairs, she could still feel him. His body diminished in size, but his spirit omnipresent. The space between them grew larger as she watched him go, but she felt as though they were still connected. Her body splintered: Part of her went with him, and the rest of her was left behind. Alone. Afraid. She thought she would shrivel up and die.

She stood unable to move for a long while; she didn't know how long. Time was lost. She stood in the exact spot he left her when they last kissed goodbye. Sometimes when she really missed him, she would step into her hallway and stand there, remembering exactly how she felt when their lips last met.

She told herself that she had to go inside. She felt like a bullet had blasted through her heart, leaving a big hole in the middle. She squeezed at her chest, tried to get the pain to dwindle. She needed to lie down. Maybe she should call Viv to come over.

"He's gone, he's gone," she repeated it in a whisper. It petrified her, made her feel nearly catatonic.

Then she remembered his words: *Maybe someday, we'll be together again.*

*Maybe someday, we'll be together again.*

"One, two, three, four, five, six," and she took six steps toward her bedroom. "One, two, three, four, five, six," and six more steps. She felt some relief.

*Maybe someday, we'll be together again.*
*Maybe someday, we'll be together again.*
*Maybe someday, we'll be together again.*
*Maybe someday, we'll be together again.*
*Maybe someday, we'll be together again.*
*Maybe someday, we'll be together again.*

Something in her mind shifted, like a moment of recognition as the truth came to her. *This is just temporary. We will be together again, Jacob. I just know we will.*

She didn't know how it would happen, or when. She just knew that it would. She would wait. Patiently. Unwearyingly. She would wait for that time to come.

In the meantime, she would stay close to him. *Not too close, but close enough*, those words echoed in her mind in a voice that was not her own. She nodded *yes*, to the unfamiliar voice that spoke in her own head. "Yes. Yes. I know what I have to do. This is all going to be OK," she responded to herself. Then, she went into her refrigerator, pulled out some chicken, and began to prepare her dinner.

*It's all going to be fine. I know what I have to do now. One, two, three, four, five, six.* She washed her hands six times.

Jane followed Jacob. It wasn't stalking. Viv told her that it was, but Jane explained that she needed to stay close to him, "Not too close, but close enough."

"You're fuckin' nuts. Do you know that?" Vivian would say. Jane would tell herself that Viv didn't understand. Vivian, with her stars all aligned just right, couldn't understand. It was OK, she loved Viv anyway.

She didn't follow him every day or all the time, just enough to know what was going on his life. She also called his cell phone quite a few times. Lots of times, actually. She didn't like caller ID. *What a crappy invention,* she would say to herself. She had to block her number to call and hear his voice on his voicemail.

Maybe she called with that blocked number a few too many times because one day, even without caller ID, he knew it was her. She and Jacob had not lost their connection. And yet, Jacob called her and asked her to stop.

He wasn't mean about it. He understood how hard their separation was. It was hard for him too. He called one afternoon. When Jane heard his voice, her throat clogged with tears. "Hi, Jacob," she managed to say.

"Hi, Jane," his voice warm. For a moment, she felt his arms around her.

"Jane, this is very hard for me to say…" He paused. The silence overpowered the sound of their breathing. "You need to stop calling me so much. It would be nice to talk every once in a while, catch up and stuff. But you can't call ten times a day. Fiona's getting angry. It's causing problems here. I'm so sorry." His voice trembled on the last few words.

"I miss you." Tears streamed down her face.

"I miss you, too. I'm sorry. I will call you. Sometime soon. To say hi. I promise."

"OK, Jacob... um... OK."

Another pause. Blaring silence. A painfully loud silence. Then: "Bye, Jane." He hung up.

*One, two, three, four, fix, six.* She pushed the call-end button six times.

She knew that Jacob and Fiona got married quickly. Jane assumed it was because of the baby. A couple of weeks after that, they moved into their new home: the brownstone on the Upper Eastside. Fiona Peoria's family was in real estate and wealthy. Her father had bought them the brownstone. The announcement of the wedding and the purchase of the brownstone were in the local newspaper. Jane bought six of those papers, cut the articles out and saved them.

Not long after that, Fiona fell down the stairs in front of their brownstone. Jane read it in the paper. She bought six copies, and saved those articles too.

Part of her felt sad for Jacob. His unborn child had died. She couldn't help but feel terrible for him. He had sacrificed his and Jane's future to be with his baby. But there was another part of her that felt relieved, part of her believed this was when they would be together again. *That didn't take very long at all*, she thought.

The stars must have corrected Fiona's meddling. Jacob was coming home.

She called him.

"Jacob. Hi. I read about Fiona in the paper. I'm so sorry. Are you OK?" She needed to express her concern first. It would be impolite to just ask him when he was coming back before asking about the baby.

He sounded distant, far away at first. "Hi Jane. Yes, thank you, I am OK."

"Jacob?"

"Yes?"

"When I read about Fiona in the paper, I thought it was a sign...a sign, that... um... well... that we would be able to be together again."

"I understand, Jane. But I don't know. I'm married now and own a home. Things have gotten... I guess life just took over. One thing happened, and then the next, and the next. I don't know. Everything is more complicated now. I don't think that I can leave. I do miss you, though."

"I miss you, too. But... but I just don't understand. You were going because of the baby, but the baby... well... the baby is gone now. You said that *maybe someday, we'll be together again.* You said that. Do you remember? Maybe now is that someday."

"I did say that, and I meant it. But life is messy sometimes. What we want to happen and what happens aren't always the same. Sometimes, the only choice we have is to adjust to the cards we are dealt and not dwell too much on the past. Sometimes you have to make the best of things. I have had to do that my whole life, you know? Make the best of things."

"Jacob. Please... Pleeeazzze... don't say that. We will be together. We will. I just know we will. Don't you still want that?"

"I… I wish… I just don't think it can happen, though. At least not now. But I will call you soon. Please don't make this harder than it is."

"When is soon?"

"As soon as I can. I promise."

He hung up. She pressed the call-end button six times. Her counting became worse.

*Not too close, but close enough. Maybe someday we'll be together again.*

Her following — stalking, really — of Jacob increased. Maybe she wasn't trying hard enough. He said he wanted to be with her. He did say that. Maybe she needed to get a little closer. She followed him to the gym a few times, waited outside while he exercised, then followed him back home. She followed him and Fiona to dinner a few times. Those times were very painful. Watching them together ripped her heart nearly in half, but she would remind herself of the ephemerality of the situation.

*One, two, three, four, five, six,* she would count to feel better.

*Not too close, but close enough. Maybe someday, we'll be together again.*

One day he paused for a moment and looked over his shoulder. Jane's body stood stiff, almost like her legs were caked in cement and attached to the ground. She didn't know what she would say if he saw her. But he just turned and kept walking.

Sometimes when she would watch him going about his life, living everyday without her, she felt incredibly lonely. She wondered how he was surviving without her and why his life looked so complete from the outside looking in. Meanwhile, she was barely breathing without him.

She had one of those dark feeling again, one afternoon when she watched him laughing with Fiona as they walked home from the gym. For an instant, she thought he looked happy with her. Emotions overwhelmed Jane. Confusion. A chill of horror. A flash of dread that made her heart thump, thump, thump. Anger. A deep, red-hot anger. She did not like being angry at Jacob. In fact, the anger could cause her to become misaligned from the destiny the stars had planned for her and Jacob. She pushed the thought out of her consciousness. She didn't want the universe to receive mixed messages from her.

Later that day, she decided she should call him. He said they could talk occasionally, and she really, really wanted to hear his voice. She wanted to hear her name roll off his tongue. She tingled when he said her name. Maybe she needed to reach out, to remind him that they were meant to be.

It turned out to be their last phone call. Well the last call until she started calling the radio show. Things deteriorated for Jane after the call. Only a week after, she was served with court papers stating that Jacob had filed for a restraining order. Despite her best efforts, or perhaps because of them, Jane had caused her destiny with Jacob to be derailed from the plans her stars had forged.

It didn't make any sense. He didn't know she was following him. Even if he suspected it, she had never threatened him or anything like that. She would never threaten Jacob.

During that last phone call, Jacob spoke with her as if she were a stranger. Unlike his usual warmth, he sounded detached. His last sentences were: "Jane, I'm sorry. I know I have hurt you, and this was never my intention. But, it's over between us. I am with Fiona now. We both need to move on with our lives. Please do not call me again."

He hung up. *One, two, three, four, five, six.* She pushed the end call button six times. Went into her bed and stayed there for days.

Vivian finally came over one day after her repeated phone calls to Jane went unanswered. She pulled her out of bed and made her go out. "You need to let this go. It's over. I know it's hard. Havin' your heart broken is a traumatic thing, but you have to pull yourself together. He has moved on. And now you need to also."

"But, I know he loves me. I know we're meant to be. I don't know why he's doing this, but there must be a reason. And the reason isn't because he doesn't want to be with me. I'm sure of it."

Vivian raised her voice. She wasn't being malicious, just stern. Her voice nasally and shrill. "If he wanted to be with you, he would be with you. It's ovvveeerrr! I'm sorry to be harsh, but you must accept it."

*One, two, three, four, five, six. Maybe someday we'll be together again.*

"I can't expect you to understand, but I'll try, OK… I will try." She had to placate Viv or she was never going to stop saying those bad things.

That voice that ricocheted back and forth in her mind re-minded her that she had to keep following him. She had to stay connected. *Not too close, but close enough. Maybe someday, we'll be together again.*

She continued to follow him on and off over the years. When Facebook started, she was able to watch his life more closely with less risk of being seen. She did still go to his apartment sometimes. She would stand, squeezed between the two high rises across the street, wait for him to leave and walk. With her hair all pulled up in a hat, big round glasses, she followed, making sure to stay at least a half block behind him.

She did not like thinking about the night she saw Jacob talking to that woman. She enjoyed watching him. It wasn't him. It was the exchange that she observed which distressed her.

He walked past East 76th Street. Jane, a block behind him. He stopped in front of a brownstone right on the corner to talk with a woman. Jane walked closer. She hid behind a long staircase two buildings away.

The woman had dark hair pulled back off her face. She wore a skin-tight cat suit, all black. She looked like she was in a big rush. Jacob called her name. It was Yvonne Tracy, a woman that Jacob was friends with on Facebook. She called herself Y.E. Tracy on her profile, and she also graduated from Columbia University. Jane was almost certain that she was a friend of Jacob's, someone that he had met while he was in graduate school. But she couldn't be sure.

She watched them talk for a few minutes. She couldn't hear what they said. Yvonne Tracy held a bag, large and heavy looking. She turned to leave. Jacob called her name. Yvonne Tracy shook his hand and dashed away. She looked like the bag weighed her down as she hurried off. Jane wondered what they talked about. She so wished she could have heard their conversation.

Jane became temporarily disoriented the next day when she saw on the news that a murder had taken place right inside the building that Yvonne Tracy came out of. She had a dark feeling about it, especially when she looked on Facebook and saw that the victim was a doctor who graduated from Columbia University.

That bad feeling lasted for a couple of hours, pulled and nagged at her, but she did not like where her mind went. She did not like that at all. It made her feel trapped, like she was yanked into a dark, ominous tunnel.

That was a bad, evil thought. It frightened her. So, she blocked it out, made herself forget what, deep down, she knew was the truth.

# CHAPTER 15

*Some say that sex is the most intimate act between two*
*people. I don't agree. I think it's murder.*

*Emily Goodyear*

**M**onday daybreak. Cold, sunny, a luminous yellow ball lit the sky. Kadee felt groggy from the weekend. She opened the blinds, welcomed the natural light into her living room. She reached her arms all the way up in the air, stood on her tippy toes, extended her abdomen. She stretched away her sleepiness. Alex had already left for the office. Her coffee brewed. It was definitely a two-cup, maybe even three-cup morning.

She read the news on the Internet, then logged on to Facebook. There was a message from Yvonne.

> *Hi Kadee,*
> *Aren't you sweet offering your shoulder to lean on. If anyone*
> *understands the depth of my distress, it would be you. Don't you*

miss him sometimes? I know I do. However irrational it may be, there is a part of me that will always love him. But I guess, love isn't rational, now is it? He was so much of my life, it's hard not to think of him fondly sometimes.

Anyhoo, things with John are moving right along. I was wondering what it's like to be engaged to Alex? Do you feel ready for that level of commitment with someone new? I mean, I just don't know that I could shift gears that quickly. But then again, it's not good to linger in the past, now is it? And Alex is quite a dish, if you don't mind me noticing. ☺

I'm thinking about moving too. I thought to myself, "Now maybe if I leave this place, this place that holds so many memories of Noah, it will be easier for me to move on." That's what I'm thinking. Then again, I can't leave the space in my heart that throbs with pain. Unfortunately, that goes with me wherever I go. We can't run away from ourselves, now can we? ☹

On the flippity-dip side, things are heating up between me and the handsome detective. I can tell he is in love with me. *Sigh* I am trying. I really am.

Let's grab lunch this week?

Oh, by the way, I hope you don't mind that I reached out to your friend Vanessa and to Alex. I'm just trying to make connections with some new people. My therapist recommended that as part of a rebuilding process. You know, putting all those itsy-bitsy pieces back together. Just call me Humpty-Dumpty, LOL.

Lovey Dovey, Yvonne

She sat back in her chair, released her hair from her nighttime ponytail and ran her fingers through. *Lovey Dovey? Whaaat?* Vanessa was right; there was something strange about Yvonne. She couldn't quite formulate what it was, but something.

She laughed: *Flippity-dip? Humpty-Dumpty?* She almost spit coffee on her computer screen. But it was creepy too. Strange. Something.

She wondered if Yvonne had always been this way. Of course, her initial perception of Yvonne was limited to seeing her in therapy sessions. *Everyone has eccentricities, little oddities that make them unique*, she thought. If not for that, the world would be sterile, an antiseptic, vanilla place filled with automatons. Boooring. And for Christ's sake, Kadee was far from perfect. *Flawed, flawed, everyone is flawed in one way or another.*

Yvonne was broken. Maybe it began with her brother's suicide, how her parents idealized him following his death, immortalizing his strengths to the extent that Yvonne felt she would never measure up. Never be good enough. When Kadee read Yvonne's book, she had tears in her eyes during that chapter. Emily Goodyear went into detail about never feeling as good as or as loved as Teddy, the James character in *Circle of Betrayal*. Maybe what happened with Noah just opened the floodgates. Emily Goodyear's narrative implied that.

But of course, that part could have been fiction. It did make sense, though. She wished Yvonne hadn't asked for the book back. If she read it again, she might be better equipped to help

Yvonne. Was that her responsibility though? *It's our responsibility to help others who need it…*

She wrote back.

*Dear Yvonne,*

*It is difficult moving on (as we've discussed), and I do still think about Noah, too. More than I would like to. I do miss him, too, some part of him, anyway. But that part wasn't real. The part I miss was a visage. I have recently been letting go of my anger. As I have done that, I'm feeling less weighed down by it. Forgiveness is freeing. It's very hard, though. Now I have been processing my feelings about the way he was killed. I know it's hard to talk about. But his own mother killing him… I do feel so sad about that. Maybe we could discuss this more when we meet up?*

*I'm happy with Alex. It's a different situation for me because Alex and I dated in college. Remember? We've known each other a looong time. And we had been in love before. So maybe it's easier for me to move forward with him.*

*Loving and feeling loved may be two of the most important things in life. If John loves you, I think you have to try your best to be open to him, his loving you and even you loving him. Just because we miss Noah doesn't mean we can't also move on with someone else. You deserve to feel love. I promise you do.*

*Moving? Really? Wow! Where to? I think it's a fabulous idea. Nothing like a fresh start. I would love to hear more. How about lunch tomorrow?*

*Cheers,*
*Kadee*

*P.S. When is "Circle of Betrayal" coming out? I kept meaning to ask you. I am looking forward to reading it again.*

Kadee hit "Enter," the message sent. She hurried into the shower to get ready for work at the station.

Around the same time that Kadee left for the station, Jane Light stood in the shower counting and counting. "One, two, three, four, five, six, one, two, three, four, five, six." It took her over an hour to stop counting the rubs of shampoo through her hair. Then another half hour to stop counting the scrubs of soap down her arms and legs. She skipped her conditioner; she was pretty sure that would set her back another hour. After an hour and a half in the shower, her fingers tips soft as spoiled fruit, she turned off the water. She dried herself one hundred times, six times: six hundred times. Finally she left the bathroom and got dressed.

After Jane was dressed, she sat on her bed. She touched her cheeks. They were moist. She was crying. She hadn't even realized she was crying until she felt the tears run down her cheeks.

Following that devastating night when Jacob told her never to call him again, she cried consistently for more than a month. Her face swelled up. Viv told her that she looked like the inside of a watermelon, her face was so red and puffy. Then one day, she stopped crying. In fact, a few times after that she had tried to make herself cry, thinking about that last conversation with Jacob. But the tears wouldn't come. It was like she had used them all up. She wondered if people were only allotted a certain amount of tears in a lifetime. If so, maybe she didn't have any left.

Nevertheless, she cried the morning she planned to go to the police. The tears trickled sparsely, but they fell nonetheless, rolling silently down her cheeks. She missed him. "He's gone," she said it out loud. "Jacob is gone. And someday will never come," and then they flowed heavily, poured down her face like a heavy summer rain.

It was the first time that she felt the depth of her pain in nineteen years. It felt good to feel something. She had been closed for so long. She felt like she lived in a bubble of water. Everything moved slower outside the bubble. Exterior noise was muffled. She tried to clear the fogginess before she left to go uptown to the police station. She wanted to be straight in her own mind on what she was going to share and what she wasn't.

There were those dark things that slid in and out of her mind. Some of them she remembered, even though she tried really hard to not. But others were more just a feeling. She sort of knew there was something behind those feelings, those chilling sensations, but she didn't really know what they were. Every once in a while, when she had the chill, there was a visual flash of something happening, and then a shooting sensation from her head down to her toes. Then the image disappeared, leaving her wondering what it meant. She wouldn't tell them about those. She didn't know what they meant, and they scared her. But she would have to tell them other dark thoughts, the one's she didn't like but was able to recollect. Like the kiss between Fiona and Sally. She did not like thinking about that at all, but she wanted to help Jacob and that kiss could be important. She at least knew that. She did not like it, but she knew it was the truth.

*It's all coming together so perfectly*, Yvonne thought as soon as she received Kadee's response message. She almost felt guilty that Kadee was being so charitable with her support. But it *was* owed to her. Wasn't it? *It was.*

Kadee stole her life, her future; the least she could do was listen to Yvonne. And wasn't Kadee almost pathetic believing that Yvonne was torn into itsy-bitsy pieces. *Ha!*

*I just loved my Humpty-Dumpty metaphor. Being a murderess has made me a clever lass. Hasn't it? It has.*

She *was* torn to pieces, though.

Noah's eyes appeared, hovering in the air like a ghost from her past.

An ominous moment. A flash of guilt. Her body tensed. She squished her whole face as hard as she could, shook her head, her eyes closed tight. Darkness and vulnerability overwhelmed her. She squealed: "No more, no more, this time ole Kadee it's my time to score." She opened her eyes. They vanished. Her shoulders relaxed.

Wasn't Kadee precious asking when Yvonne's book would be out? As if Yvonne was actually foolish enough to publish something so close to the truth. Of course, no one could ever prove it. She had covered every track, crossed every "t," dotted every "i." Belle Donovan leaving that suicide note and admitting to killing her husband, both added bonuses that had been both coincidental and fortunate.

She was working on her second book. Title still unknown. This one also had Emily and Elle in it. Like the first one, the stream-of-consciousness, first person narrative was both therapeutic and exhilarating. She planned to meet John at the station in the afternoon, so she worked hard to finish off the chapter she was currently writing.

She was quite pleased with how it was shaping up. Emily's words flew off the keyboard onto her computer screen. Yvonne's heart rate accelerated with each sentence. She wrote fervently, madly, with the velocity of a cheetah chasing down its prey.

It was onomatopoeia-worthy. Drum roll (Bada-Boom).

Yvonne worked on Emily Goodyear's narration: *My mind was a whirl of chaos when I found out about Oliver and Elle. Oliver was my greatest love, my only love; he held the key to my dreams and my future. My mind was a circus of commotion. I couldn't separate him from her: Who was the one who stole my life? Was it Oliver or Elle? It was all a big, black hole of emotional darkness.*

*Elle was that woman, that woman from grade school who all the teachers liked more than me, that woman from high school who effortlessly, with one flip of her long, shiny hair and the flash of a smile, got the attention and admiration of every boy I ever desired. She was that woman who broke my brother's heart with her careless use of sentimentality, pretending to love him, only to leave him, causing him to take his own life. Elle was that woman, the one who was everything I wasn't and took all that I had.*

*I thought Oliver had rescued me from ever having to suffer at the hands of that woman again, but it was naïve of me. Elle was the prototype, the archetype of that woman. There she was again, stealing my life with her beauty, her adventurous spirit, her exquisiteness, her style, her marvelous ease with men.*

*And she was his secret. They shared a bond that he and I could never have, a secret bond, which held them together making it impossible for him to ever leave her. I thought I was his favorite, but this wasn't true. I wanted to be his favorite, but I would never be. I would never be her, and she was his favorite. It was her. That woman again. I wanted to annihilate every piece of her.*

*I wanted to kill her. Destroy her. The her that was every other woman that she represented. Every woman who was that woman, that woman who existed within her, she embodied all of them. If I killed her, I would finally be free of the pain and suffering. And it was her fault, for her attractiveness, her allure, her splendidness.*

*Then it hit me that it was Oliver who needed to be murdered. I realized that it was him whom I needed to kill. Oliver needed to die, not Elle. At least not yet.*

*So I killed him. That's right, I Killed him! (Capital K). And now that some time has passed, I will consume her. I will do everything I can to become that woman. I will follow her. I will do what she does, practice her laugh, her walk. I will get close to her and eat up who she is. Become a version of her. I will devour all that she is, take it away from her and keep it for myself. I will eat her, drink her, until finally, like a new budding flower, I will finally become her, the her that is that woman. My life will never be stolen again; I will take back what belongs to me by becoming that woman.*

She smiled. Satisfied. Deviant. Writing was so therapeutic. She reread it a few times. Clicked "Save." She poured herself an orange tea, sipped it. The tang lingered on her tongue. It was going to be a good day.

Kadee arrived at the station, went into her small office and picked up where she left off in the recordings of *On the Couch with Jacob*

*Temple.* They were certain that the murderer knew Jacob Temple. There was no forensic evidence found at the crime scene. Yet. They were still analyzing Jacob's body along with some items taken from the brownstone. There was no break-in. No real leads.

They had been curious about Oscar Piedmont. But when Poole and Gibbs drove over to the restaurant in New Jersey with a photo of Piedmont, the bartender confirmed that he had been there with a tall, blond woman. The bartender vividly remembered them because the woman was dressed ostentatiously: ruby red boots with a stiletto heel and a white fur coat. He told Poole and Gibbs that they had been at the bar all night.

Then there was this woman Beth, who was a regular caller on Jacob Temple's show. Kadee had a hunch that Jacob knew Beth, but they had no way of finding her. No way of finding the caller Thomas, either. He had practically threatened Jacob Temple on the air. There were so many callers in the two and a half years that he was on the radio. It was a tough case because Jacob came into contact with so many people.

But it *had* to have been someone who knew him, even Dr. Puffin confirmed that. It was someone who knew him personally, not just on the air, someone who he either let into his apartment or knew how to get in. Gibbs was going to do some digging into Jacob Temple's life to see if he could make any connections.

Poole's first choice had been Fiona. But her alibi checked out. Even Poole had to concede that it was rock solid. It wasn't her. Then there was Sally Stringfellow, the unusual cat-lady neighbor. They had no proof it was her, but she had no alibi, which made her a person of interest. They needed to hunt into her background a bit too. If she did do it, what could her motive have been? Hopefully her background check would reveal something.

Then there was what Dr. Puffin had said. *"Perhaps Jacob Temple saw something he shouldn't have or didn't see something he should."*

Naturally, she thought Dr. Puffin was right. He had served as an expert witness for more than twenty years. He had seen a lot of murder cases. So if that was the motive, then *who?* That was a gigantic question mark and she wondered if they would ever be able to erase it. And what had he seen or not seen?

She decided to listen to a few of Beth's calls again. Poole hated hunches with nothing to substantiate them. He always gave Gibbs a hard time about that. "Evidence. Concrete evidence," he always said. But as a researcher, Kadee knew that instincts often led toward the evidence.

Yvonne's message said things were "heating up" between her and Poole. For a millisecond, which was more than enough, she pictured them naked having sex. *Why, just why did my mind go there?* She shook her head like an Etch-A-Sketch to erase the image from her mind.

The recording started. Kadee heard Beth's voice, dull and adenoidal. It sounded like her nose was stuffed up. Maybe she had a cold, but then she always sounded like that. She couldn't have a cold for two and a half years. Kadee assumed that it was her regular tone.

Her conversations with Jacob, at least the few Kadee had listened to, were pretty much the same. She had been with this guy, Matthew. They had to separate after a long love affair. The circumstances surrounding their breakup were never made explicit in her calls. She mostly talked about how her life had fallen apart without him. She wondered if Jacob Temple thought it was possible for Matthew to come back to her.

"Hi Jacob. It's Beth again. How are you today? I so enjoy our talks," Beth's voice her usual nasally sound.

"As do I, Beth. I'm doing great today. Thanks for calling. How are you doing?" Jacob maintained an upbeat tone.

"It's the same with me. I'm home alone. I just can't seem to get myself to do anything. I miss Matthew so much. Usually, the only thing that makes me feel better is staying home and thinking about the times we shared when we were together. I wish he would come barreling through my door this instant. You know, break it down and tell me this was all a big mistake."

"I understand, Beth. We've talked about Matthew before."

"Yes."

"And we have talked about doing things for yourself, things that make you feel good about your own life."

"I know we have. And I have tried some things. It's just so hard sometimes. Just when I start to feel a little better, I remember how he touched me, how he looked into my eyes, and I just feel like I can't take another step without him. It's very hard."

"I understand, Beth. I really do." Jacob's voice adopted a more somber tone. He sounded like he really did understand.

"You do?" her voice had a flash of life to it.

"Of course. Many of us have had our heart broken at least once. Sometimes more. And it's always terrible." Jacob turned to a more elated tone. "But you have to find reasons to move on, to let go of the past and accept it. If you can do that, you might meet someone new."

"I don't know about that. I don't know if I could be with anyone except Matthew. He was my whole life."

"Of course he was, Beth. But I believe there is always hope for a better future, if we allow ourselves to be open to it. Can you try to be hopeful? Can you try to think about what I'm saying?"

"Yes, Jacob... I always think about what you tell me. Every word. I know I said this before, and it's a little embarrassing, but in my heart I believe someday me and Matthew will be together again. Isn't that being hopeful?"

"I guess it is. I wonder if you'd enjoy your life more if you put your focus on other things. Not just Matthew."

"I know you're probably right... it's just very hard. Easier said than done, if you know what I mean."

"Change is hard, and so is letting go. If you stay on the line, my producer will give you the name of some books that might help you with this. Will you read them and see if they help you?" He sounded really sincere, a warm tone.

"OK... Yes, I will."

"Great, Beth. I hope we'll talk again soon. And remember to always have hope that things will get better."

"I will. And talk to you soon. Thank you, Jacob."

"And thank *you* for calling *On the Couch with Jacob Temple*."

Kadee removed the headphones, exhaled a frustrated sigh. She found Beth's calls heart-wrenching. Clearly the woman was suffering, but the idea that she would hold on for twenty years, just seemed abnormal. Sure, people have great loves that always stay with them even years after it's over, but most people move on and create a life without the person. She wondered what the real story behind Beth's life was. It almost sounded like Matthew, whoever he was, had put Beth under a spell.

Her thoughts moved to Noah. "Ugh," *Why? For the love of God, why did you just go there?* If he hadn't been… killed, would she still have strong feelings for him after twenty years? The thought sickened her. Noah was damaged. Maybe Matthew was too.

Noah's death forced grief upon her. She had no choice but to move on. He was gone. But she would have moved on anyway.

Absolutely. One hundred percent. Positively.

She knew deep down Noah was never going to be a permanent fixture in her life. But, it would have been harder if he was still alive. No doubt his presence would have made it more difficult. And what if he just kept calling and coming over for sex? *Well, don't even go there.* It could have dragged on for months, and he would have married Yvonne anyway. Or would he?

*Of course, he would have.*

Poor Yvonne. She placed her hand on her heart. She couldn't even imagine the depth of despair Yvonne must have experienced when she found out about Noah's deception. Naturally, her moving on process was harder. She had lost more than Kadee. In a way, Yvonne lost her past, present and future.

Sort of ironic that Kadee thought Noah picked Yvonne and Yvonne thought that he had picked Kadee. *We're not that different.*

Then her mind associated to Beth. Her thoughts shifted, entertaining the possibility that Beth killed Jacob Temple. She didn't want to be that type of person who made judgments about someone else's life without having the whole story. But in the privacy of her own thoughts, she admitted to herself that she thought Beth was nuts, unstable. Maybe even filled with seething rage, unhinged by her own emotions, and possibly in a catathymic crisis. Did Beth know Jacob, though? And if she did, what was their connection?

Maybe Beth had erotomanic delusions about Jacob Temple? Maybe she believed that they were in love, that Jacob Temple expressed secret love signals toward her through the radio show. Erotomanic delusions are most common with celebrities. *Look at John Hinckley, Jr.'s delusions about Jodie Foster. He shot President Reagan under the belief that it would impress her.*

Beth clearly had some emotional difficulties. She had been holding on to a lost love for twenty years. Maybe she became obsessed with Jacob Temple, then created the false reality that he reciprocated her feelings. Until one day, she got frustrated and killed him. Or if she was totally psychotic, she could have thought that she was supposed to kill him. But how would she have gotten into his apartment? Jacob Temple was intelligent enough to not open the door for a woman that was in the throes of an erotomanic delusion.

Gibbs was right. They needed to dig into Jacob Temple's life. Maybe he knew Beth. Even if it wasn't her, it had to be someone from his life. Listening to the shows was good for generating hypotheticals, but the real truth would be discovered by learning more about Jacob Temple.

She looked up. Poole waved her over. An unfamiliar woman stood beside him and Gibbs. Kadee left her office, walked toward them. The unfamiliar woman had long brownish hair, a web of grays at the roots. She had cat-like eyes. The woman shifted on her feet, played with the pockets of her sweater. She seemed distressed.

She introduced herself as Jane Beth Light. In a hesitant voice, like it was painful for her to get the words out, she explained that she might have some information that would help with Jacob Temple's murder. *Jane Beth? Was that Beth? Her voice sounded different? But that didn't mean it wasn't her.* Either way, maybe she would be the break they needed in the case.

Poole guided her into the consult room. Kadee and Gibbs followed. They sat around a rectangular table. Jane on one long side, the trio on the other. She took her sweater off, pulled her hair away from her face. The purplish crescents under her eyes made her look exhausted.

She dropped her gaze and introduced herself again. Staring down at the table, she started her story. "I'm Jacob's ex-girlfriend and... well... and... this is so hard for me," she took a heavy breath. "I'm not sure, but maybe I know some things about Jacob that could help you find who did this. My sister encouraged me to come because of... um... because of my history with Jacob. But I'm not sure if what I know will really help. But I'd like to try."

Poole led the questioning. He stood up, adjusted his belt. "Thank you for coming in, ma'am. What can you tell us?"

She began a long and curious story. She told them that she met Jacob Temple in the summer of 1996 in Miami. They were together in New York City for six months and very in love. She was sure they were going to get married. It was a serious relationship. Her eyes flickered like the flame of a candle when she spoke about their relationship.

She swallowed. The flame extinguished, her eyes now broad and dull. "Then something unexpected happened and my whole life fell apart…" She looked at Kadee and asked, "May I ask that what I am about to tell you will remain confidential? I have done some things that I probably shouldn't have. Nothing bad. But I am very ashamed."

Kadee squinted, curious. She also felt compassion for this woman. Kadee looked at Poole for the answer to Jane's question.

He responded, "For now, we can keep it private. And we can try our best to protect your identity throughout the investigation. That's the best I can offer. We do need you to continue, though."

The trio leaned forward in unison. Jane Light continued.

It took her awhile to get the story out. She fumbled on words, and it almost looked like she talked to herself under her breath between thoughts. She told them about Jacob and Fiona's friendship. Fiona's girlfriend, Stacy. She detailed Fiona's seduction of Jacob, even the specifics of their sexual encounter, and Fiona's pregnancy.

Poole stopped her for a moment. He wanted to get the story straight. He rubbed his hand over his head and asked, "Let me make sure I have this straight, Mrs. Temple was living with a woman named Stacy and was in a romantic relationship with her. She took Dr. Temple home with her and seduced him. They had sex that one time, and she became pregnant with his baby? Is this correct ma'am?"

"Yes," she responded to Poole but looked at Kadee. Her eyes wincing.

Kadee gave her a comforting smile. Her heart went out to her. Her mind immediately connected Jacob Temple to Noah. Maybe he had been totally deceiving Jane. *For Christ's sake, stay objective.*

Poole jotted down some notes, then asked her to continue.

Kadee noticed Jane's lips moving subtly. No sound came out. Then in her same flat tone, she continued. She explained that Jacob was raised in a conservative home, on a farm in Roxbury, New York. His father was pro-life, against pre-marital sex, and would disown Jacob if he didn't marry Fiona and raise his baby with her.

She told them about *that night:* the night Jacob came over, told her what happened, and ended their relationship, even though he really loved her. She described how sad they both were, how they hugged and cried for more than an hour before he walked out of her life.

Poole nodded. "But the Temple's don't have a child?"

She gulped. Then told them about Fiona's fall and how she lost the baby. She admitted that she had called Jacob to come back. She believed that they were meant to be together.

She wrinkled her brow. "I don't really understand why, but he said he couldn't leave her. It didn't make any sense, but he said they were married and owned a home and that… that it all was just more complicated. And that even though he missed me he couldn't leave. I thought there was something he wasn't telling me. Or maybe it had to do with his father again. Jacob's father was an intimidating man and Jacob…" she averted her eyes for a moment. "Jacob was a very sensitive person. Maybe he believed that his father would not accept a divorce."

Poole looked up. "Sounds terrible. Did you carry resentment for all of these years because of this?" He sounded matter-of-fact. Kadee knew he had to ask her. It was a good question, but she felt bad for Jane. She seemed so mixed up.

"Oh no, detective. No. I was never angry at Jacob… sad, very sad. I'm still sad. I loved him with all my heart. He was always trying to do the right thing. And he really wanted his father to be proud of him. He was just doing what he thought was right. It's part of what I loved about him. I should tell you, though — my sister told me it was important to mention — Jacob did file a restraining order against me after that last phone call." She looked away. Kadee noticed her silent lip wiggle again.

Poole's voice took a more forceful tone. "Yes, ma'am, that is very important. Did you threaten Dr. Temple?"

"No. NO!" she shook her head. "Like I said, I wasn't angry, and I would never threaten Jacob. It didn't make any sense when the papers were served. I was so hurt, and yet I couldn't call him to ask him about it because I wasn't allowed to call him anymore." She hid her face in her hands, shook her head. "It didn't make sense. It still doesn't. There has to be something he didn't tell me. I guess a part of me was hoping that you would be able to tell me what happened." She looked down. "I know that probably sounds pretty selfish right now, with Jacob's passing and all…but this has been bothering me for the last nineteen years. And then…"

"Yes?"

Jane scrunched her face so tight with bitter distaste for the story that would follow. They waited. When she resumed, she told them about the kiss between Sally and Fiona. She described Sally's book, *The Wolf Cries: A Memoir*, and how Sally had stabbed her uncle with a fork to escape from him.

Poole stood up, adjusted his belt, sat down again. His next statement sounded harsh. "Ms. Light, I have to ask you, how did you wind up in a writing class with Sally Stringfellow? Your "love of your life turned murder victim" ex-boyfriend's neighbor?"

"It was one of those strange coincidences that happen in life. We are both writers and just wound up in the same group. But I never told her I knew Jacob. I didn't want it to be… you know, weird or awkward or anything."

"You do realize that this does not sound good for you?"

"I guess. But I didn't hurt Jacob. I want to help and I didn't want to tell about the kiss. In fact. I like Sally. I don't even want to think about it, but I… I… I dunno… I thought it was important. And there's one more thing. This one I don't like thinking about."

"Yes," Poole asked.

She then revealed that she had been calling the show as Beth, putting a clothespin around her nose and tissue over the receiver to disguise her voice. She wanted to talk to Jacob. She said that she thought he knew it was her, but couldn't be sure.

She put her face in her hands. "I'm so ashamed. I'm… I… I just wanted to talk to him so badly. I didn't know what else to do. I feel horrible that I was deceiving him."

Then the icing on the cake came when she told them that she was almost positive that Thomas McPherson was the 'Thomas' who called the show and threatened Jacob. She told them about the bottle-stabbing altercation on South Beach nineteen years ago.

Jane had one of those dark feelings as soon as the words about Thomas escaped from her mouth. No, she did not like that at all: *stop, stop, stop, stop, stop, stop.*

Kadee thought Poole looked ready to scream at her. He shifted in his chair, his eyes intense. He asked, "Where were you the night Dr. Temple was murdered?"

She looked askance. "I was home."

"Alone."

"Yes, alone."

"Did you talk to anyone? Is there anyone that can confirm that, ma'am?"

"I don't think so. Not that I remember."

"That's not good, Ms. Light."

"I didn't do anything. I would never hurt Jacob, detective. I loved him."

"I understand that, ma'am. But from where I'm sitting, this doesn't sound good. Can you give us a few minutes? We'll be right back."

She nodded. Kadee noticed her mouth moving again.

As soon as they stood outside of the consult room, Poole and Gibbs started bickering. Poole thought she wasn't telling the truth. Gibbs thought she was. Kadee wasn't sure.

Poole was adamant: "She's holding back. She's lying or only telling us the part of the truth she wants us to know. And she has the perfect motive: jealous rage."

Gibbs rubbed his hand along his forehead. "I see what you're saying, but there isn't any concrete evidence. Which, just to remind you, is always what you are looking for. There's none here. Just a story. And that motive is flimsy. Why a jealous rage after nineteen years? It just doesn't fit. Even if she was following him on the show, calling every week, what made her snap now? After all this time? We can keep her for more questioning, but we can't make an arrest. And I think we need to step back and explore all of the leads, Stringfellow, this McPherson, and maybe even give Fiona Temple another look. There's more to this story."

As the banter went back and forth, Yvonne strolled into the main office. A smile and head nod exchanged between Kadee and her. Poole excused himself. He was on his way toward her when an odd exchange took place.

Jane Light came out of the consult room. She asked if she could use the rest room, then she stopped in her tracks. Her eyes widened, like a shock of electricity had jolted through her. She stared at Yvonne. And stared.

Kadee observed the whole thing. Yvonne and Poole embraced. Gibbs walked toward them. Kadee went toward Jane.

"Is there something wrong?"

"No, Ms. Carlisle. Well, yes. I'm quite upset about Jacob. And the detective accusing me of hurting him is really painful… I…" with an ashen face, her eyes focused on Yvonne.

"Do you know that woman?"

"No. No."

"Are you sure? You're staring at her."

She looked at Kadee, her pupils big black saucers. "Oh, sorry... um... I do that sometimes. I don't know her."

Kadee wasn't sure she believed her. But why would she lie? And then Yvonne didn't appear to recognize Jane. Yvonne barely looked at her. *Strange.* Then it occurred to her that Jacob Temple also went to Columbia University. They weren't in the same programs. Yvonne studied for her M.D. and Jacob for his Ph.D., but they could have crossed paths. They both studied within mental health.

*Maybe Yvonne met Jane with Jacob nineteen years ago when they were a couple? Maybe she doesn't recognize Jane? But that's downright ridiculous. If Yvonne knew Jacob Temple, she would say something. Wouldn't she? Her boyfriend is working on his murder investigation, for Christ's sake. Certainly, she would mention it.*

Poole interrupted her flight of ideas. To Kadee's astonishment, he walked toward Jane, who was on her way back from the bathroom, and told her that she was free to go. They would be in touch after they followed up with some leads.

Kadee thought*: Whaaat? "They would be in touch after they followed up with some leads." Someone snatched his body. That was totally out of character. Totally.*

Jane looked at Yvonne one more time, her face misshapen and white as a cotton ball. She pulled her coat tight and left.

The whole scene was odd, interesting, *something.*

Yvonne approached Kadee. "Thank you so much for your messages. You really are a blessing. And lunch tomorrow sounds delightful. Shall I pick a place? Or would you prefer to choose?"

"Either one…" Kadee was distracted.

"Ka-**Dee**." She accentuated Dee.

"Yes?"

"Shall I pick a place? Or would you prefer to choose?" A pinch in her tone.

"Right. Sorry. I was thinking. How about that new Greek place… or you know what… what about the same diner we met at last time? It's convenient for both of us and we can sit and chat relaxed there."

"OK, yes, that makes sense. It's a plan then."

Gibbs called Kadee over.

"Back to work."

Yvonne nodded, "Yes."

Kadee and Gibbs sat down and shut the door, about to discuss some impressions about Jane Light's statement when a call came through to Gibb's cell phone. It was Oscar Piedmont. Gibbs put it on speaker.

Oscar Piedmont's voice trembled. "Detective Gibbs. I wasn't totally honest when we spoke. And I do apologize. I was scared. There are some things about Jacob Temple that you should know. And I'm ready to tell you. Can I come down today?"

"Yes, please, Mr. Piedmont." Gibbs responded. He and Kadee shared a deliberate glance: There was definitely more to the story.

# Chapter 16

*There is a thin line between fact and fiction, truth and
lies. For some, they are indistinguishable.*

*Emily Goodyear*

Yvonne sat with Poole in the main office. Kadee and Gibbs were in
her office discussing Jacob Temple's murder. Jane Light gave
them quite a bit of information, which created more questions
than answers. But she did provide them some direction. They
were in agreement that she had been truthful in what she report-
ed, but they thought there were some pieces missing. Or perhaps
her story was distorted by her relationship with Jacob.

Kadee couldn't help but wonder what really happened between Jane and Jacob. She held on for nineteen years. Nineteen
years!

It seemed as though her feelings for him never faded, the way
feelings usually wane years after a relationship has ended. She

desired so much to be close to him that she concealed her identity using a clothespin on her nose to talk to him so that he would continue to take her calls. Add to it the restraining order without a substantial reason, then the kiss between Fiona and Sally, and they hit the story jackpot.

Kadee thought there was a strong possibility that Jane imagined her relationship with Jacob to be more serious than it was in reality. Maybe she became infatuated with him, ultimately creating the truth that they were in a serious moving-toward-marriage relationship, while Jacob considered Jane a casual fling. Then one day he met Fiona, fell in love and married her. Regardless, a piece of Kadee couldn't help but identify with Jane. Like her, she had become enamored with a man who chose another woman for marriage.

Then there was her peculiar reaction to Yvonne. Kadee wondered if she knew Yvonne. But then why would she say that she didn't? Maybe it was a lie. Or maybe Yvonne reminded her of someone else. Perhaps Kadee was overthinking it — *me overthink things? Nah.*

Regardless, Jane was clearly uncomfortable. Maybe it was simply a reaction to her own internal angst and had nothing to do with Yvonne. *Could Yvonne have been her therapist?* Yvonne didn't appear phased by Jane's presence. Would she have acknowledged Jane if she was a former patient? Maybe not. Some therapists adamantly oppose public social interaction with current and former patients to maintain patient privacy. Even so, Yvonne gave no signal of recognition. It was probably nothing, but she asked Gibbs his opinion.

Gibbs also noticed Jane stiffen up when she saw Yvonne. But he thought it probably held little significance. His instinct told him that Jane was just overwhelmed by the whole situation.

They agreed Jane Light most likely did not kill Jacob Temple. They weren't totally ruling her out. She had no alibi and possessed an obsessive-like attachment toward Jacob, but it just didn't make sense that she would kill him now. If anything, she still held on to hope that they'd reunite. Consequently, the motive was missing. She appeared genuinely upset that he was killed.

Perhaps there was more to her story. Maybe she was hiding something Oscar Piedmont could shed light on. They certainly wanted to know more about this restraining order. Gibbs would be able to retrieve the information through the computerized database. It probably wouldn't reveal much, but it was worth pursuing, especially since Jane said she didn't understand why it was filed. A curious statement.

They were going to do some digging, see if they could find anything else connecting her. But they also wanted to know more about Sally Stringfellow, Fiona Temple and Thomas McPherson. So while they waited for Oscar Piedmont to arrive. Gibbs went to his desk to conduct research on the three.

From her cramped office, Kadee observed Yvonne and Poole, who were on his computer doing something. Her curiosity tugged. She opened up her laptop and began searching the Internet for potential connections between Yvonne and Jane Light or Jacob Temple.

On Facebook, Kadee found some information. She looked at Yvonne's information on there and noticed that she had done her internship at Columbia's Psychiatric Institute. The same place where Jacob Temple had done his. She looked at the dates, which showed, in fact, that they were there for one whole year together. They must have known each other. Or maybe not. It was a big hospital and they were in different programs. She couldn't be sure, but the odd coincidence gnawed at her.

She could just ask Yvonne about it tomorrow at lunch. But if she did know him, surely she would have said something. Should she mention it to Gibbs? She didn't know. She was probably making a mountain out of a molehill.

Elbows propped on the table, Kadee rested her chin in her hands as she squinted at Yvonne's Facebook profile photo. Large blue eyes, long dark hair draped over her shoulders, tight skinny jeans, and knee-high black boots. Yvonne looked sexy. Back arched, chest out, hand on hip, she appeared different, less conservative.

Poole opened the door to the office. He and Yvonne walked in. Gibbs followed behind them.

Kadee's stomach cart wheeled as she inconspicuously switched her screen to Google.

Yvonne titled her head and smiled, "Hi there girlfriend." She released a giggle. A little silly and a lot not-Yvonne-like.

Kadee met her eyes. Not the warm, compassionate eyes she remembered from therapy. They seemed frivolous now. "Hey."

Gibbs sat next to Kadee.

Poole pulled his knit hat down below his ears. "I'm heading out for about an hour. We have a lot of work to do when I get back."

Gibbs shifted in his chair. He spit back a response. "We *are* working. Where the hell are *you* going? We have someone coming in to talk with us in thirty minutes."

"Right. Well, Yvonne here's looking to move." He pulled Yvonne toward him, wrapped his arm around her back. "Her old place reminds her of Donovan." He squeezed her across her shoulders, pulled her closer.

Yvonne gazed admiringly at Poole.

He kissed the top of her head.

Yvonne in her calm, breezy tone looked at Kadee and said, "The place I am looking at today is right across the street from you and Alex. The broker just called about it. We are meeting her there now to have a look. Life is so strange sometimes. Isn't it? We just might become neighbors."

Kadee looked up, cocked her head to the side. An uneasiness coursed through her body. *Across the street?* "You said you were thinking of moving. I had no idea you meant so soon."

"It all happened so suddenly. Isn't it always that way for rentals in this city? It's like as soon as you contact a broker, it's one, two, three, and you're signing a lease. John had contacted his broker friend for me just to get an idea of price range and availability, when this one across the street from you popped up. It's all so exciting actually."

Kadee shifted in her chair. "Cool. Well, I hope it goes smoothly. It can be a nightmare apartment-searching in Manhattan."

"We should get going. Patricia will be waiting out in the cold for us." Poole gently nudged Yvonne. Looking at Gibbs, he said, "I'll be back when I'm back."

Gibbs gave him a hard look, but said nothing.

Yvonne smiled at Kadee. "See you tomorrow. Noon, OK?"

"See you then." *There is something so strange about her...*

"She's a little odd. Or is it just me?" The words flew out of her mouth as soon as Poole closed the door behind them.

"That's just her way. To be honest, I think she's still torn up over Donovan's murder."

"I guess. I was thinking the same thing. She has this calmness, but it feels like... I don't even know how to describe it. I appreciated that way about her when she was my therapist... but now as I get to know her more, it feels almost too calm... like she's holding back or something. And her demeanor recently seems a little school girlish. It's probably me. We are becoming friendlier. I guess I'm really only just getting to know her."

"She seemed overly calm to me during the Donovan investigation, so that's probably just her way. She's stoic *and* quirky. Many shrinks are. I have a couple of friends who are shrinks and they are just about as off-beat as it gets. Like you. You're a weirdo." Gibbs threw her a wink.

Kadee chuckled "Yup. No doubt about that."

While they waited for Oscar Piedmont, Gibbs went back to his desk. Kadee returned to Facebook, an irresistible pull of curiosity. She scrolled through Yvonne's wall.

Her most recent post put up that morning: "*I'm moving*!" Twenty-two people on her page liked the status.

Kadee scrolled down the page and saw a dozen posts from people offering condolences on September 20th. The day after Noah was found murdered.

Yvonne had posted a status the following day: *"My life was stolen from me."* People offered comments of compassion and sympathy.

*That's an interesting choice of words. His life was stolen, not hers. Then again, he was her life.* The nagging guilt resurged. It wasn't her fault, Kadee tried to remind herself. She was also hurt, "a victim," as Vanessa had said.

Gibbs peeked his head in. Oscar Piedmont had arrived. He waited in the consult room to speak with them. Kadee closed her computer. She pulled her cardigan sweater tight around her body to get rid of that chill that crept along the inside of her skin. She was so sick of winter. She accompanied Gibbs into the room to meet with Piedmont.

Oscar Piedmont appeared rattled and sweaty. His thick-rimmed glasses kept sliding down the bridge of his nose. He sipped a large cup of tea. His thin lips curled around the rim. A backpack sat at the corner of the table. It was filled with spiral notebooks packed with the inner thoughts of Jacob Temple: his journals.

Oscar slid the bag toward Gibbs and said, "I found these when I was cleaning up some of Jacob's things over the weekend." He paused, looked down for a moment. "I probably shouldn't have read any of them. But… I didn't know what they were at first. Once I realized that they were his journals, his private thoughts… it was hard for me to stop reading."

Kadee made a mental note: *Dispose of your journals as soon as you get home. First Noah's journals, now Jacob's journals. Clearly it's not safe to keep a written diary of your inner life. I don't need people rummaging through my private thoughts. Ever.*

Gibbs opened the zipper, peeked in the bag and said, "Thank you, Mr. Piedmont."

"I didn't read all of them. There are years of entries, but I skimmed through most of it. Some of the stuff in there... well, some of it I knew already. Jacob had told me some things about his life." He wiped his forehead with a handkerchief. "I should have told you the whole truth when you came down to the station, but... but..." he wiped his forehead again. "I was afraid, you see... but when I read Jacob's thoughts in those pages... then it became really clear that I was only thinking about myself and that was not the right thing. I realized that I had to stand up and tell the truth. For Jacob."

Gibbs nodded. "I'm glad you came in. Please tell us what you know."

Oscar Piedmont sipped his tea. His eyes turned reddish behind his glasses, tears welled. He pushed against his eyelids with his fingers. Then he proceeded with a long, convoluted tale, exposing more layers to the story that was Jacob Temple's life.

Oscar began his account by exposing the details of the relationship between Jane and Jacob. He told them that Jacob met Jane in Miami in 1996 and that he immediately fell for her. He explained that Jacob was a sensitive young man, handsome, but sort of a misfit, always struggling to fit in with his contemporaries.

He said that Jacob told him that when he met Jane, it was the first time he felt that he could relax and be himself.

Oscar continued trying to fight back tears. Kadee noticed he also seemed shaken, like he feared for his life. He then revealed that Fiona Peoria, soon to be Temple, was Jacob's friend at the same time that he was dating Jane. "Fiona Temple is a manipulative woman. I personally think she had her eyes on Jacob all along. Jacob told me about the night that she seduced him." His voice dropped to a whisper. "He thought she might have drugged him…"

Kadee sat on the edge of her chair.

Gibbs glanced at her. "Mr. Piedmont, do you know why he thought that?"

"Well… it didn't make sense to Jacob at the time, you see. It was one of those things that he was only able to understand a few years later when he looked back on it. He writes about it in his journal. I was in tears just reading about it."

Gibbs scribbled a few notes. "Please continue, Mr. Piedmont."

"Well… Fiona's father is a bigwig real-estate mogul and well-connected, if you know what I mean." Oscar pushed against his nose with his finger to indicate mob affiliation. "Back then, he was trying to break into politics, maybe run for mayor. Well, he learned that Fiona was with a woman. Fiona is gay, you see. He was convinced it would reflect poorly on him, so he urged her to marry a man. He said he would disinherit her if she didn't leave her girlfriend and find herself a man. She finally told Jacob about her father's threat a few years into their marriage. Could you imagine? She was very nasty toward Jacob. Abusive, if you want my opinion. She told him that she didn't love him, that their marriage was a farce, and that she was only with him because of her father. Obviously Jacob wanted to leave her. At least in his heart. Because of his values — or rather his parents' values — he couldn't bring himself to divorce her. Jacob was a tormented fellow caught between what he wanted and what he thought was the right thing." Oscar's cheeks burned red, his brows furrowed in anger.

"To add insult to injury, Fiona made her father pull some strings and get a restraining order against Jane even though Jane never threatened or harassed Jacob in any way." He raised his voice. "You see, Fiona *knew* Jacob really loved Jane, and she knew they still talked on the phone. She didn't want them to be able to talk anymore. So she had it handled. It just pisses me off that with money and the right connections, people can get just about anything taken care of. Jacob wrote in his journal about his anguish following that restraining order. He felt so guilty for hurting Jane, but he also felt like there was nothing he could do. Fiona is a coldhearted woman, coldhearted as they come. After that restraining order, well… Jacob felt powerless in his own life. He battled a near life-threatening depression for years after that. Excuse me."

Oscar blew his nose. A heaviness hung in the room; it was that heaviness that looms in the air right before a torrential downpour. Gibbs went to comment, but Oscar kept going, almost like he was alone in the room reciting a monologue. Kadee thought that perhaps he was relieved to get the whole story out of his head and into the air, unburdening himself by sharing it with other people. It must have been a lot to bear. So tragic to think that Jacob Temple died without ever having lived.

"After Jacob's radio show started… a woman Beth started calling. For two years, Jacob spoke to her like any other caller. But about six months ago, he started thinking that it was Jane calling. To be honest — I don't like saying this — at first I thought he was off his rocker. Jane must have moved on by then, but there were a few things that she said on the show. Certain phrasing that reminded Jacob of Jane. Once he believed it was her, he couldn't stop believing it."

Gibbs began to ask a question, but Oscar spoke right over him.

"Aaand then… then… Beth, or rather Jane… repeatedly talked about not being over a man she had been with nineteen or twenty years ago. Jacob thought — no, Jacob knew — that she was talking about him. As it turned out, he was not over her, either. He said, that once he realized that it was her, once he realized that she still loved him, he felt hopeful for the first time since he was raped… excuse me… since he slept with Fiona."

Gibbs slipped in, "You don't seem to like Fio–"

Oscar blurted, "Please, detective, you can ask me whatever you want when I'm done, but I need to tell you the end of this. I just can't hold it in anymore. Please…"

Gibbs acquiesced with a nod.

"About a week before his murder, he came to me and said that he knew Fiona was sleeping with and probably in love with Sally Stringfellow. Their upstairs neighbor. Very strange woman, but nice enough. He had suspicions about them. But when he asked Fiona, she denied it.

"One night, he told her he would be in a meeting and wouldn't be home until eleven that night. But he went home around seven. He found Fiona and Sally naked in their bed!" Oscar took a deep breath. "Right then, he told Fiona he was leaving her.

"She's not the kind of woman that you leave, if you know what I mean. Fiona likes to be the one calling the shots. She told Jacob he would be sorry if he left her. When he told me what she said, I was concerned. I told him that he might want to take her threat seriously… but… I think he was just so fed up with the stuff she had done to him for all those years. He said he wasn't afraid of her. He said he was relieved.

"He also said… and this piece really hits me in the heart… he said he was going to call Jane to see if they could rekindle their relationship. I had never seen him as happy as he was for the days leading up to his murder. I thought for sure he and Jane would be together. That finally Jacob would be living the life he always wanted. *His* life. On *his* terms." His voice shook. "What a tragedy."

Kadee sat astonished by the story as Gibbs finished his notes. Oscar was right, it was a tragedy. Not just Jacob's murder, that alone was awful, but his life was destroyed by Fiona and the restrictions imposed upon him. Then to hear that he had just made the decision to start living the life he wanted right before he died, that was almost too much to bear.

She thought back to the day when Jacob Temple smiled at her while she stretched at the gym. She was irritated by the exchange at the time. She wrongfully assumed that he was just some wealthy celebrity with some perfect life, who was probably ogling her. Meanwhile he was actually a tortured soul trapped in a life he didn't want, and feeling like he didn't have the freedom to change his circumstances. *It just proves that you never know what the truths behind people's lives are.*

Her mind shifted to Jane. *Did she know he was coming back to her? It sounded like she didn't. She hadn't mentioned it when she came in.* Although Kadee knew better than to get involved in people's personal affairs, she couldn't help but feel compelled to call Jane and tell her. Maybe it would free her if she knew that after nineteen years, her love wasn't in vain. Jacob felt the same as she did.

It was so strange, she thought, how the space between people can seem really far, and yet be incredibly small. The physical space between Jane and Jacob may have grown wide over the years, but emotionally they were still connected. It was like there were invisible lights connecting people to other people who impacted their lives, past and present. Especially the people who they truly loved.

In some ways it cleared her thoughts about Alex. They rekindled their relationship after many years. Clearly something remained between them even though they were separated for a long while. Maybe they, too, were joined together by an everlasting bond. Maybe she was too afraid to admit that Alex had always been her love. He had hurt her in college. Unlike Jane, who forgave Jacob for his flawed character, Kadee had remained angry at Alex for many years.

*But things are different now.*

They had both grown and changed since college. Now she felt secure in their relationship. Maybe the Noah thing clouded her judgment, made her question the depth of her feelings for Alex.

*Sometimes, we miss the truth when it's right in front of us,* she thought. *Sometimes the closer we are, the harder it is to see.*

*Alex had always been the one.*

It was an epiphany that she normally would be anxious to write down in her journal. But she reminded herself: *You are disposing of them.* She would have to hold her insight in her head for the time being and remember to never, ever forget it.

Gibbs started asking Oscar a few follow-ups. Kadee needed to snap out of her preoccupation. Be focused. She wanted to know the truth behind Jacob Temple's murder more than ever. She thought of Yvonne's Facebook post: "My life was stolen from me." *Yvonne must really feel that way, but she has another chance. Noah doesn't, and neither does Jacob Temple.* She wanted the loss of Jacob Temple's life to be avenged.

Gibbs spoke with an eyebrow raised. "You don't seem to like Fiona much. Do you think she had something to do with this?

"I can't say that she killed Jacob, but ... let me rephrase that. I'm no detective, but I know that woman. There is not a doubt in my mind that that woman is responsible for Jacob's death. Whether she did the stabbing or had someone else do it. Trust me, detective. I would not put anything past her. I was afraid... I'm still afraid that when she finds out that I came down here and told the truth... I'm afraid she might kill me, too."

Gibbs responded. "We will try to keep your involvement in this confidential for as long as we possibly can, Mr. Piedmont."

He wiped his forehead. "Thank you. Is there anything else you want to know? I'm exhausted."

"I understand. Just a couple more questions. Anything about Sally Stringfellow that might help us."

Oscar placed his hand on his chin, contemplated. "Not much. I know she had a real bad time of it. Her whole family was killed. She never talked about it. But she did write a book about it."

"Yes. We're aware of her book."

"It's a terrible story. And she's strange from it. I guess anyone would be strange if they went through what she did. But did she kill Jacob? She's not a strong type. Not like Fiona. It's hard for me to think of her being so violent. But then she did stab her uncle." He looked thoughtful. "It was in self-defense, but she did stab him with a fork… oh, the same as Jacob. I um… I guess it's possible she did it or was involved somehow."

Gibbs opened his mouth to speak. Oscar cut him off.

"Actually, I wouldn't put it past Fiona getting Sally to do it. It's hard to imagine it — she's so fragile, like she's about to topple over — but, I guess when someone's got enough adrenaline pumping through them, anything is possible."

"Thank you. Do you know anything about Jane other than what you already told us? Do you know if Dr. Temple had called her before he was killed?"

"I know Jacob loved her. He said that she was just about the best person he had ever known. Once he realized it was her calling the show he admitted to me that he thought about her all the time. He writes about her in his journal." He rubbed his forehead.

"Do you know if they spoke before he was killed?"

"I'm not sure. He didn't say they did. I think he would have told me. It's not in his journal, either. Although it looks like he stopped writing in it once he told Fiona he was leaving. That's the last entry. But... I got the feeling that he was waiting until he moved out of the brownstone. I don't think he wanted Fiona to know about Jane. I think he was trying to protect her from the wrath of that woman. But I could be wrong."

Gibbs leaned over and shook Oscar's hand, "Thank you for coming in, Mr. Piedmont. We'll be in touch."

All three of them stood up.

"I hope I was helpful. Please find out who did this."

Poole came back just after Oscar left. Gibbs filled him in on what they learned. Poole seemed more concerned with the news that Yvonne found a new apartment, which was, in fact, right across the street from Kadee's place.

"Yvonne is so excited about it. That will be nice for you two ladies, huh?" Poole flashed a rare smile to Kadee.

Poole missed Kadee's hesitation, but Gibbs caught it — and her slight eye roll.

"Ah, sure." Kadee forced a smile.

Poole clasped his hands together. "Great. The paper work still has to go through, but Patricia said it's a done deal."

"I'm sure Kadee's enthralled by the news, but can we get back to doing actual work?" Gibbs flashed a knowing half-smile to Kadee.

Kadee put her energy into finding out who was responsible for killing Jacob Temple. They had more research to conduct on Fiona and Sally before calling them in for questioning. They would be interviewed simultaneously, but in separate rooms. They were still going to look at Thomas McPherson, too. With such a clear motive for Fiona and maybe even Sally, it was hard to think about other possibilities, but Gibbs reminded them that Thomas McPherson had made a threat. They should not be blindsided by circumstantial evidence or hearsay.

Fiona had a rock-solid alibi, but given the information that Oscar Piedmont revealed, they had to consider other conspiratorial options. Though the killing seemed to be rage-driven, Fiona could have hired someone to do the kill. Apparently, she came from a family that felt they were entitled to rise about the law, using money and power to do whatever they wanted.

And that's precisely what Gibbs suggested. He hypothesized that Fiona had instructed a hit man to make the kill look rage-filled to set the investigation astray. Anything was possible. It was an unusual pattern of criminality, though. Poole was convinced it was Fiona. That fit with his initial theory, and it was the way his mind worked: *It's almost always the partner.*

It was a busy afternoon filled with research, phone calls, and conversations about who the killer was. Kadee's thought processes fatigued as the hours wore on. She had a ton of statistics homework to do that evening, which required unwavering concentration.

She grabbed a large Starbuck's coffee on her way home. It was close to forty degrees, balmy after the arctic cold front. She opened her wool coat, sipped her beverage, strolled home. She needed to clear her head. She had to get schoolwork done after dinner.

Alex planned on cooking a chicken dish. He had texted her earlier about it. But she hadn't heard from him, so she wasn't sure if he was home yet. It was almost 7:00, and she was starving. Food preoccupied her mind as she jiggled her key in the doorknob. She opened the front door. Her jaw nearly hit the ground.

Kadee found Yvonne in her living room, perched on her couch, sipping tea and chatting with Alex. Yvonne looked at Kadee. "Alex, it's the woman of the hour. Kadee, were your ears burning?"

# Chapter 17

Jane arrived home from the police station in a state of disorientation. Her thoughts and emotions tangled, her mind raced. She couldn't calm herself down. She counted in sixes. That almost always unruffled her, but this day no matter how much she counted, she could not find any quiet. She felt like she was trapped in a storm cloud. Her body released deep thunderclaps of force, her thoughts a crowded web of lightning flashes. She didn't fully understand them.

The images in her mind burst through her consciousness. She tried to block them out, but they blasted through so quickly. Short clips that alternated scenes, her mind on fast forward. They flipped so fast that she couldn't fully comprehend the images. It felt like a dream. She wished — hoped — that it was. She grabbed her knitting needle, poked herself six times in her stomach. Still asleep. Still dreaming. *Wake up!* She poked herself six times in her right leg. This time, blood came out of the puncture wound.

It hurt, but the pain calmed her. And despite her hope, she was, in fact, awake. She watched the blood ooze from her insides. She stabbed herself again, six times in the left leg. She watched as red seeped out of both punctures. The sensation of fluid releasing from her body almost felt euphoric. She laid back on her couch, breathed in and out, deep breaths to temporarily relax her.

Then came that voice again. She couldn't distinguish whether it came from her own head or if it was outside in the air of her apartment. She grabbed both sides of her head and squeezed. She tried to push out the voice, to quiet it.

*You know the truth*, the voice said. She shook her head, hollered, "I can't, I can't, I can't, I can't, I can't, I can't."

She took the needle, stabbed her right leg again. Harder this time. Instead of a trickle of blood, this deeper wound poured out a stream of blood. It dripped over her thigh, down her calf, and across her foot. She watched it flow. She breathed deeply, counted in sixes until her mind became quiet. The sound of the voice vanished into the air.

It was seeing that woman Yvonne, Jacob's friend, that shook her up. Jane lived on the precipice of emotional instability since that last conversation with Jacob nineteen years ago. His abrupt termination of their contact combined with the unexplained restraining order severely wounded her. The world as she knew it, the safe, predictable world where people who loved each other stayed forever connected, was shattered by Jacob's departure. Her world became an unsafe place filled with emotional hazards, making her ability to stay grounded in reality precarious.

She managed a semblance of functioning through her counting, her collecting and even her writing. But, she always teetered on the fine line of a complete emotional break-down.

Seeing that woman Yvonne made her feel like she might totally decompensate. She needed to slip into a reality that was safe, a reality created by her own mind to protect her from the truth. This false reality would shelter her. It would save her from knowing the actual reality.

That image of Yvonne at the police station wouldn't go away. Jane didn't know why she was there. It made no sense. She knew that woman did something bad. She did not like knowing that information.

There was something else too, something even more petrifying that her mind was still able to protect her from.

The pictures of Yvonne blazed through her mind. There were more than one; the scenes kept changing. Jane felt that chill come over her. That something else felt like it might be a memory of some kind. It was something she really did not want to remember, something that could cause her to lose her grip on reality. It tried to intrude into her thoughts. Her subconscious knew it was something scary, so it blocked the thoughts from her consciousness at all costs. Even if the cost was her grip on reality.

Viv came by after work that day. She brought spaghetti and meatballs for dinner and a bottle of red wine. She said she was really glad Jane finally went down to the station and told the truth. But Viv could tell something was bothering her.

"What is it Jane? You did the right thing."

"Yeah, I know. It's just so hard. Having to tell about the restraining order and all. It just made me feel the same way it felt nineteen years ago. I still don't understand why — how — Jacob could do that to me."

"We discussed this ad nauseam. Remember? We finally agreed that we are nevah gonna know. I know it's really hard. But you gotta let it go. He's been fuckin' murd– sorry… he's passed on now, and you have no choice but to let it go."

"We always have a choice…What if I don't want to let it go? What if letting it go feels like I'm letting Jacob go? And what if I don't want to let him go?"

"Jane. Listen to me." She held Jane's chin. "Listen. To. Me. You have to let him go. He's gone now. You understand that, right? He's gone."

Jane's eyes became moist. That chill emerged and wouldn't go.

A shrieking voice came off of her tongue, "Viv, stop it! Just stop it! It's been a long and difficult day. I feel like I'm losing my mind. You need to stop it! I don't know how much more I can take today."

Those memory flashes returned.

She couldn't make out anything specific. They flickered through too fast. She thought she saw blood. Or maybe not. She couldn't tell what the images were, but she knew they were scary.

Her mind flashed to Yvonne Tracy at the police station, then to Kadee Carlisle asking her if she knew Yvonne. The kiss between Sally and Fiona. Thomas McPherson. A flash of herself taking a picture with her cell phone…

That voice came for a minute again, said: *You know the truth.*

"No, no, no, no, no, no," she yelled.

Viv's eyes welled. "Jane… I'm sorry. Are you gonna be OK? You looked like you left your body or something. Your eyes had this blank look. Like a zombie or somethin. What's goin on?"

Jane's brow wrinkled. "This is very hard. I miss Jacob's voice on the show. I don't know if I'm ever going to be OK. I am trying. I'm really trying."

Vivian fought back tears. She needed to be strong for Jane. Her dear sister, so fragile. She didn't know what to do for her except to let her know she was on her side. "OK, Jane. I'll ease up. You tell me what you need when you need it."

When Viv finally left, Jane dug deep into one of her boxes and pulled out another smaller box. She put it on her couch. She poured the remainder of the wine into her glass. She opened the box and pulled out the huge pile of printouts: email exchanges between her and Jacob from when they were together.

She read through them all, every single one. She could practically recite them by heart she had read through them so many times. They always made her feel better. His words reminded her that their love was real, that someday they would be reunited.

It was harder for her to hold on to that now because he had transitioned, but she reminded herself that their love was eternal. She had hoped that they would have more time together in this world, but there was always the next. She was sure he would wait for her.

She fell asleep on the couch. Jacob's written words soothed her into a slumber. But her unconscious interrupted the tranquility with images that both soothed and disturbed her.

It was a dream. A voice screamed. There was blood everywhere. She didn't know where she was, but everything was covered in red. She saw Fiona and Jacob. Fiona reached for him, but he pushed her away. He reached out for Jane instead. Jane went to him. They embraced. He was crying. Then a blinding light behind him pulled him into a radiant tunnel. His hand reached out to Jane. She screamed, "Please don't go, Jacob. Please don't leave me here all alone. I love you so much."

"I love you too, Jane. You were always the one. Maybe someday, we'll be together again." Then the image of him dissipated into the illumination behind him. His voice gradually fading, moving further and further away. But Jane heard him say, "Tell the truth, Jane. Tell the truth. It will free you just like it freed me. Tell the truth, Jane…"

When she woke up, she was standing in her living room, reaching forward, reaching for the Jacob in her dream. For a moment, the most terrifying moment she had ever experienced, she knew what those images meant.

# CHAPTER 18

Yvonne dropped another box on top of the third stack lining the far wall. She marked it *BOOKS,* then taped up the top. She wasted no time sealing up the contents of her life. She decided to keep all of her furniture except her bed. It reminded her too much of Noah. She wanted to start fresh. She would throw out the old mattress and order a new one. She couldn't believe how easily she found an apartment across the street from Kadee. Ha! Proximity (Capital P). Once her perfect credit was approved, *which it would be,* she would sign the lease. The next step of her plan would begin.

*Moving right along.* A scathing sound left her throat (*ahahaha*), as she recognized her witty play on the word *moving.*

She passed the time packing up her old life, the life she wanted to leave behind. A new life waiting for her just across the street from Kadee. She waited for evening to fall. She thought she would make her way over to Kadee's at around 6:00. If Kadee wasn't home from the station yet, maybe Alex would be there to welcome her. She thought it was high time they met in person, anyway. They were going to be neighbors after all. Right? *Right.* She nodded to herself, a wily grin. Alex was the most important extension of Kadee. If she was going to consume Kadee's life, naturally, she had to have a rapport with Alex.

Yvonne expected Kadee to do what Yvonne wanted. Kadee had Stolen (capital S) her life, after all. Because it was Kadee's fault, she felt entitled to take whatever she wanted from her. Kadee owed her. Yvonne's eyes grew dark, fuming with rage. An internal furnace of hate heated her insides. She thought about how much had been robbed from her. Her whole life. *Everything.*

She imagined stabbing Kadee over and over, watching the blood gush out of her. Yvonne's mouth curled, her eyes burned. She rubbed them. She certainly wasn't going to risk going to prison for killing someone who had already taken so much from her. *If* she ever decided to take her life, she needed to be very calculated.

Or *when…*

She went through some of her cosmetics, getting rid of what she didn't use anymore. *Nothing like a move to get you to throw out the old and the useless.* She tossed out a handful of old eye shadows. Noah liked when she wore blue on her eyelids. Her face grew long. She snatched the plastic container filled with all her eye makeup off her shelf and dumped it in the garbage. She would purchase some new products as part of her moving-out and moving-on process.

As she reached for her perfumes, Noah's eyeballs emerged. She squeezed her eyes shut, but Noah's eyes wouldn't go away. He always commented on how much he enjoyed the way she smelled.

She thought of his dead body, the way she stood over him after he was gone, wiping his blood on her skin. She took the bottles of scented oils, threw them in the garbage bag with her makeup, took it outside and tossed it in the dumpster next to her apartment. When she went back inside, his eyeballs disappeared.

But thoughts of him loitered in her mind temporarily. She was reminded of those last few conversations with him. Those dreadful talks where he tried pitifully to explain why he had been carrying on an affair with Kadee. Naturally, he never thought he would get caught. *They never do.* Dashing Dustin (he liked to be called that – Loser, capital L), the prototype of the cheater, also thought she would never find out. And she did. Didn't she? *Yes she did.*

Dustin did come in handy for her alibi though. *At least he was useful for something.* Bowled over by her new sexual prowess after they spent the day naked having sex, he asked her to come back to him. How timely. Wasn't it? *It was.* She smiled.

She told him that lil' ole her didn't have an alibi for the day of Noah's death because she was home alone trying to sort through all her feelings after learning that he betrayed her. Integrity was never one of Dustin's fine points. He agreed to lie for Yvonne. He would say he was with her all day and night on September 19th, if she agreed to move in and give it another try. *Deal.*

She wondered if she would have to stay with Dustin for the rest of her life because they shared that secret. But naturally, Dashing Dustin did what he always did. *So Predictable.* Yvonne stopped being so sexually open. She went back to that militant, woman-on-the-bottom-man-on-the-top-only sex. He got bored, began a relationship with Sabrina, another young resident. That was that.

When Yvonne confronted him, he wasted no time ending it with Yvonne, said he wanted to be with Sabrina. Her secret was safe. She was free, *and* he thought it was his decision. *Fool.*

Secrets. Secrets. In some ways, they bind people. Don't they? *They do.* Head bowed, her lips a quivering frown. She sat on the corner of the bed. Noah had told her that he was trying to end the relationship with Kadee. He said he was having difficulty because he was concerned that Kadee might kill herself. He said that Kadee had been threatening to take her own life if he left her. Yvonne probably would have believed him. She loved him to her very core. He was everything to her. *Everything.* And she trusted him.

*She trusted him.* Except no matter how hard she tried to lie to herself, telling herself that *his* Lie (capital L), was the truth, that Kadee was suicidal, Yvonne knew it was a total fabrication. Kadee had been her patient. Yvonne knew with complete certainty that she was not going to kill herself. She wasn't even expressing suicidal ideation.

Noah made the whole thing up because he just couldn't leave Kadee. Yvonne read his journal entries. He wanted to stop sleeping with Kadee, but he felt like he couldn't. *He couldn't stop.* When she read those words, her heart broke into thousands of itsy-bitsy pieces. How could he, the love of her entire adult life, best friend, man of her dreams, how could he be writing those words.

She wanted to believe him, but the truth kept seeping into her mind. On top of that, Kadee and Noah had a secret bond:

they shared a private life, one where Noah expressed sides of himself that he never showed Yvonne. In a way, he was more honest with Kadee. This destroyed Yvonne. She always believed that Noah was the closest with *her*, shared his innermost thoughts with *her*. It turned out that he showed Kadee things about himself that he never showed *her*.

Yvonne's whole life with this man transformed from truth to illusion. Fiction. An invention she made up to feed some childish fantasy of ideal love. What could she have been thinking? She wasn't thinking back then, was she? *No, she wasn't.*

She was now. She stood up, went to her desk and wrote down a stream of words — a poem. She scratched out a few lines, then added a few more. She hoped that once Kadee and she were neighbors, Kadee would do things according to Yvonne's plans. If she didn't, Yvonne would have to be creative in figuring out just how to get away with her murder. Of course she would be able to come up with something. She was garnering the sophistication of the most extraordinary of killers. She was reading all of the research Kadee gave her. *Thank you for your services, Miss Carlisle. I'm so glad you trust me. Ha!*

*Trust is never a good thing.*

Yvonne felt a sense of power that she never experienced before, but her strength wasn't integrated. It was a false sense of control, one that only came from the most heinous of actions. Inevitably, this type of all-pervading grandiosity fails. But Yvonne was starting to believe that she was invincible. It was becoming her truth.

And she did have some secrets of her own.

Didn't she? *She did.*

Would Yvonne become too confident in her murderous talents and make a careless mistake? Or would her tactics become increasingly refined? Only time would tell.

Yvonne looked up at her clock: 5:46. She grabbed her new coat, steel gray, and her red hat. She surveyed the mess of boxes. She had a lot of packing to do when she got back home and more papers to burn. *Moving right along.* She shut the light and left for Kadee's.

# CHAPTER 19

Kadee opened her apartment door to find Yvonne seated with Alex, the two chatting like old college roomies. Nothing could have been more surreal. She needed a second to register Yvonne's unexpected presence. Yvonne looked strange sitting in Kadee's living room. Out of context, like a tiger walking down Second Avenue.

Kadee blinked. "Yvonne. Hi. Wha– What are you doing here?" *That doesn't sound right.* "Sorry... I meant... I'm just surprised to see you here. What's up?"

Yvonne stood up. "Hi neighbor," she reached in to give Kadee a hug.

Kadee gave a tentative hug back. She got the creeps, like bugs crawling all over her skin.

"I thought I'd stop by to give a warm hello and tell you that I got the apartment. We'll be seeing more of each other now. I wanted to meet Alex, too. Funny how life works, isn't it? Us being neighbors?" She flipped her hair off her shoulder, let it flow down her back.

Yvonne's demeanor was even and calm. It tempered Kadee's uneasiness. Yvonne always seemed so easy-going. Despite everything she was going through, for the most part, she carried herself with a proud sort of composure. That was one of the things Noah found so endearing. Kadee thought he probably wanted a poised, relatively undemonstrative wife, a woman who was not as emotionally expressive — *is that a euphemism for emotional basket case* — or demanding as Kadee.

She thought of Hailey's words: "Yvonne is the type men like Noah marry." *I will not let her obnoxious attitude and comments effect me. Ever. I probably shouldn't spend too much time with her. Besides, Alex loves my complicated emotional nature. Loves it! Fucking Hailey.* Kadee's lips smiled, her eyes sad for an instant. She took her coat off and sat down with them.

"It *is* a crazy coincidence. I'm really happy that you found something so quickly." She looked at Alex. "So, what were you two talking about?"

"Nothing much. Yvonne was just telling me about her new place. Sounds like a good deal. Maybe we should have a look in her building. There is a large one-bedroom available."

"Um, I don't know Al. We discussed this. We are fine here for now."

"But we could just have a look…"

"Sure. We could. But I thought we agreed that we wouldn't look for a new place until after the wedding."

Alex looked at Kadee. "That's true. But it's worth a look. Sometimes it pays to do things out of the order you planned. Especially when it comes to real estate in this city."

She smirked at him. "Let's talk about it later."

"OK." He gave her a loving look.

Yvonne observed their interaction. She let out a sigh. "You two seem so good together. I'm happy for you, Kadee. I really am. After everything you've been through, you deserve to have joy in your life. I don't think I've ever seen you so content."

Yvonne's statement made Kadee's heart heavy. "You deserve happiness, too. I hope this move will be a new start, and you will be able to create a new life for yourself."

"Absolutely! That's the plan. It really is. Life is funny. You just never know how it's going to play out. You know what I mean? Sometimes, a tragic event has a deeper significance that's part of a larger life plan unbeknownst to us until after time has passed. And sometimes... that which you think is the happiest, most joyous, most fantastic event turns out to be nothing that it seemed, perhaps even the heartbreak of your life." She gazed down, dabbed the inner corners of her eyes with her forefinger.

Kadee put her hand on Yvonne's shoulder. "It's going to be OK."

She nodded. "I expect that it will. This move is a big step, and I am optimistic. I really am. Naturally, it's quite stressful. Going through some of my things has brought up memories of... of Noah. I just knew him for so long. The entire time I have lived here in New York. It's a painful process. Do you know what I mean?" Her tone lifted when she added, "But on the flippity-dip side, it is a type of cleansing too. I anticipate feeling much better once I've finished and moved in."

"I totally understand. Listen, if you need any help just let me know."

Alex got up to inspect the defrosting chicken. "Why don't the three of us go out for some sushi?"

"Jeez, sweetie, that sounds fun, but I have a shitload of statistics homework I need to get done."

Alex had his "this is non-debatable" lawyer face on. She knew she would inevitably give in. "Come on, Kade. A quick bite. You have to eat."

"OK. Sure. Let's do it. But no lingering over sake afterward. I need to come right home, 'kay?"

"Yeees, ma'am." He kissed Kadee, then wrapped his arms around her body. "You up for dinner, Yvonne?"

"Oh, yes. Thank you for the invitation. It sounds delightful."


The dinner was pleasant. Kadee wanted to ask Yvonne if she knew Jane Light. It felt like a ridiculous question in most ways. Of course, she would have said something if she knew Jane *or* Jacob Temple. Still, Kadee was curious. Jane's reaction combined with Kadee's discovery that Yvonne and Jacob Temple worked at the same hospital for one year, sat impatiently in the back of her mind through the dinner. It was probably a coincidence, but those sorts of happenstances never seemed satisfactory to her. As a researcher, she liked to practically dig a tunnel to China, excavating every possibility she could think of. Maybe it was chance. But she wanted to ask Yvonne anyway.

She wondered, though, how exactly she would ask. She had perused Yvonne's Facebook page. That's how she found out that she and Jacob were in the same program. Suddenly she felt like she had invaded Yvonne's privacy. Of course, that was nonsense. The profile was up publicly, and they were Facebook friends. Anyone could read it. Yet, her purposeful inspection left her feeling a tad contrite.

Her statistic homework nagged at her, too. She decided her brain could only handle so much at once. She would wait to ask Yvonne after she had a little time to think about how exactly she would broach the topic. *Sometimes, Kadee, you really are your own worst enemy. Why do I always make e-v-e-r-y-t-h-i-n-g so goddamned complicated?*

After dinner, Yvonne came back to their apartment. She had forgotten her hat. She had her coat on, but hung around. She didn't seem to want to leave. Kadee assumed she didn't want to go home and deal with going through all of her personal items, everything that she said stirred up feelings about Noah. Kadee empathized, but she had to get her homework done.

She tried to use indirect, understated cues to let Yvonne know that she needed to leave without actually asking her to.

Alex even said, "Well, it was nice to meet you, Yvonne," and shook her hand.

Kadee moved closer to the front door.

Silence. Yvonne didn't budge.

"What is it, Yvonne?" Kadee asked finally.

"Oh, nothing. Nothing, really." She stood still.

"I'm sorry, but I have to get this homework done."

"Oh, yes, yes, of course. I understand. I really do." She put her hands up to her cheeks. "It's just difficult right now. Very difficult. And it's been so lovely to be with the two of you. I just think to myself how fortunate it is for you that you have been able to get past everything that happened between you and Noah. Do you know what I mean? You seemed so distraught. And now look at you. It just seems that you moved on so quickly. I wonder to myself how that's possible given the way... the way you said you felt about him."

Kadee's eyes narrowed. She looked at Alex. "I'm not sure what you're getting at. Things with Noah were awful. You know that better than anyone. It was nothing like what Alex and I share." She reached for Alex and put her arm around him. A flash of heat ran up her back. "Listen, I have to get my work done. We are meeting for lunch tomorrow, right?"

"Yes. I didn't mean anything by what I was saying. I guess I'm just struggling to move on, too."

"I understand. And you *are* moving on. You've got a new place, a new boyfriend. Maybe you should take a break from going through your things. You have time before you move. Maybe go through your stuff a little at a time. It might make it easier."

"Of course you're right about that, Kadee." She turned toward the door. "Well, thank you two for a lovely dinner. It really was most enjoyable." She gave Kadee a hug. "See you tomorrow."

"OK. See you then."

Yvonne pulled her hat on and left.

As soon as the door closed behind Yvonne, Kadee sat down, scrunched her forehead. That statement about her moving on and getting passed Noah, felt passive-aggressive. She sensed that Yvonne veiled some resentment toward her for moving on with her life. She said it in front of Alex, too. It didn't feel right. Of course, Yvonne said she was glad for Kadee, but the comment suggested otherwise.

But Kadee still had that lingering guilt. Perhaps she was being overly sensitive. She couldn't be sure if she just misperceived what Yvonne meant because she, too, had been wondering how she was able to move on while Yvonne was still reeling and broken.

Then, Kadee thought about Yvonne going through her belongings and all of the memories stored up in her apartment. Yvonne had known Noah for so many years and they shared intimacies that Kadee had never experienced with him. His death must have left Yvonne with a hole that remained raw, maybe never to be filled.

A stomach pang, a stitch, a moment of envy. She hated that feeling. Jesus Christ, did she hate it. But it stung her whenever she allowed herself to think of Yvonne and Noah together.

Alex looked at her. "What is it?"

"Nothing."

"Don't 'nothing' me. What is it?"

She didn't want to get into the complexity of everything swarming around her mind. Men were never great at understanding the intricacies of female friendships, and her relationship with Yvonne had obscure threads that were woven into a tight knot, possibly impossible to disentangle.

Alex couldn't let things go easily. He sat across from her, waited for an answer.

"I don't know, Al. It's... it's complicated."

"You always say that. Let's flesh it out. It's her, isn't it?"

"What do you mean?"

"It's simple if you break it down. She was your therapist. You were in a bad relationship with someone you couldn't trust. You go to her for help. Then you find out she's involved with the same man. Then he's murdered. It must be a little weird to be spending time with her now. Plus, you have your whole save-the-world philosophy, which is making you want to help her in some way. She isn't your responsibility."

"I didn't love him. Not the way I love you. You know that, right?"

"Is that what's bothering you?"

"She made that comment."

"It was a bad relationship. Not so different from my relationship with my ex-wife." He leaned toward her. "Filled with passion, but based on lies. Hell, I didn't even know who that woman was when I married her. By the time we divorced, I couldn't even stand to be in the same room with her. I thought I loved her, just like you thought you loved him. But that's not love. Not like what we have. C'mere." He pulled her on his lap, her long legs dangled. She rested her head on his shoulder. "Yvonne is nice enough, but she's going through hard times. It's not your job to fix her. It just seems to me that she wants something from you. She definitely didn't want to leave our apartment tonight. Maybe she thinks you can help her because you knew him. Who knows. Just don't get too involved. You've got enough on your plate. OK?"

She squeezed him. "I love you." Alex was always so rationale. It all made sense when he said it. *I love this man.*

Alex felt her relief. "Back atcha."

Alex opened the blinds. "It's a full moon tonight."

She walked over to have a look, a perfect white disk suspended in the sky. Alex pulled her close, kissed her along the side of her face. They gazed at the moon appreciating its splendor. Alex snapped a picture.

She kissed him. "Now to get this damn stat homework done." She plopped her book on her desk, rustled through the pages. She began reading about correlations and chewing on her pen cap.

Yvonne wandered back home. She mumbled under her breath: *no more, no more, this time, ole Kadee, it's my time to score. I will pierce your skin and watch you bleed. I will do it slowly so I can stare as you plead...*

It was a poem she was calling, *Ode to Kadee.* She sat on a stoop, pulled out her small note pad. She jotted down another verse. *Oh, the joy, oh, the glory, this, dear Kadee, is the end of your story. I will crack you and knife you, until no more will you be...*

She paused, stuck on the words. She wrote a line, then scribbled it out. It was almost done, but not quite. She noticed the moonlight glistening off her jewelry. The night was quiet, her eyes daggers. She got up and continued walking.

Yvonne fumed. In her mind, Kadee asking her to leave, saying in that high-pitched, "being teased in the schoolyard" voice, "I'm sorry, but I have to get this homework done" was a complete dismissal. The perceived rejection was too much for her. It shifted any desire to be close with Kadee into a venomous hate.

When she arrived home, she went inside and packed. She hummed *Ode to Kadee*. She tried to come up with the last verse, *the grand finale*. She released an acrimonious laugh. Kadee must never treat her so cavalierly. After everything she had done to her, the least she could do was give Yvonne the attention she deserved. *No more, no more*, her mind thundered repeatedly.

How could she get away with this one? Killing Kadee would not be easy. The detectives knew they had a relationship. Unfortunately that complicated things. *Well, twiddle dee dum dee*, she said to herself as she packed dishes, *I will figure this out. I'm just as smart as can be*. She scampered to her desk and jotted that down.

She fantasized different schemes, none of which seemed appropriately perfect. She needed to calculate this correctly. Naturally, she didn't have to do it right away. She could wait a few months. In the meantime, maybe she could destroy Kadee's relationship with Alex. *Ooh, La, la. Wouldn't that be a delight!*

She let out a cackle. She was absolutely certain that her last comment about Noah caused some problems between them after she left.

Obviously, there was quarreling going on back at Kadee's right now. She wished she was in her new place and would have that unobstructed view into their living room. It was such a fortunate situation she had fallen into: First, an apartment became available on the same block as Kadee; second, they'd both have apartments facing the street. Once she moved, whenever Kadee left her blinds open, Yvonne would be privy to the entire front room of their apartment. *Oh the joy, oh the glory.*

Naturally, Kadee and Alex were fighting right now. He would be upset after hearing Yvonne's comment. Didn't she have flair? *She did.* It was subtle enough that it wouldn't be obvious that she was trying to cause a disruption, but direct enough that it had to raise an eyebrow.

*Oh, did lil' ole me cause all that ruckus between you two. I'm so very sorry that I did something to inconvenience your life, Kadee. I didn't mean to. Just like you didn't mean to steal Noah and my future. You did make that itsy-bitsy, pathetic apology to me, now didn't you? You did. Well, I'm sorry, too, Kadee. I'm so very very sorry that your life is breaking down into itsy-bitsy, teensy-weensy pieces.*

Another idea. She scurried to her desk and jotted down her brilliance. The ode was almost finished. She cupped her hands, shimmied her shoulders. A satisfied grin crossed her lips.

She wanted to know what was going on between Alex and Kadee. She wanted some confirmation that her comment had an effect. She needed to feel that she had power over Kadee that Yvonne's existence mattered to her, that Yvonne occupied space in Kadee's thoughts, and that her presence had a direct impact on Kadee's life. She *had* to have that. Must have that. It was only fair. If she was suffering, Kadee had to also. If she couldn't kill her *yet*, she would indulge herself by watching her world shatter, just like Kadee had destroyed Yvonne's.

She signed onto Facebook. It was unlikely that Kadee posted an update. She had to get all that homework done. *I'm sorry, but I have to get this homework done*, a sarcastic squeak in her voice. She wanted to check anyway. It was the only way she could feel connected and observe Kadee's life to possibly find out what was going on over at her place.

Alex had posted a picture. Yvonne enlarged it. She placed the back of her hands on her cheeks, the flesh scorching. He tagged Kadee in it. *What a darling he is.* Her eye twitched. It was a picture of the moon, round and full amidst darkness of space. The photo showed the reflected image from the window. It was Alex, one arm out taking the shot, and the other arm wrapped around Kadee. The two stood shoulder to shoulder.

People commented on what a great photo it was. She read the thread. Her lips curled, a foul taste in her mouth. Her eyes poison darts waiting for a target to attack. Perhaps her Noah comment had no impact on Kadee and Alex. Her face sizzled, an inferno. She went to the freezer, grabbed a few ice cubes, rolled them in a towel and pressed it against her cheeks.

She leaned against the kitchen container, hoping to cool down. She glanced at the kitchen sink. She had more papers to burn, a distraction, a sudden sense of purpose. She retrieved a folder containing a huge chunk of paper from her desk, threw it in the steel basin. She ignited it with a lighter. She watched the corners incinerating, her eyes glassy from the flames. She would find a way to demolish Kadee. It was just going to take some time. And she was good at being patient, wasn't she? *Oh. Yes. She was.*

She watched the paper turn into ashes. Her mind was working out the last verse of her ode when an image of herself and her brother running through the high grass in their backyard entered her mind. It was a childhood memory. She didn't understand why it emerged. She tried not to think about James. It was too painful.

She blamed herself. They were so close. She should have known he was suffering.

She looked at the tips of the flames, orange, red, blue, a mesmerizing mix of color dancing in her sink. James and she used to light campfires in their backyard in the summers. They'd roast marshmallows and sing along to James' fumbling guitar accompaniment.

That changed when Bettina came on the scene. James spent all of his time with her; Yvonne was so jealous. The image of her brother hanging from the ceiling beam entered her mind. Yvonne's scream. Her mother rushing in. She gasped. It wasn't her fault. Was it? *No, it wasn't.* It was Bettina's.

She pulled her hair away from her face, inhaled deep from her gut, shook off her vulnerability. She stopped the thoughts about James by returning to her poem. She walked around her apartment. Her mind now preoccupied with reciting different variations of the last verse until it felt finished. *You will scream and you will...die...no...*

*You will cry...you will cry...I will not stop until you...die.*

She wrote. And wrote.

*I'm a crafty one, aren't I? Yes, I am.* She sat up straight, chin raised, a proud glow. She wrote down the final line. She put her pen down. (Bada Boom).

*No more, no more, this time ole Kadee it's my time to score. I will pierce your skin and watch you bleed. I will do it slowly so I can stare as you plead.*

*Oh, the joy, oh, the glory, this, dear Kadee, is the end of your story. I will crack you and knife you, until no more will you be. I will rip you apart, too, twiddle dee dum dee.*

*You will scream and you will cry, but I will not stop until you die. Never again, no more, no more, this time, ole Kadee, it is my time to score.*

*I'm becoming an exceptional writer. Aren't I? I am.*

The flames still burned. She went in the freezer and took out a frozen apple pie, stuck it in the microwave. She was in the mood for something sweet.

While Yvonne worked out the end of her ode, Kadee sat at her desk nibbling on her pen cap. She couldn't concentrate. Alex was in the bedroom listening through a deposition. She picked up her phone and called Vanessa.

The phone rang. "Pick up. Pick up."

Three rings, then: "Hey, Kade."

"Heeey. Whatcha doing?"

"Nothing much. Working on some edits. What's up? I thought tonight was correlation night."

Kadee sighed. "Yeah. Me, too." Her voice thin.

"What is it? You don't sound good."

"It's Yvonne. I dunno, Ness. Something's bothering me about her. I'm not even sure what it is exactly. She's moving across the street from me and Alex. I feel uncomfortable with it, I guess."

"Wait. What? You didn't tell me *that!*"

"I just found out. She got the apartment today. Then… Jesus… then I come home from the internship and she's sitting in my living room with Alex. Said she wanted to pop in and say hello. Something like that. Then we go to dinner. The three of us. She comes back to the apartment afterward and wouldn't leave. Then she made this weird comment in front of Alex about me moving on so quickly. She mentioned how messed up I was about Noah. It felt, I don't know... hostile. I don't like saying that about her. Clearly, the woman is suffering. And she *was* my therapist. But still. Something feels weird."

"I can't believe she's moving across the street. I have to say that *is* kinda weird. Almost stalkerish. I don't think you should spend too much time with her. She's strange."

Kadee bit a cuticle. "Yeah. Alex said something similar. It bothers me that it bothers me. People move all the time. I don't own the block. She's allowed to move here. And I do really feel bad for her. She's all messed up about Noah. I really understand how she feels. It's hard for me to turn my back on her because I know how hard dealing with his betrayal and his murder has been for me. It's got to be worse for her. I dunno, Ness."

"I understand. It must be horrible for her. I agree. But don't make her feelings more important than your own. You do that sometimes. It's not good. If you feel weirded out by her, or uncomfortable, it's OK to spend less time with her."

"I'm probably making too much out of this. Just because she's moving across the street doesn't mean I have to hang out with her all the time."

"Exactly."

"Thanks, Ness. I couldn't stop thinking about it. It feels good to say everything out loud."

"Try not to dwell too much in the past. You've got so much good stuff to look forward to. Speaking of which, have you and Alex decided if you're going to elope or not? Eloping is so romantic. I will miss sharing the day though."

"I *think* we're going to elope. Maybe Hawaii. You and Henri could come with us."

"I like that idea. Let me know when you decide, and I'll talk with Henri about it."

"'Kay. Listen. Don't say anything to Hailey, yet. I don't feel like dealing with her opinion on nontraditional wedding ceremonies."

"Of course, I won't. Lunch or dinner over the weekend?"

"Sounds great."

"Get your work done. And talk tomorrow."

"Ness. Thank you."

"No prob. Talk to you tomorrow. Bye."

"Bye"

Kadee leaned over her statistics book. Of course, Vanessa was right. Yvonne moving across the street didn't have to be a big deal. *Kadee, love, sometimes you really are your own worst enemy.*

Everything was fine. She looked at her engagement ring, smiled. She went into the bedroom. Alex sat over his desk with headphones on. She leaned over and kissed him.

"I love you so much."

He turned in his chair and embraced her. "Me too."

Within minutes they were under the comforter, naked, ravaging each other.

Kadee felt so safe with him. *I have so much good stuff to look forward to,* she thought. Vanessa was so right.

Unfortunately, Kadee let herself feel safe too soon. Kadee's safety: one big illusion.

# Chapter 20

**Gibbs had spent** the prior evening ripping through Jacob Temple's journals. The content matched Oscar Piedmont's story. Jacob's interior monologue poured out on the pages. He described in painful detail how he felt trapped in his life while not knowing how to change it. Hundreds of entries described how Fiona treated him. He wrote that she was abusive, manipulative, uncaring, controlling.

When Kadee got in, Gibbs summarized it for her. There was no time for Kadee to read through the journals. They had called Fiona and Sally in for questioning. The two had arrived together earlier that morning and were placed in separate interrogation rooms. Poole and Gibbs had already begun to talk with them. Gibbs had a hunch that they were hiding *something*.

Kadee sent Yvonne a quick text letting her know that she wouldn't be able to meet for lunch. It was already 10:00 in the morning and they were just getting started. Gibbs assured Kadee they wouldn't be done by noon.

*Can't make it to lunch. Caught up at internship. Sorry for the short notice. Reschedule?*

Yvonne responded within minutes.

*Sorry to miss our lunch. ☹ I understand though, I really do. Maybe you can come by my place after work? I have a stack of old books you might want before I throw them out. We could grab dinner near me. What do you think? YT*

She contemplated. She still hadn't finished her statistics homework, and it was due the next day. It was early in the day and she was already tired. It was a busy semester and the winter was getting to her. But she thought about Yvonne alone in her apartment, all her past memories haunting her as she went through her personal effects. If she could get there by 6:00, she could be home by 8:00.

*Sure. 6:00-6:15?*

Yvonne responded immediately.

*Wonderful, 6:00-6:15 is perfect. Wine and dine, we'll have a good time. ☺ Toodles,*

*YT*

Kadee rolled her eyes at the response. *She is definitely strange. Stop thinking about it. Jeez Kadee, focus.*

That was that. She gave Gibbs her full attention.

He showed her two of Jacob's entries, both written just a week before his murder, and referred to his finding Fiona and Sally in bed together. The first one read: *It should have been a devastating moment when I saw my wife in bed with someone else. I guess I always knew she didn't love me. Did it bother me? I guess it did, but then again, I have made so many mistakes in my life and marrying Fiona was one of the biggest. But I was a weak man then, always in need of my father's approval. And for what? Nothing I ever did was good enough for him. I internalized his critical voice and, over the years, I didn't need him to judge me. I did it myself with his same harsh and impossible rules. Life is messy. No matter how hard we try to create order, something happens to cause the structure we created to falter. Maybe that's the only way for us to learn. If everything stayed neat and orderly, then we would never be forced to grow and change. We need something unexpected to help us make sense of where we are and to guide us to where we need to go. My therapist was trying to help me leave Fiona, and I wanted to, but felt like I couldn't. So seeing her in bed with Sally was a life-shattering moment. But, instead of my world falling apart, it actually came together. Confirmation of Fiona's cheating gave me that final burst of courage I needed to go back to Jane, where I should have been all along. God, I've missed her. I realize now that it was my rigid moral conscious that forced me to live in a way that was not meaningful or true. I'm the only one who has the power to change my life. I now have the emotional strength to do it. I can't wait to move out of this place and start over.*

Jacob wrote a second entry the same night: *I told Fiona that I'm leaving. I feel so liberated. It's like I've been living someone else's life and finally have the courage to change that. I've always known that I wasn't living the life I wanted, but I tried my hardest to pretend everything I had was what I wanted. If I didn't, I would've lost my mind. Maybe even killed myself. But the moment I told her I was leaving, a burden lifted. I finally faced the truth. I was living a lie that I created to make my unhappy circumstances bearable. I'm relieved. I'm excited. Now I know things are going to change. She tried to scare me with all kinds of threats. Physical. Emotional. Professional. She said she'd expose me as a fraud. That everyone would learn that I came from a poor, rural community. That she'd make sure I lost my radio show. It's funny how people project things. She is the fraud, not me. I was never ashamed of where I came from. Fiona made up that lie about my roots. She lied about herself, too. To me and everyone else, including her family. She said, "You will be sorry if you leave." And for the first time, I said, "You know what, Fiona? I don't care anymore. Threaten me all you want. As long as I know the truth about myself, there's nothing you can do to hurt me anymore. My lawyer will serve you the papers. I'll be out of here within a week and I never want to see you again after that." It felt so good to have the final word. She's screaming at me through the door as I'm writing this. And I don't care. I've never felt more sure of myself. And I can't wait to see Jane. I have missed her so much over the years. I hope she forgives me, though I wouldn't blame her if she didn't. My life starts now.*

Kadee shivered. She pulled the front of her cardigan sweater tight as she looked at Gibbs. "This is tragic to read. That last line, heartbreaking."

He nodded. "He was a troubled guy."

"But he was finally making changes. Life can be so cruel. Killed right before he was ready to start living." She closed her eyes to concentrate. "This really makes it look like Fiona had motive."

"We checked her alibi again. She definitely was in Miami visiting her brother. We checked the airlines, and they confirmed she was on the plane in both directions. We also called her brother, who said she was there visiting."

"Is there any way she could have done the deed?"

"She couldn't have. The forensic report established the time of death at least twelve hours before she landed in LaGuardia airport. I have this feeling that she did have something to do with it. I just need to figure out who else was involved. The one piece that bothers me is the nature of the kill. It was clearly rage-filled. Very personal. Whoever did this held strong feelings for Jacob Temple. If she didn't do it herself in an out-of-control fury, then whoever she convinced to kill him either felt that fury or wanted us to think they did."

"Or maybe the person who did this isn't even on our radar." Kadee felt a morose excitement in getting caught up in the mystery.

Poole walked toward them, his eyes squinting from his frustration-induced headache. He shook his head. "That woman is so manipulative. From your notes about Piedmont's description and the entries in Jacob Temple's journals, she sounds like a control freak. Maybe even sadistic, but she talks all meek, in a soft voice with large innocent eyes." Poole made big puppy-dog eyes and a childlike frown, imitating Fiona. "She has to be involved in this."

"Kadee and I agree, but she has a rock-solid alibi. And there's no evidence showing any involvement, other than motive. C'mon, you're the one who always wants something solid. There's nothing here."

"I know. I know," he rubbed his bald head. "What about Stringfellow? Did you find anything?"

"Nope. Nothing other than what we already knew from her book. She's had a horrible go of it."

Kadee jumped in. "She has no alibi."

Gibbs looked at Kadee, then at Poole, said: "But that alone is not enough."

"For fuck's sake, Gibbs, I know that. I'm just trying to sift through what we *do* have. She and Fiona Temple were having an affair. Stringfellow could have motive, wanting to get rid of the competition. She stabbed her uncle with a fork. Those forks were a signature of some kind. Could be a coincidence… but what are the chances. Given her relation to Fiona and the victim, it just seems like there's more to it."

"She's still not talking?"

"Nope. She's saying that she had no involvement, she has no idea who would do this to Dr. Temple, and is heartbroken over his murder."

"What about the wife?"

"She refused to say anything more without her attorney. He's on his way. I could just image who her father hired for her. Without any evidence and with a solid alibi, he's probably not going to let her talk, and she'll be outta here an hour later."

Kadee skimmed through some of Jacob Temple's journal entries. "Jacob made reference to 'my therapist,' a number of times, but there was no name for this person. Maybe this person knew something that could help the case."

"Do we know who he or she is?"

"Yeah, I noticed that too," Gibbs responded, "I didn't see a name either."

"So he was in therapy, just like ninety percent of Manhattan." Poole's tone sarcastic.

"Maybe his therapist knows something that could help the case."

"I'll see if his insurance claims can give us a lead."

"Good idea, Kadee. We haven't got much else, unless the two ladies start talking. Or McPherson tells us something when he comes in."

Just as Curt Gibbs completed his sentence, a man's voice bellowed from across the office. His tone bit with antagonism. "I'm looking for John Poole or Curt Gibbs? My office told me that I had to come up here and answer some questions. Where are they?" All three turned around. The belligerent voice belonged to a tall man with a mess of red hair and a face full of freckles.

"I'm Detective Poole. You must be Thomas McPherson."

McPherson walked toward them. His long legs took gigantic steps, which matched his aggressive presence. He grabbed Poole's hand, and shook it with unnecessary vigor. "Yes. Mr. McPherson. What am I doing here? I'm a busy man and, frankly, I don't have time for arbitrary bullshit. This better be important, officer."

"It's detective. Sir. And it *is* important. It's about Jacob Temple's murder."

McPherson looked straight into Poole's eyes, his brow furrowed.

"You do know who Jacob Temple was, don't you?" Poole's voice took an acerbic tone.

"That radio psychologist quack? Sure, I know who he was. Doesn't everyone in Manhattan? It's a disgrace the things we are forced to be exposed to. His synthetic looking grin is on posters all over the city. But what does his murder have to do with me?"

"We have reason to believe that you had a personal vendetta against Dr. Temple. Let's go into a room and discuss this." Poole motioned his hand toward a private office.

"That's utterly preposterous. You have called me up here to waste my time on an absolutely superfluous claim."

"Mr. McPherson, I suggest that you choose your words wisely because I know for a fact that you knew Jacob Temple. Let's go talk about this in private." Poole extended his right arm, directed McPherson toward an interrogation room.

McPherson followed along with Kadee and Gibbs. The four sat down at a rectangular table. Poole opened a file and continued his line of questioning. They had confirmed the charges against McPherson from Miami Beach in 1996. Using that report along with Jane Light's statement, they all thought it possible that McPherson was the Thomas who called the show and threatened Jacob Temple. He had stabbed Jacob in Miami, after all. Of course, that could have been a coincidence, but it was definitely worth pursuing further.

They would get a voice analyst if they needed to. Kadee had listened to McPherson's calls a handful of times. She didn't think McPherson's deep voice matched the caller's tone, which had a croaky sound, almost like he had sandpaper stuck in his throat. However, he could've intentionally disguised the sound of his voice. Jane had done that.

Kadee found McPherson off-putting. He had that awful combination of haughty egotism — his chin slightly raised, looking down on the masses — and flashes of rage. His eyes inflamed whenever Poole nudged at him with probing questions.

He definitely seemed the type that would feel entitled to take matters into his own hands if he needed to. Of course, it didn't mean he killed Jacob Temple.

When Poole asked him about the incident in Miami, McPherson's body stiffened. He sat for a moment, glared at Poole. Then, haunches raised, he practically spit out his response. "That happened twenty years ago when that imbecile interfered in a private matter."

"It says here that you were charged with sexual assault." Poole stared him down. "Doesn't sound very private to me."

"The charges were dropped. I surmise that it does say that in your file. You've called me here to discuss some nonsense that happened twenty years ago? And for the record, Temple threw the first punch. He swooped in like some wannabe hero, trying to rescue a woman who was engaged in an S & M role play with me. It was farcical. A misunderstanding. I never saw the likes of Temple again. Well, that is until I was exposed to his puss-face on the side of the bus."

"Mr. McPherson, do you not take this seriously? Dr. Temple was murdered, and your name has come up as a possible suspect. Maybe you want to take a minute to calm yourself and reconsider your confrontational attitude."

"Take it seriously? Yes, detective. I do take it seriously. You must think I'm some kind of idiot. Temple was killed. Of course that's serious. What I do *not* appreciate is being called away from my busy work day and questioned about a petty dispute that happened twenty years ago. It has nothing to do with his murder."

"I'll be the judge of that. We have reason to believe that you called the show and made a threat toward Dr. Temple on the air."

"That's insane."

Poole leaned forward; hit a key on his tablet. The recording of McPherson threatening Jacob Temple played.

It didn't sound anything like McPherson.

"That's not even me! Clearly it doesn't take a rocket scientist to recognize that that doesn't sound like me *at all*." He stood up. "Unless you have something further, I'm leaving. This is exploitation!"

"Mr. McPherson you do realize that we will uncover the truth. And if you had anything to do with Dr. Temple's murder, which I think you did, and you do not cooperate with our investigation, you will be in more trouble than if you admit the truth now." Poole stood up and met his blazing eyes.

"I have already told you the truth. And I will not speak with you again without my attorney present."

Just as he went to reach for the doorknob, Poole spit out one last question, "Where were you on the night of January 29th?"

The question hung in the air for a moment. McPherson stared at the door. He grabbed the doorknob before he turned around. "I was home with my wife."

"We'll have to confirm that."

"I'm sure you will." He moved into the hallway. "Good day, detectives." His long legs had him back on the street in a handful of strides.

"What an arrogant fucking asshole," Poole sneered at the empty space where McPherson had been standing.

"No doubt. What do you think?" Gibbs closed the file and pushed back his chair.

"Let's check out his alibi. The altercation with Dr. Temple was a long time ago. And the voice does not sound like him at all."

Kadee shook her head. "Oh, it's definitely not him, but I'll have it analyzed anyway if you want."

"I will say, though, that with his combative attitude, I'm surprised he doesn't have a jacket full of assault charges. I still think that it was Mrs. Temple with someone she hired to execute the crime."

"No evidence. I know I keep saying it. But it's the truth."

"Right," Poole stood up, adjusted his pants and sat back down. "Right. She has the strongest motive. And given what we've learned about her character versus her manner during our questioning, I don't believe a word she's saying. I'm just trying to figure out how she did it."

"You're getting tunnel vision, Poole. Sure, she had the strongest motive, but there's nothing else. Let's not get blindsided. We could miss something." Gibbs flipped his notebook open and mulled over an entry. "You know, there is something about her demeanor though…"

"The voice on the show definitely doesn't sound like McPherson. Just check out his alibi to confirm. Kadee, don't bother with the voice analyzation for now. Let's focus on Stringfellow and Mrs. Temple." Poole checked his phone and said, "It's Yvonne. She's outside. I'll be back in a few minutes."

Gibbs threw his pad across the desk. "We're in the middle of an interrogation. Fiona Temple's attorney will be here soon.

You're slacking off during a complicated investigation. It's not like you."

"Just give me a few minutes."

When Poole left, Gibbs looked at Kadee and shook his head. "I've never seen him like this before."

Her mind flashed through an inventory of her conversations with Yvonne about Poole, Noah, and moving on with her life. "Looks like love to me."

Suddenly she felt a rush of warmth, a thin layer of sweat along her palms. She wiped her hands along her pants and took her sweater off. *PMS or too much coffee? Or something else?* She opened her water bottle and took a big gulp.

# CHAPTER 21

Yvonne had just mastered her best "I'm glad to see your face" for Kadee before pulling on the precinct station's door when John Poole walked out. She saw yearning in his eyes, *a lil' ole puppy dog*, as soon as he saw her. *He's wrapped around my itsy-bitsy, teeny-tiny finger*, she thought, smirking. He smiled, kissed her lips, and tucked her small frame under his arm. She played along, nestled comfortably against his body. "How's my handsome fellow today?"

Poole looked at her, pulled her even closer. "You're an oasis in a desert of a day."

"Oh handsome. Do I sense the heart of a poet? You're full of surprises."

She had decided earlier that morning, after looking through all the pictures of Kadee and Alex, that if she couldn't come between them, she would try a different approach in her plan to emotionally trespass on Kadee's life.

She and John walked around the corner to the coffee shop arm-in-arm. She still straddled the fence about killing Kadee. If she was going to do it, she needed time to plot the slaying.

Part of her could not stop seething; she was absorbed in fantasies of rushing into Kadee's apartment and stabbing her over and over, until every ounce of life bled out of her. Yvonne employed her practiced emotional fortitude to wait. It had to be a calculated decision. One engineered with the care of an experienced killer. Act sloppy and risk getting caught? Not Yvonne. That would defeat the purpose. She had every right to do what she was doing, but she was rational enough to understand that the legal system would not see it her way.

She attempted to assuage her mounting rage with an "in the meantime plan." She would be creative, executing different ploys to impinge upon Kadee's life. The tension continued to build. It was painful, but she alleviated some of the pressure by reminding herself that disrupting Kadee's life would be a gratifying activity. She wondered if it wouldn't be more satisfying to have Kadee alive so she could emotionally torture her. *Ha!* A wicked grin formed whenever she thought about that. Maybe she could drive Kadee so mad that she would ultimately kill herself or wind up in a psychiatric ward.

Although that scenario would place Yvonne in less danger than murder, it would be a far less rewarding outcome. Should she kill Kadee, Yvonne wanted to watch her beg and squirm. She wanted to be the one who had the final decision about whether Kadee lived or died; she wanted to watch Kadee's eyes drain of vitality. Yvonne needed Kadee to know that She (capital S) was the one in control of Kadee's flight from this world. Yvonne was the one calling the shots now, and she needed Kadee to die knowing that.

The connection between Kadee and her had been the major obstacle that Yvonne needed to navigate with care. *To die, or not to die? That is the question. Ha! I'm so clever, aren't I? I am!* She hated her. However, she also wanted to be close to her, be more like her, be important to her. *Be* her. It was an untidy braid of contradictory emotions, errant strands sticking out everywhere, chaotic and unruly.

When Kadee acted toward her the way that Yvonne desired, she eased up on her decision to slaughter her. But when Kadee didn't do what Yvonne wanted, like kicking her out of her apartment the night before — *really, how dare she be so insensitive* — then cancelling their lunch at the last minute — *so self-involved* — thoughts of stabbing her violently, recklessly, maniacally, consumed Yvonne. Kadee teetered at the edge of a steep cliff, the slightest misstep could be deadly.

Yvonne's relationship with John Poole offered the perfect opportunity to create disorder in Kadee's work life. She wouldn't kill her… *yet.* Instead, she would try emotional torture first. If disrupting her romantic life turned out to be too difficult to do without being overt, with John Poole as her involuntary partner, she would unbalance the stability of Kadee's career ambitions.

*I am fucking the shit outta him.* She giggled to herself. *It's not like he's not getting something in return for his generosity, for his participation in the destruction of Kadee's emotional world.*

So, she commenced Operation: Kadee part II. She dropped by the station unannounced after Kadee insensitively cancelled their lunch at the last minute. Kadee seemed to think it was Yvonne's purpose in life to sit around and wait for her. Kadee responded based upon Kadee's flighty whims of when *she* wanted to be with Yvonne and when *she* decided to discard Yvonne and her feelings. *No more*, that was *not* acceptable. Clearly, she could have left the station to meet Yvonne if she was important to Kadee. John rushed out as soon as she showed up proving her theory that if he could leave, so could Kadee.

It was a subtle beginning to her plan, but she was just getting started and needed to remain inconspicuous. She showed up to meet John around the time that Kadee was supposed to meet her for lunch. The subtext — *if she was intellectually sophisticated enough to read between the lil' ole lines* — was that Yvonne could not be brushed aside so easily. More important, Yvonne could show up at her place of employment and intrude whenever her lil' heart desired.

They sat down at the coffee shop. Yvonne decided it was a good idea to tell John that Kadee harbored residual jealously toward her. She wanted to influence the way he saw Kadee and manufacture a reason why she should spend more time with him at the station.

More time with him at work meant more occasions to be near Kadee. More chances to observe her. Control her. Delicately infiltrate her space and life.

Yvonne sipped her tea. "I'm starting to believe that Kadee is afraid I'm going to steal Alex from her. You know, because of Noah wanting to marry me instead of her. It makes me quite sad, actually. I think she's worried that Alex will want me instead of her if he gets to know me better. But… I would never do that to Kadee." She kissed John on the lips. "Besides, you're my fellow now. I don't want anyone else."

He squeezed her body. "I could see how Kadee might feel insecure next to you. My ex-wife, Felicia, was a lot like that. She constantly accused me of being attracted to her friends. And in the end, she was the one having the affair. Just give her a little time. I'm sure once you two spend more time together, she'll realize she's just being silly."

"I don't know. She can be stubborn when she wants to be. She was that way with Noah, never letting go, even when he so clearly wanted nothing to do with her. I know it might sound odd to you, but it means so much to me to have her in my life and to trust me. I can't have her feeling threatened. But honestly, I don't know what to do about it. Perhaps if I spend more time with you at the station, she would see that *you* and I are serious and, consequently, has nothing to worry about." She batted her eyelashes.

He squeezed her again, "I wouldn't worry too much. These sorts of disagreements usually work themselves out."

Yvonne cheeks flushed. Her big toe went up and down inside her boot.

She gazed up at him demurely, "What do you think about me spending more time at the station with you? I really think that may neutralize the situation."

"Oh Yv… you know I can't have you with me while I'm at work. I wouldn't get anything done. I would be too distracted. You two will work it out. She seems to be a level-headed girl. Why not have a summit meeting with her?"

Yvonne's toe hit the top of her boot harder and faster. "I don't know, John. You do love me. Don't you?"

"Of course."

"I really like it when you say it to me." She leaned in and whispered in his ear. "It turns me on when you say it."

"I love you, Yvonne."

"And…"

"And you will always be my number-one lady."

She kissed him. She slipped her tongue inside his mouth and wrapped it around his.

John Poole's phone vibrated. He didn't notice Yvonne's face redden as he pulled away from her to glance at the phone: *FT's attorney is here. Ready to talk. Get back here now.*

"Duty calls."

"Perhaps I'll walk you in."

"C'mon, Yv. I'm in the middle of an interrogation." He smiled. "You know how easily you distract me."

"Oh, yes. I understand. I really do. The Jacob Temple murder? Is there a suspect?"

"We're questioning a few suspects, but we still have no concrete evidence. I was hoping for a confession today, but I doubt it's gonna happen."

"If anyone can get a confession, it's you, handsome fellow. You still think it was his wife?"

"I do. But the woman has an alibi. I think I mentioned that."

"You did."

"She couldn't have stabbed him unless she is capable of being in two places at once. I'm thinking she got someone to do it."

"Oh. A conspiracy? Do tell." She reached for his hands. A ploy to keep him close for a little longer.

"Something like that." He pulled away from her and got up. "I'm not supposed to be discussing aspects of an ongoing investigation. It goes without saying that you shouldn't repeat any of this."

"Of course, handsome. It's our secret. I'll walk back over with you. That way we can spend a lil' more time together." She grabbed and squeezed his hand.

They walked back around the corner, faster than Yvonne would have cared for. When they got to the front door Poole kissed Yvonne. "I'll call you later."

Yvonne felt hot. She wanted to go in with him, but could tell he was anxious to get back inside to work. Her toe hit her boot again. It hurt, but she couldn't stop it.

"OK, yes, talk to you in a while." She gushed over him, giving him doe-eyes as he left her on the steps.

"That did not go as I had planned," Yvonne muttered as she walked home, determination in her long strides. "He should have invited me in. Even if it was just for a brief goodbye. Naturally, I know he's busy at work, but he could have let me inside just for a moment. Especially since I said it was important to me.

I *am* providing vast amounts of sexual gratification after all. Aren't I? *I am.* I have been twisting my legs all around to satisfy that man. My goodness, I even used a douche last week to make sure I smelled fresh for him.

"Well… he did say he loved me. *He did.* So did Noah, though. As a matter of fact, Noah used to say it all the time." Her pupils small, two beads. She took her hat off and picked up her pace.

*Twiddley dee dum dee, I hope he acts accordingly.*

# Chapter 22

**Poole, Gibbs, and** Kadee filed into the interrogation room to meet with Fiona Temple and her attorney, Carl Tunis, a tall man with a tuft of brown hair and long sideburns. Fiftyish. A potbelly tugged at the buttons on his shirt. He stood up, introduced himself, then announced that his client had information to share.

He signaled Fiona. Black lines of mascara hung under her weepy eyes. She shredded the last bit of tissue clutched in her hand and spoke, her voice small, her manner apprehensive. She covered half of her mouth as she mumbled behind her hand. The group strained to hear her.

Poole balled his fists while containing his aggravation. He didn't buy Fiona's bereaved widow act for a moment. Through gritted teeth, "Mrs. Temple. Please take your hand away from your mouth and speak louder so the recorder can pick up your voice."

"Go on, Mrs. Temple. It's OK," Tunis coaxed.

"This is so difficult." She took a new tissue out of her bag, wiped her eyes and began ripping it to pieces. "It is true... everything you said before," she looked up at Poole, then gazed down at a spot on the table as she continued.

"When I met Jacob, I was living with a woman named Stacy. I saw him at the gym one day and liked him immediately," she looked at the ceiling, her nose red. She sniffled. "I was attracted to him, but he wasn't available. He was in a relationship with a woman named Jane. He seemed to really love her. He talked about her all the time."

"Did you ever meet Jane?" Poole asked.

"No, I never did. Honestly, it was a difficult situation for me. I started to fall in love with Jacob, so when he would talk about loving someone else... well... that really hurt me. I didn't tell *him* that, though. And... and... I did do something that I'm very ashamed of." She covered her whole mouth. Her words shivered.

Tunis put his hand on her back, "Take your time."

"I lied to Jacob," she sighed. "I did. It was not the right thing to do, but I was so young then. I told Jacob that Stacy was my girlfriend. I told him that I was gay and involved with Stacy. You see... he seemed to be guarded in the beginning. We really only saw each other at the gym. The few times I asked him to go for a drink or coffee, he declined. I figured it had to do with his girlfriend. So I thought if I told him I was a lesbian, he would feel more comfortable with me. I knew he was attracted to me. And I think it scared him... that is until I told him Stacy was my girlfriend. That's when everything between us changed. We started spending more time together. Became good friends. Slowly, he began to fall in love with me," she paused, wiped her eyes with the tattered remains of the tissue.

Kadee scratched a few words on her pad, angled it toward Poole, and pointed to what she just wrote: *I don't believe her.* He nodded.

Fiona took out another tissue and twisted it as she continued. "I shouldn't have lied to him. Sometimes when I look back, I feel so guilty that I did that. But like I said, I was young and, honestly… a bit selfish. I never thought he would leave his girlfriend for me. He seemed to really love her. Honestly, I just thought we would spend more time together. I didn't really have any expectations. But when it happened, well… um... I was thrilled."

Poole rubbed his hand across the top of his head. It was quite a different description of the events that they got from Jane Light and Oscar Piedmont. "Let me get this straight, ma'am. You were not in a relationship with the woman you lived with, this Stacy. You are saying you lied to Dr. Temple in order to get him to feel more comfortable spending time with you?"

"Correct, detective."

"And that over time, he fell in love with you and left his girlfriend, Jane, to be with you?"

"Correct."

"Did you ever tell him the truth?"

"No."

Poole opened up a file where there were some entries from Jacob's journal. "Ma'am, how do you explain the words of your husband here? He mentions in his journal that he didn't know what happened that first night with you, and that he never meant to cheat on Jane. You threw yourself at him. Didn't you?"

"No, detective. No disrespect. But I would never throw myself at a man."

"Well, in his journal, he wonders why he was so drunk that night," he took a page out with a highlighted part and showed it to Fiona.

*I was so drunk. I know I am a lightweight, but I almost felt drugged. I don't think Fee would drug me, but I just don't know how to explain what happened. I never meant to sleep with another woman while I'm with Jane. I have always prided myself on my integrity. I may have made bad decisions in my life, but I have always tried to treat people with kindness and compassion. Jane is the very last person I would ever want to hurt. The whole night seems really unclear to me.*

"I see. I can explain that. Jacob had this issue with making his father proud. It haunted him his whole life. And I think in many ways he was deeply troubled. He wasn't always open with me. I guess he wrote it all down instead of talking to me. I know he had a really hard time coming to terms with what happened between us. He felt so guilty for betraying Jane. Maybe he needed to lie to himself in the beginning. Like, if I was the one that pursued him, then he didn't violate his own code of honor. As I said, he didn't always talk to me… but that was my impression of his struggle our first few months together."

"I don't believe you. Your story is inconsistent with your husband's journal entries. And unlike *you*, *he* had no reason to lie. But let's come back to that. Tell me about the night when your husband found you naked in bed with Ms. Stringfellow. How did that affair happen?"

Fiona looked at Tunis, who signaled her to continue.

She covered her entire mouth with her hands. Her speech muffled. "It jaahhapaaahed."

"I need you to take your hand away from your mouth so we can hear you. Don't make me ask you again."

"It just… happened," she looked down at her hands, ripped apart another tissue. "Jacob and I were having problems. We weren't happy for a long time. We had discussed divorce, but because he craved daddy's approval, he didn't want one. I still loved him, but we were fighting all the time. Honestly, we were making each other miserable. I would confide in Sally a lot. Some nights I would go upstairs to her place just to stop the yelling between us. Jacob started staying late at work and I started spending more time with Sally. Then one night after a few drinks, it just… happened."

"What just happened?"

She sighed. "We slept together."

"So you were not involved with your roommate, Stacy, but you entered a sexual relationship with Ms. Stringfellow?"

"Correct about Stacy. We were platonic friends, roommates. With Sally, it wasn't… *isn't* a relationship. We had sex a couple of times. I know it's terrible. I was cheating on my husband, but honestly, the marriage had run its course. We were barely able to be in the same room."

"Ma'am, as I mentioned to you earlier, before your attorney came, your husband says in his journal that you threatened him when he told you he was leaving." Poole looked at Tunis, then stared down Fiona. She averted her eyes. "He was killed a week later. From where I'm sitting, that doesn't look good for you."

She blinked, fought off tears. "I understand how that might seem, but I was just emotional. Like I said, I knew it was over, but I did really love him. I just rambled off a bunch of words in the heat of the moment, but I didn't mean any of it."

Poole shoved the page of Jacob's journal in front of Fiona. "Do me a favor. Read this out loud?"

"Detective, is this really necessary?"

Fiona patted Tunis's hand. "It's fine, Carl." Her eyes scanned the page. Her hand covered her mouth as she fought back tears.

Poole cleared his throat, immediately prompting her to move her hand away from her mouth.

Her voice hushed as she read. *"She tried to scare me with all kinds of threats. Physical. Emotional. Professional. She said she'd expose me as a fraud. That everyone would learn that I came from a poor, rural community. That she'd make sure I lost my radio show. It's funny how people project things. She is the fraud, not me. I was never ashamed of where I came from. Fiona made up that lie about my roots. She lied about herself, too. To me and everyone else, including her family. She said, 'You will be sorry if you leave.'"*

She wiped her eyes, strands of black stained her cheeks. "It's so painful to read this. I didn't mean any of that. I was upset. To think I said those things. That he was killed before I could tell him how much he really meant to me." She hid her face in her hands, a flood of tears pouring down her cheeks.

Tunis put his hand on her back again.

Kadee did not want to believe Fiona's story, but her reactions to her husband's journal seemed so heartfelt. Could she be wrong about Fiona? Her emotions seemed genuine, that she really loved her husband. This picture of Fiona sitting in front of her was quite a different portrait of a woman than Kadee had painted in her mind. She remembered Piedmont's statement that Fiona was ruthless and manipulative. Maybe Fiona was a total psychopath. If she wasn't telling the truth, she was really good at controlling the impression she inspired in others. She certainly had Kadee sitting on the precipice of believing her story.

Kadee assumed Poole didn't trust Fiona. Naturally, he would stick with his conviction that the most likely suspect was the partner. She quickly shifted back to the present as Poole continued his interrogation.

"I know you had something to do with your husband's murder. If you confess now, we can help you. I'd advise you to choose your decision wisely. Even if you weren't the one who actually stabbed him, conspiring to commit murder carries a life sentence. You will be rotting in prison for the rest of your life. If you start talking, we can help you. Do you understand?"

Fiona looked at Tunis. Her eyes pleading, dripping.

Tunis patted Fiona's hand to assuage her growing anxiety. "Cut the intimidation tactics, detective. There is absolutely no evidence implicating Mrs. Temple. Stop the bullying if you want this meeting to continue." He looked at Fiona, "Go ahead. Tell them. It's OK."

She shifted her gaze, her eyes sunken, from Tunis to Poole. The tension grew thick in the room as they waited for her to continue.

Kadee leaned forward, sliding to the edge of her chair. The ticking clock counting down to the end of the life that Fiona Temple enjoyed.

Fiona released the breath she'd been holding. She blurted, "It was Sally. Oh, holy Moses… I can't believe this… I'm sorry." She crossed her arms, plopped her face down into them. Her shoulders shook as she sobbed.

"What?" Kadee couldn't contain herself. She did not expect *that*.

Poole looked at Kadee and Gibbs, raised his eyebrows, then returned his attention back at Fiona. "Ma'am, what do you mean it was Sally?"

She blew her nose. "Sally. She killed him," tears poured down her face. "She killed my Jacob."

Poole took out a handerkerchief and wiped the perspiration from his bald head. The closed room was getting hot. They all felt it. "And how do you know this?"

"She told me. The other day. She told me. She said she couldn't take the guilt anymore. She begged me not to say anything… but I just… I just couldn't let Jacob's death not be vindicated. Oh, may God forgive me."

"What did she say, Mrs. Temple? I need to know exactly what she said." Poole raised his voice.

"When she first called me, I was busy with a client, so I didn't pick up. She left me a voice message saying she had something important to tell me."

Poole asked her to play the message.

She took her phone out, put it on speaker. Sally's voice played: "Fee, I need to talk to you. It's really important, really important. Call me as soon as you can, you can."

Poole stuck his neck out, moved his face closer to Fiona's. "That doesn't mean anything. She's your girlfriend. Ms. Stringfellow was just leaving a message for *you: her girlfriend.*" He looked at Kadee and Gibbs. Then to Fiona: "You've gotta have more than that."

"She told me, detective. She admitted it to me later that day when I got home. I called her back. She asked to come down. Said she had something to tell me. She came down a few minutes later. She looked pale as a ghost, and weak like she might fall over. I asked her what was on her mind. That's when she told me."

"I don't believe you!" Poole pointed to Kadee and Gibbs. "And I don't think they believe you, either. But humor us. What did she say? Tell us, to the best of your recollection, her exact words."

"She said, 'I am so sorry, Fee. I didn't mean to do it. I lost control.' She told me that while I was away, Jacob had come up to her apartment a few times, badgering her about catching us together. I guess he wanted Sally to admit that she was in love with me. Which she is. Sally has asked me over and over to marry her, but I don't feel that way about her. It's caused some tension. So when Jacob kept asking her, she became unnerved. She is not a stable woman, detective. It doesn't take much to tip her over, if you know what I mean."

"No, what do you mean?"

"I mean, she gets stressed out very easily. Sometimes even aggressive… like throwing things. One time, she became frustrated with me, she ripped her mattress apart. She looks fragile, but when she's upset, she's very strong."

"What else did she say about the murder?"

"She said that Jacob told her that he wanted the truth. She wouldn't tell him. And he became increasingly forceful. He cornered her against the wall in the den. She said she felt the exact way she felt when her uncle attacked her that last time. The time she stabbed him and ran away. She said she doesn't really remember anything about the knife wounds, that she must have blacked out. The next thing she remembers is coming to, her hands on the forks that were sticking out of Jacob's… oh, God… out of his eyes." Fiona's lips trembled. "God forgive me. I promised her I wouldn't say anything. But I had to… it's the right thing to do."

Tunis said, "That's enough for now. My client needs time alone to mourn."

"This is a murder investigation, Mr. Tunis, and your client has just revealed some compelling information implicating Ms. Stringfellow. Interesting that she takes herself out of the entire equation and blames Stringfellow for the whole thing. But I have another theory. I think *you*," he pointed at Fiona, "conspired to kill your husband. *You* were enraged that he was leaving, that you lost control over a man you had been manipulating for nineteen-years. *You* decided that he must die. But you didn't want to risk getting your own hands dirty, so you convinced Ms. Stringfellow to do it for you. You probably told her some ridiculous lie, like it needed to be done so you two could be together without Jacob in the way. That's what happened, isn't it?"

"No! No! I had nothing to do with Jacob's murder."

Tunis slammed his fist on the table. "Detective, that's enough. There is no evidence that my client had anything to do with this. You're just badgering her now."

"There is evidence that she threatened him, written in the victim's own words."

"And Mrs. Temple explained that she just said those things because she was upset. Certainly, you have had arguments when you have said things in anger that you didn't mean. Those entries mean nothing. Now, Mrs. Temple will cooperate in any way you need her to, but I will not have you bullying her into a confession for something she had nothing to do with. Unless you have something concrete to hold her on, we are leaving. She's been through enough already."

Poole glared at Fiona. "We know you tricked your husband into marrying you. We have journals entries where Dr. Temple writes that you admitted to him that you manipulated him into the marriage. Again, he had no reason to lie. Not nineteen years ago. And not nineteen days ago. But *you* do."

"I already explained that. Jacob needed to lie to himself. It was the way we got together. That he cheated on Jane. He could never quite get past it." She sniffled.

Poole threw his arms up. He knew they couldn't hold Fiona. "I know your lying. We will get to the truth."

"You better. My client expects her husband's death to be vindicated." Tunis took Fiona's arm, ignored Poole's glare. He and Fiona brushed past them and exited the room.

Fiona walked alongside Tunis, her eyes glazed, lips tight. As soon as they stepped outside, her mouth curled up at each corner: a small smile.

# Chapter 23

Despite her confession in the interrogation room, Fiona failed to convince Poole of her innocence. In fact, Poole held strong to the idea that she masterminded her husband's murder. His gut told him that she fabricated her story, implicating Stringfellow to conceal her own involvement. Something about her account of Stringfellow as perpetrator seemed contrived. But they had to pursue the lead regardless. Poole was pissed off that he couldn't slam her in cuffs immediately.

Based on the journal entries, Kadee and Gibbs felt compelled to agree with him. Fiona as the architect of a homicide conspiracy was a viable hypothesis. She definitely had motive. But as her lawyer, Carl Tunis, pointed out, they lacked evidence.

Kadee played devil's advocate to reason out Fiona's statement. What if Fiona told the truth about her and Jacob? What if Jacob had skewed the reality of Fiona's sexuality to Jane to avoid the guilt over his indiscretion? What if he really did fall in love with Fiona while committed to Jane, then lied to himself?

It seemed highly unlikely. Maybe impossible. Then again, *anything* was possible. If nothing else, it did shed reasonable doubt, which would make building a case against her all the more difficult.

After Fiona and Tunis left, Gibbs called Jane Light and asked her to come in the next day. They wanted to pick over Fiona's story with her to see if she had something more to tell them, possibly even poke holes in Fiona's story. They speculated that Jane had held back some information. Perhaps learning of Fiona's statement would push her to disclose anything she may have been hiding.

Fiona's story didn't make sense over the long term. It was clear from Jacob's journal that he always loved Jane. He planned to go back to her. Even if he had fallen in love with Fiona nineteen years ago, as she had alleged, he always held Jane close to his heart. Something didn't add up.

There were large chunks of time where Jacob hadn't written in his journal. Was it possible that he only wrote things down when he was distressed in his marriage? That would make the story his words told only part of his experience. It was hard to interpret bits and pieces of his life, creating an entire narrative over the years, when there were parts missing. Besides, those were his private thoughts. Who knew what his actions were like. So much was left open to conjecture, which meant the diary entries could only be used for speculation.

Even if Fiona lied about her relationship with Jacob, it didn't mean she murdered him. Hypothetically, there was reason to believe Fiona was involved somehow, but a theory wasn't enough to arrest her. Given her alibi, they needed to mount hard evidence against her. Otherwise, she just might get away with it. The thought that she would not be held accountable left Poole fuming.

Gibbs called the district attorney, requested a search warrant for Sally Stringfellow's apartment. Even though they didn't know if Fiona's statement was the truth, they were going to interrogate and investigate Stringfellow. It could have been Fiona and Sally in a conspiracy or perhaps Fiona was telling the truth: Sally was the murderer and acted alone.

Stringfellow didn't have an alibi and she did have motive. The forks, a signature weapon for her, could have been some sort of reenactment of the trauma with her uncle. Maybe a disagreement with Jacob triggered her past ordeal, then she grabbed the forks in a dissociated state because she thought she was protecting herself. The same way she had defended herself against her uncle.

Poole was out for blood; he held steadfast to the conspiracy theory. If Stringfellow killed Jacob in a dissociated state, it likely meant Fiona Temple wasn't involved. It also suggested that it was *not* premeditated. If the trauma reaction could be proven, then Stringfellow had a good chance at an insanity plea. Poole did not like that theory at all, but he knew they had to explore it.

"I still say Fiona is behind this in some way. She's a manipulative, conniving shark who thinks she's smart enough to get away with murder. And what an actress. For fuck's sake, she was able to turn her tears on and off with the control of a faucet."

Gibbs didn't even look up from his paperwork. "No evidence, though, just motive and you know that's not enough."

"What do you say we get Stringfellow to give us some. Maybe she'll spill it when she finds out her girlfriend turned her in for murder."

The questioning of Stringfellow not only turned out ineffective in support of their theories, it was excruciating. Stringfellow sat and listened to Poole relay the details of Fiona's statement. They wouldn't allow Pip in the station, even though she had the paperwork classifying him as a therapy cat. She had a stuffed white cat on her lap. She stroked it, back and forth, back and forth.

Her stare remained vacant, and her voice flat. "I would never kill Jacob, kill Jacob."

Even Poole's usual caustic interrogation style was tempered. Her fragility, obvious.

But her manner, her flatness, her disconnectedness, also suggested that she was someone who could snap in a dissociated rage. Kadee didn't want to believe that that's what happened. Although it did seem a possibility, she felt bad for Sally. *Objective, Kadee, stick to the objective.*

"Ma'am, Mrs. Temple played a message from you where you said you had something important to tell her. What were you referring to?"

"I…I don't remember, don't remember."

"Think about it for a moment. This is very important."

She looked down. She petted her stuffed white cat.

Silence, except the clock ticking away the seconds until this torturous interview ended and she could return to the safety of her apartment, locked securely behind her door chain, two dead bolts, and door wedge.

"Ma'am?"

"I really don't remember, don't remember. I'm sorry. I'm not hiding anything. I just have a bad memory sometimes, sometimes."

"I understand. Then isn't it possible that you forgot that you killed Dr. Temple?"

"No," her eyes giant pockets of terror. "I would never forget something like that. Sometimes I forget small things. Like where my keys are. Stuff like that, like that. Why would Fee say I did this, did this? It doesn't make any sense, any sense." Tears dripped out of sunken eyes.

"Maybe she's covering for herself. Do you think that's possible? If you know anything about Mrs. Temple's involvement in this, it will help you. Do you understand? We are going to search your apartment for evidence of this heinous crime, and as soon as we find something, you will be charged with Jacob Temple's murder. If you know something, anything about Mrs. Temple I highly recommend telling us now. I don't think you did this all by yourself."

"By myself? I didn't do it at all!" She dabbed at the tears. "I feel so confused. I think I'd like that court-appointed attorney now." Sally heaved, the waterworks falling like a torrential storm. "I don't understand. Why would Fee say such a thing, such a thing?" She buried her face in the stuffed cat and sobbed.

Poole kept going. "She made you do this. Didn't she? Now she's putting the whole blame on you. Do yourself a favor and tell the truth."

She looked up. "No, no… please, get that attorney, that attorney. I feel confused. Please stop, please stop." Her mouth agape, her face frozen in horror at the accusations laid before her.

"OK. But we're not finished here. We will get to the truth. I hope after you discuss this with your attorney, you come clean with the whole story. Otherwise, you may be rotting in prison while Mrs. Temple is living the high life."

Stringfellow stared at him with a vacant look, her hands never leaving her stuffed cat. She stroked the fur back and forth, back and forth, soothing her exasperated spirit.

As soon as they left the interrogation room, Poole and Gibbs started bickering. Poole still thought Fiona was behind the murder, enlisting her lover Sally to assist. Gibbs didn't think Stringfellow was capable of premeditated murder.

"She's too disorganized, Poole. I don't think there is any way that woman would have been able to carry out a conspiracy plot, especially alone. I know you don't want to hear this. If she is our killer, then it happened just like Mrs. Temple said. Stringfellow snapped and killed Temple in the heat of the moment."

"But look at Dr. Temple's own words. His wife threatened him. She was abusive toward him throughout the marriage. Hell, the bitch manipulated him from the very beginning, lying about being involved with her roommate, seducing him into bed and…"

"No doubt, Dr. Temple was in an unhappy marriage. But even if she was an awful wife and a terrible person, it still doesn't make her a murderer."

"For fuck's sake," Poole threw his arms up in the air in frustration.

"Maybe Stringfellow isn't involved at all." Kadee looked at the two men for approval. "Maybe Fiona is setting her up as a patsy."

Poole's phone buzzed. He looked at the screen. "It's Yvonne." He went back to his desk to talk with her.

When he came back a few minutes later, his whole demeanor changed. He was calm, docile. "On second thought, you might be right about Mrs. Temple."

"What did she zap you with? Cell phone love potion? Kadee, is there an app for that?" Gibbs nudged Kadee, who couldn't contain her chuckle. "Poole, even though it's easier to agree, it's our disagreements that often get us to the truth. We push each other out of our own way of thinking. I need you to focus while you're here. Save the puppy love for home."

"Shit. It's not about Yvonne, you ass. I gave it more thought, and I think your theory makes sense. Let's get the search warrant. See what we can find out. Kadee, call her an attorney."

Gibbs nodded. It was a high stress day, but he made a mental note to discuss Poole's relationship with Yvonne with him. No doubt, Poole was letting his personal life affect his work. Gibbs felt it was his responsibility, as his partner, to say something.

It was Mrs. Temple's word against Stringfellow's. Public defender Marc Forrestt arrived in the late afternoon. He insisted that Stringfellow be released. He argued that Fiona Temple lied, and without evidence to back up her story, they didn't have enough to make an arrest. Poole tried again to get a confession, but Forrestt continued to profess his client's innocence.

Forrestt was right. They didn't have enough to hold Stringfellow. In fact, they really didn't have anything. Fiona Temple's story was hearsay and from someone who probably had the strongest motive.

Poole rubbed his hand back and forth along his bald head as they watched Sally Stringfellow be guided out of the station by her attorney. They would have to see if any evidence turned up during the search once the warrant was issued. They needed something. It was all just speculation at this point.

Gibbs planned to continue his research into Fiona, Stringfellow and Jacob Temple's backgrounds to see if anything turned up. It was a messy investigation and with Jacob being a celebrity they all knew there was a chance — albeit an unlikely one — the killer could be someone they hadn't considered. Someone off their radar. Maybe a caller on the show or an erotomanic fan.

# Chapter 24

*Oh, no. Jane* hung up the phone and grabbed her head.

Detective Gibbs called. He asked her to come down to the station the next day for more questioning. She had been counting and knitting, occasionally reading Facebook updates and watching the local news looking for information about Jacob's murder. She missed him so much. It was as painful as that last time he came to her apartment. *That night*, that awful night when her life suddenly ended. *That night* when Jacob and she shared their final kiss.

And he walked out of her life.

She touched her mouth. Even with the passage of time, if she concentrated really hard she could still feel his smooth lips against hers. She tasted that butterscotch flavor that he often had from sucking on candy. His lips always felt warm and soft. When he kissed her body, it felt like silk brushing along her skin. Sometimes she would take her fingers, rub them along his mouth, studying every crease on the raised pinkish skin, thinking how lucky they were to have found each other.

She did not want to go to the police station. The memory flashes were coming with more frequency. The truth of what she knew slipped in and out of her consciousness. She did not want to fully comprehend what they meant, so she spent her time absorbed in her own world: counted, knitted, tried not to think about those bad, dark thoughts or images. *Knit and count.*

It was the dream. The dream where Jacob visited her from the otherside. He must have found a way to come to her during sleep, to see her and talk to her. Seeing him triggered her memories of what happened. It was as if he came to show her, to remind her of what she witnessed.

She was there that night. The night Jacob transitioned. Jane knew Fiona was away in Miami. She decided to go over to the brownstone to see if Jacob came out so she could follow him. When she got there, she saw something she shouldn't have. And then she saw other things the day following Jacob's passing. She didn't want to keep seeing those images, bits and pieces of visual information that flashed through her mind that she didn't want to register. She had to block out those pictures. She didn't want to know those things, those bad, bad things. *Knit and count.*

If she knew those terrible things, she might become angry. She did not want to feel mad at anyone. If she admitted to herself what she knew, she feared she might lose control. Jacob had told her to tell the truth, though. She wanted to be loyal to Jacob, so the images were getting harder to push down. *Knit and count.*

She felt her grip on reality slipping. Her mind repeatedly constructed new ways to block out the thoughts. But the truth persisted, creeping in through the cracks of her splintering psyche.

She felt increasingly muddled. *Knit and count.* She tried to lose herself in a very organized and predictable routine. *Knit and count.* She tried to ignore the chill she felt along the inside of her skin. *Knit and count.*

The detective's call fractured her fragile structure. Suddenly, she felt flooded with memories: images of her and Jacob in love, then Fiona stealing Jacob, Fiona kissing Sally. But there was someone else. Another vague impression of colors. For a flash, she had a clear thought. A recollection. She saw herself with her cell phone, taking photos. She watched herself snapping pictures. Her insides felt cold, then hot. The fog rolled back in.

She couldn't recall what happened after she hung up with Detective Gibbs. At first, she didn't know where she was. She wondered if she was dreaming. Then she felt water lapping at her cheek. She found herself in her bathtub with water up to her neck. The warm bath enveloped her. It pulled her down toward oblivion.

Her knitting needles sat at the side of the tub. *How did they get there?* She picked one up and stabbed herself in the leg to make sure she wasn't dreaming. She couldn't tell if she was alive or if she was even real. She felt like she was outside of her own body. She wondered if she had died. She poked herself six times. A sharp sensation: a piercing, a throbbing. She cleared her lungs, rested her head against the tiled wall.

A thread of red swirled up to the surface. A thin line at first. Then it dispersed, turning the entire bath pink. Her mind split in two. She could not go to the police station, but Jacob told her to tell the truth. Two voices argued back and forth.

*"You shouldn't go."*

*"But you have to. The pictures, the pictures."*

It was too much. She shifted her body all around. Water washed over the sides of the tub, spreading the pink death into the hall. She squeezed her hands around her head. "Stop it. Stop it. Stop it. Stop it. Stop it. Stop it."

She took her knitting needle. This time she stabbed herself in her neck. She pierced a vein, blood gushed out, an endless spurt, a violent red stream.

The voices wouldn't go. Their banter continued making Jane feel like her head was a ticking bomb. Her body weakening, her eyes burned. She squeezed them shut and stuck her head under the bath water. At first it hurt; she couldn't breathe. She choked.

She saw Jacob. He reached for her. *"I love you, Jane."*

Her nose and mouth came above the water. She gasped for breath. With a faint wheeze, "Jacob."

*"I love you Jane,"* she heard again.

She went back under. She reached for him. The bathwater, thick and idle. Her strength waning, her life evacuating her body.

Her arm went limp, but she could feel Jacob's fingertips as he reached for her. She opened her eyes. She saw the bathroom ceiling, dark and blurry.

*"I love you, Jane. You were always the one."*

A gurgle. A gasp. Small bubbles of breath above her. Then... Peace.

# Chapter 25

Kadee left the station and walked up to Yvonne's apartment. Her mind shuffled through the details of the day. The question mark of who killed Jacob Temple hung heavy. The theory that Stringfellow was the murderer made everything tidy, a quick close to the case. However, it did not make sense when you took into account Stringfellow's physicality and psyche. She seemed so frail in body and mind. Kadee found it difficult to imagine her perpetrating such a violent killing. Then there were the discrepancies between Jacob's journal and Fiona's story. Of course, Jacob wasn't there to tell his side. All they had were his words on the pages, which may have been his truth at the time he was writing. *But* was it the reality? She remembered her conversation with Yvonne when they discussed that sometimes truth and reality aren't the same.

She thought about Fiona turning Sally in. Fiona said her motivation was to vindicate her husband's murder. That certainly was a realistic incentive. Yet, Kadee wasn't sure she was telling the truth. She jumped to Vanessa. Would Vanessa turn her in under similar circumstances?

She modified the scenario. If she had killed a man Vanessa was married to, would she turn Kadee in? When she thought about it, the situation was too outrageous to even consider. As she flipped it back and forth, she decided: a big *NO*. She could not come up with any viable circumstances where she would ever murder someone Vanessa was involved with.

If Kadee had killed Noah and told Vanessa, would Vanessa have gone to the police? Kadee couldn't be sure, but she surmised that Vanessa would not turn her in. But if Vanessa killed Alex would she tell? *Well, that would never happen. I'm not even going there. Besides the Fiona-Sally-Jacob situation is totally different.*

Sally's unfortunate history suggested she could be violent if her safety was threatened. But Jacob Temple appeared to be a sensitive and compassionate person. History did not paint him as intimidating or a bully. Of course, Sally could have had a flashback and misinterpreted his desperate attempt to know the truth as aggressive.

She shifted to thinking about Jane and Jacob. He clearly loved her. Would he really have left Jane for Fiona without Fiona having manipulated him? That didn't seem likely. Yet, Fiona was convincing when she described her side of the story. *Well, if she's a psychopath, she would be believable.*

Kadee decided that she didn't trust Fiona. But was it her over-empathizing inclination again? She wondered. She didn't like the idea of Sally going to prison, rotting away in a cell, her scrawny frame wilting until she died from starvation. Given everything she had been through, it did not seem like a fair ending to her life. But then again, life didn't balance out much of the time. Things just happen. No logic required.

Kadee stuck her knit glove in her mouth, nibbled at the threads. She hated when circumstances held no reason. It was one of the things that made research appealing. She could find and assign value and meaning to abstractions, create order where there was none.

She turned the corner onto Yvonne's block; her cadence slowed. She had never been to Yvonne's apartment before. It hadn't occurred to her until she walked down her street. This was the place where Yvonne and Noah had spent much of their time. Yvonne's memories stored in the walls, their sexual intimacies shared in her bed, her kitchen where they had meals and conversations. Her stomach tossed. *Maybe I shouldn't go in.*

But why? She edged slowly toward the building. She *was* over Noah. She had accepted what happened and moved on. Or at least she told herself so. But it could bring up residual feelings of rejection, reminding her at her core that Noah planned to marry Yvonne while he used Kadee to gratify his sexual appetite.

She imagined her and Yvonne sipping tea, boxes of items that Noah touched all around them. Even so many months later, she still had trouble integrating the reality that he had been murdered. It was hard to believe the chain of events that unfolded in all of their lives, her, Yvonne, Noah, even Belle Donovan.

She had told Yvonne that she would help her sort through her belongings if she needed it. Maybe some of Noah's belongings, too. *What was I thinking?* "Get over yourself, for Christ's sake," she mumbled. "It might sting for a minute, but you'll be fine." She rang the buzzer. "Just imagine what Yvonne's going through."

"Hello," Yvonne's voice bellowed out of the speaker.

"It's Kadee."

"OK."

The door droned. Kadee walked into the lobby, noticed the high ceilings, and two beige couches as she passed by. The elevator doors stood straight ahead. Once in, she pressed "2." The cart grinded and lurched upward.

When she got out, she noticed how spotless the narrow corridor was. The brown rug didn't have a speck of lint, the walls looked freshly painted, a blah off-white. A few paintings hung along the walls, nothing special. It didn't have much character, yet it was tasteful.

She thought of Noah walking through the hallway to Yvonne's apartment. In that moment, she felt his presence next to her, his long legs took big steps, his arm wrapped around her back as he whispered to her how beautiful she was. She removed her hat, blew her bangs off her forehead, thought: *How many times had he left my place and went over to Yvonne's right afterward?* She puffed her bangs out of her eyes. *Too many.*

*Stop it.*

Kadee shook off the sensation of Noah beside her. She arrived at Yvonne's door just as Yvonne poked her head out and smiled.

"Hi, Kadee. It's lovely to see you. Please come in." she widened the opening, gesturing Kadee inside.

Yvonne's long hair flowed over her shoulders. She looked sexy, clad in a fitted red sweater, tight skinny jeans, high boots with a narrow heel. She appeared less conservative than Kadee was used to. Kadee wondered if Yvonne had always been more risqué in her personal life than how she was in their therapy sessions. Or maybe John Poole was bringing a less conventional side out of her.

Kadee's eyes scanned around the living room and into the kitchen. There was a closed door to the far left: *the bedroom?* Boxes were scattered along the bare walls, a brown leather couch with two matching love seats and a long glass table in the middle. An empty bookcase and desk positioned to the far right. She wiped her palms along her pants. She looked at that closed *bedroom* door, discomfort burned from the inside.

Kadee wanted to leave. A fantasy of bolting out rushed through her mind. Yvonne insisted that they have one glass of wine before they headed out to dinner. She had a box of psychology books that she was getting rid of; she wanted to see if Kadee wanted any of them before she tossed them out.

Kadee conceded. She sat down on the love seat, and accepted the glass of red wine that Yvonne handed her. They tapped glasses. Kadee shifted in her chair, tried to keep her search for a position of comfort discrete.

Yvonne noticed. "It's hard being here. Isn't it?"

"Um, no... um... I guess, a little... yes," She let out a nervous laugh followed by a large drag of wine. "I'm sorry. I know it's hard for you. I don't want to make it any harder."

"No, silly-willy. You're not making it more difficult. It's the memories that live here. I miss him, you know. I really do."

"I know. Of course you do."

"I wonder to myself if he... if he were still here would I have married him knowing about the two of you. Do you know what I mean? I ask myself that all the time."

"Um..." Kadee felt punched in the gut.

"I think I would have, to be honest. I know it sounds weak, but I think I would have. I really do. He was my greatest love. We knew each other for so long."

Yvonne's blue eyes pierced Kadee's heart, two bullets hitting her chest. Kadee dropped her head and rummaged through the box of books. "You loved him. Love can lead us toward forgiveness. That's not weak. It's strong." She flipped through a book, avoided eye contact. Her voice small.

"It's funny. I know all of that, but... I even tell patients these things. Sometimes it's difficult to take your own advice."

"Agreed." Kadee toasted the air and took another sip.

"John told me he loves me. I adore him. I really do. I'm just not sure I can love him yet."

"It takes time."

"Yes, but not for you... you love Alex, don't you? Or perhaps I am making a false assumption based on the fact that you accepted his proposal. *Am I*?" her tone had a slight cut to it.

Kadee moved in her seat. "Thanks, Yvonne, but I have a lot of these books. Maybe donate them to the library instead of throwing them out." She closed the box lid. "I do love Alex. Our situations are different."

"Are they different? Well... I suppose they are. Aren't they?" She placed her hand on her cheek. "It's easier for you because you weren't planning a future with Noah. Instead, you were trying to separate. Noah hadn't promised you anything, but he held my future in his hands. It's all been taken away. Him. The sacredness of our bond. Our life together."

"It's unfair, Yvonne. I'm sorry for what you're going through." She finished off the wine and poured another glass. *I feel like drinking directly from the bottle.* "What I meant was that it's different with Alex and me because we have a history. Don't you remember? I told you this before. Alex was my first love, really. You and John are still getting to know each other. It takes time. It will get better. It has to."

"You think so, Kadee? I suppose. At least easier."

"It will." She polished off the second pour. "Maybe we should get going. I have to get home early to finish up homework for tomorrow night's class."

"Oh… I was hoping to have a second glass too, before heading out."

"Another night? OK? I promised myself I'd be home by 8:00, 8:30 to work. You know grad school. You've got to keep strict discipline. If you fall behind even a little, you're struggling to catch up all semester."

"Right. Yes, of course. I understand. I really do." Yvonne's tone was calm, but her gaze was prickly. "Let me use the rest room and get my things. Give me a couple of minutes."

Kadee could not wait to get out of there. Thank God Yvonne wanted to go out to dinner rather than have Kadee go through Yvonne's belongings with her. Sweat accumulated along the back of her neck. A memory suddenly popped in her head. It was from a therapy session with Yvonne. "Women don't sweat, Kadee. We glow." Kadee rolled her eyes at the memory. She wanted to take her sweater off, but didn't.

She wasn't quite sure why she felt so disquieted, something about being in the space that Yvonne and Noah shared. It was Yvonne's expression too. There were subtle bites in Yvonne's tone. She wasn't certain. There was *something*, though, *something* she couldn't quite put her finger on that made her uneasy. She brushed it off and tried to distract herself.

Kadee fiddled with her cell phone, checked her email. She crossed her legs. Uncrossed. Recrossed. She picked up *The Interpretation of Dreams*, a Freudian classic, from the box of books. She flipped the pages, put it back. The time felt long. She got up and started looking around the apartment.

She heard the muted sound of Yvonne's voice through the closed bedroom (it had to be, she decided) door. "Yvonne?"

Yvonne came out, phone to her ear. "Just give me a moment. It's John. I'll be right with you." She gave a half curtsy, went back in, and shut the door.

*A curtsy. She's so strange sometimes.*

Kadee browsed. She imagined Noah there in that apartment with Yvonne. *Did he touch her the same way he touched me? What were their conversations like?* She had considered these questions before. Most often, they were upsetting, bringing up all of the insecurities of why he chose Yvonne instead of her. This time the inquiries were more intellectual, a detached curiosity, almost like her research inquisitions. They lacked the emotional poignancy they usually had.

*Maybe I'm finally moving past this. For the love of God, I hope so.* She walked into the kitchen.

She opened Yvonne's refrigerator. *OK, now I have hit snoop rank. Maybe I should change my Facebook status to: Curiosity is a euphemism for nosy,* she thought to herself. She quickly scanned the shelves.

Kadee believed that you could garner vital information about a person by looking at the contents of their fridge. In a way, it was a metaphor. The outside: the visage shown to the world. The inside items: the private self. For example, Kadee always had hers stocked up because she was an over-planner, someone who had to be prepared *just in case.* She kept all of her leftovers, just in case, even though half the time she never touched them again.

Of course, the inside of her fridge looked different now that Alex had moved in. He was more of a *live-in-the-moment type,* often picked up items at the grocery store only as needed. When needed. She would catch him in the middle of tossing out her saved half-eaten food. His response: *"You're never gonna eat this Kade."* He'd give a warm, knowing smile and kiss her. He ate super healthy, too. Supplements now occupied the shelves, fuel for his gym sessions.

The freezer revealed another dimension of Alex: chocolate ice cream. Lots of it. He always made sure he had extra. He could eat a whole pint after dinner in less than fifteen minutes. She had decided that one of the best ways to conceal your real self, as shown by the inner world of your refrigerator, was to have someone else move in, mixing all of their eccentricities with yours.

Yvonne's shelves were nearly bare, probably because she was moving, Kadee thought. There was a half loaf of whole-wheat bread, peanut butter, two yogurts, prepared egg salad from the grocery store, a Tweedy Bird mug with red jelly in it and five un-opened bottles of white wine. She opened the freezer: three small apple pies and two bottles of vodka.

She couldn't make a full evaluation of Yvonne's fridge because she had probably cleared it out preparing to move. However, it did appear that Yvonne either drank frequently or was a *just in case you have company and need to offer a drink type*. Or perhaps it meant nothing. She turned around, unsatisfied with the results of her inspection.

*But...* she noticed something.

A small white board, with a list: call bank, dishes and sil-verware, organize paperwork. Finally, underneath in big black letters: KEEP MOVING FORWARD!

Kadee tilted her head when she saw *it* dangling from one of three small hooks at the bottom of the white board: *Noah's key*.

She had always wondered what happened to it. It never turned up during the investigation. She had assumed that Belle Donovan had gotten rid of it. *That can't be his key. For Christ's sake, get a grip.*

*But* it was.

It was on a ring with three other keys. She lifted it up. It was unmistakable. The key had the monogram *B.D.* in curly white letters with the black laminated background. Belle Donovan had those keys customs made. Kadee almost lost her footing. She grabbed the side of the counter. *So she has his key. Big deal.*

Her mind flooded, a ubiquitous dread, a wave of hor-ror, a rewind of Yvonne's book, the voice of Emily Goodyear committing the murder, the detail, the vivid emotionality, the perspicuity. The exchange they shared underneath the oak tree that day in the park:

Kadee: "Sounds like the truth."

Yvonne: "It is."

Their conversation in the diner when Yvonne said she didn't mean that she was actually Emily, that it was a fictional story used to get at her feelings. A form of therapy. Their interactions over the past couple of weeks: Kadee's feeling that something was strange about Yvonne's calm demeanor, almost too contained. Yvonne showing up unannounced at her apartment. The comment she made about Noah in front of Alex.

Blood rushed to her head. Kadee felt sticky with sweat. The floor looked like it was rippling in waves. A flash of heat.

*I have to get out of here.* She wiped her hair from her face, grabbed her coat and hat and…

Stopped.

She needed to act nonchalant. *Is that even fucking possible. You need to get out of here stat!* She coughed. Her throat clogged with phlegm, she swallowed hard. "Yvonne?" She tried to keep her tone steady. *Is my voice shaking?*

Yvonne popped out of the room, "Oh yes, Kadee. My sincerest apologies. John was filling me in on his day. I didn't want to cut him off abruptly."

Kadee could feel her face perspiring.

Yvonne noticed. "Are you OK? You looked flushed." She moved to put her hand on Kadee's forehead. Kadee flinched away.

"Actually, Yvonne, I'm not feeling so well," she backed away from Yvonne.

"Maybe it's just the wine on an empty stomach. You did drink those two glasses pretty quickly. Dinner is just what the doctor ordered."

"I don't know, Yvonne. I think I have a fever. I really need to go home and lie down."

"Oh, yes. Of course. I understand. I can see that you don't look well. Let me take your temperature. Perhaps I can help. I *am* a doctor." She smiled.

"Thank you, Yvonne. But I think I need to lie down. I'm probably just run-down."

"Are you sure? I'd like to help."

"I'm sure. I've got to go. See you later."

"OK, I understand. I really do."

Kadee opened the door, tried to keep her stride from becoming a run until she made it around the corner of the hallway and Yvonne could no longer see her. Then she ran down the stairs and out the door as fast as she could. Her heart racing, her breath catching as the cold hit her throat. *She killed him? Yvonne really killed Noah?*

The question hung there as she leaned over, staving off hyperventilation. She needed to do something about Yvonne. But what?

Yvonne stewed in a cauldron of contempt. She could not believe that Kadee completely and utterly dismissed her. She left Yvonne's apartment abruptly without a care, abandoned their dinner plans without an appropriate discussion. *Did she even give any consideration to what I might want? No, she didn't.*

She seethed. Her nostrils expanded as she walked back and forth in her living room trying to silence the eruption of hate that poured out of her. She could not kill Kadee yet. She needed to sate the rage or she might make a grave error.

She reminded herself that she still had ample opportunity to spend time with Kadee and destroy her life. However, Kadee must behave according to *her* plan. *Her* plan! Not some inconsiderate variation of Kadee's own device. *And why did she leave so quickly? She said she wasn't feeling well? Oh, poor lil' ole Kadee, not feeling well. You felt fine when you got here. I guess you decided that you wanted to go home and made up a feeble lil' ole excuse, selfish and self-serving egomaniac that you are. It's my time to score, Kadee. My time!* She shook her head, ran her fingers through her hair, threw her shoulders back and went into the kitchen. She started packing up the rest of her dishes.

It would be much harder for Kadee to discard her once she moved in across the street. She stood still, a story in her mind. A daydream. Yvonne would go over, stop by whenever it was convenient for *her. That's right, for Me. (Capital M).* No worrying about Kadee's agenda. She imagined herself hanging around with Alex, too. Perhaps if she spent a little more time with him, a trust would build.

*Naturally a trust would build.*

She was a master at earning trust. She had the lead homicide investigator wrapped around her finger. Ha! John totally trusted her. Kadee, pathetic loser, trusted her. Soon Alex and even

Vanessa would trust her. She would use this to her advantage, naturally.

*We must always hone in on the gifts we have. Ooh La La!*

Once she earned Alex's trust she would use it to slowly damage the relationship between him and Kadee. These fantasies calmed her. She pulled the edge of her sweater down and continued packing.

It would be fine. This was a temporary setback. And there was always her ultimate plan, the grand finale: killing Kadee. Her eyes danced. She was the one in control, and at any time she could decide it was time to eliminate Kadee from this world. She would figure out a crafty plan, perhaps use John Poole as an alibi, and do it.

With that thought, she stopped packing. She snatched up a notebook, sat on her couch, and scribbled furiously, her hand racing across the page. She needed to devise her plot. She would create an outline. This way she wouldn't make any mistakes. She would start with her plan to take over Kadee's life, then write down how she would kill her. Naturally, she would wait for the right time to do that.

She wrote. Her letters full and bubbly. What weapon would she use? *A knife, naturally.* She would enjoy watching Kadee beg for her life, the blood draining as Kadee registered that Yvonne was the one who had the final word. Yvonne was the one with all the power in the end. Ha!

She would get a look at Kadee's knives next time she went over to her place. She would kill Kadee using a knife from Kadee's own kitchen. She would leave it inside her, protruding right out of her body. A quietness washed over her. The pen propelled across the page, the plan evolving faster in her mind.

Maybe she would use the outline for another book. She leaned her pen against her lip. Now that would be an interesting twist. Wouldn't it? *It would.* She was in the middle of the draft of her second book. It was mostly about the relationship between Emily and Elle, but she added a lot of fictional details. She thought she just might have this one published.

She wasn't sure how it was going to end yet. Maybe Emily would kill Elle in this book. Perhaps not. She enjoyed writing about stalking so much, she wasn't sure she wanted to kill Elle off. At least not yet.

She continued developing her outline. Well, she was certainly creative enough to end the second with an opening for a third.

Certainly she was. *Ha!*

# Chapter 26

Curt Gibbs' day kicked off with a shit show. Kadee called in sick. Poole was running late and the district attorney denied the search warrant for Stringfellow's apartment due to lack of evidence. There needed to be something more concrete before going through her apartment. A statement made by another potential suspect was hearsay. He had known it was a long shot, but without the warrant the investigation was at a standstill. He rustled through some of the paperwork on the case, looking for something he might have missed.

Jane Light had said she would come around 2:00. Maybe she would disclose new information. He rested his elbows on his desk, fingers on his forehead. He had never seen Poole become so consumed in a relationship. His work was slipping. An occupational hazard of their job was that it often affected personal relationships. He suspected that Poole blamed himself for Felicia's affair, though he had too much pride to admit it.

He guessed that Poole didn't want to make the same mistake with Yvonne Tracy, investing so much time in work that he neglected her needs. However, he planned to have a serious conversation with him, and soon. He couldn't work cases alone all morning while Yvonne was getting Poole up with the sunrise… and again in the shower.

*Was Fiona telling the truth about Stringfellow?* He opened his computer.

Fiona rolled over. Her auburn hair draped over one eye. She gently shimmied away from the man lying a little too close to her for her liking. The cold, blustery weather whipped against the windows of her room in The Plaza Hotel. She rarely ever stayed there, which was how she liked it. "Why don't you put the room in your name, dear," she recalled telling her bedmate. "I don't know the people here, and they don't know me. Let's keep it that way."

She picked up her cell phone: 7:49 a.m. Time to sneak out. Carl Tunis had mentioned that her statement likely would not be enough for a search warrant. Her daddy was calling one of his friends down at the district attorney's office to see if they could do anything to remedy the situation. She called him in tears yesterday, begged him to help her avenge Jacob's death.

Most likely he would be able to get her what she wanted. Her daddy always knew how to finesse people. As a young girl, she studied him intensely. She admired the way people looked up to him, listened to him, his commanding presence. She aspired to be like him.

And she was.

Since neither her daddy nor Tunis had called her yet, she assumed that Sally was still home, not arrested. It was only the beginning of the day. She hoped it would happen that afternoon. She didn't want to have to deal with Sally. At some point she might have to, but not yet. She would go over to her parents' apartment on Park Avenue and wait to see if Sally was charged.

Sally's shrink told Sally that she suffered from dissociative episodes. Fiona thought that she was enough of a mastermind to convince Sally that she killed Jacob in a blacked-out rage. Sally was always fearful about snapping.

Fiona had come up with the whole scheme just one week before. She and Sally had been strolling down Madison Avenue when a man checked out Fiona, ogling her up and down. Sally had noticed and lost control, berating the stranger with the blinding fury of a nuclear explosion. Passersby skirted around them, giving Sally an especially wide berth. Sally occasionally had outbursts like that. When Fiona observed Sally crack, Fiona knew she could use it to her advantage.

Sally feared men. Jacob called it hypervigilance. Jacob was always too soft. Fiona preferred the word paranoid to describe Sally's fear of the opposite sex. Sally did have a comfortable rapport with Jacob, though. He always had a way with people, particularly with the fragile and the wounded. It appealed to Fiona when they first started spending time together at the gym, especially when he was unavailable, and she had the challenge of seducing him.

In the end, *that* turned out to be an easy endeavor. In the earlier stages of their relationship, she even thought that she might have loved him. Once they were married, however, she found him weak. He was so easily controlled. She could make him do just about anything she wanted. It turned her off.

He did look good on paper though, and really, that's all her daddy cared about: What the public thought of you and how to act to manipulate their perception. It was all she ever heard when she was growing up. She became quite an expert at it. She could control exactly what people thought, get them to do what she wanted, and mange the immaculate and uncontaminated image that her daddy expected of her.

Daddy had taught her well. She couldn't have Jacob leave her, especially not to go back to an ex-girlfriend. If they were nobodies, maybe she could have accepted his departure from their marriage. But their breakup would be all over the media. The images of the headline disturbed her: *Radio psychologist Jacob Temple leaves wife for former lover.*

She tried to get Jacob to stay. For the first time, she couldn't convince him to do what she wanted. He was so steadfast, so determined; it was actually a turn on. She had to masturbate after the conversation when he stood his ground about the divorce.

She also knew right then that she had to have him killed.

That's what her daddy would have done in her circumstances. It was all so hush-hush, but she knew that her daddy had had someone killed back when she was in high-school: Tabatha, one of his business partners.

Fiona knew that her daddy was having an affair with Tabatha. Fiona speculated that Tabatha threatened to go public if her daddy didn't leave her mother to be with her. So he paid someone to kill her.

She listened in on a few phone conversations where there was talk about money exchanging hands for a *service*, and other comments about *when the business is taken care of.*

Of course, back then, getting away with murder was a little easier, but her daddy made it appear effortless. When the police came to question him, Fiona listened from the top of the stairway. The detectives asked her daddy about the affair. He denied it. Fiona knew he wasn't telling the truth because she had heard him on the phone with Tabatha, making plans to meet at The Plaza Hotel a dozen times. Her daddy had an alibi, which checked out. That was that. The police never bothered him again, and they never caught who did it.

Fiona knew who, though. She was a precocious teenager and an excellent eavesdropper. From listening in on some of those telephone conversations, she surmised that it was her daddy's childhood friend Earl McPherson. They didn't see Earl and his family that often. Occasionally, they would meet for dinners. He had one son: Tommy. He was Fiona's age.

It was the summer before they both went off to college when Fiona lost her virginity to Tommy. It was no grand love affair, but she enjoyed the experience. She had initiated a date with him, wanting to know him: the son of the man who her father trusted to kill for him.

Tommy served another purpose. At the time Fiona felt more of an attraction toward women. Her daddy would never accept that. She suspected that he would disown her if he found out about Margie, a girl she had been dating her senior year.

So she feigned an attraction to Tommy. He was good-looking enough, but she preferred Margie. Nevertheless, she continued to have sex with Tommy throughout the summer as she heard her father's words echo in her head: "Let the public see what you want them to see."

One night while they lay in Tommy's bed, Fiona told him that she knew that his father had killed someone. Tommy became defensive. Whenever he felt backed into a corner, he used big words to try to sound smarter than he was. He was insecure, which made him easy to influence. Besides, Fiona was an English wiz. Tommy was going to need more than a few eloquent vocabulary words to intimidate her. She wanted him to know that she held secret information about his family, just in case she ever needed a *favor*. That's what her daddy had called them: *favors*.

Over the years, she would meet with Tommy, who now used his formal name, Thomas. She continued to have sex with him. It only happened a couple of times a year, but she thought it was a good connection to keep going in case she needed a *favor*. As it turned out, she did.

Fiona slid out of bed. Thomas pulled her back. "Are we done so soon?"

She kissed him and sat up. The sheet covered her otherwise naked body. "I've got to go. We can't risk being seen together. We're almost in the clear. I don't want to take any chances."

"So you think Sally takes the fall?"

"I'm sticking to my story. Either way, it will affect the direction of the investigation. They'll never figure out the truth. We both have alibis. Worst case scenario is that no one gets charged and the case goes cold. Just like what happened with your daddy."

His face crinkled. "I dislike when you bring that up."

"I know." She flashed him her breasts, then began dressing.

"The rest of the money? Next week?"

She tucked her waves of red under a bob length black wig. "We should wait. I know, I know. I had said half right after and the rest in ten days. But three hundred grand is a lot of money. I think we should wait, just in case the detectives start probing my and Jacob's bank accounts."

"There're not going to do that."

"Probably not. But are you really willing to take that chance? They have already accused me of a conspiracy. We need to be really careful right now. Besides, the three hundred grand I already gave you should keep you busy for awhile." She pulled her coat on, leaned over and kissed him. "I want to find out what's going on with the warrant."

"I'll call you from the disposable cell in a few days."

"OK. Remember, think about your every move. Do not be careless." She pressed the sides of the wig down, and walked out.

Thomas grunted. He looked over the side of the bed at his duffel bag. He pulled the bank check out and rubbed the corner, smiling. He folded his pillow in half. *I got you this time, Fiona Peoria. You might have great tits and an award-worthy ass, but I've got the superior I.Q.* He reached his freckle-covered arm across the bed to feel the edge of that check again. *Cha-cha-ching.* He pulled the comforter over his back, rolled onto his side, and went back to sleep.

Gibbs looked for information, anything that might give them a lead. Although the conspiracy idea made sense theoretically, he didn't think Stringfellow was capable of premeditated murder. His search resulted in nothing new or relevant. Aside from the Web links to the radio show and her real estate business, Gibbs only uncovered a handful of items about Jacob and Fiona Temple, including several fund-raiser events they attended with accompanying photos. Nothing significant. The links relating to Stringfellow and Light's books turned up nothing he didn't already know.

He read through comments under one of the show's links. His tendency to pursue multiple leads, his non-systematic method of getting to the truth, had him considering other suspects. It was probably Stringfellow alone. Mrs. Temple in a conspiracy scheme with someone else. Perhaps Jane Light. He didn't think so, but she had no alibi. He wasn't even sure what he was looking for, a deranged fan perhaps.

Poole came in just as Gibbs' phone rang. It was district attorney Melanie Pierce. She let Gibbs know that a search warrant for Stringfellow's apartment had been granted. Gibbs questioned why the decision was changed. It was initially denied due to a lack of substantial evidence. Pierce kept her response short and encrypted. "I got you what you asked for. Don't question it *detective*."

Gibbs had been at the job long enough to realize that it was code for "Randal Peoria. No more questions allowed."

He told Poole about the warrant, a knowing glance exchanged.

Gibbs grabbed his coat. They would pick up the paperwork and head over to Stringfellow's.

"Kadee not in today?" Poole asked.

"She's sick, a flu or something."

"Right." Poole adjusted his pants. "Yvonne had mentioned that she wasn't feeling well last night. Let's go then."

Gibbs wanted to talk to Poole about his relationship interfering with his work, but he decided to wait until after their search. He wanted them to concentrate on the investigation.

Stringfellow opened the door holding Pip. She looked over the paperwork. A thin frown quivered. She let them in. Gibbs and Poole spent the morning into early afternoon searching through the apartment. A couple of crime scene experts worked alongside them looking for evidence. Nothing.

Stringfellow sat on her couch the whole time, petting her cat. Her eyebrows raised, gaze stationary, a fixed expression of confusion and horror. Poole tried to get her talking a few times, but she refused to speak without her attorney present.

They walked out discouraged.

Poole's phone rang just as they got into the car. He glanced at the screen. "It's Sheehan." He swiped the screen to accept the call. Put it on speaker. "What's up?"

Detective Sheehan's voice filled the car. "There's a Vivian Hill here asking to speak with the detectives handling the Jacob Temple case. She's real upset."

"We're on our way." Poole turned off the phone. "Who the fuck is Vivian Hill?"

Gibbs sneered at Poole. "If you didn't have your head up Yvonne's ass half the day, you might know that she's Jane Light's sister. The name's in her statement as the one who prodded her to come to us. Remember? She's also listed as next-of-kin. And she's mentioned numerous times on Light's web–"

"OK. Point made." Poole smirked at Gibbs. "Fucker."

# CHAPTER 27

Poole and Gibbs hurried back to the station debating what Jane Light's sister would have to add to Jacob Temple's murder investigation. When they entered, bringing the cold in with them, they saw a woman pacing by their desks, wearing a path in the floor. As they approached her, she looked at them and pulled off her wide-framed sunglasses. "Are you Detectives Poole or Gibbs?"

Poole gave her a once-over. "Poole. And you're–?"

"Vivian Hill." Her eyes bloodshot, her face creased. "I'm Jan–, I'm Jan–" she took a breath. "I'm Jane Light's sister." Her voice, nasal and hoarse.

"Let's go into a private space to talk," Poole gestured her toward one of the consult rooms.

"I can't stay long. I... um... I don't even know how to say this, so I'm just gonna say it. My sister..." her eyes welled up. "My sister, Jane... she died last night. Killed herself. At least that's what the doctors say happened. I found her this mornin...I

called 911, but it was too late. She stabbed herself in the neck...
um... she um... bled out while drowning in her bathtub." She
put her hand over her heart, a few tears dripped down her cheeks.

Poole and Gibbs looked at each other.

"Oh, I'm sorry to hear this, Ms. Hill. Your sister's all the way
downtown, right?" Poole asked.

"Yes. The police were already there. They said... they said
it was suicide. There's nothing suggesting anything else. This is
beyond hard detectives." She sniffled. "I have to get back downtown. My sister's body is with the medical examiner... but she
left this for you." She pulled a manila envelope out of her bag and
handed it to Poole.

"There was a note?"

"No. Not really. Just what this says." She pointed to ink
words written on the envelope.

*For: Detectives Poole and Gibbs*
*From: Jane Light*

"That's why I don't know if she really killed herself. I mean, Jane
was a writer. Why wouldn't she leave a note, somethin' to explain
to me and my family about what happened? Why she did it? Or
to say goodbye." She sucked in air. "I dunno... I keep thinkin'
it was an accident, like she didn't mean to do it or that someone
killed her. But I'm not an idiot. The detectives downtown are
sayin they can tell it was a suicide. I can't tell myself something
that isn't true just to make myself feel better. I just came to give
this to you. They're pictures. I thought they looked important."

"Thank you for bringing these and I'm very sorry."  Poole said.

Gibbs put his hand on her shoulder. "I'm truly sorry, Ms. Hill."

Her eyes glassy, she gave a half smile. "I hope you find out who killed Jacob. I know that would be... um... I know that would be Jane's wish. I hope her pictures help. Will you let me know?"

"Yes, of course." Poole responded

She produced her card. "Thank you." She put her sunglasses on and hurried out.

# CHAPTER 28

Kadee worked up the fortitude to attend her morning statistics class. After that, she didn't have the emotional stamina to go to the station. She had tossed and turned the night before, reviewing in her mind all the facts she had on Yvonne and her professional opinion on Yvonne's behavior. Despite that she was convinced the truth didn't match the submissible evidence, deep down she knew: Yvonne killed Noah.

She attempted to creatively argue herself out of it. It was a frightening reality, but try as she might, the combination of the book, the conversation in the park, Yvonne's comment that *it is* the truth, her odd behavior and Noah's custom-made key made the reality impossible to deny.

She paced around her apartment, the thoughts that kept her awake once again replaying in her head. The culmination of these unofficial facts put her in an awful predicament. She felt naïve. *How could you be so stupid?* She prided herself on her intuition. She couldn't understand how she let herself deny the reality of Noah's death.

Yvonne wrote the book with such detail of the murder scene. She had said "it is" the truth. *She fucking said it. She pretty much confessed. Did I need to be spoon-fed the information in order to register it?* She felt like a failure having let herself miss something so obvious.

Yvonne was clever asking Kadee to return the book. She *was* clever. She had nothing to show the detectives. Nada. Not a thing! Only her word. With Poole head-over-heels in love with Yvonne and no evidence, he was never going to believe her. He wouldn't even consider it. Ever. This placed her in a jam, stuck in a jar of thick marmalade with no way out.

Then there was the narrative. *Jesus Christ, that narrative.* She paced. She couldn't remember the details, just a vague summary of Emily's (Yvonne's) anger toward Elle (Kadee). It didn't say anything directly about revenge or a retribution plot — *I would have recalled that* — but there were plenty of descriptions about Emily's envy and her resentment toward Elle. Kadee did remember reading that.

Of course, Yvonne took the book back, so Kadee couldn't re-read it with a fine-tooth comb. She needed to extrapolate from the content what Yvonne's real feelings were toward her. She pulled her hair back, continued her pacing.

She checked the locks on her door numerous times. It almost felt compulsive. Pace, check the locks, pace, check the locks. She knew she was overreacting. Yvonne wasn't going to come after her physically. Rather, she seemed to be purposefully emotionally intruding on her life. Noah's murder was likely a direct reaction to his betrayal after her loving him for all those years. And though Kadee also had lied to Yvonne, Yvonne didn't have the same level of emotional investment in their relationship. She wouldn't feel strong enough rage to drive her to kill Kadee. She checked her locks on her door again. She also checked the front window lock. Part of her couldn't be certain about Yvonne.

She wouldn't be able to avoid Yvonne. She was dating Poole. Dating Poole! *Ugh!* She popped up at the station all the time. Kadee checked the locks again, plopped on her chair and rocked back and forth. What was she going to do? Yvonne was moving across the street. "This is not good, Kadee." She gnawed on a cuticle.

*Normal people would go to the police.* But she couldn't do that. Yvonne was dating the lead investigator. Besides, she couldn't be 100% sure Yvonne did it. She didn't want to go around making false accusations. There really was no evidence. Just the book. A fictional account. Who knows where Yvonne had it anyway? She may have destroyed it. The key was something, but Yvonne could just say she took it sometime before the murder. Kadee had nothing. She pulled her sweater closed, rocked back and forth. Deep down she knew the truth: *Yvonne killed Noah.*

Kadee would have to go back to the station at some point. She could be sick for a couple of days, but eventually she would have to face the reality of what was happening. That included seeing Yvonne and finding a way to interact with her without breaking out into a frenzy of fear, without becoming totally petrified. She needed to act normal while she decided what to do about the whole calamity.

She tried to convince herself that it would all work out, not to worry too much. She reminded herself that she only allowed herself a certain amount of rumination time per week. Although this time, she didn't think she was being neurotic. This time her worries were justified. *This is about a murder, for Christ's sake.*

Her phone dinged. A voicemail. She looked at the screen. It was Yvonne. *Of course, it was,* her inner voice tart. Her hands shook as she gripped the phone. *She's probably not going to go away. Probably? She is NEVER going to go away. What does she really want from me?* Her body rattled. She listened to the message.

"Hi Kadee, it's Yvonne calling. I just wanted to see how you were feeling. John said you didn't come into work today. You must be quite unwell. Please let me know if there is anything I can do. I could stop by with some food. Chicken soup always makes me feel better. Anyhoo, let me know, and I do hope you're getting rest. Call me. OK. Bye-bye." Yvonne's voice sounded full of concern. *But is it an act?*

Her chest felt tight. She thought to call Alex, but what would she say? That she knew Yvonne killed Noah? She had never even mentioned the content of Yvonne's book. She was too afraid to admit to herself the feelings that Yvonne's narrative triggered. Her own need to deny Yvonne's potential murderessness led her to keep the storyline of the book to herself.

She didn't know if she should just play along with Yvonne or if she should totally distance herself from the relationship. She definitely wasn't going to spend too much time with her. However, she had to give the semblance of friendliness or Yvonne would know that she had figured out the truth. The deadly, felonious, wicked truth.

Maybe Kadee should confront her. Yvonne could even be feeling guilty. Perhaps she would be relieved by the conversation.

But Emily Goodyear did not describe *any* remorse. None. Not one iota.

She sent a short Facebook message. The last thing she needed was Yvonne coming by with a container of chicken soup trying to nurture her back to health dressed in her Dr. Jekyll uniform.

> *Hi Yvonne,*
>
> *Thank you for your message. I have a flu. I'm resting today. Hopefully I will bounce back in a day or two. I appreciate your offer to stop by, but I just want to sleep. Besides, Alex is taking good care of me.*
>
> *Cheers,*
> *Kadee*

She needed to chill out. She had time to figure out the best way to handle this quagmire. Yvonne had been walking around, a facade of sanity concealing her murderessness since September 19th. She would distance herself from Yvonne — just enough so as not to rouse suspicion — and take time to formulate the best option.

Another thought came to mind, perhaps the most disturbing: Jane Light's strange reaction toward Yvonne. The memory played in her mind. Did Jane know Yvonne? And if so, why had she lied and said she didn't? Her synapses fired. Links made, concluding with a leap to Jacob Temple: *Did Yvonne know Jacob? Could she have killed him?*

*No! You're being ridiculous. That doesn't even make sense.* Yvonne killed Noah because of his not treating her as his favorite, his deception, and the depth of her love and attachment to him. Surely if she was romantically involved with Jacob Temple, it would have been discovered in his journals or some other way already. *No! Not fucking possible!*

She checked her locks again: *OK, now you are really overreacting.* She decided to make a casserole for dinner to keep herself distracted from her ruminations. *Kadee, love, sometimes you really are your own worst enemy.* It would all workout. She just needed to stay calm.

# Chapter 29

Vivian Hill left the detectives flabbergasted by the bombshell she dropped on them concerning her sister, Jane Light. Gibbs made a quick call to the precinct near her apartment to confirm that they were considering her death a suicide. The medical examiner would still have to confirm it. But based on the scene at her apartment, lack of break-in, the angle of the injuries and the blood stain patterns, they felt confident with their preliminary findings.

Poole shuffled through the photos. He absentmindedly rubbed his bare scalp as he focused on the images. While Gibbs exchanged information on the phone with the downtown precinct, the receiver cradled in the crook of his neck, Poole dropped a few of the pictures in front of him.

Gibbs examined the photos, his brow furrowed. He picked one up, turned toward Poole, his eyes wide. He put his forefinger up to him: *one minute.* Gibbs spoke into the phone. "She's with the M.E. now? Right. I see..."

Poole grabbed the memory stick that accompanied the photos that Jane Light had slipped into the envelope that she left for the detectives. Her last heroic act before she checked out. Poole popped the stick in the computer and opened the files. As he leaned forward, a pleased expression spread across his face. The computer images were the same as the printed pictures, and they were time stamped.

Gibbs hung up the call and wheeled his chair to Poole's desk. They looked at the enlarged images their mouths' agape. The first few showed Fiona Temple — her hair, short and black — side-by-side with Thomas McPherson walking into The Plaza Hotel on January 30th at 7:03 p.m., the same day she found Jacob's body. Then there were three of Fiona alone. Her auburn hair flowing down her back as she walked out of Bank of America at 4:32 p.m. on the 30th. Just hours after Poole, Gibbs and Kadee questioned her.

There were eleven photos all snapped in succession between 10:20 and 10:21 p.m. on the night of January 29th.

The night of the murder.

The photos showed Thomas McPherson leaving the Temples' brownstone. His red hair peeked out from underneath a black knit hat. Instantly identifiable.

"I knew it," Poole blurted out. His thick finger pointed to one of Fiona Temple and McPherson in front of The Plaza.

Gibbs absorbed the photographic data, piecing together what it meant. "Holy shit, man… I'm wondering how Jane Light got these shots. She must have been following them. But why? And she must've known about Mrs. Temple and McPherson when we questioned her."

"She's not here to tell us. We'll probably never know. It's a good thing her sister found these and brought them in."

Gibbs contemplated the discussion. He did not like loose ends. "I guess I'm wondering if she was involved somehow. Maybe the guilt got to her, and she killed herself. Then turned in the other two."

"What was her motive to kill him?"

"I dunno. Something just doesn't fit. She was calling Dr. Temple's show. She was clearly very attached to him. Probably obsessed. She said she came in to help us, but then didn't tell us that she witnessed McPherson leaving the scene? Just doesn't make sense."

"Right. But Piedmont's statement and Dr. Temple's journals both suggest that Dr. Temple was going back to her. Why would she want him dead?" Poole crossed his arms.

"It's unlikely she knew that. She wouldn't wait — pine — for a man for nearly twenty years, then kill him when she learns he's coming back to her."

"True. And now, thanks to her, we've got proof of McPherson leaving the crime scene on the evening of the murder, and him and Mrs. Temple together, going into a hotel the next evening. They were working together. We'll have them down for more questioning. Call the bank and ask for information about her transactions on the 30th. Look through their phone records. If she withdrew a large sum of money, we've got her. She'll probably turn him in. She's the type that will use anyone she can to get away with this. Hell, she threw her neighbor-slash-lover under the bus yesterday. She'll turn on him in a heartbeat. There ain't a doubt in my mind."

Gibbs rolled back to his desk. "Yep, true. Seems likely that they conspired the murder and McPherson was the executor.

And here we didn't even know they knew each other. Jane Light told us who McPherson was and about the Miami Beach altercation. I'm just trying to figure out what the truth is."

"Mrs. Temple wanted her husband dead. That's what the truth is. The motive? He was gonna leave her. The woman threatened him. We have it in the victim's own words. She hired McPherson to do it. We'll find out how they know each other when we question them. They won't be able to deny that part. Pictures don't lie." Poole took the photos back from Gibbs. "They are so screwed."

"We should question Mrs. Temple first. Now. It's already after three. If we call her and McPherson to ask them to come in tomorrow, it will give them a chance to talk. They could come up with a story."

"Right. But she's not going to talk without Carl Tunis there. Besides, they can't corroborate a story if they don't know what we have on them. There's no way they know about these pictures. And there's no way they're going to be able to make up a story to cover their asses with this kind of evidence."

"They could if Jane Light was involved and they know of her death."

"Don't matter. We've got time-stamped pictures."

Gibbs nodded. "Tell them they have to come in tomorrow. I'll get a warrant for Mrs. Temple's bank records. Hopefully, I'll be able to do that before her father gets wind of it. The more we have the better."

"Peoria can't mess with the investigation with this kind of physical evidence. Pierce'll issue the warrant."

Gibbs raised his eyebrows.

"Call now. Not even Randal Peoria can interfere with the investigation with time-stamped pictures."

Poole looked at the photos again, shook his head. "I knew it was her."

"We can't be sure of that… yet."

"*I'm* sure. Tomorrow will be interesting."

"Agreed."

# Chapter 30

Kadee arrived at the station a little after 9:00 in the morning to learn that Jane Light had committed suicide and that there were pictures connecting Fiona Temple and McPherson, which suggested a conspiracy. She was speechless. One day out and she had missed all the action.

For the average person, it was just *a* day. But in the Jacob Temple investigation circle, the previous twenty-four hours had been jam-packed. Jane had taken her own life and left an envelope of photographs behind. The said photos served as evidence not only implicating Thomas McPherson as the murderer, but Temple's own wife, Fiona, for at least solicitation to commit murder and possibly even as an accomplice to the act. There was likely a long history between McPherson and Fiona Temple. And Sally Stringfellow may have skirted all charges. In addition, Kadee was hauling around a huge secret, an oversized piece of emotional baggage: *Yvonne killed Noah.*

Yvonne hadn't responded to Kadee's Facebook message from the day before. She had no idea what Yvonne was thinking, but she knew it was only a matter of time, probably only a few hours, before she had to deal with her again. She kept telling herself to stay calm — *cool like a cucumber* — her new mantra. She thought her mother would approve. She just needed a little time to process what she knew and figure out how best to handle it.

She couldn't refrain from looking at Poole. *If he only knew.* And what was her responsibility in this matter? If anything happened to him, she would never forgive herself. Her hope was that he would not betray Yvonne, that he would treat her as his *favorite*. She reassured herself that he was attentive toward Yvonne. He did treat her as important, even at the risk of it affecting his work. Besides, she knew Yvonne didn't feel as strongly toward Poole as she did toward Noah. The love wasn't intense enough to turn into hate. In an ironic sort of way, the fact that Yvonne didn't feel as passionate for Poole most likely would keep him safe.

She sipped her coffee while looking over the photos. Thomas McPherson leaving the scene at the time of the murder. Fiona Temple in a black wig. She had read case studies where there were circumstances like this. But to witness it unfold right in front of her, the connections between potential suspects, the malevolence, a planned murder, to purposefully take a life for monetary gain or whatever else, it was evil.

They would need more than the photos to have McPherson charged with pre-meditated murder, but the truth seemed undeniable. McPherson was already in an interrogation room with his attorney, MaryAnn Smithers.

Poole salivated. He couldn't wait to get in there to interrogate McPherson. Poole and Kadee waited for Gibbs to return from the bank. The warrant had been granted, so he was retrieving Fiona Temple's financial transactions from the past year. The more evidence they had for the interview the better.

Kadee thought about Jane. Had she died without knowing that Jacob Temple always loved her, that he had planned on going back to her? She rested her chin on her steepled arms. Her stomach churned from the gut-wrenching story. She had thought of telling Jane the truth: Jacob never stopped loving her. She would never have that chance now.

Jane and Jacob's missed chance at love reminded Kadee of her and Alex's upcoming wedding. The thought exacerbated the churning in her stomach. They still hadn't decided if they were going to have a destination wedding or elope. They leaned toward eloping, but wavered. They lingered over the decision like they had all the time in the world. Time, the luxury of youth. *The things we take for granted. Didn't you learn anything from your jail stay? We should elope. And soon.*

She wondered if Jacob's murder caused Jane to take her own life. Perhaps it was too much for her to handle? Or maybe she felt she had no reason to live with him gone. That was an awful notion. To think the only reason she wanted to live was for someone else. What a sad, singular existence. Or was it? Kadee was always so insistent on her independence. Maybe she couldn't love as selflessly as Jane loved Jacob, holding on for years even though he was with another woman.

She might have thought Jane was someone who just couldn't let go or create a life for herself. Someone possibly unbalanced or with attachment issues. But knowing that Jacob Temple felt the same about Jane contradicted her initial hypothesis. They had an enduring bond, one that sustained the years and separate, independent lives.

It was a testament to the power of love. A type of love Kadee never believed existed. Maybe she just didn't understand it. Kadee, being a researcher, always looked for order and meaning. She found it hard to accept the mysteries of love. Perhaps that was her main problem with Noah. She got sucked into his craziness because she wanted his behavior to make sense and it didn't. Well… it didn't until after she knew the truth. Until after Yvonne killed him. Her mouth puckered at the thought, like she had just sucked on a sour candy.

Gibbs walked in.

*Thank God, a distraction from that line of self-examination.*

"Got 'em," Gibbs said. He swung paper up in the air.

He laid the paperwork down on the table. On the 30th of January, Fiona Temple got a bank check for three hundred thousand dollars. The money was shown as withdrawn from her account. They had no proof that the money exchanged hands between Fiona and McPherson, but it was a substantial withdrawal and a bank check was suspicious. The only explanation that seemed true: Fiona paid McPherson to kill her husband. They would use the information as leverage to get them both to tell the truth.

"It does seem strange that she would be careless and leave this evidence trail. Don't you think?" Gibbs wiped his brow.

"I think she's the type who thinks she's above getting caught. Perpetrators like her always shoot themselves in the foot. She's over confident. We've seen this before and we'll see it again."

Gibbs nodded. "Suppose so. She just seemed smarter than that, but I guess if we see her as believing she's entitled, than she's probably deluded herself into thinking she is above the law." Poole prompted Kadee with a glance.

"She does appear to match the character type."

Poole nodded. "Man, they always do. She's probably been getting away with shit her whole life. She never learned that she could be held accountable for the consequences of her behavior. We're going to bury that woman. Now let's go get him to talk."

The three entered the interrogation room. McPherson's attorney, MaryAnn Smithers, jumped out of her chair. She stood tall, had a severe haircut, piercing blue eyes and thin lips. She started on the offensive before anyone could say a word. "My client has answered all your questions already. This repeated interrogation is bordering on harassment."

McPherson leaned back and folded his arms, a smug smile settling in.

Poole smirked back. "Mr. McPherson. Where were you at around 10:20 p.m. on the night of the murder?"

McPherson huffed, making a big show of how he was being put out. "At home. With my wife."

Poole dropped the photos in front of McPherson and Smithers. "I thought you might say that. How do you explain these?"

McPherson looked at the time-stamped photos of him leaving the Temples' on the night of the murder. He rustled in his chair, chewed on his lower lip as the smug smile evaporated.

"Mr. McPherson?"

Smithers held up her head. "I need a minute with my client."

McPherson glanced at her, his arrogance tempered. "No. It's OK."

"Thomas." Smithers shot him a fierce look, a "don't say anything" glower.

He looked at Poole, then Gibbs, then Kadee. "I was going to tell you. I was just waiting for a little time to pass. Fiona Peoria is a frightening woman. I didn't want her to know I turned her in."

Kadee leaned forward.

Smithers tried to stop him again.

McPherson's voice slightly raised, his palm up, "MaryAnn, please."

He began his story: "Fiona and I go way back. A childhood kinship. We have maintained some contact over the years and she had confided in me about her matrimonial disharmony. I never knew what she saw in that jock looking…" he paused, straightened his back, "…excuse me…in Jacob Temple. I had that incident in Miami with him and then I heard his show on the radio, but I had no personal affiliation with him. Fiona — she likes to be called Fee, but it sounds infantile — Fiona would fill me in on bits and pieces about their life together. In my opinion, he didn't seem on par with her. She had the money, the brains, the family legacy. He was just going along for the ride. I don't think he ever loved her. He was enamored with the life she provided for him. But not her. Over time it wore her down. When he decided that he was going to leave, I think she just had had it. *So*, she decided that she wanted him killed.

"She phoned me. We met for lunch. She asked me to do it. I agreed… but only so she didn't hire someone else. I said I would do it, but I didn't. I went to Temple's that evening at the time Fiona and I had agreed upon. I was going to tell Jacob Temple about the plan. Let him decide what he wanted to do about it. Give him a chance to protect himself.

"When I got there, I rang the bell a dozen times. No Temple. I went to use the key Fiona had given me when I noticed the door was unlocked. I thought it was strange. But no big deal. I went in. Called Temple's name. Walked around. I found him on the floor of his den. He was dead, stab wounds, loads of blood and forks sticking out of his eyes. I must have come right after it happened."

Frown lines formed on Poole's face. McPherson read the doubt in those deep crevices.

"I didn't kill him. I swear. She must have done it and just used me in case it came to this," he gestured to all of them sitting around the table. "Being questioned. There is no way Fiona would take the fall for something like this. I know she has an alibi, and I'm not sure how she managed to finagle that. But I know her. Fiona *always* gets what Fiona wants."

Poole glared. "Mr. McPherson, you lied about your alibi. You didn't come forward after the murder. We had you down for questioning, and you said you had nothing to do with this. From where I'm sitting, this does not bode well for you."

"I know how this looks, but you have to understand. Dealing with Fiona Peoria — Fiona Temple — means you're dealing with Randal Peoria. That family takes matters into their own hands. I was afraid if I told the truth about her involvement, they might have me disappeared."

"If that's the case, why come forward now?"

"I don't have much choice now, do I?"

"I suppose not. And I don't believe a word you're saying other than the conspiracy between you and Mrs. Temple. If she denies that and we can't prove it, you may be serving a life sentence while she is free. How would you like that for an ending?"

"I have something else." He took out his cell phone, placed it on the table.

Smithers put her hand on McPherson's forearm, "Thomas, don't." She looked hard at Poole, "We need a moment."

McPherson put up his hand to stop her. He looked at the detectives. "In for a penny, in for a pound, right?" He played back the recording.

The group heard Fiona Temple's voice: "Tommy, it's me. Thank you for taking care of the arrangement. You did a fine job. Let's meet at our regular spot this evening. I know you want your money. I will try to get it before we meet tonight. The detectives just left. I need to wait a few hours before I go out. But I should be able to get it before the bank closes. See you tonight."

The message was recorded at 1:40 p.m. on January 30th; right after Poole, Gibbs and Kadee had left the Temples' residence. It was only hours after Fiona called in the murder.

Poole looked at Gibbs and Kadee. *They got them.*

"Mr. McPherson, that message just sealed your fate." Poole counted off on his fingers. "Overwhelming evidence to conspire with Fiona Temple. Going to the Temples' at the arranged time. Accepting the money. All part of a plan to commit murder. Now I highly recommend you confess to committing the murder. We know you did it. If you tell the truth now, it will help you. Do you understand?"

"Please, I was *never* going to kill Temple. Did I like him? Not particularly. But I didn't want him dead. I was just humoring Fiona so she wouldn't get someone else to murder him. He didn't deserve that. You have to understand what I was dealing with. Fiona had a look in her eyes when we met for lunch. When Fiona gets that look, you know she's not going to relent until she gets what she wants. I didn't kill Temple, nor was I ever planning to do so. She did it. She must have. Who knows with her. Maybe she and someone else plotted to pin the murder on me. But I swear it was *not* me." Thomas's shirt had huge sweat marks under the arm pits.

Gibbs ignored his pleas. "Those forks were a nice touch. Making it look like it was Stringfellow in a rage. You thought you had it all figured out. Didn't you?"

"I didn't even know about that woman's past until after I found Temple murdered. Fiona knew about Sally Stringfellow's past. Maybe she got Stringfellow to do it. Do not put anything past that woman. She's Charles Manson in a skirt," he screeched. "That's it. Maybe the two of them planned this. Fiona got Stringfellow to do it, and they set me up to take the fall."

A nod exchanged between Poole and Gibbs. Gibbs: "Convenient explanation, Mr. McPherson. I'd almost believe it except for those pictures, which point only to you."

McPherson became flustered. "You have no idea what that woman is capable of. No idea."

The detectives and Kadee spent the next hour trying to get McPherson to confess to the murder, but he continued to profess his innocence. None of them believed him. They thought he was just covering his own ass, and turning on Fiona to serve his own best interests. But Fiona had an alibi, confirmed both with the airline and her brother; she couldn't have done the kill. It had to have been McPherson.

The nature of the kill was rage-filled: the numerous stab wounds, and the forks in the victim's eyes, in particular. If Fiona didn't have that rock solid alibi they would have considered her as the perpetrator rather than the solicitor. They decided that McPherson must have lost control, having carried resentment for Jacob Temple since the assault on Miami Beach. He stuck the forks in Jacob Temple's eyes to try and frame Stringfellow.

Fiona Temple and Carl Tunis arrived. They were going to see what she had to add to his story. Maybe something more concrete connecting him to committing the actual murder. Either way, Poole could not wait to arrest her for conspiracy.

Gibbs called the district attorney and was given the green light. A warrant was being issued to charge McPherson with conspiracy to commit murder and second degree premeditated murder and another for Fiona Temple for conspiracy to commit murder and aiding and abetting. They would need more evidence to uphold the murder charges at arraignment, but there was enough for an arrest.

Poole slammed the evidence down on the table: the pictures, the bank statement, and the disposable cell phone message that

McPherson provided. "We know you conspired to kill your husband. What we want to know is… are you the one who stabbed him, too? Mr. McPherson seems to think you did."

Tunis slid his chair back and covered his mouth, stupefied, by the bombshell of Fiona's involvement. Fiona burst out in tears; water poured out of the creases of her eyes. She looked at Tunis.

Tunis asked for moment alone with Fiona.

Poole flung his arms up in the air. "I don't know what there is to discuss. It seems clear what happened from this evidence. Your client is being charged with conspiracy and aiding and abetting. The only chance she has now is to tell us the truth about the execution of the murder." He gave Fiona a vicious look: *I am going to eat you alive. I don't care who your father is.*

"I need to speak with my client." Tunis stood up.

Fiona ignored Tunis. Her voice strong: "Thomas did it. Not me. He killed Jacob. That's the truth."

Tunis gave her a grim look. "Mrs. Temple we should discuss this."

"But I didn't do it, Carl. Thomas did this. It was all his idea." She turned to Poole. "He was holding a grudge against Jacob for nearly twenty years for an incident that happened between them in Miami. Thomas had a short stay in jail for that. He lost some business as a result. He blamed Jacob. When he found out I was dating Jacob, then married him, he was so jealous. He always had a thing for me. May God forgive me, this is all my fault. I always had a feeling that he might hurt Jacob one day. I should have said something." She took a tissue out and dabbed her eyes before ripping it to pieces.

"Mrs. Temple, you pulled *three hundred thousand dollars* out of your account on the 30th," he pointed at the bank statement. "You were disguised in a black wig. You called Mr. McPherson and thanked him for carrying out an arrangement. Then you tried to blame your girlfriend, who you knew had a history of using a fork as a weapon in self-defense." He smirked at Tunis. "Clever touch, don't you think?"

Gibbs took a gentler tone with Fiona. "Now we know you are behind this. We know it was your idea. This is your chance to tell the truth about your involvement. It's your only chance."

"I am telling the truth, detective. Thomas did this." Her doe eyes two flooding pools, her voice crackly.

No one believed her. Not even Tunis.

She didn't have anything, but her word. After her previous lies, the evidence of the conspiracy and trying to frame Sally Stringfellow her word held no credibility. She continued to blame Thomas.

Poole persisted. He wanted her to admit her involvement. A half hour later, the air thick and stifling, they were still in a Mexican standoff.

Poole, Gibbs and Kadee retired to the hallway for a brief convening. They agreed she probably wasn't going to talk. They went back in and gave McPherson one more chance to confess. Nothing.

Gibbs arrested McPherson, who surprisingly went quietly. His hair moist, sweat beads around his forehead and ears, his shirt saturated. His manner almost seemed resigned. His head hung down, beaten and defeated. He repeated, "I didn't do this. I didn't do this."

Smithers patted his hand. "Don't worry, Thomas. I'll take care of this. It's going to be OK. I'll work on getting you bail."

Poole arrested Fiona Temple. With an accomplished grimace, he banged handcuffs on her wrists. "You're under arrest for conspiracy to commit murder and aiding and abetting…"

As he finished reading Fiona her Miranda rights, she cried, insisted relentlessly that she didn't do it. They knew she was just grasping at straws. There was no question she was the instigator. Poole spit out, "I'm guessing you thought you would get away with this, but you didn't count on having your husband's ex-girlfriend there to snap some pictures of you."

Fiona looked riled. Her eyes morphed from desperation and fear to flames as Poole cuffed her. "What?"

"That's right. Jane Light provided those pictures. I'd say your husband got the final word." He pushed her out the door.

"Wait till my daddy finds out about this. You'll be sorry. You don't know who you're messing with!"

They had a lot to do to prepare for the arraignment. They needed to retrieve video recordings from the bank and The Plaza Hotel, as well as the phone records. They were going to do more research into Fiona Temple and McPherson's backgrounds.

Kadee had thought she would feel total satisfaction when they arrested the perpetrator of Jacob's murder, a closure, a comfort that the story ended with justice. Though there was resolution, she felt sad.

Nothing would bring Jacob Temple back. His dreams left unfulfilled. His life unfinished. The senselessness of his life having been taken so abruptly and before he could go back to Jane, left Kadee feeling like a chunk of her heart had been removed. A burning hole. Nothingness. She wondered if anyone ever felt their life was lived to the fullest when it ended.

Poole and Gibbs appeared to be without conflict. They caught the bad guys. They were ready to grab lunch and then begin putting together the case for arraignment. Period. It was that simple.

Poole said he wanted to give Yvonne a quick call before they headed out for lunch. Kadee felt her body stiffen. She had been preoccupied with the investigation and had temporarily forgotten that Yvonne was a murderess, was dating John Poole and soon would be living across the street from her.

Gibbs went to his desk for a minute. Kadee looked over at him. *Maybe I should tell him. But what would I say? Give yourself a little time to figure out what you want to do. Don't act impulsively and do something you'll regret. Cool as a cucumber. Remember.*

Poole and Gibbs walked toward her, a welcomed distraction. The three headed out for lunch.

# CHAPTER 31

John Poole called Yvonne, his tone energized. He told her that they arrested Fiona Temple and Thomas McPherson, the two responsible for Jacob Temple's murder.

"That is terrific news John. I knew you would figure it out."

"Dinner tonight?"

"Yes. I mean, I'm busy packing today, but I do want to see you. I really do."

"I'll pick you up around 7:00. Is that good?"

"Oh, yes. Sounds perfect. So... Kadee's feeling better?"

"She's here. So I think so. She seems fine."

Yvonne's big toe moved up and down, tapped her floor. "Oh, good. I'm glad to hear that she's no longer unwell. I'll see you at 7:00."

"See you then, sweetheart."

She hung up the phone. Her lips bunched up like a tulip, her eyes two narrow slits, bitterness and animosity practically seeping from her pores.

*Were you ever really ill, Kadee? It appears that you have recovered rather quickly from your so-called ailment. And responding to my phone call with a Facebook message is quite dismissive in my opinion. Do you consider my feelings to be so trivial? You do, don't you? Yes, you do.*

*I'll play your pathetic lil' ole game. For now anyway. Soon I'll be right across the street and your neglect and abuse of my emotions won't be so easy to implement. I'll make sure of that.*

She opened her Facebook and sent Kadee a message.

> *Dear Kadee,*
>
> *John mentioned that you are back at work today. I'm pleased to hear that you have recovered from your illness so quickly. Maybe you just needed a lil' rest and relaxation. Anyhoo, I'm moving right along over here. \*wink, wink\* I'm not sure if I mentioned this, but I'm moving in this weekend. All the paperwork finally went through. In just a couple of more days, we'll be neighbors. ☺ I very much look forward to that. I wanted to invite you and Alex over on Sunday for a champagne toast to celebrate this hurdle in my transition. You know better than anyone how difficult this path has been. The new apartment is a tremendous step forward in my recovery process. I do hope you two love birds will join me. It's always so lovely to see you.*
>
> *Lovey Dovey,*
> *Yvonne*

She really hoped Kadee behaved accordingly.

She returned to her packing. Her mind wandered. The temptation to kill Kadee swung like a pendulum back and forth, in leaps. Fantasies of being close with Kadee and intruding upon her life were perhaps the only things keeping Kadee alive. Yvonne knew she had to be careful, so she indulged in the ideation; it was gratifying and sadistic. It made her feel powerful. It also kept her from acting on her urges too impulsively. She would not risk a mistake that could get her caught. She had her plan outlined. She needed to stick to it.

While enveloped in her visualizations she suddenly became aware of her hands gripping something. She glanced downward. Two forks. She had been packing her silverware, and hadn't registered the emotional significance of the forks. In that moment, she observed herself almost as an outsider.

Her mind flashed back to the time when she stabbed Jacob Temple in each of his eyes with the fork tines.

Jacob was already dead when she did that.

But she felt compelled to show him, and everyone else, what happened if they didn't see her, if she was pushed aside, dismissed, made to feel unimportant. No one would ever not notice her again — and live to tell about it. *No more.*

Yvonne's mental state was severely compromised and becoming worse. The kinetic experience of holding the forks propelled a new image into her consciousness that situated itself as a hallucination projected onto her refrigerator: Jacob Temple's eyes right before all the life washed out of them. His brown irises being drained of all vitality, right before she witnessed his empty stare of death.

His eyes were alive on the white door, the pupils pulsated. Then a last shutter of desperation turned into a vacant imprint of color, brown melting like a candle, drooling, dripping, then stiff. It was just the way he had looked the day she killed him. She remembered checking his pulse to make sure he was gone, right before she took the two forks and stabbed them right through each eye. Those were an afterthought: an important message to anyone who was listening, that she would never feel unseen again.

Her grasp loosened. The forks dropped to the floor, clanged against the tile.   Yvonne didn't hear it. She tried to wipe the door clean of Jacob's eyes, but they would not wash away. She ran and got the paper towel. She drenched it with kitchen cleaner, went back to the refrigerator and continued scrubbing, harder and faster. But his eyes just sat there. Staring. Petrified. Lifeless. She felt something, something uncomfortable, but she was losing touch with her emotions. Everything felt overwhelming.

She scrunched her whole face together and held it for at least a minute. When she opened her eyes, Jacob's irises were gone. She placed her hands on her cheeks, pulled the skin down. Her eyes sagged. Her jaw hung.

It was such an unfortunate chain of events that Jacob unwittingly became a participant in, leading her to have to eliminate him. A shiver of vulnerability: *no more*. She pushed her chest out: *no more*. Her voice, shrill in her head, demanded that she wipe away any sense of weakness. She continued packing, deciding to leave the silverware for last.

Jacob's murder was a little different than Noah's. It involved more planning, more engineering. It wasn't a detached sort of methodical kill, like in organized and/or contractual crimes, where the murder is seen as a job responsibility. There was some unbridled passion in this one also, but it was a slower percolation than with Noah's death. It involved more thinking and less emotion. It was more calculated in the sense that she could have stopped herself. But didn't.

It was good thing that she had decided to live without the obligation of any morality because Jacob Temple had been her patient. She had felt bad about that when she decided she had to take his life. He had trusted her with his innermost thoughts. She really had liked him. Quite fond of him, actually. She thought he was a genuine, authentic person. A down-to-earth man struggling to survive in a life he had become trapped in.

And he had that awful wife. She treated him without an iota of respect. Yvonne was positive that Fiona had manipulated him into marrying her. He was a handsome man, the type who would look good on the front page of the newspaper if and when Fiona Temple's father needed a shot of that proper-looking family for his political agenda.

They terminated his therapy about six weeks before Noah's murder. Jacob had achieved his treatment goals and decided that he was ready to end his therapy. He had been working through the conflict between what he wanted and what he believed was expected of him. He had discovered that his former girlfriend still loved him. At almost forty-five years old, he was done living the lie that had become his existence. That included, perhaps most important, being reunited with his first love. A lady named Jane. He was prepared to deal with the consequences of leaving his wife. She was probably going to try to take everything he had from him. He just needed a little more time, but he was emotionally ready to make the change.

It was an untimely coincidence when she bumped smack into Jacob as she was leaving Noah's the night that she killed him. Yvonne did feel conflicted about how to handle it. She didn't want to have to murder Jacob Temple. She wasn't the type to just randomly take the lives of others. If she was going to kill again, it would only be for a particular purpose.

Yvonne's rationality was terribly compromised since Noah's murder, but her thoughts still held a glimmer of discretion. It was a twisted sort of reasoning. Murdering someone is never a righteous act, but in Yvonne's mind her kills made sense. They were emotionally based offenses geared toward others who had hurt her or otherwise taken something from her. If she was going to slaughter anyone else, it certainly would be Kadee. In Yvonne's new reality, if she killed Kadee, it would only be because Kadee deserved it.

Originally, killing Jacob didn't fit into the schema she created where her murders held personal merit. But she also couldn't have a loose end lurking in the shadows. She needed to know if Jacob had figured out the truth. At first, she tried an alternative approach to killing him. She sent Jacob a couple of friendly Facebook messages. Established a sort of casual rapport with him.

She knew not to communicate too much over the Internet. She learned from Noah's investigation that the detectives could get their hands on just about any and all digital communication. So after a few short exchanges, she called him.

It was a leap she had to take. So she dumped whatever remained of her ethical responsibility out the window in lieu of saving herself. It was all part of her moral decline. These were concessions she was going to have to make if she planned to live out her new life, the type where she was completely free of any sort of authority.

She called under the pretense of a clinical follow-up: to see how he was doing since their therapy termination. Jacob was cordial, but distracted. Yvonne couldn't ask him directly what he knew, that would be like admitting culpability. So she tried her best to figure out what he knew by gauging his reactions toward her. But it was impossible to know anything from a phone conversation. She needed to read the nuances in his manner, observe his eye contact, gestures and the like. So she asked to meet with him.

They met at a bar one evening in midtown near the radio station. When Yvonne arrived, Jacob was already at the bar sipping a beer. For a moment, Yvonne recognized Noah in Jacob. They were similar physical types, tall with dark hair and dark eyes, both handsome men. She shook her head violently to wipe away the image, but then Noah's eyes emerged and would not go away. They manifested over and over throughout her time with Jacob. They disoriented her. She tried to focus. She tried to ignore them, look past them, but it was impossible.

As she talked with him, Noah's eyes displaced themselves onto Jacob's. Yvonne became increasingly confused. Suddenly she leaned in to kiss Jacob on the lips.

He stopped her. "What are you doing?" He moved his head backward avoiding the kiss.

"Nothing," she responded unemotionally, then leaned forward, attempting to kiss him again. Noah's eyes bobbed in front of Jacob's nose, further muddling her thoughts.

Jacob pulled back. "Yvonne, this isn't right. Please stop. I'm sorry."

"What's wrong?"

"Nothing's wrong. This just isn't right. C'mon, you know that. Is this why you insisted that we meet?"

"No." The eyes went away. Yvonne realized what she had done. "Oh my. I apologize. This is awfully embarrassing." Her cheeks turned pink.

"No problem," he said, seeming uncomfortable. He took a step back, created a larger gap between them.

After a few minutes of casual, but awkward chitchat, they moved past the discomfort and regained a rapport. Jacob continued his story about Jane. He told Yvonne how he planned to call Jane later that week, that he could not remember the last time he had felt so alive. He had Yvonne to thank for that.

He couldn't have known it, but his dialogue about Jane, following Yvonne's failed kiss, and his resemblance to Noah fed right into Yvonne's new psyche diagram of who she had the right to kill.

It didn't matter anymore whether or not he knew she killed Noah. In fact, Yvonne had surmised that he did not know. It was clear from spending time with him that Noah wasn't even on his radar, never mind that she killed him.

Unfortunately that was no longer her concern. Yvonne listened to him. She watched his lips release sentences filled with enthusiasm about his decision to call Jane. She seethed. Clearly, this Jane woman was Jacob Temple's *favorite*. Even after all of the years that had passed and Jacob's marriage to another woman, he still loved her.

Jane was his one. His only. His *favorite*. It left Yvonne with a lump of poison in her belly. The rage emerged into her consciousness, blasted through, polluted her mind. At that moment, she decided Jacob Temple needed to die. He was one of them, one of *those people* who pushed her to the side, leaving her feeling undervalued. Unimportant. Expendable.

Yvonne tried her best not to think about the night that she killed Jacob Temple. She stuck those images into their own compartment and instead became interested in the investigation. John Poole was quite generous in the amount of information he shared with her.

She wondered how it would all play out in the aftermath. As the search for the truth unfolded, she was flummoxed by what they discovered. Just like Noah's murder, someone else was charged with her crime. Clearly she had a natural aptitude for killing.

Naturally, she wouldn't even be considered. No one even knew Jacob was her patient. She knew he didn't tell anyone about his therapy. He didn't want his wife to know. He paid in cash. Yvonne burned up his file in her kitchen sink. She burned that paper until it was nothing but itsy-bitsy ashes that she washed down the drain. She blocked him from Facebook to eliminate their message exchanges. Just in case they looked through his interactions on there. Besides, John would never believe she was capable of such a violent act. He trusted her. *Ha!*

It was too bad that Thomas McPherson was being held responsible for Jacob's murder. He must have been manipulated by Fiona Temple. Yvonne was sure she was one of *those* women.

*He probably didn't even see it coming.*

*They never do. Do they? No, they don't.*

What a mystery. Something that might be worth writing a book about someday. There were pictures taken by Jacob's ex-girlfriend, Jane, who John said killed herself. She left the photos behind. Those images led them to the other evidence: the information that revealed a conspiracy to kill Jacob.

The data was so overwhelming that if Yvonne hadn't killed Jacob herself, she would have felt certain that Fiona Temple had paid Thomas McPherson to kill him. They practically framed themselves for a murder they didn't *get* to commit. *Oh, the irony!*

Everything just fell into place, in a nebulous, strange sort of way. All of those itsy-bitsy pieces coming together, leading someone else to take the blame for her murder. It almost led her to question her own culpability. She wondered how she could have come upon such good fortune.

Their unproven innocence was not much concern for her. Why worry about someone else's life? She got away with her second kill. On to the next chapter: Continue building her circle of trust so that she could emotionally torture Kadee, eventually kill her and be sure to get away with another murder. *It's funny how things in life work out sometimes. Isn't it? It is.*

She ran her fingers through her hair, a contented expression. When she finally decided to slaughter Kadee, she would most certainly get away with it.

Yvonne continued her packing. She was free as a bird and *moving right along.*

Kadee, Poole and Gibbs were out at lunch when Poole received a phone call. It was Julie Brown from the crime scene lab. Trace amounts of DNA were found underneath two of Jacob Temple's fingernails. He must have been fighting to defend himself and scratched off some of the perpetrator's skin.

Poole hung up the call. "We got him. There was DNA under Temple's nails. Now we just need a warrant for a DNA sample from McPherson and we have our evidence. There is no way he can talk himself out of that. DNA doesn't lie. I think this calls for a drink." He hailed their server and ordered a round of beers to celebrate.

They raised their drinks, clinked glasses. "They. Are. Finished," Poole cheered. "A toast to proving their guilt and making sure that justice is served."

"To justice," Kadee and Gibbs chimed in synchrony.

# AFTERWORD

Thank you for reading *Circle of Trust*. I am always grateful to those who take the time to read my work. I hope you enjoyed your experience.

I know I left my readers dangling on a bit of a cliff this time. But… hold on tight. The third book in the series, *Circle of Truth*, will be released in the fall of 2016. So you won't have to wait too long to find out what happens.

Below is an excerpt from the afterword in *Circle of Betrayal*, for those of you who have not read it. It gives a bit about my background and the inspiration for writing the *Close Enough to Kill* trilogy.

Although the story is entirely fictional, the content explored is one of my long time interests. As an alumna of John Jay College of Criminal Justice, like Kadee Carlisle, I entered the graduate program in forensic psychology with a curiosity and fascination for what I believe to be one of the most paradoxical crimes:

Passionate homicide. How does love turn to murder? I couldn't learn enough about it. And the question remained without a satisfactory answer.

My original career ambition was to work for the FBI's Behavioral Science Unit (now the Behavioral Analysis Unit) as a criminal profiler, but I eventually decided to pursue my doctorate in clinical psychology instead. Academics seemed more of a natural fit for me. And so it goes...

I worked in the criminal justice system as a psychotherapist and forensic evaluator for years, picking and probing the psyches of violent offenders, writing papers, evaluating insanity plea acquittals, journaling thoughts, formulating hypotheses.

After finishing my dissertation, then authoring two non-fiction books, and co-authoring two more, I found myself feeling limited in what I could learn. In psychology we conceive an idea, explore, research, hypothesize, write, but we are always looking to find what we set out to look for. In this way, it is somewhat formulaic, or at least it felt that way to me.

So I decided to use my knowledge of psychology and my clinical experience a little differently. I created characters, set a background, let my mind wander freely, allowing the characters to drive the story. I wanted them to provide the answers.

I submerged myself in the inner world of each character, allowing them to guide me through the narrative. They offered me the opportunity to experience firsthand what I was interested in knowing more about. There was love, rage, envy, obsession, risk, chance, loyalty, fear, betrayal, redemption all coalescing. I experienced it *all* as I went through it with each of them; I *knew it* in a way I couldn't possibly have understood it before.

I wasn't even sure who would be responsible for the murder in the beginning; I just gave each character the motivation. They did not disappoint. As the story went on, it became clear who did it and *why*. Each one of them left me fascinated, surprised, disturbed, exhilarated. And I loved ever moment with them, even the highly emotional scenes, when I could feel my own heart racing.

Thank you again for reading!

# ACKNOWLEDGEMENTS

**W**riting is a journey, each story, every chapter, the interior world of all of the characters, even the art of stringing words together are all a type of adventure. I wake up in the morning, a subtle sense of where my characters are and what will ensue on a particular day, and suddenly, I'm surprised with where they take me. As my imagination draws conclusions and my unconscious pours out onto the pages, I am filled with wonder, awe, excitement, and, in the case of writing while inside the mind of a murderer, disturbed. Fascinated, too.

Writing is a solitary process. When I'm not *actually* writing, I'm often thinking about the characters and their story, trying to fit all the pieces together, *where are they going, what's going to happen.* My mind needs a quiet space to work through the many complexities. That being said, I have a whole team of people behind me who have helped me along this journey, making the creation of this book possible.

Much gratitude to my favorite editor, friend, and creative collaborator, Carlo DeCarlo. I know I've said it before (but I like reiteration when I'm emphatic), this book would not have been possible without your help. Thank you. Thank you. Thank you. Lovey, Dov... *uh... ahem...* I mean, Thank you. *wink, wink*

To my husband, Joseph Gunn, for another great cover image. I am so grateful for your support, for your tireless listening and feedback as I tried to work out plot hurdles, conversing about my characters for hours, reading excerpts, and believing in me. A million times thank you.

Thank you to my wonderful father, Philip Simon, for the tremendous support, reading parts of the book, listening to my thoughts as I tried to piece loose ends together, for believing in me always. I am forever grateful.

Many thanks again to my trusted consultant, James Flanagan, formerly an Assistant Essex County Prosecutor and formerly an Assistant US Attorney, for contributing his knowledge of criminal investigations and the legal system, and for helping me through a few plot holes. Your expert advisement was an integral part of this process. Much gratitude for your time and expertise.

To many friends who have joined me on this journey, Pamela Frank, Melinda Gallagher, Mike Alonzo, Ross Kenyata Marshall, Lisa Vainieri Marshall, Tyla Loria, Gina Jorge Valentin and Dahlia Gordon. Thank you for reading, re-reading, providing feedback, letting me bounce ideas off of you, making suggestions, and listening to the story as I was creating it. Your time and support are greatly appreciated. I couldn't have done it without your help!

# About the Author

Jacqueline Simon Gunn is a clinical psychologist in Manhattan and a freelance writer. She is the author of four non-fiction books, including co-authored, *Bare: Psychotherapy Stripped*, as well as many articles, both scholarly and mainstream. *Circle of Trust* is Gunn's second work of fiction, and book two in her *Close Enough to Kill* trilogy. In addition to her clinical work and writing, she is an avid runner.

# OTHER BOOKS BY JACQUELINE SIMON GUNN

**Non-Fiction**

*In the Therapist's Chair*

*Bare: Psychotherapy Stripped* (co-authored with Carlo DeCarlo)

*Borderline Personality Disorder: New Perspectives on a Stigmatizing and Overused Diagnosis* (co-authored with Brent Potter)

*In the Long Run: Reflections from the Road*

**Fiction**

*Circle of Betrayal* (Close Enough to Kill Series – Book One)

Made in the USA
Monee, IL
09 August 2023

40716235R00207